## Praise for Minerva Spencer's Outcasts series:

**[DANGEROUS]** *Booklist Top 10 Romance Debuts of 2018*

**[BARBAROUS]** *Bookpage 14 Most Anticipated Romances of Fall 2018*

*"Minerva Spencer's writing is sophisticated and wickedly witty. Dangerous is a delight from start to finish with swashbuckling action, scorching love scenes, and a coolly arrogant hero to die for. Spencer is my new auto-buy!"*
**-NYT Bestselling Author Elizabeth Hoyt**

*"[***SCANDALOUS*** is] A standout...Spencer's brilliant and original tale of the high seas bursts with wonderfully real protagonists, plenty of action, and passionate romance."*
**★Publishers Weekly STARRED REVIEW**

*"Fans of Amanda Quick's early historicals will find much to savor."*
**★Booklist STARRED REVIEW**

*"Sexy, witty, and fiercely entertaining."*
**★Kirkus STARRED REVIEW**

# "How would you like your tea today, Mr. Worth?"

"Stephen. I know you can say it."

Elinor set the teapot down with a thump. "Why? Just tell me why you've chosen to honor *me* with your attentions?"

He rose from his chair and moved to the settee so quickly she didn't realize what he was doing until he was beside her. "Is it so hard for you to believe that I've come to love you?"

"Yes."

He laughed, his green eyes dancing. What sort of man enjoyed rejection this much?

"Why?" he asked.

"I know myself, Mr. Worth. I am *not* that loveable. Certainly not enough to make you ignore the dozens of pretty, young girls who are flinging themselves at your head. I am a widow with no fortune, I am no beauty, I am lame, and I am two and thirty."

His lips curved into a smile; *that* smile. "First, I have fortune enough for the two of us. Second, I'll be the judge of who I find beautiful. Third, you do not appear to let your foot get in the way of much. Fourth, I will be two and thirty on my next birthday. And, fifth," he said, cupping her jaw with one big, warm hand, "I never take no for an answer, Elinor." He lowered his mouth over hers.

# S.M. LAVIOLETTE

Crooked
Sixpence
CS
P
Press

CROOKED SIXPENCE BOOKS are published by

CROOKED SIXPENCE PRESS
2 State Road 230
El Prado, NM 87529

First printing April 2020

ISBN: 978-1-95166

10 9 8 7 6 5 4 3 2 1

Photo stock by Period Images

Printed in the United States of America.

# Chapter One

*London*
*1802*

Iain Vale was examining a marble statue of some poor armless bloke when the door beside it flew open and a whirlwind in skirts burst into the hall.

"I *will not!*" the whirlwind yelled before slamming the door, spinning around, and careening into Iain. "Ooof." She bounced off him and stumbled backward, catching her foot in the hem of her dress in the process.

Iain sprang forward, reached out one long arm, and caught her slim waist, halting her fall. He looked down at his armful of warm female and found surprised gray eyes glaring back at him. Her mouth, which had been open in shock, snapped shut. Iain hastily righted his bundle and took a step back.

"Who the devil are *you?*" the girl demanded, brushing at her dress as though his gloved hands might have soiled it.

"I'm the new footman, Miss."

The gray eyes turned steely. "Are you stupid?" She didn't wait for an answer. "I'm not a *Miss*. I am Lady Elinor, your employer's *daughter*."

Iain's face heated under her contemptuous eyes. He'd been spoken down to many times, but never quite so . . . effectively.

"You are welcome, *Lady Elinor*."

"What?" she demanded. "*What* did you say?" Her eyes were so wide they looked to be in danger of popping out of their sockets.

"*I said*, 'you are welcome, my lady.'"

She planted her fists on her slim hips. "I'm welcome for what?"

"For saving you from a very nasty fall," he retorted, unable to keep his tongue behind his teeth even though he was breaking every rule in the footman's handbook. If such a thing existed.

The unladylike noise that slipped from her mouth told Iain she was thinking the same thing. "You are an intolerably insolent *boy*. Not to mention the most ignorant footman I've ever known."

Iain couldn't argue with her on that second point.

"Besides," she added, looking him up and down, "I wouldn't have needed your clumsy rescuing if you'd not been listening at keyholes."

Listening at keyholes? *Why the obnoxious little—*

Iain had just opened his mouth to say something foolish and most likely job-ending when the door Lady Elinor had exited so violently opened and Lady Yarmouth stood on the threshold. Her gray eyes, much like her daughter's, moved from Lady Elinor to her newest footman and back again.

"What is going out here, Elinor?"

The girl scowled. "I have just asked our new footman to run away with me, Mama."

Iain's jaw dropped.

Lady Yarmouth's lips thinned until they were pale pink lines. She raked the younger woman with a look designed to leave her quaking in her slippers. Her daughter glared back, un-quaked.

"Come back inside this instant, Elinor." The older woman turned and retreated into the room without waiting to see if her daughter obeyed.

# The Footman

Lady Elinor gave an exaggerated sigh and rolled her eyes at her mother's back before limping toward the open doorway. She stopped and turned back to Iain before entering the room.

"You'll catch flies if you don't close your mouth." She slammed the door in his face.

*Bloody hell.*

***

Iain yawned. It was almost three in the morning and the festivities showed no sign of abating. Other than his encounter with Lady Elinor earlier, the evening had been quiet. Disappointingly quiet not only for his first ball, but also his first day as footman.

The only other entertainment had been watching an overdressed dandy cast up his accounts on his dancing slippers while trying, and failing, to make it to the men's necessary.

Iain adjusted the lacy cuffs of his fancy new shirt and examined the stranger who looked back at him in the ornate mirror. The black livery made him appear taller than his six feet and the well-tailored coat spanned his shoulders in a way that made him look lean and dangerous rather than scrawny and puppyish. His wiry red hair had been cropped to barely a stubble and was now concealed by a white powdered wig that gave him dignity. Of course his freckles were still there, but there was nothing he could do to hide them—unlike his age.

"You don't look five-and-ten, Iain," his Uncle Lonnie had said upon seeing Iain in his new clothes earlier today. He'd then grinned and squeezed Iain's shoulder. "Go ahead and give us yer story one last time, lad."

The story was one his uncle had concocted when Iain first came to work in Viscount Yarmouth's household three months ago: Iain was nineteen and had spent six years in Mr. Ewan Kennedy's household, two as a scrub boy, two as a boot boy, and two as a footman, even though he was unusually young for that last position. Uncle Lonnie also told Lord Yarmouth that Iain had come to London seeking employment after Mr. Kennedy died and there weren't any other suitable positions in the tiny town of Dannen, Scotland.

That last part was the only *true* part of the whole story. Dannen was more a collection of shacks than a real village and there'd never been any Mr. Kennedy, nor any work as scrub boy or footman. Iain had written the letter from "Mr. Kennedy" himself, under his uncle's direction.

"Admiring your pretty face?"

Iain yelped and jumped a good six inches. Female laughter echoed down the mahogany-paneled corridor. He turned to find Lady Elinor behind him, her small, almost boyish, frame propped against the wall in a very unladylike manner. Her white gown looked limp and tired, as if it were ready to go to bed. Her hair, a nondescript brown, had come loose from its moorings and fine tendrils wafted about her thin, pale face. Only her large gray eyes held any animation.

Iain drew himself up to his full height and glared over her shoulder at nothing. "How may I be of service, my lady?"

"Oh, stuff! You're angry with me, aren't you?" She didn't wait for an answer. "I'm sorry for being beastly earlier. I was wrong. Pax?" She held out her hand and limped forward. Iain stared, not because of her limp—he already knew she was lame—but because of the gesture. Surely a footman wasn't permitted to shake a lady's hand?

Besides, he hadn't forgiven her. His mother and uncle both accused him of being too grudging and slow to forgive. He looked down at her little hand and chewed his lip. Maybe they were right; perhaps it might be advisable to *appear* to forgive her. He'd just decided to say 'pax' when Lady Elinor grabbed his hand.

"Don't be angry with me. I apologized."

"I'm not angry," he lied, tugging not so subtly on his hand to free it from her grasp. He suspected it would not do to get caught holding the hand of the daughter of the house at three in the morning, or at any other time of the day or night, for that matter.

"Why aren't you in there," he gestured with his chin toward the ballroom, "dancing? Er, my lady," he added a trifle belatedly.

She snorted and hiked up her dress, exhibiting a shocking amount of leg. "With this?"

Iain gawked. He'd seen girl's legs, of course, but never a *lady's* leg. Her stockings were embroidered with flowers—daisies, perhaps. His groin gave an appreciative thump as he studied the gentle swell of her calf. She had shapely legs for such a tiny thing.

She dropped her skirts. "Are you ogling my limb?"

# The Footman

"What do you expect if you go around hiking up your skirt like that?" The words were out of his mouth before he could stop them. Iain squeezed his eyes shut and waited for her to start screeching. But the sound of giggling made him open them again.

She eyed him skeptically. "You're not like the other footmen."

What was Iain supposed to say to that?

"You look *very* young. How long have you been a footman?"

"Today is my first day."

"You shan't keep your job very long if you argue with any other members of my family. Or ogle their limbs."

His face heated and he pursed his lips.

She looked delighted by whatever she saw on his face. "How old are you?"

"Nineteen, my lady."

"What a bouncer!"

"How old are *you?*" Iain bit out, and then wanted to howl. At this rate, he would be jobless before breakfast.

"Sixteen." She stopped smiling and her eyes went dull, like a vivid sunset losing its color. "But I might as well be forty. I shan't even have a Season."

"I thought all young ladies had at least one Season." What drivel. What the devil did *he* know about aristocrats, Seasons, or any of it? It was as if some evil imp had taken over his body: some pixie or spirit determined to get him sacked. Or jailed. He clamped his mouth shut, vowing not to open it again until it was time to put food in it.

Luckily his employer's daughter was too distracted to find his behavior odd.

"Tonight was my betrothal ball." Her shapely, shell-pink lips turned down at the corners. "Why should my father go to the expense of a Season when he can dispose of me so cheaply without one?"

It seemed like an odd way to talk about a betrothal but Iain kept that observation behind his teeth.

"The Earl of Trentham is my betrothed," she added, not in need of any responses from him to hold a conversation. "He is madly in love."

The silence became uncomfortable. Iain cleared his throat. "You must be very happy, then," he said when he could bear it no longer.

5

Her eyes, which had been vague and distant, sharpened and narrowed. "He's not in love with *me*, you dunce. He is in love with a property that is part of my dowry. Some piece of land that is critical to a business venture he and my father have planned."

Iain's flare of anger at being called *dunce* quickly died when he saw the misery and self-loathing on her face.

"Lord Trentham will have his land, my father will get to take part in the earl's investment, and I? Well, I will have—" She stopped, as if suddenly aware of what she was saying and to whom she was saying it. She glared up at him, her gray eyes suddenly molten silver. "Why am I telling *you* any of this? How could you ever know what it is like to be an ugly *cripple*? You will never be forced to marry someone who is twice your age. A man who views you with less pleasure than he does a piece of dirt." Her mouth twisted. "I am no more than a broodmare to him."

Her expression shifted from agonized into a sneering mask. Iain hadn't thought her ugly before—plain, perhaps—but, at that moment, she became ugly. Fury boiled off her person like steam from a kettle and Iain recoiled, not wanting to get burned.

She noticed his reaction and laughed, the sound as nasty as the gleam in her eyes. "What? Do I scare you, *boy*?"

Iain felt as if she'd prodded him with a red-hot iron and he took two strides and closed the distance between them, seething at the undeserved insults and bile. He stared down at her, no idea as to what he planned to do. Not that it mattered. The second he came within reach, her hands slid up the lapels of his jacket like two pale snakes. He froze at her touch but she pushed closer. Small, firm mounds pressed hard against his chest.

*Breasts! Breasts!* a distant, but euphoric, part of his mind shrieked.

His breeding organ had already figured that out.

Iain looked down into eyes that had become soft and imploring.

"What is your name?" she asked, her voice husky.

"I—" He coughed and cleared his throat. "Iain, my lady."

"Would you like to kiss me, Iain?" It was barely a whisper and Iain wondered if he'd heard her correctly. He cocked his head and was about to ask her to repeat herself, when she stood on tiptoes and pressed her lips against his.

# The Footman

Iain had kissed girls before. Just last week he'd done a whole lot more than kiss with one of the housemaids in the stables. But this kiss was different. It was a gentle, tentative offering, rather than a taking. To refuse it was somehow unthinkable. He leaned lower and slid his hands around her waist, pulling her closer. She was so slim his hands almost spanned her body. She made a small noise in her throat and touched the side of his face with caressing fingers, her pliant body melting against his.

"You bloody *bastard!*"

The girl jumped back and screamed just as Iain's head exploded. He staggered, his vision clouding with multi-colored spangles and roaring agony. When he reached out to steady himself on the wall, he encountered air. A foot kicked his legs out from under him and he slammed onto his back, his skull cracking against the wood floor.

"Lord Trentham, *no!*" Lady Elinor's voice was barely audible above the agonizing pounding filling Iain's head.

A body—Lord Trentham's?—dropped onto Iain's chest with crushing force. Soft but powerful hands circled his neck and squeezed.

"You rutting pig, how dare you touch *my* betrothed?" The choking eased on his throat just before a fist buffeted the right side of his head. "How *dare* you put your filthy hands on your betters?" Another blow slammed into his left temple.

"*Stop it! Stop this instant, he did nothing wrong. It was me!*"

"I'll deal with you next, you little whore," the earl said, his tone even harsher than his words as his fists cracked against Iain's head over and over again. Iain's mouth filled with blood and he struggled to spit it out before he choked on it. And then a knee jammed between his thighs and he screamed, the world going black.

"*You're going to kill him!*"

Iain retched and Trentham scrambled off him, clearly wishing to avoid becoming drenched in blood and vomit. Iain rolled to his side and cupped his hands protectively over his aching groin, his stomach convulsing until there was nothing left to expel.

He wanted to die.

"What the devil is going on here?"

Iain distantly recognized Lord Yarmouth's voice.

"Make him stop, Papa, he will kill him!"

"I will certainly make him *wish* he were dead," Trentham snarled just before a foot made contact with Iain's side.

"*Ooof!*" Iain groaned and rolled away, unwilling to take his hands from his groin and risk more gut-churning abuse.

"Trentham, what is going on?" Yarmouth asked again.

"This lout was in the process of mounting your bloody daughter when I caught them."

"That's not—" Lady Elinor began.

"Silence!" her father roared.

"Is this the kind of household you run, Yarmouth? Has this happened before? Is she even *intact?*"

"I assure you, Trentham, this is the first time such a thing has happened. Look at her. Do you think she poses much of a temptation to any man?" The viscount continued without waiting for an answer. "Besides, this is a mere boy. I told Lady Yarmouth he was too young to be fit for the position. We shall discharge him immediately and forget this ever happened."

"I won't forget it, Yarmouth. And I won't marry this lout's castoffs—not unless my doctor examines her and swears she is intact. And I want *him*—"a kick glanced off Iain's shoulder—"put where he belongs."

"We did nothing wrong, Papa. It was just—"

"Another word from you, Elinor, and you will regret it most severely." The viscount's normally soft voice was thick with disgust and rage. A pregnant pause followed his words before he spoke again. "Very well, Trentham."

"*Papa, no.* It was only a kiss. He didn't even want to, I begged him—"

"*Enough!*" The word was followed by a loud crack and a muffled cry.

"I want him taken in for attempted rape," Trentham said, his voice suddenly cool and collected.

"Very well," the viscount said. "Thomas, Gerald, take him. You can put him down in the cellar while one of you fetches the constable."

Four hands closed around Iain's arms and began to lift. He struggled weakly against their efforts, squirming and thrashing his way across the plush carpet.

# The Footman

"You incompetent fools." The Earl of Trentham's voice came from behind. "Let me ensure this piece of rubbish gives you no trouble." Something hard slammed into Iain's head and the world faded to black.

# Chapter Two

Elinor washed the blood from her hands and turned back to the young boy. His eyes were crusted with dried tears and his lids had become heavy. He would sleep soon enough. She motioned to the boy's mother to step outside.

"He'll be fine, Mrs. Carruthers. It was only a shallow cut. The skull tends to bleed quite freely, so it appeared worse than it was. He will sleep the day through from the small amount of laudanum I gave him. Tomorrow he can resume his normal diet but keep him indoors and quiet for a few days."

"Oh thank you, Lady Trentham!" The older woman wiped tears from her weather-reddened cheeks and took Elinor's hand and kissed the back of it before Elinor knew what she was doing. "I was *that* frantic when I went to Doctor Venable's house and learned he was off helpin' Squire's eldest with her first labor. But for you my boy would have died. I know he would."

Elinor gently tugged her hand away from the woman's viselike grasp. "No, no, he most certainly wouldn't have. It was only a small cut, ma'am, nothing life-threatening. Now, you should take him home, before he wakes up."

"I've got no money, my lady." Her ruddy cheeks darkened even more.

"Please don't concern yourself with that, Mrs. Carruthers."

"Mr. Carruthers is fixed to bring in the lambs soon. I'll bring you a fine leg of lamb."

"That will be lovely."

Mrs. Carruthers finally left, taking her sleeping child and embarrassing gratitude with her, leaving Elinor to tidy up her surgery. She'd learned to take the gifts her patients offered, even when they couldn't afford to give such things away and Elinor didn't need them. But she didn't wish to insult the goodhearted folk and she always found a place for the offerings, usually in some other needy household; God knew there were enough of them on the current Earl of Trentham's lands.

Elinor frowned as she bundled up the soiled linen. She liked thinking about her dead husband's nephew—the current earl—almost as much as she liked thinking about her dead husband, which was to say not at all.

Instead, she turned her mind to the work she had yet to finish today. She was studying the human digestive system and had not completed the essay Doctor Venable had assigned her.

She finished cleaning the small surgery and was about to commence her studies when Beth bustled in, her plump, rosy cheeks bright with two spots of color.

"You must come with me, my lady. Quickly now. His lordship approaches with a guest." Beth glanced around the room, her mouth tightening with disapproval. "You know how the earl feels about, well . . . about what it is you do here."

Elinor closed the medical text she'd only just opened. "Fortunately I don't need to concern myself with his lordship's likes or dislikes, Beth. I am free of all male interference and direction in my life until I shuffle off my mortal coil."

Beth frowned. "Well I don't know nothin' about those kinds of coals, my lady, but I *do* know you've blood on your second-best muslin. Come now, we must make haste."

Her maid scolded Elinor nonstop as she dragged her from the outbuilding that served as her surgery toward the Dower House, which was her home. Beth did not stop when they reached her chambers. Instead, she yanked off the offending gown and then clucked and fussed as she garbed Elinor in her third-best morning gown.

"This dress is shameful, my lady. I can't turn the hem again, it's all but threadbare."

"Where did you speak to Lord Trentham?" Elinor asked, before Beth could launch into her favorite topic: the dismal state of Elinor's wardrobe.

"He was bound for town when I was coming back from the market, my lady." She paused in the act of fastening the small buttons to cast a rapturous glance at Elinor. "With him was the most handsome man I have seen in . . . well . . . maybe ever."

"Oh? Who is this paragon?"

"He's not a foreigner, my lady, but a proper gentleman."

Elinor bit back a smile. "A paragon is something of unsurpassed excellence, Beth, not a foreign dignitary."

"He has the most beautiful green eyes," Beth continued, not interested in a vocabulary lesson. "And hair the color of polished copper. He was dressed bang up to the nines, my lady, and made his lordship look quite dull. His coat was a dark mustard shade with—"

Elinor held up one hand. "Green, copper, mustard? He sounds quite vulgar. Did his hat have bells?"

Beth grunted. "Oh you do like to tease, my lady." She gave Elinor's shawl a few twitches before stepping back to admire her handiwork in the mirror. Her smile faltered.

"Poor Beth," Elinor chuckled, patting her maid's hand. "I don't give you much to work with, do I?" She stumped toward the door, her leg heavy and awkward from standing too long in her surgery.

"Oh, my lady, what a thing to say. Why, you've a sweet figure and such lovely eyes. And beautiful, thick hair, if you'd only let me—"

"I suppose I must offer them tea," Elinor said, stopping her maid before she could get started on yet another of her favorite harangues: Elinor's person and how she failed to make the most of it. "Will you have Hetty send in some of her currant buns. They are just the sort of thing to appeal to gentlemen. I shall receive them in the library," she added, closing the door on her servant's protests before limping down the narrow stairs to the second floor.

She would receive her visitors in the book-lined room no matter that it defied convention—or maybe *because* it defied convention—and would irritate her dead husband's successor.

Elinor loathed Charles Atwood, the Fifth Earl of Trentham, and he loathed her right back. He was a greedy, self-absorbed man who did a dreadful job caring for the estate and its people. He'd never been satisfied that he'd inherited the title, the properties, and the bulk of the wealth from his dead uncle—the fourth earl—and he still resented Elinor's meager jointure of a thousand pounds per annum and the use of the Dower House.

The man would like nothing better than to see her cast out of house and home. Luckily for Elinor, the only way he could get his wish was if he sold off the estate; finding somebody willing to purchase the dilapidated house and estate would be next to impossible in the current environment.

Elinor pushed the matter from her mind as she dropped into her chair and began to tidy the clutter that seemed to accrete on her desk no matter how hard she tried to be neat.

She'd just finished re-shelving a pile of books when the library door swung open.

"The Earl of Trentham and Mr. Stephen Worth," Beth announced, flinging out the names with enough pomp to satisfy a prince.

Charles strode into the library as if he owned it. Which he did, of course. Behind him came the most striking man Elinor had ever seen. His hair *was* the burnished hue of copper and his eyes *were* the vivid green of emeralds. If that wasn't enough, his features and person were the stuff of mythic heroes. It was hard work dragging her eyes back to the earl's less-than-appealing figure.

Charles gave her a perfunctory bow. "Good afternoon, Elinor. You are looking lovely today." He smirked at his own lie. "Mr. Worth, may I present to you my aunt, Lady Trentham. Elinor, this is Mr. Stephen Worth."

The paragon towered several inches above Charles, his broad shoulders, buckskin-clad thighs, and highly polished boots dominating the room. He fixed his beautiful eyes on her face and his full lips curved in a way that resurrected her long-slumbering heart and set it hammering against her ribs like a lunatic pounding on a cell door.

"It is a pleasure to meet you, my lady." His accent was unusual and Elinor struggled to place it as he took her hand and bowed over it. She refused to wear gloves, much to Beth's chagrin, and her hands were not those of a lady. For the first time in memory, Elinor felt the urge to hide her calloused, chapped fingers from this perfect, elegant creature. She settled for removing her hand as quickly as politely possible.

"You are not from England, Mr. Worth?" She was pleased to hear her voice sounded normal, no matter how strangely the rest of her body was behaving.

His teeth were a flash of white in his tanned face. "No, my lady, I'm from England's prior upstart colony." His cocky smile belied his humble words.

"One could hardly call the United States an upstart."

His smile turned wry. "I thought the same thing until I spent a Season in London."

Elinor couldn't help smiling. What a shock the burnished, gorgeous creature must have given the pale aristocrats who dominated the *ton*.

"Mr. Worth is here on business, Elinor," Charles broke in, clearly in no mood for social banter. "He represents Siddons Bank of Boston." His pale blue eyes, so like those of Elinor's dead husband, watched her with the cold intensity of a snake.

"Naturally I've heard of Siddons," Elinor murmured. Did Charles mean the man was in *England* for business? Or in *Trentham* for business? Just what was Charles up to?

The door opened and Beth entered bearing a large tea tray.

Elinor gestured to her desk and Beth's frown told Elinor what her servant thought of such a barbaric notion, but Elinor ignored her. For some reason, she was not inclined to leave the safety of her desk to serve tea today.

"Mr. Worth recently assisted the Duke of Coventry with his, er, entail issue," Charles said the instant the door closed behind Beth.

Elinor's hand shook at the word 'entail' and tea sloshed over the rim of the cup and pooled in the saucer.

"How clumsy of me," she murmured, her hand trembling as she lowered the teapot. She looked up to find two sets of eyes on her. One pair was, predictably, malicious and the other? Well, she didn't know what she saw in the American's eyes. Curiosity? Boredom? Thirst?

"Do you take milk or sugar, Mr. Worth?"

"Milk and two sugars, please."

Elinor fixed his tea, filled a plate with an assortment from the tray, and looked up. The American rose and came to take the cup. He was tall and well-formed and moved with the grace of an athlete.

"Much obliged, my lady," he said, his unusual accent pleasing to her ear. Indeed, there was nothing about him that did *not* appear pleasing; except perhaps his reasons for coming to Trentham.

Elinor turned away from his disturbingly appealing person and prepared Charles's tea. She was relieved to have something to busy her hands with as she asked her next question.

"But Blackfriars is not entailed." She lifted the cup and saucer toward him, grateful her hand was no longer shaking.

Charles took the proffered cup and waved away the plate of food.

"No, it is not. But that is not the only service Mr. Worth's bank offers."

A sick feeling began to expand in her stomach. "Oh?"

"I need to consider my options," Charles said with a smirk. "You, more than anyone, should know the property is a horrific drain on my purse, Elinor. You watched for almost a decade as it drained my uncle of his resources. It will hardly get better as crop prices continue to fall. We beat the French in battle but they will have their revenge with the plow. We simply cannot compete with them when it comes to agriculture and it is foolish to try."

Elinor ignored his self-serving argument.

"The property is vastly underutilized, Charles. Blackfriars would provide far more revenue if you made the necessary repairs to attract more tenants. Easily half the land goes un-worked and many of the cottages are—"

Charles waved his hand, his thin lips twisting into a condescending smile. "Things are far different now than they were even five years ago. Landed gentry are an anachronism and the sooner men of sense and vision recognize that fact, the better it will be for all of Britain. Farming is a thing of the past, isn't it, Worth?"

The American set down his cup and saucer and gave a slight shrug of his broad shoulders. "Perhaps you have oversimplified the matter, my lord." He turned to Elinor, his smile apologetic. "Even so, I'm afraid the earl has the right of it, Lady Trentham. English agriculture was under assault even before Waterloo. The economy is far from robust and the great landed estates of England can no longer survive decades of mismanagement as they have in the past."

Charles blinked at the other man's words and then frowned, as if he couldn't possibly have heard the American correctly. He turned from the American to Elinor and continued with his argument.

"It is manufacturing we should turn our attention to now. I say let the Frenchies do the farming."

Elinor ignored the earl's foolish bravado and smoothed the fabric of her skirt. Beth was correct; her blue muslin was no longer fit to be seen. The seams had been turned so often they were visible even from a distance. She must seem like a ragamuffin to the wealthy, beautifully attired American.

She looked up and caught the object of her ruminations staring, his green eyes intense with something that looked like . . . fury? Elinor flinched back and he dropped his gaze to his plate, depriving her of a better look. He picked up a piece of biscuit and placed it between his shapely lips before looking up again, his expression as mild as milk.

Elinor realized she'd been holding her breath and exhaled. She must have misread his expression; what would he have to be furious about? It was Elinor who should be angry with him, particularly if he was here for the reason she suspected.

"You helped the duke break entail? Is that something bankers do in your country, Mr. Worth?"

He didn't smile, but somehow Elinor knew he found her rather tart question amusing.

"Not in the general way, my lady, but I am also a lawyer. As such, I find antiquated property law matters diverting." His eyes flickered across Elinor, her desk, and the rest of the shabby room, as if entails weren't the only quaintly amusing thing England had to offer. "You could almost say the topic of entails is something of a hobby for me."

Elinor opened her mouth to ask him what it was he enjoyed so much about destroying ancient estates but Charles cut in before she could speak.

"Mr. Worth isn't here to talk about entails, Elinor. He believes his bank might be interested in acquiring Blackfriars."

Elinor was not stupid. She knew the only reason Charles and his weak-chinned son—a man as devoid of all sense and decency as his father—hadn't already sold Blackfriars was because of the dearth of eager buyers for such a property. The land was in bad enough condition, but the house itself would require a monstrous amount of money to repair and operate.

She gave the American a coolly appraising glance, hoping it hid the sick feeling that had begun in her stomach and was rapidly migrating out to the rest of her body.

"Is acquiring unprofitable estates another of your hobbies, Mr. Worth?"

He smiled at her chilly tone. "Our bank is always looking for good investments. I will need to do a great deal of research before I can assess a proper value."

Elinor found his smooth, confident manner more than a little annoying, especially since he was talking of selling her home out from under her, although she wondered if that were legal.

"If the English agricultural model is so *antiquated,* why is your bank interested in acquiring an agricultural property?"

"We invest in a wide variety of interests, Lady Trentham. I did not say we had decided to offer for the property. It is far too soon to say whether Blackfriars and Siddons Bank will be a proper fit. I will have to spend some time in the area before I can make such a determination."

His bland expression would have done a parson proud. Why, then, did Elinor suddenly feel breathless and anxious, like she was racing along the edge of a cliff on a skittish and unpredictable mount?

She looked away from his placid but disturbing gaze. "Do try a currant bun, Mr. Worth, they are quite delicious."

\*\*\*

Stephen tossed his hat and gloves onto the rickety walnut console table and yanked on the tattered bell pull. He had only been a guest at

Blackfriars a few days but already knew it was best to summon a servant long before you had need of one.

He struggled out of his close-fitting riding coat, yet again cursing the absence of Bains, his valet of six years. He'd hated to leave the man behind in Boston, but he'd had little choice in the matter. His business in England was far too sensitive to jeopardize with loose talk, and nobody knew better than Stephen how servants liked to talk.

No, the only employee he could trust on this venture was Fielding, a man so close-mouthed he might as well be mute. But Stephen had foolishly sent the taciturn man away on a fact-finding mission, so now he didn't even have Fielding's rather savage ministrations. It had been a bloody long time since he'd had to valet himself.

Stephen could almost hear Jeremiah, his old mentor, laughing at him. "You are a vain, comfort-loving creature, Stephen," the old Puritan had scolded him many times.

Even though he'd been one of the wealthiest men in America at his death, Jeremiah Siddons had lived like an ascetic, viewing most luxuries as un-Godly and a sign of weakness.

Stephen did not suffer from such qualms. He'd worked hard and sacrificed much to afford the luxuries he could now command. He frowned at the dusty, yellowed drapes and threadbare carpeting around him and sighed. Well, luxuries he could command everywhere *except* Blackfriars, a house whose amenities were as gothic as its appearance.

It irked him beyond bearing to sleep on damp sheets and take shallow, tepid baths. Fielding might be a disaster when it came to clothing or barbering, but the man did an adequate job of ensuring Stephen had the bare minimum of comforts.

Still, he'd not hired Fielding to be his valet. He'd engaged the man to manage sensitive business matters, which the taciturn man handled with absolute discretion, tact, and ruthless efficiency.

Stephen had also promised his surly servant ample time to pursue his own affairs. Private affairs Stephen knew little about and wished to keep that way.

No, Fielding was not a valet. He was not even a normal employee. Fielding was not a normal anything.

# The Footman

Stephen pushed away thoughts of his enigmatic servant and surveyed the gloomy, moth-eaten chamber, no doubt the best one the earl had to offer. While the obvious decay might be uncomfortable, it was a good sign for Stephen's purposes. Lord Trentham was desperate for money—ripe for the picking, as Jeremiah would have said, and then chuckled quietly, as though he'd gotten away with something criminal by speaking the vulgar cant of the streets.

Yes, the greedy Earl of Trentham was as good as in Stephen's pocket.

He turned his mind to the real purpose for his visit: the Countess of Trentham, the earl's aunt, who was actually younger than her nephew.

Seeing *her* after all these years had been like a kick to the throat and Stephen had hardly been able to breathe when he'd entered her library and found her standing there.

For fifteen years this woman had dominated his thoughts. He'd seen her face first thing when he'd woken up every morning and he'd drifted off to sleep with her, often carrying her into his dreams. She'd grown to monolithic proportions in his mind over the years. Today he'd realized the Lady Elinor of his memory was nothing like the reality.

Somehow, she'd grown in stature in his mind and Stephen hadn't recalled her being so . . . slight. Fairy-like, really. Not that any of that mattered. After all, she was, without a doubt, the same person. For fifteen years he'd planned this, wondering countless times whether she would recognize him when the day came. She *should* have recognized him: the man whose life she'd ruined. But there hadn't been even a flicker of recognition in her silver-gray eyes.

Well, why should there be? He'd been nothing but a servant—little more than a serf—and hardly worth remembering. Indeed, in many aristocratic households all the footmen were utterly stripped of their identity and given the same name for the convenience of their employers. The grand Lady Trentham had probably forgotten about the incident entirely.

Stephen's lips twisted as he contemplated Lord Yarmouth's arrogant little daughter, the woman who'd turned him into a criminal on the run, banished him to another country, forced him to change his bloody name, and left him blind in one eye.

And she'd done it all with only a kiss.

Not even a good kiss, if his memory served him correctly.

Stephen thought back to her as she'd looked in her cramped, shabby library today. It was clear his recollections had been those of a fifteen-year-old boy. His younger self—that poor, frightened servant—had built her into an irresistible siren in his memory. In reality she was nothing but a diminutive, somewhat colorless, aging matron.

So why had there been such a frisson of excitement when he'd touched her hand? The sharp, jolting sensation had been out of proportion to her size—a mere dab of a woman—and also for a woman possessed of her plain looks.

Oh, she was not homely, he admitted. But neither was she beautiful—hardly the type of woman a man would *choose* to ruin his life for. Not that he'd been given any say in the matter.

Still, he'd experienced an uncomfortable squeeze in his chest and a definite twinge in his cock when she'd looked up at him with her silvery-gray eyes.

Stephen shrugged away the momentary attraction. It was just his body's reaction after so many years of anticipation. Besides, he was not, in the main, attracted to slight women. He preferred his women to be more substantial. He was a large man and he appreciated full figures and generous curves—a healthy armful beneath him in his bed.

Not that it mattered what his preferences were. This was business, not pleasure.

The only part of Elinor Trentham he'd remembered correctly was her eyes. They were large, clear, and gray. The last time he'd seen them they'd ranged from haughty to amused to desperate in the span of a few moments. Today they'd been unreadable.

Well, not quite. Stephen smiled. Her eyes had narrowed quite expressively whenever they'd rested on the current earl. Who could blame her? Trentham was a bullying worm of a man. Worse, he was stupid. Only a stupid man would blithely consider selling Blackfriars, one of the finest examples of late Gothic architecture in all of Britain, if not the world. Still, the rambling house would be a drain on a healthy estate, and the Earl of Trentham was not operating a healthy estate. Stephen grinned; the earl's stupidity and venality worked in Stephen's favor and would make taking the man's birthright a true pleasure.

His venality would also help Stephen in his dealings with Elinor Trentham. There was no love lost between the dowager countess and her nephew and he had no qualms about dispossessing *her*. Trentham had been gleeful when he'd told Stephen the countess had no life estate on the house she occupied.

Yes, the man was lower than pond scum but he would serve Stephen's purpose admirably.

A pale face with silvery eyes thrust aside all thoughts of the despicable earl. Stephen had spent years doing his research and had read everything written on the English peerage. He knew, for example, the wife of an earl did not take her husband's surname upon marrying. She was not Elinor Atwood, but Elinor Trentham. She was also not quite what he'd expected, a realization that was a bit . . . unnerving.

He poured himself a stiff brandy from the decanter Fielding had had the good sense to pack. The Earl of Trentham's spirts and food were as poor as the condition of his house and property.

The dowager countess had spoken the truth today; if the earl had bothered to properly manage his land it would yield more than enough to take care of his people and maintain the house. Unfortunately for Blackfriars and those who relied on it, the revenue could never be enough to support the earl's most expensive habit: himself.

Not that Stephen was complaining. The earl was so greedy for money it would take no great effort on Stephen's part to convince him to take the proceeds from the sale of Blackfriars and parlay it into a once-in-a-lifetime investment opportunity. A feral grin twisted Stephen's lips and he took a deep pull on his glass. Yes, ruining the stupid, grasping earl was almost too easy. Unlike the second, and more important, part of his plan: Elinor Trentham. The countess was far smarter than the earl and another kettle of fish entirely.

Not only did she speak intelligently and knowledgably, but she seemed to lack what the earl possessed in spades: greed. She appeared not only contented with her worn gown and moth-eaten house but managed to project an image of serene superiority. Stephen knew from experience how difficult it was to manipulate people who weren't greedy for more: more money, more power, more something.

But there had to be *something* she valued, something he could take from her. Some way he could hurt her.

Stephen would keep looking until he found it.

A soft scratching at the door pulled him from his reverie.

"Come in."

The door opened and a wench stood in the doorway: the overly friendly maid from the evening before.

"You sent for me, Mr. Worth?" Her blue eyes sparkled and her full lips parted. Wild tendrils of autumn-gold hair escaped from beneath her cap. Her uniform did a similarly unsuccessful job of restraining her ripe body.

Stephen ignored her inviting lips as well as the sudden heaviness in his groin. He had nothing against a quick fuck with an attractive woman—servant or otherwise—but not when he was intent on business, especially business he'd been planning for fifteen long years.

"Have a bath prepared for me." He tugged his cravat loose and tossed it over the back of a chair. "I prefer water that is almost scalding." That way it might actually arrive before ice could form on the surface.

Her eyes dropped to his exposed neck. "Very well, Mr. Worth." She inhaled so deeply Stephen swore he could hear threads popping. "Do you wish for me to . . . attend you?"

The tightness became a genuine swelling as he imagined water sluicing over her bounteous curves and down toward what would most certainly be—

"No," he said sharply, quashing the fantasy before it could form. "I will attend myself."

He turned away and waited for the sound of the door shutting before tossing back his drink.

There would be plenty of time for women later.

# Chapter Three

*Coldbath Fields Prison*
*London*
*1802*

A loud, agonized moan jolted Iain awake. When he opened his eyes, he realized the sound must have come from him.

Dirty brown light filtered through the wooden slats of the shed, just enough that he could see the others in the big room, most of whom appeared to be sleeping. The day had been unseasonably hot and muggy and a nauseating miasma of foul breath, shit, piss, and desperation hung over the cramped room.

Iain tried to breathe through his mouth as he lowered his head back to the damp, stinking straw. He fingered his pounding skull and winced. It felt as if it had been broken into a dozen pieces and reassembled with a few chunks missing. His vision was strange and hazy—as if he were looking through a grubby window. Still, he felt better than he had yesterday or the day before that—when he'd believed he would die.

Of course, he still might die.

He listened to the heavy, measured breathing of sleeping men and gathered his strength to face the others when they woke, which they would sooner than he'd like. They were locked in the oakum shed, perhaps a dozen of them. It appeared Iain had had the bad luck to be tossed into prison the same night on which Edward Despard and his revolutionary associates had been arrested. The regular cells were full to bursting and Iain, as well as several others, had been relegated to one of the many outbuildings that comprised the prison known as 'The Steel'.

Food arrived erratically and was immediately snatched up by the strongest. He'd had nothing but a heel of bread and a dipper of water, and that thanks to his inscrutable savior. He turned and squinted at the man—or boy, really—who leaned against the wall not far from him: the hulking convict who'd saved Iain's life more than once in the past days.

Eyes as black as the pits of Hell greeted his and Iain blinked at the cold, hard stare. What had happened to make a boy not much older than Iain look so dead inside?

He pushed himself up to his elbows. "I wanted to—"

The boy gave a slight shake of his head and raised a finger to his lips.

Iain tried again, this time speaking in less than a whisper. "Thank you."

The young giant shrugged his brawny shoulders.

"My name is Iain Vale. What is yours?"

For a moment he thought the boy wouldn't answer.

"John Fielding." His lips curved into a self-mocking smile, as if he'd disappointed himself by speaking.

"How long have—"

The loud jingle of keys and the screeching of rusty hinges cut off the question and caused the other boy to scramble to his feet. Iain followed suit, albeit far less gracefully.

The gray light of dusk slanted into the room and a stooped, ragged figure loomed in the open doorway.

"Here's yer damn dinner, ye bastards!" The guard flung a bucket of slops into the middle of the dirty straw floor. Bodies that had been sleeping mere seconds earlier sprang into motion. Before Iain could reach the food, the larger chunks of bread had been snatched up.

"You," the guard growled, pointing a wicked looking cudgel at Iain.

Iain flinched back. "Me?"

"Aye, you, come 'ere!"

Iain shuffled closer, expecting the club to fall at any moment. Instead, the jailor grabbed the front of his filthy shirt and yanked him close enough that Iain could smell sour ale and rotting teeth on his breath.

"Be ready, boy," the jailor threatened, shoving him back so hard Iain's head banged against the stone wall behind him and he slid to the floor, bells ringing in his skull.

The door slammed shut, plunging the hut back into near darkness.

Fielding sidled up next to him. "What did he want with you?"

"I . . . I don't know." Iain's head was throbbing so bloody badly he would have vomited if there'd been anything left in his stomach to bring up. He scrambled to sit up and something scratched against the skin of his chest. When he felt the front of his torn shirt his hand encountered a crumpled piece of parchment.

"He put a note in my shirt," Iain whispered to his friend and savior. Excitement pulsed through his weakened body as he smoothed out the small piece of paper and tried to read it in the gloom.

"You know your letters?" John Fielding asked, surprise coloring his voice for the very first time.

"Aye." Iain lurched to his feet and staggered to the narrow slit that served as a window. He stepped on somebody's foot and earned a volley of curses as he collapsed against the far wall, holding the precious paper to the line of gray light.

*"Be ready to leave when the moon is at its peak tonight. Feign sickness and—"*

A hand shot over his shoulder and tore the paper from his fingers right before a body slammed him against the wall.

"'Ere then, wot's this?" an amused, grating voice demanded.

Iain twisted and lunged for the paper but another hand grabbed his ankle and yanked him off his feet. He landed on his back in the filthy straw, his head once again screaming.

"A love note, my lord?" the same voice mocked while a foot descended on Iain's chest and held him pinned to the reeking floor. "Anybody 'ere as can read a lovey-dovey letter?"

The others laughed while his tormentor peered through the gloom at Iain, who lay gasping for breath under his hobnail boot.

"I fink maybe 'is nibs ought to read it out loud. What do you fink, boys?"

"Bloody right, Danno!" another voice yelled while loud cheering shook the small shed.

His persecutor—Danno—tossed the letter down just as a big arm snaked around Danno's neck and yanked him off his feet before flinging him against the far wall.

Iain drew in a ragged gulp of air once the boot disappeared and scrambled for the note. He snatched up the precious scrap of paper and held it to his face.

*Be ready to leave when the moon is at its peak tonight. Feign sickness and scream for the guard. He will take you to a small side door in the prison wall. I will be waiting in the prison cemetery.*

It wasn't signed, but Iain recognized his uncle's small, careful handwriting. He tore the note to bits just as scuffling and yelling filled the room. He looked up to find John facing not just Danno, but another three who'd sprung up like noxious weeds from between the cracks in the flagstone floor. The huge boy was holding his own, but he couldn't take on the entire group.

Iain scrambled to his hands and knees just as a shadow broke away from the group of cheering boys and circled behind Fielding. Iain launched himself across the filthy floor, managing to lay hands on the shadow's foot as he raised it to kick John in the back. He yanked with all his strength and the man lost his balance and hit the floor, taking Iain down with him.

John turned at the sound and flicked at glance down at Iain, his face a terrifying mask of hatred and rage. His huge fists made fast work of his aggressors and their own cowardice took care of the rest, until Fielding was left standing alone.

Iain flailed and punched, landing one or two good hits to the other boy's head and neck before kneeing him in the groin, an action he knew to be all too effective. He scooted back toward the rear wall of the hut, leaving the boy curled up on his side.

Fielding slid down the wall not far away, his chest heaving like a bellows as Iain crawled crablike until he was beside him.

"Thanks for saving me yet again."

John ignored him, his eyes fastened on the now silent group across the room.

"They're coming for me tonight," Iain whispered. "You can go with me. My uncle will help you."

The boy's bitter laughter spilled out of him like a dead, bloated body floating to the surface of a deep, dark lake.

"What?" Iain asked, stunned by the other boy's ill-tempered reaction to an offer of freedom.

"The only place I'm going is Norfolk Island."

Even Iain—bumpkin that he was—had heard of the infamous penal colony. "You're being transported?"

"Aye, on the morrow, as *yer* luck would have it." He gave Iain something that passed for a grin. "I doubt you'd have lasted another day without me," he added.

Iain already knew he wouldn't have lasted five minutes.

"Come with me tonight, John. We'll talk the guard into it by promising him more money from my uncle. Surely the guard won't care if two go rather than one if it means more coin in his pocket?"

John snorted. "'Tain't the guard puttin' me on the boat. My life ain't worth a bucket o' warm piss after getting' on the bad side o' Fast Eddie. Leavin' this miserable shitebox of an island is the only chance I 'ave left."

"Fast Eddie?"

"Aye, Fast Eddie. 'E runs it all—from gin t' whores."

"What happened?"

"Never you mind. Just keep yer mind on getting out o' 'ere tonight." He turned away to indicate the discussion was over.

Iain stared at his harsh profile in the dim light, trying to think of something to make him change his mind. Transportation? What a horrible thought—to leave everything and everyone you knew and head to a dangerous new land alone. It had been bad enough to leave Scotland after his mam died, even though he knew his Uncle Lonny was waiting for him in London. How would it be to go half-way around the world to some strange place where nobody knew you?

His eyes began to tighten and water just like they always did when any thought of his mam passed through his mind. It would be the end of him in this cell if he started blubbering; John Fielding would probably beat Iain himself if he broke down. He swallowed down the tears and drew on the anger that came after the pain. His mother would still be alive and Iain wouldn't even be in this godforsaken city if not for The MacLeod kicking them both off their land. Thoughts of the Highland lord made Iain boil and gave him strength.

"You angered him, Iain. But he's your real father," Mam had reminded him as she lay dying in a filthy room in Edinburgh. "You can always go back to him if you need help. Him or your Uncle Lonnie."

Iain had chosen his uncle over the bloody bastard who would get a child on one of his housemaids and then marry her off to one of his tenant farmers. Not that John Vale had been anything but kind to his adopted son, treating Iain as though he'd been his own blood.

Iain squeezed his eyes shut on the old pain, turning his thoughts back to the boy who'd saved him so many times these past few days.

Transportation.

*Bloody hell.* What a nightmare that would be. He massaged the back of his aching neck. Thankfully Iain would never have to face such a thing, not with his Uncle Lonny looking out for him.

# Chapter Four

*Village of Trentham*
*1817*

"Y"ou're doing very well, my lady," Doctor Venable murmured, stopping behind Elinor's shoulder to watch while she carefully stitched the jagged wound shut. "That is the perfect tension," he added, a slight puff of breath warm against her temple.

Elinor lifted the needle and pulled the thread slowly taut. "I learned with the Carruthers boy that this is far more challenging when the patient is alive," she said dryly.

The usually staid doctor chuckled before coming to a halt across the table on which the lamb's body lay.

"Yes, a live patient tends to add a certain degree of urgency. Now, make sure that last stitch is tight, but not so tight as to score the skin. Recall that living flesh swells after trauma." He handed her a dainty pair of embroidery scissors before she needed to ask for them.

Elinor cut the thread and leaned closer to examine her work.

"It's not bad," she declared, looking up from the unfortunate lamb and meeting the doctor's velvet brown eyes.

His shapely mouth twitched into a slight smile. "It's certainly better than any of my first dozen attempts."

"No doubt it's all my years of needlework showing." Elinor lowered her hands into the basin of hot water Doctor Venable's servant had brought into the room a few minutes before. The doctor was adamant about the frequent washing of hands and Elinor was eager to comply with what others might consider a rather obsessive attitude on the matter.

"I hear we have a rather important visitor in the area," Venable remarked as he covered the lamb's body with a heavy canvas sheet. It had begun to stink and this would be the last time they would use it for their purposes.

The doctor's comment surprised Elinor as they rarely discussed anything other than medicine. She picked up a clean strip of rough cotton and dried her hands as she looked up at his attractive face. "You can only mean Mr. Stephen Worth. Have you met him?"

"I've not had that pleasure, although I've seen him several times from afar. He was inspecting Jason Beck's farm with Lord Trentham when I paid a call on Beck's youngest child." Venable lifted the lamb's body onto a small cart, which would be picked up later by the village renderer who would make use of the small animal. The lamb had suffered an unfortunate run-in with a neighbor's bull. Elinor had practiced her skills on any number of creatures, most of them dead.

"I understand Worth is an American banker of considerable repute," the doctor continued.

"Yes, he's associated with Siddons. I believe he's the scion of the family which started it, although I'm not quite clear on the relationship between him and the bank's founder, Jeremiah Siddons."

"I recall reading of Siddons's death last year. Apparently, his bank was involved in a rather large undertaking involving coal mining in Yorkshire. I understand the project ground to a halt after he died. Is Mr. Worth here to resume the project?"

"As to that, I could not say." Elinor paused to consider what she knew and how much she should admit to knowing. No doubt Charles was not behaving with any circumspection; why should she maintain silence on the subject? Besides, the doctor was one of her closest associates—maybe even a friend. "I believe Lord Trentham has lured him here with the hope of selling him Blackfriars."

Venable nodded as if he was not surprised but said nothing.

# The Footman

Elinor was accustomed to the doctor's unwillingness to use more words than were absolutely necessary. His laconic nature was even more pronounced when it came to his own person and past.

Elinor took a seat at the low table that served as her desk during their lessons.

"I completed the anatomical representations you assigned last week," she said, removing a sheaf of foolscap from her medical portfolio and handing it to him.

She studied the doctor while he studied the drawings. He leaned beside the glass-fronted cabinet that covered one wall, his tall, powerful body graceful in his well-made but worn garments. She'd seen him wearing his shirtsleeves and breeches last fall, at a harvest picnic where he'd helped the farmers. Women had swooned.

Not for the first time did Elinor wonder about her mysterious tutor. It was obvious from his speech and bearing that he was a gentleman but she could discern nothing from his accent as to what part of the country he called home.

She'd known him for five years and had surreptitiously studied medicine under him for more than three. And still she knew nothing about him other than he'd attended medical school in Edinburgh and moved to Trentham from Manchester. And that he was pulse-poundingly handsome in a tortured, brooding sort of way. His dark eyes, pale skin, and unruly thatch of pitch-colored hair were the stuff of gothic romance novels.

Elinor admitted to more than a little curiosity as to where Doctor Venable had been spending a week each month since this past January. She wished she knew him well enough to ask what he did on his week-long absences. But she kept her questions to herself; she'd hardly like it if *he* went poking about in *her* secrets.

"These are very good, Lady Trentham," he murmured, his black lashes lush against his cheeks as his eyes moved over the pages. Elinor realized how odd their formality was. They'd studied together for many hours and discussed—even argued—over hundreds of matters. She'd assisted him with operations, some of which had lasted hours and left them both exhausted, sweaty, and less than civil. And still they were as formal as they'd been the first time they'd met. The same night her husband had become bedbound.

He looked up from the drawings. "I believe you are ready to move to the digestive process next."

Elinor placed a hand over her heart. "Has a woman ever heard sweeter words?" She was pleased when he returned her smile. She genuinely liked him, but his reserve was an insurmountable wall. Whatever it was he protected, he protected it from her as well as the rest of the world.

"What will you do if Lord Trentham sells Blackfriars?" he asked.

Elinor leaned back in the old cane chair, astonished by the unprecedented personal question. "I suppose I will find a smaller house and go on much as I do now."

The silence stretched between them, broken only by the sounds of Venable's servant moving around in the next room and the insistent cooing of a morning dove in a tree outside the surgery window.

"You could marry me."

Elinor's jaw sagged.

Venable threw back his head and laughed, an action which astounded her almost as much as his proposal. Had she ever seen him give such a genuine laugh before? It took ten years from his age and made him even more attractive.

"That is hardly a flattering response, Lady Trentham."

Elinor's face reddened and she closed her mouth. "I apologize for what was probably a singularly unattractive expression, doctor."

"Not unattractive, merely speaking. Please forgive my impertinent suggestion, if you cannot actually forget it." He turned to his already neat desktop and began straightening the few items on top of it.

Elinor reached out and laid one of her hands over his. He froze. His hands were strong and elegant with long, graceful fingers but the skin was chapped and red—like hers. They were the hands of a gentleman who worked. He looked up but did not remove his hand, his dark eyes impenetrable.

"You are *not* impertinent, doctor, but kind. You wish to help me, to save me. I'm honored by your offer to sacrifice your person—" She held up a hand when he opened his mouth to deny it. "Please, do not say it would not be a sacrifice. A man like you could secure any woman he wished for a wife. You cannot be in a hurry to marry an impoverished gentlewoman well-past her prime. While I appreciate your offer, I cannot, in good conscience, accept it." She smiled to soften her rather bald words. "At least not yet. Perhaps *I* will be begging *you* to repeat your offer if Charles really does sell the Dower House from beneath me." She shrugged. "That time has not yet come. What you can do for me is continue my tuition. Who else would spend the time you do on a mere female?"

"It is an honor to instruct you, Lady Trentham. You are more naturally talented in the field of medicine than most of my colleagues. It would also be an honor to offer you whatever protection and security a marriage might afford should you ever need it. Marriage to you would pose no hardship, I assure you." His black brows were drawn down into emphatic slashes, making his normally impassive face commanding and unbearably handsome. Something hot flared in his dark eyes and she swallowed, flushing at this unexpected demonstration of admiration. She hurriedly looked away and removed her hand from his. He almost managed to convince her that he spoke the truth. Not that it mattered. She would never marry again, even to a man as kind as Doctor Venable.

She gathered up her possessions. "Shall I work on diagrams forty-seven through fifty for next time?"

"Yes, of course." He glanced down at the medical text he had studied from as a student and now used to instruct Elinor. "I also want you to take a look at the discussions regarding esophageal functions." He flipped several pages, his tone once again cool and businesslike. "Let me direct your attention to a section in Appendix B which you might find helpful."

\*\*\*

The sky was an ominous shade of gray by the time Elinor left Doctor Venable's.

"Are you sure I cannot run you home in the gig, my lady?" he asked for the third time.

"That will not be necessary. I shall see you on Monday, doctor." Elinor hurried away before he could offer again. She enjoyed the short walk from town to the Dower House as it gave her time to think over the day's lesson before she reached home and the inevitable questions and concerns Beth would greet her with at the doorway.

She'd only gone a few hundred yards down the quiet lane when the trees off to the left rustled and a horse and rider emerged. Elinor immediately recognized broad shoulders and a flash of flaming red hair beneath a tall black hat. She stopped, foolishly hoping Mr. Stephen Worth would continue on his way without noticing her. Instead, he turned toward her as if she'd called out his name.

"Ah, Lady Trentham." He lifted his hat.

Elinor cursed inwardly. To say she found the handsome American an unwelcome distraction was an understatement. But what else could she do—run away? Pretend she hadn't seen him?

She pasted a welcoming smile on her face and resumed walking. "Good afternoon, Mr. Worth. You are out inspecting the countryside? Perhaps considering additional business investments?" Elinor could have bitten off her tongue at her waspish tone.

Worth smiled. "I'm always considering investments, my lady." He swung down from his horse, a magnificent russet-colored beast whose coat was remarkably similar to his master's hair.

"You are on your way home. May I accompany you?" Piercing green eyes bored down into hers and her breathing quickened, as though his intense stare had incinerated the air between them. Did he always burn so very brightly? It must be fatiguing—to those around him, if not him.

Well, she could hardly say 'no,' could she?

"Thank you, I should like that," she lied.

He held out his hand for her basket. "I shall carry that for you."

Elinor wanted to argue but, again, could not think of a good reason to refuse. She handed him the basket and they resumed walking; her limp was more pronounced than ever.

"You have been shopping in Trentham, my lady?"

"I have been visiting."

"Bestowing bounty on the neighborhood's needy-but-deserving residents?" His expression was all that was amiable but the barb in his words was impossible to miss. No doubt he'd heard of her small charitable endeavors and thought her yet another useless aristocrat who delivered calf's foot jelly and improving religious pamphlets to the earl's neglected farmers.

Two could play at that game.

"I hear you've been busy inspecting the local tenantry as well, Mr. Worth."

"I make no secret of how I spend my time, Lady Trentham." His taunting smile told her he'd heard otherwise about her.

Elinor sighed. Charles and his big mouth, no doubt. What had her repulsive relative told the charming Mr. Worth about her relationship with Doctor Venable? She gave a mental shrug. Why did she care what he knew or thought?

"When will you be leaving us, Mr. Worth?" It was a question that had more than one toe over the line of rudeness.

"That depends on you, Lady Trentham."

Elinor stopped walking. "I beg your pardon?"

"Lord Trentham is planning an entertainment to introduce me to the neighborhood."

"How kind of him," Elinor said, not bothering to restrain her impatience. "But I'm afraid I don't understand what that has to do with me?"

"I've told him I will only postpone returning to London if you agree to honor me with at least one dance."

Elinor laughed before she could stop it. "What rubbish."

He grinned down at her. The man had dimples and he was brandishing them quite shamelessly. Elinor quickly looked away.

"Not rubbish at all, my lady. And I've accomplished part of my object."

"Oh, what part is that?" She resumed walking.

"I made you laugh."

Elinor shook her head at his foolish banter. How long had it been since anyone had flirted with her? Decades, if ever.

"And that was your intention, was it? To make me laugh?" Elinor didn't bother to hide her skepticism.

"Well, I wanted to see what you looked like when you smiled. The laugh was merely an added bonus."

Her face flamed in the coolness of the day. Was the man so bored he had decided to inflict his considerable charm, his *dimples*, on an aging cripple?

"You are truly wasted here in the country, Mr. Worth. Your gallantries would be far more appreciated in London. Indeed, *you* would be greatly appreciated in London."

*And I would be considering esophageal anatomy rather than pondering the felicitous combination of musculature necessary to produce such devastating dimples.*

"Are you saying you don't appreciate my gallantries, Lady Trentham?" He'd sheathed his dimples and was frowning down at her with mock severity.

"Not at all, I'm saying they are wasted. Those are two completely different things." A small drop of rain struck her cheek, and then another. Thankfully the Dower House was almost within view.

"It was not a gallantry, ma'am. I *would* like to dance with you."

"My dancing days are behind me."

"You make yourself sound ancient—I know for a fact we are barely a year apart in age."

Elinor didn't want to think about *how* he knew such a thing. "For obvious reasons, I do not dance, Mr. Worth."

"Because of your foot, you mean?"

The power of speech deserted her and it was a long moment before she could respond. "Such astuteness must serve you well in the world of banking, Mr. Worth," she said tightly.

"Why should a mere limp keep you from dancing?"

Elinor's breath caught at the casual way he dismissed her physical impediment. Fury followed shock. How easy it was for a person like him to hold forth about another's misfortunes and then minimize them. What difficulties had *he* ever faced in his gold-plated life?

He sighed. "Now you are angry with me. I can tell by the way your chin is jutting out."

"I don't know you well enough to be angry with you, Mr. Worth." A drop of rain hit her chin. She lowered her head a fraction. "Nor is my chin jutting out."

"Do you only get angry with people you know well?" He appeared to be fascinated by such a claim.

Elinor stopped and looked pointedly at the front steps of the Dower House.

"I am home, Mr. Worth. Please, let me relieve you of your burden." When she moved to take the basket, he lifted it out of her reach.

"I insist on delivering it to your door." He moved ahead of her, taking long strides toward the entrance, easily outpacing her.

The door opened before he reached the steps.

"*There* you are, my lady," Beth exclaimed, as if the other woman didn't know perfectly well that Elinor took tuition at Doctor Venable's twice a week on exactly the same day and at exactly the same time. "And just in time, too, as it appears the heavens are about to open."

As if on cue, rain began to pelt Elinor's straw bonnet.

"And you've brought Mr. Worth with you." Beth smiled up at the American as though she'd only just that moment noticed the six plus feet of man towering beside her. "You can enjoy a nice warming cup of tea while this nasty bit of weather blows over." She opened the door wider and ushered them both inside.

"I should love to," Worth murmured, sounding, for all the world, as if that was what he'd hoped for all along.

***

*Christ.* Stephen had not exerted this much charm, and to so little effect, since he'd been ten and Sister Mary MacEwan had caught him and Angus Baird red-handed with the sacrificial wine.

Lady Trentham's servant—Beth, she'd called her—on the other hand, now there was a woman amenable to being charmed.

If not for Beth, Stephen would have found himself riding hell-bent for shelter through the vicious storm which had sprung up in the blink of an eye.

The countess sat as far away from him as the little room allowed. Other than the brief moment when she'd laughed, Stephen could see nothing of the lively girl he'd known so briefly fifteen years before. She was wary. Whether it was of him or life in general, he could not say.

He'd lingered at Blackfriars for a week and this was only the second time he'd seen her.

He'd meant to seek her out every day and begin ensnaring her bit-by-bit. Instead, he'd become entangled with his annoying host every damned day. The earl was most eager to cement their association—and Stephen's money.

Stephen told himself the delay was fine; charming the dowdy little woman should not take much time. He was not vain, but he was practical. He knew women found him physically attractive. His appearance, combined with his extreme wealth, made him a package most women found hard to resist. How difficult could it be to captivate a woman well past her prime? A woman who'd never been much to look at even when she'd been *in* her prime? A woman who'd thoughtlessly stolen a kiss that had wrecked his entire life?

He glared across the small sitting room to where his reluctant hostess was gazing out a rain-spattered window.

*Calm yourself, Stephen.*

He shifted restlessly in his seat at the chastising voice. Indeed, it never did a person any good to get emotional. About anything.

Besides, the past week had hardly been a waste. He'd spent his time prowling the estate and the house, avoiding its owner when possible. One thing had become clear the more he saw: he wanted Blackfriars—badly. For whatever reason, the house had worked its way into his bones.

Stephen knew himself well enough to recognize the hungry, clawing feeling in his gut. Jeremiah had called the feeling *ambition* but the word was too tame for what Stephen felt. Once the yawning hole within him opened its maw, bared its teeth, and latched onto him, it could not be appeased, paid off, or ignored. It required one thing and one thing only: satisfaction.

Stephen would have Blackfriars.

The servant entered with the tea tray, cutting Stephen an encouraging smile. *Ah, I have an ally in the countess's household.* He gave her a smile that left her blushing.

"Thank you, Beth. That will be all." Lady Trentham said, dismissing her meddling servant and pulling his attention back to the gloomy, shabby little room. "How do you like your tea, Mr. Worth?"

*I don't.*

Stephen gave his hostess his most charming smile. "Three lumps of sugar, no milk, please."

The woman raised an eyebrow to show what she thought of that.

"I confess to a bit of a sweet tooth," he explained. Besides, maybe enough sugar would make the wretched beverage palatable. Tea, tea, and more tea. It tasted no better than used dishwater and generated a ferocious need for a piss after the first tasteless sip.

"Biscuit?" She gestured toward a plate filled with the tiny food items women seemed so fond of foisting on hungry men.

Once they both were in possession of cups, saucers, and food, the room grew uncomfortably silent. Only the heavy patter of rain and occasional gust of wind broke the stillness.

"What have—"

"How often—"

They both began at the same time, and then laughed, easing some of the tension.

"You first, Lady Trentham."

"I was only going to ask how long you planned to stay in our country."

Stephen considered pointing out that she'd already asked him that, but decided it wasn't a worthwhile avenue of discussion. "I will remain in England for the foreseeable future."

Like every other aristocrat he'd met since coming back to England she was unfailingly polite and utterly unreadable. Even so, the very slight tightening around her eyes said his admission had surprised her. Had it displeased her, too?

She sipped her tea and hid her eyes from him.

"We have an office in London and I will be spending a good deal of time there when I'm not traveling." Stephen picked up a small bun studded with currants. He'd had one the last time he'd visited and it had been quite delicious.

"Traveling? To the Continent?"

Stephen finished chewing and took a mouthful of scalding, cloying beverage. "Mostly I will visit properties across Britain to assess their potential investment value."

"Ah, investments." Her teacup hid her mouth, but he was certain he'd seen a contemptuous smile.

"You say that word like many others of your class. I'm afraid the members of the English aristocracy can no longer afford to disdain commerce or finance." The words came out harsher than he'd expected, but her superior attitude irked him. He could buy Blackfriars and everything around it twenty times over. How dare she treat him with the same insulting condescension she'd done on that long-ago night?

Her cool voice cut through his building anger. "You would have the *English aristocracy* joyfully embrace the destruction of our way of life, Mr. Worth?" She nibbled on something swathed in pink-and-white icing.

"Change is an unavoidable part of life, Lady Trentham." Stephen had not come here today to discuss philosophical issues, but he was nothing if not adaptable. "Whether you would embrace it or not, change has come to *you*."

She put down her saucer and cup with more force than was necessary. "Is this your indirect way of telling me you are purchasing Blackfriars?"

"What has Lord Trentham told you?"

"Nothing."

"Nothing?" Stephen could not believe that was true. At the very least he would have expected Trentham to boast about the windfall he would receive from the sale.

"The current earl and I are not close, Mr. Worth."

"Even so, you live here. I would have thought it was his duty to inform you of his intentions."

A ghost of a smile flitted across her face. "And what is the procedure when a property with tenants changes hands? Will we have some period of time to make arrangements or will men simply arrive one day and put us out on our front steps?"

Stephen laughed. And then realized she wasn't laughing with him. Her question had been serious.

"I understand your father and brother are still alive, my lady. If you were to leave Trentham surely you would return to your family?"

Her frosty glare told him that *never* would be too soon to ask her such personal questions.

He'd known her relations with her father and brother were strained, and he'd lost any tiny bit of ground he'd made by prodding her on such an obviously sore subject. He glanced out the window. It was gray and raining, but it was beginning to look far more hospitable than the atmosphere inside the room. His approach with her had been ham-handed in the extreme. Between her wary attitude and his own inept bungling he was beginning to feel quite foul-mooded. How the devil would he ever be able to seduce the blasted woman if he kept setting her back up?

"What will you do with Blackfriars after you acquire it?" she asked, breaking into his black thoughts. This small, uncharacteristic sign of curiosity was promising.

"*If* I were to acquire Blackfriars it would be to live in it myself."

Her lips parted and her gray eyes widened. Stephen had to suppress a smile. Emotions—progress indeed.

"It surprises you that I would desire such a house, Lady Trentham?" The two spots of color that sprang to her pale cheeks were the only answer he needed. He chuckled, genuinely amused by the gentle fluster he'd managed to elicit. "Even pushing cits like myself must have somewhere to live, you know."

She took cover behind her teacup before responding to his taunt. "I am merely surprised you should choose to live in England, Mr. Worth."

"Why is that?"

"Will you not miss your family and friends in . . . is it Boston?"

"Yes, Boston. But I have no family there, Lady Trentham." *And precious few friends*, he could have added. "I am unencumbered and free to live wherever I choose."

"And you would choose Blackfriars." Her voice was oddly meditative.

Stephen neither confirmed nor denied her statement.

The clock chimed the half hour and he realized he'd been in the sitting room longer than the strictly proper. He stood. "I have imposed on your hospitality long enough, my lady."

Her eyes flickered to the window as she rose. It was still raining, but lightly now. He thought she might extend her offer of shelter, but she merely led him toward the door, which opened before she could touch the handle. Lady Trentham's maid stood in the open doorway, a slight frown on her face.

"Please have Tompkins fetch Mr. Worth's horse, Beth." Lady Trentham spoke firmly, as though to forestall her servant, whose expression had turned mulish, as if she were considering whether she might suggest an invitation in spite of her mistress's obvious reluctance. At the end of her brief struggle the maid turned away, leaving them alone together in the small foyer.

Stephen took one last shot at piercing the countess's not inconsiderable defenses. "I was serious about Lord Trentham's party, ma'am."

Her gray eyes were assessing but her words, when they finally came, were dry and vague. "You are too kind, Mr. Worth."

Stephen found himself hatted, gloved, and in possession of Brandy's reins almost before he realized it. The countess stood beneath the small *porter cocher* beside her maid and watched as he cantered away from the shabby house.

Stephen waited until he reached the lane before giving Brandy his head.

The gelding shot forward, as eager as his master to leave behind the uncomfortable gaze of a pair of gray eyes.

***

"You should have invited him to stay longer, my lady."

Elinor pulled her gaze away from Mr. Worth's disappearing form and turned to stare at her servant.

"Well, why shouldn't you?" Beth protested, although Elinor had not spoken. "It was unkind to throw him out in such dreadful weather. You've had Doctor Venable to dine on more than one occasion. You are a widow; a certain amount of freedom accompanies that position."

Elinor turned away without answering. "Please tell Hetty I'll take a cold dinner in my room." She shut the door to the library on Beth's muttering and collapsed in her favorite chair. What the devil had all *that* been about? Could the man really be so bored as to flirt with her? Or had he merely been taking shelter from the storm?

No, he'd been behaving oddly before the rain began to fall.

Elinor absently picked at a thread on her gown. His face came to mind without any effort on her part. Indeed, his face *crowded* her mind. How could it not? When was the last time so much male beauty had been focused on her?

Oh, Doctor Venable was certainly a very attractive man, but he did not fill every inch of space in a room. His brooding manner was retiring, his presence almost . . . soothing. At least to her. There were times they worked together in the same room for several hours without speaking. Stephen Worth rattled her, and not just because of his compelling green stare and imposing masculine body. There was something about him. Elinor shook her head. What? What was it? Why did she feel like he was wearing a mask?

She pushed aside her fanciful imaginings. Was Charles really going to sell Blackfriars? Such news shouldn't surprise her. His son, Martin, was another just like him. They were both selfish men far more interested in town life and town pursuits than responsibilities to their land and people.

"Greedy fools." The sound of her voice took her out of her reverie. And what would she do when that happened? Where would she go?

*Will you return to your family?* His question floated through her mind.

Just what did Mr. Stephen Worth know of her family? Had Charles told him anything? That seemed unlikely. Charles enjoyed talking of himself too much to spare any time for other people. Besides, what was there to say about her family that was of any interest to anyone? Her father and brother lived in London, only occasionally visiting their country seat and never Elinor. Father had his horses, his clubs, and his mistress. And her brother, Stuart? Well, who knew what or whom Stuart had? Certainly not Elinor. Relations hadn't been very good before her mother died, and they'd become almost non-existent after that.

It had been years since she'd spoken to either of them. The same night she'd hosted her last ball at Blackfriars. She recalled that dreadful evening as clearly as if it had been yesterday.

Elinor had no interest in exhuming memories of that long-ago night and turned her thoughts to the man who'd summoned them. Stephen Worth was a powerful, formidable man. His hands had dwarfed the cup and saucer the same way his presence had overwhelmed the room. And her.

What did he want?

*He is interested in you*, Beth had said.

Warmth pervaded parts of her body she generally did not notice and left her feeling anxious. Beth's observation was nothing more than proof of her servant's affection. Beth loved her and believed her to be worthy of interest, even from such a man as Stephen Worth. He was a golden creature—or perhaps copper would be a more accurate description—who glowed with confidence that he was master of all he surveyed. Or soon would be, if he acquired Blackfriars.

As pleasant and attentive as he'd been toward her, Elinor could not shrug off the feeling something dark lurked beneath his polished, friendly surface. Beth would *pooh-pooh* such a worry and tell her it was merely the result of too much time spent with her own company.

Was Beth correct? *Had* marriage to Edward left her hardened and suspicious of any man who might show any genuine, decent interest in her?

Elinor recalled the American's arrogant dismissal of her crippled foot and her subsequent anger and knew he'd been correct, for all that it had irritated her at the time. She *could* dance, she just never had. At least not in public. She'd learned all the steps like any young girl anticipating her first Season. While brisk dances had proven difficult for her, those with a slower pace had not burdened her foot beyond bearing.

She bit her lip at the ridiculous thoughts he'd managed to sow in her mind with so little effort. A ball? And at Blackfriars of all places.

What nonsense.

# Chapter Five

Elinor sat in the most formal of her family's three drawing rooms, her gaze fixed on the Ormolu clock on the mantle. If she closed her eyes and concentrated, she imagined she could hear the murmur of voices two rooms away, where her father and her betrothed—or was he her former betrothed now?—haggled over her future. Or, rather, haggled over the chunk of land that mattered to both of them far more than she ever would.

She tried to keep her mind on the land in question rather than the terrible words she'd heard come out of the Earl of Trentham's mouth two nights ago. Had it really only been two nights? Was she really only sixteen? She felt all of sixty today.

"You strumpet, you little *whore*! How many times did you spread your thighs for him? Are you already carrying his bastard?" Trentham had demanded after the footmen had dragged the boy's unmoving body from the hall and her father had ushered them all into his study.

"Now Trentham, I will tolerate no more of that kind of talk," her father had belatedly—and rather weakly—interposed.

The earl had turned on him like a mad dog, his urbane façade a distant memory by that point. "*You* will tolerate no more, Yarmouth?

What about me? Am I to be satisfied with the sullied leavings of a servant?"

Tears had rolled silently down her face as she'd watched her father's feeble efforts to calm the almost demented man.

"She shall be examined by a physician of your choosing, Trentham."

His words, so horribly mortifying to Elinor, failed to pacify the furious peer.

"And what if she is not intact? Or what if she is *increasing?* What then? You have no other daughters; will you try to marry me to your *son?*" Spittle flew from his sneering mouth.

*Strumpet. Whore.*

The words had paraded through her mind the entire time the cold, judgmental doctor had prodded and poked at her. A procedure which had left her feeling exposed and eviscerated, like a corpse on an autopsy table.

Elinor had wished she were dead when the doctor's cool, alien flingers had invaded her, not stopping until she'd bled all over his hand and satisfied him, her father, and the man who would be her husband.

The door to the sitting room opened and jerked her away from the nightmarish memory.

Her mother stood in the doorway, the Earl of Trentham beside her, his sharp, handsome features arranged in an expression of weary ennui. He was unrecognizable from the vicious beast he'd been a few nights before. Except for his eyes, which were the same hard, pitiless pale blue.

"His lordship would like a few minutes with you, Elinor." Lady Yarmouth's words were foolish, considering it had been she who'd put Elinor in this room a full two hours ago to sit and wait for him.

Elinor rose on legs that felt too shaky to hold her and curtsied low as Edward Atwood gave her mother a barely civil nod and strode into the room. The door closed and Elinor sat. The earl took a chair some distance away.

"I have acquired a special license." His voice was clipped and cool. "We will no longer have the ridiculous ceremony your parents desired in St. George's. That is all to the best, in my opinion." He stopped and Elinor wondered if he expected her to say something. But then he continued. "We shall spend one night in Trentham House before you are removed to Blackfriars, where I will return every month until you are breeding." His eyes flickered over her and he made no effort to hide his distaste. "You will remain in the country until such time as you have delivered two male offspring of *mine*, not the footman, groom, or stable boy. Is that clear?"

Elinor's face was unbearably hot, but she refused to look away from his contemptuous stare.

"I am well aware what is required of me as your wife, my lord."

His pale eyes glinted like a lighthouse warning. "You would be wise not to employ such a tone with me ever again, my lady. You will find my household far less indulgent than your father's. I will not hesitate to discipline you should you fail to obey me in even the smallest way. Is that understood?"

His dispassionate threat was even worse than his rage.

Elinor swallowed. "I understand, my lord."

He stood. "Very good. I shall see you on the morrow."

Elinor watched his slim, stylish form until the door closed behind him and then slumped against the settee, tears rolling down her face yet again. She couldn't seem to stop them, and her weakness sickened her. She closed her eyes, but that only brought an even more upsetting vision: that of a handsome young face masked with shock, pain, and blood.

"Oh, God," she whispered, as the footman's face wavered in her mind's eye. What would become of him? What had she done to an innocent man in a moment of carelessness?

# Chapter Six

## Village of Trentham
## 1817

Stephen was in a foul mood after a second unsuccessful attempt to catch Lady Trentham on her way back from the good doctor's house. He was certain the woman had purposely thwarted him. He'd not been able to find her either in the small village or on the only road that led from the doctor's to the Dower House. He could hardly pound on her front door and demand entry, so he'd finally admitted defeat and aimed Brandy toward Blackfriars.

Stephen was not surprised when he cantered beneath the arched entry of the massive stable block and nobody came out to greet him. Indeed, he'd become accustomed not only to caring for his own horse, but most of his other needs.

He'd just finished filling Brandy's feed bag when the sound of horse hooves on cobbles reached his ears.

"Damn it," he muttered under his breath. He'd managed to avoid Trentham's annoying company since breakfast. It appeared his luck had run out. Grumbling, he went out to face the toad-eating aristocrat.

But the huge back that greeted him did not belong to Trentham.

"So, you've finally decided to return, I see."

# The Footman

John Fielding's massive shoulders swung around in a remarkably fluid motion. For all his size, the man moved like a cat.

His dour, hulking servant merely grunted. "Aye."

Stephen looked up a good two inches into eyes blacker than a Lancashire coal pit. He knew the single word was likely the only one his terse servant would freely offer until he was good and ready. Getting Fielding to speak was a lot like mining. But just like that laborious activity, it could also yield precious ore if a person had enough patience.

A stable boy wandered into the covered yard and froze when he saw Fielding, his placid features rearranging themselves into a mask of terror.

Fielding had that effect on people.

"Here, lad, take Mr. Fielding's horse." Stephen said gently, nodding to the reins Fielding still held in one giant gloved hand.

Fielding tossed the reins to the boy without looking at him and then unstrapped his bag from the saddle. The man's heavily mud-spattered coat told Stephen he'd ridden through the rain that had passed through the area last night rather than taking shelter. His mount, an enormous dun-colored creature with a disposition to match his master's, bared its teeth and lunged at the stable boy when he tried to take his bridle.

"Enough!" Fielding snapped. The beast, whom Fielding had not bothered to name, stiffened at the harsh command, his posture offended rather than chastened. But he did allow the boy to lead him away.

Fielding stood silently, bag in hand.

"Have you news for me?" Stephen asked, turning toward the house, the larger man falling into step beside him.

"Aye."

Stephen rolled his eyes. Had he really missed the surly bastard? "Come to my chambers after you've cleaned yourself up."

Fielding broke away without answering, making his way toward the servant's entrance.

Stephen cast off his coat upon reaching his chambers, wishing for the fiftieth time he'd taken the opportunity to engage a new valet when he'd last been in London. Now it appeared he would not be leaving for London at least until Trentham's wretched ball.

He was considering the possibility of sending Fielding back to London to engage a servant on his behalf when the man himself knocked and entered.

Stephen looked pointedly at his watch. It had been less than ten minutes since they'd parted. Hardly long enough to clean up or change clothing and make himself presentable. Fielding ignored the not-so-subtle gesture.

"Sit," Stephen said, motioning toward the two ragged chairs that flanked his dormant fireplace.

Fielding looked from one chair to the other before choosing the larger of the two. The man was enormous, his body a compact collection of muscles that made him appear almost as wide as he was tall. While he was only a few inches taller than Stephen, he probably outweighed him by at least three stone. He took the glass Stephen offered, his distinctive six-fingered hand dwarfing the cut crystal.

Stephen took the chair across from him. "So?"

Fielding threw back the liquid and bared his teeth as it burnt a path down his throat. The grimace tightened the scars that radiated out from both corners of his mouth, deep cuts that would have required dozens of stitches to hold the wounds closed. John Fielding had been a handsome young man before he'd been carved upon. Well, Stephen supposed Fielding was still handsome, in a dangerous, terrifying sort of way—at least based on the number of women who fought to warm his bed. Fielding didn't want for female company, although he never seemed eager to prolong any relationship beyond a few nights.

Stephen had never asked the man how he'd come by such dreadful scars—a Cheshire Smile, as it was called among the members of the criminal class. No, theirs was not that kind of relationship. While they might be more than master and servant, they were certainly not friends. He supposed it would be most accurate to call them conspirators.

Fielding fixed his perpetually sullen gaze on his employer. "Yarmouth has taken the bait. He's also noised about it to anyone who bothered to listen and many who haven't."

"Has he taken any steps to acquire money for the scheme?"

"He's not yet found anyone daft enough to loan money on his London property, but he's generated a tidy sum from the lands that came to him on Lady Yarmouth's death."

"As to that, did you ever find out anything more about her bequest to Lady Trentham?"

"There was none."

Stephen blinked. "How unusual for a mother to leave her daughter nothing," he mused.

"Not in that family. Her father and brother behave as if Elinor Trentham died years ago."

"I know that, already, Fielding. Have you learned *why*?"

"No. But I've a few lines in the water, I've just had no bites yet."

"You'll let me know the moment you learn anything. Even the smallest thing."

Amusement flickered in the other man's Hell-black eyes. "Aye, 'course."

Stephen tamped down his irritation. Fielding was correct to find his desperate need to know even the tiniest detail about Viscount Yarmouth's family amusing. Stephen was foolish to show his obsession to anyone—even his own servant. He would need to hide his emotions better.

"Has Lord Yarmouth managed to attract any other investors?"

"Aye. He's roped more than few silly buggers into his scheme." Fielding raised his hand and ticked off the names. "Lords Bryce, Fenwick, Stockton, Piermont, Leonard, Singleton, and—" he paused, saving his sixth digit for last "—the ailing Duke of Falkirk is said to be tossing a few bob his way."

"Falkirk? I thought he was too ill to be interested in such matters."

Fielding's mouth twisted into a sneer and it was not a pretty sight. "Falkirk's young pup has brought the matter to his papa's attention."

"Lord Gaulton?"

Fielding's eyes kindled like burning coals at the sound of his legitimate half-brother's name.

Had Stephen been wise to tell Fielding about his relationship to one of the most ancient families in Britain, albeit on the wrong side of the blanket? Stephen was no longer so sure his decision had been a good one. The hatred he saw in the Fielding's eyes was . . . worrisome.

As if hearing his thoughts, doors slammed shut over the raging furnace in Fielding's eyes and once again they became the flat obsidian wall he usually showed the world.

Fielding shrugged his massive shoulders. "I daresay he's eager to impress his father with his business acumen. Given the state of the Duke of Falkirk's affairs, he cannot afford to lift his nose at commerce."

"That may be so, but I'd like to dissuade all but Fenwick, Piermont, and Stockton from sinking money into this venture. From what I know about those particular men they deserve whatever they get." Indeed, given the stories he'd heard about the lecherous peers and the trail of suffering they'd left in their wake, it would be a pleasure to take their money.

His giant servant seemed to double in size like some venomous jungle reptile. His muscles were taut and tense as his body expanded in the rickety chair.

"I want Falkirk," Fielding growled, giving him a look that said Stephen was something he would be picking out of his teeth soon if Stephen wasn't careful.

This was what the man must have looked like in a boxing ring before he dismembered yet another opponent.

Stephen relaxed in his chair, crossing one booted foot over his knee. "Tell me, John, will you be able to keep your feelings about the Duke of Falkirk from interfering with *my* business?"

Fielding rose, blocking the sun from the study window with his broad back and casting his face into shadow. "You may pay me, Worth, but you don't own me. No man does. What I do on my own time is my own business."

"There's no need to fly into a pucker, John. I'm not saying you may not play your little games." Stephen put his half-full glass on the table and rose. He closed the gap between them, not stopping until he was close enough to see the subtle color difference between Fielding's narrowed black pupils and the dark brown of his irises. "I may not *own* you, Fielding, but I have financed this endeavor—including freeing your wretched carcass from somewhere south of Hell, transporting you half-way across the globe, and giving you every goddamned thing you now call yours. Have a care your games do not interfere with *mine*.

Are we understood?" Stephen didn't bother to conceal his barely suppressed fury.

The muscles in Fielding's jaw were so taut Stephen swore he could see the individual striations. The nostrils of his once patrician, but oft-broken, nose flared. After what felt like twenty years, he lowered his eyes and took a tiny step back. "Aye. I understand."

Stephen felt almost light-headed with relief. He'd not stood chest-to-chest with a man in many years, and never against one who unsettled him as much as John Fielding. Stephen was pleased to learn he still had the stones when necessary.

He sauntered back to his chair and dropped into it, picking up his glass. "Good. Now, get the hell out of here and find me a damned bed that doesn't leave me a bloody cripple every morning, even if you have to tear the house apart."

# Chapter Seven

*Coldbath Fields Prison*
*London*
*1802*

I ain struggled for breath, the heavy burlap bag as easy to breathe through as mud.

"Quit yer squirmin'!" the guard hissed above him. "I've a mind to dump yer worthless arse right 'ere." The rickety gurney tilted to one side to illustrate his intentions.

"Oye," his partner said, "mind ye wait 'til we've got the blunt, first."

"Shut yer gob. 'Course I'll get money in 'and first."

The two bickered in loud whispers while they lugged Iain's bagged corpse across the cobbled prison yard.

"What have ye there?" a voice called from someplace farther afield.

"This one 'as got the cole-er-ah. We're taking 'is rotting body straight to the 'ole."

A grunt of assent was all the answer they received, making Iain wonder just how many prisoners died in this wretched hellhole. And how many escaped.

So far the journey from the oakum shed had been relatively easy, with the exception of the suffocating burlap that covered him from head to toe. The evening had gone exactly according to plan. Iain had begun wailing just as the moon reached its zenith and the guards had come not long after. John had left his side earlier in the evening, when Iain had tried, yet again, to convince him to accompany him.

"Stop yer whitterin' or I'll smack you myself," the bigger boy had growled before going to sit with the same men he'd pounded earlier.

Iain had remained alone after that.

The gurney came to a sudden halt and Iain heard the distinctive sound of the creaking of rusty hinges.

"Tssst!" one of his captors hissed. "You there?"

"Aye, I'm here," Uncle Lonnie's calm, low voice called back.

Iain began fumbling with the burlap at the sound of his uncle's voice. A hand like a vise grabbed his shoulder. "Oye! Not 'til we sees the dosh."

"I've got your money." Iain heard the dull jingle of coins. "Now let him go."

"Give us the money."

"Not until he's standing beside me."

The air was heavy with violence, making it even more difficult to breathe.

"Fine." The man holding the foot-end of the gurney released his end abruptly and the wooden handles hit the ground with a crack. Not surprisingly, the head-end was quick to follow.

"Whadja do that fer?" the other guard demanded. "Ye near broke me back!"

Iain groaned and rolled to his side, shrugging off the reeking burlap in the process. Threads of rotting fiber and flakes of mud and dust clung to his eyelashes and stung his eyes. He blinked hard, peering frantically through tears and haze. A hand hovered in front of his face.

"Take my hand, Iain," his uncle said calmly.

"The money, now."

"Here's your money."

Iain heard the sound of coins striking cobblestones, followed by rapidly retreating feet and cursing.

"Come on, boy, there's no time to waste." Uncle Lonnie pulled Iain to his feet and then kept on pulling. "Run, son. Run as fast as you can." He shoved Iain roughly ahead of him.

They then proceeded to run for what felt like miles. They ran, and ran, and ran, stopping only for a few seconds now and then to regain their breath, and then they ran some more. It was too dark to tell what direction they were headed, but the streets seemed to become wider and less dangerous looking, until eventually they spotted a hackney cab.

"Do you know where *The Liberty* is berthed?" his uncle called up to the driver.

"Aye, but that's a goodly way and she's set to sail on the tide. Happens ye've already missed 'er."

"Get us there in time and I'll pay double."

The rickety carriage shot forward before the door had even closed and Iain collapsed into the torn, smelly squabs, gasping for air.

"*The Liberty*?"

His uncle nodded, but kept his face turned toward the dirty window.

"What is happening, Uncle Lonnie?"

"I've bought you passage to America."

"*What*? But, why?" Iain's voice was at least two octaves higher. "You're coming with me?"

His uncle finally turned to him and the look in his eyes turned Iain's heart cold. "No, son, I'm not. I've only got enough money for one ticket and that has to be yours. They're calling you a rapist, boy. You'll hang if you're caught in England."

"A rapist?" Iain repeated, aghast.

"Aye. They say you forced yourself on her ladyship and Lord Trentham had to pull you off."

"That's a bloody lie!"

"I know that, boy, but it will be their word against yours. And Lord Trentham isn't the only one. His lordship and Master Stuart were also there. And then there's the girl." His face was a grim mask that looked nothing like the uncle Iain knew and trusted.

"She's claiming I raped her?"

The older man shrugged. "I don't know exactly what any of them are saying, son. They've not come for me. Yet. Besides, they're hardly likely to confide in a servant."

"Do you believe them?" Iain asked, his stomach churning as if he'd just swallowed acid.

His uncle made an impatient noise. "'Course I don't, boy, but everyone else will." He grabbed Iain's shoulder and shook him. "Listen to me, we've not got much time. I've purchased you a place on *The Liberty*, but it will be rough going in steerage, boy." He reached into the pocket of his old coat and pulled out a small leather purse. "This is all I have left after buying the ticket and bribing that scum at The Steel." He pushed it into Iain's hands.

"But, what about—"

"Listen to me." His uncle's voice was harsher than Iain had ever heard it. "Your life depends on it. You must change your name—first *and* last. Make up something new—something even I don't know so I can't tell them if they were ever to come for me." His hand flexed until it bit painfully into his shoulder. "You can *never, ever* come back here, do you understand, Iain? Ever. I paid the guards enough to have you declared dead, but only truly dead men keep secrets."

Iain only realized tears were rolling down his face when he tasted salt. He dashed them away with the back of his hand, ashamed at his babyish bawling. He'd not cried even when his Mam had died.

"Aye, Uncle. I understand."

"When you get to Boston you should look for a way to New York or one of the other big American cities, they've got several. It's best you're well away from where *The Liberty* is known to dock. I can't say as anyone would put you and ships together, and I'm hoping if they do, they'll think you just hopped to France. I bought you passage under the name John Smith, but I daresay you won't be the only by that name aboard *The Liberty*." Lonnie's eyes flickered to Iain's head. "I wish we had time to do something about that mop of yours, but it's looking less red than usual with all the mud. Try to keep it hid or covered if you can, it's like a bloody calling card."

"Yes, sir."

"Good lad. Now, when you get to wherever it is you plan to settle, look for a position in service. You've a natural talent with horses and I've taught you a little. Or you can keep to your finery and serve in a rich man's house proper like. I hear things are different in America. A man can write his own ticket. You've a fair hand, write your own letter of introduction." He gave Iain a strained smile to go with his attempt at humor. "There are few enough employers who will send all the way back to England to check on you."

"What about you, Uncle? Will this put you in danger?"

The older man gave him one of his crooked smiles and patted him gently on the shoulder with his big, calloused hand. "I'm like a cat, boy. I'll always land on my feet."

An old, familiar anger reared inside him. "Why must it always be *us* who must take care how and where we land, Uncle? How come *they* always get away with trampling the likes of us?"

Uncle Lonnie shook his head and took him by the shoulder. "You need to forget that fight, Iain. It's sad but true, son, 'might makes right'." He squeezed his shoulder so hard Iain winced. "Your Mam told me what you did to The MacLeod when the man turfed you off his land. You're lucky he let you off with a whipping, boy. You need to keep a tighter hold on that temper of yours."

Iain was surprised his uncle had known about Iain's bad behavior all this time and never said anything. Iain wasn't proud of what he'd done to The MacLeod. At the time, he'd told himself the man who'd fathered him owed him the half-dozen prime sheep he'd stolen and driven to market. And then The MacLeod himself caught him and gave him the whipping of his life.

Suddenly the driver's hatch sprang open.

"Ye'd better be ready to run," he shouted through the opening. "They're pulling up the gangplank."

Uncle Lonnie flung open the cab door before the vehicle even came to a halt. He turned to Iain, his blue eyes beneath water. "Make haste boy, you've no time."

Iain tightened his hand around the small purse of money and lifted it. "Thank you for this, Uncle. Thank you for everything."

"*Run,* boy!" His uncle's voice broke and he pushed Iain out of the hackney so hard he almost fell.

"I won't forget you, Uncle Lonnie."

"*Run!*"

Iain ran.

# Chapter Eight

Elinor mounted the ancient stone stairs to the house where she'd lived for almost a decade. Lights blazed from every window, countless candles glinting behind thousands of tiny leaded panes of glass. Charles had outdone himself. Or, rather, his housekeeper and steward had.

"Elinor, my dear, how lovely you could come," the earl greeted her before she'd even taken two steps into the foyer. Elinor looked into his shallow blue eyes and it was all she could do not to turn around and leave. Why had she come?

*To see* him, *of course.*

She blinked away the thought and the face that went with it and looked at her repulsive host instead.

"Good evening, Charles. I commend you, Blackfriars looks magnificent." It would irk him that she would not compliment *him*, but instead his house.

"As do you, my dear," he said, ruining the compliment with a smirk.

Beth had done her very best tonight, but the person inside the pretty gown her maid forced her to purchase was still Elinor. The fabric—a pale peach silk—flattered her more than anything she'd worn since Edward's death. Even before her husband died, she'd worn nothing but grays and blacks. When Edward had finally noticed her somber garments—years after she'd taken to wearing them—he'd laughingly accused her of mourning a series of unsuccessful pregnancies.

By that time the comment had surprised, rather than hurt, Elinor. Who would have guessed Edward possessed such insight?

And who knew why she was suddenly interested in wearing colorful clothing again?

She handed Charles's butler her gauzy peach wrap. "You are looking well, Beacon."

The normally somber man's face creased into a pleased smile. "And may I be so bold as to say the same for you, my lady?"

"Yes, yes, very good, Beacon," Charles muttered, waving away the servant and taking her arm, guiding her past the spectacular flagstone staircase that led to the far smaller second floor. Elinor shivered, grateful she would not have to go up those stairs. To where her chambers had been.

"I have a surprise for you tonight, dear Elinor."

The small hairs at the back of her neck rose. "Oh?"

He cast her a gleeful look before flinging open one of the huge doors to the refectory, an enormous room that would be used both for dining and for the ball. The room was over one hundred and forty feet long, its ceiling supported by vast hammer beams. It had been designed on an east-west axis and a spectacular rose window complete with stone tracery faced east. Standing in the room in the morning when the sun shone through it was almost a religious experience.

But tonight her attention wasn't on the glorious window.

Viscount Yarmouth stood just inside the room, holding a glass of something ruby-colored in his white, tapered fingers.

"Hello, Elinor."

Elinor felt as though she'd been kicked in the chest by a draught horse. Naturally her excellent manners took charge of her brain and told her body to ignore the painful sensation and avoid making a scene.

"Father. What a surprise."

Her father's faded blue eyes darted from Charles to her, as if he was uncertain what to say next and was searching for cues.

A new voice came from behind Elinor and spared the viscount the effort.

"Lady Trentham, how delightful to see you again."

Elinor turned from the frying pan to face the fire.

The sight that met her eyes was every bit as glorious as the rose window. Who would have believed Stephen Worth could look more magnificent than he did in buckskins and tweeds? But of course he did. The stark black and white of his evening attire was the perfect foil for his flamboyant coloring and tall, muscular body. His black coat made him appear even broader than usual and his hair was like a live flame beneath the myriad candles.

He released his dimples in a smile so radiant she could almost believe he really *was* delighted to see her.

She dipped a slight curtsey. "Good evening, Mr. Worth."

His eyes appeared unusually green as they swept from Elinor to Charles and then lingered on her father. His lips curved in a way that made the skin on her thighs sensitive and . . . aware. Elinor tried to hide the alarming sensations with a sip of wine.

"I have just had the pleasure of meeting your father, Lady Trentham. I was both surprised and pleased to learn we share several interests."

Lord Yarmouth's pale, papery skin—so much in contrast to the younger man's vibrant glow—darkened as three sets of eyes turned his way. Elinor couldn't help wondering if her father, notorious for his ridged views on class, was quite pleased to acknowledge an acquaintance with a man of banking.

"And what are those, Mr. Worth?" Elinor asked when it appeared nobody else would speak.

"We are both avid collectors of miniatures. Unbeknownst to either of us we have crossed paths several times in recent years." The smile he bestowed on Lord Yarmouth seemed benevolent, but Elinor had learned several things about the charming Mr. Worth over the past few weeks. One of them was that his pleasant words frequently hid barbs.

Worth himself had seen to her education on the subject of Stephen Worth by popping up in the most unexpected of places.

Indeed, after the first two coincidental meetings: outside of Doctor Venable's surgery only four days after their *tête-à-tête* during the storm and then a chance encounter the day after *that* in the tiny village shop—where Mr. Worth appeared to be purchasing shoe blacking, of all things—Elinor had begun to expect him to pop up whenever she left the confines of the Dower House.

He was always charming and flattering—respectfully so, of course—but beneath his warm smiles lay a certain . . . watchfulness. Elinor had decided that was simply his predatory business nature showing through his gorgeous, polished veneer.

Lord Yarmouth gave Stephen Worth a guarded smile. "Mr. Worth acquired several specimens I attempted to procure." Her father might be smiling, but Elinor recognized the tension in his eyes. The viscount had not appreciated losing to a man he would consider no better than an upstart cit, albeit an obscenely wealthy one.

Worth took a sip from his glass and rocked almost imperceptibly from the balls of his feet to his heels, very much like a young boy whose body could not contain its joy.

"I daresay I went beyond what I should have in the case of the Cooper," Worth said, his relaxed, confident smile saying otherwise.

In that instant, his expression was as easy to read as a diagram in her medical text: Worth was glad to have outspent her father. He was more pleased by *that* than the actual acquisition of the miniature in question.

Elinor sipped her wine as that realization sank in. So, she now knew the *what*, but she still didn't know the *why*. Why did he wish to bait Lord Yarmouth by snatching a miniature from him? Why did he want to bait Lord Yarmouth at all?

"I hope all this spending hasn't put you under the hatches, old chap," Charles said, giving a bark of laughter, as though the notion of a spendthrift banker was too amusing to be borne.

Lord Yarmouth's lips tightened at the earl's gauche reference to money but Worth chuckled along with the Earl of Trentham. His green eyes, Elinor noticed, glinted behind heavy lids.

\*\*\*

Stephen could feel her presence all along his right side, even when he was turned away and speaking to the woman on his left, a Miss Susan Something-or-Other, who was far prettier than the countess but somehow far less compelling. She would also be a far easier conquest. Stephen recognized the pretty blonde's rapacious look: she wanted his money. She was like a bitch in heat—but for his wealth, rather than his person.

Stephen watched Lady Trentham's hands as he listened to the younger woman babble about some ball she'd attended in London. The widow was buttering a slice of bread, her small hands unexpectedly broad across the backs. They looked like the hands of a woman who worked rather than those belonging to a countess. Something about the competent way those hands manipulated the cutlery caused a surge of heat through his body, as if his nerve endings had imaginations of their own and were contemplating her manipulating *other things* just as deftly.

Stephen almost laughed out loud. He hadn't bedded a woman in so long that even a pair of work-worn hands made his cock hard. He wrenched his mind away from his groin and thought about what he'd learned about the owner of those competent hands in the past few weeks.

"She meets the village doctor twice every week and has done for over three years," Fielding reported a few days after he'd arrived at Blackfriars.

Even though Stephen knew about the meetings from the Earl of Trentham, hearing the words spoken out loud made the muscles of his stomach tighten. Were they lovers? He looked away from Fielding's knowing eyes and down at the ledger that lay open on his desk.

"An affair?" he asked coolly.

"He's teaching her medicine."

Stephen's head snapped up. "What?"

Fielding nodded, an honest-to-God smile lighting up his savage face. "Aye, she's learning to be a doctor. At least that's what the bird who works for Lady Trentham told me."

Stephen did not bother to keep the disbelief from his voice. "Beth told you that?"

"No, not that one. A young lass who comes from the village five days a week to do the heavy work." He snorted. "The older one isn't fond of me. *She* gave me the boot when she saw me the first time I visited the Dower House."

Stephen groaned. "When she saw you doing what, John? Please tell me you weren't trying to bed Lady Trentham's servant under her own roof?"

"Why would I do that when there's a perfectly comfortable hay loft? Anyhow," he continued without waiting for Stephen's response. "She takes lessons with the good doctor and then spends an unhealthy amount of time shut up in her room with books, according to the young maid."

*Learning medicine?*

Stephen watched her out of the corner of his eyes as she picked up a spoon and began raising dainty amounts of soup to her lips. Was that why her hands were so careworn? Medicine?

"I'm so excited to finally attend a dance at Blackfriars," the beauty on his other side chirped, pulling Stephen's attention away from the intriguing widow. "The last time there was a ball at Blackfriars was when Lady Trentham still lived here." She simpered up at Stephen before shooting a rather vicious look at said lady. "Of course I was still an *infant* then. Do you care for balls, Mr. Worth?"

*Only my own.* He smiled at the thought and turned it on the pretty blonde. "I do indeed. In fact, you could say I have something of a mania for balls."

A slight choking sound on his right side gave Stephen the excuse he needed. "Would you excuse me a moment?" he asked and then turned to his reason for being here.

"Was that a cough or were you laughing at me, my lady?" Stephen asked her profile. Her sturdy chin and regal nose were nicely offset by eyebrows that turned up at the ends with a wicked little flick. Her mouth was small but mobile, and currently pulled up ever so slightly at the corner.

She faced him and her fine brows took flight. "I beg your pardon, Mr. Worth, are you speaking to me?"

He grinned at her haughty tone. "Yes, I was. I was reminding you that I laid claim to at least one waltz when last we spoke."

Her pale cheeks tinted a delicate rose color. "I recall you asking me to reserve a waltz for you and I also recall I never answered."

"Ah, but that was because we were interrupted by that charming child—do refresh my memory, what was his name?"

Her lips twitched and her hand rose to her mouth, as it did whenever she laughed or smiled. What was she hiding? A blackened tooth or—horrors— a *missing* tooth?

"His name is Reginald Beasley. The poor child must have been eating the berries that grow in the hedge. They are not poisonous, thankfully, but they can be rather . . . unsettling."

"I noticed," Stephen said wryly.

She laughed outright and then caught her lower lip with her teeth. "I must apologize for laughing at you that day—and again, now. It was most unkind of me, both toward you and poor Reggie. But really," for the first time, he saw her gray eyes sparkle like they had on that long-ago night, "you *should* have seen your face, Mr. Worth."

Stephen had come upon Lady Trentham while she attempted to free the little urchin, a tenant farmer's child, from a particularly dense hedge in which he'd become entangled. When Stephen had finally extricated him from the foliage the child had cast up his accounts on Stephen's coat.

Stephen gave her a look of mock severity. "I'm beginning to suspect you are *not* a very nice woman, Lady Trentham."

She shook silently, her eyes shining. "I can see how you might come to that conclusion, Mr. Worth. I do hope your valet was able to get the stains out."

"My valet decamped before we left Boston and I have been woefully negligent in replacing him. As it stands, *I* am my valet, madam. At least I was that day as Mr. Fielding—an employee who sees to my needs in his own savage fashion—refused to have anything to do with the repulsive coat."

She laughed again, her fingers once more lightly touching her upper lip. It was a lovely upper lip, finely drawn and expressive. Stephen learned more from watching her mouth than he ever did from her eyes or words. He had the strongest desire to take that lip between his own and—

"You must send your coat to the woman who does our washing. She is a wizard when it comes to removing difficult stains without damaging a garment."

Stephen pulled his eyes away from her mouth with some effort. "I'm afraid it's too late, my lady. One of the stable lads is now swaning about in what was once my favorite riding coat."

She smiled. "It was a very kind thing to do."

"Well *I* wasn't going to wear it again, and throwing it away seemed like a shame, even considering the large chrysanthemum-shaped design it now sports on the lapel."

"That's not what I meant," she said softly.

Stephen knew exactly what she meant. "Whatever do you mean, my lady?"

She gave a gentle shake of her head to show she knew he was toying with her. "You needn't have helped poor Reggie; there are many men in your position who wouldn't have wasted even a thought on a tenant's child. It was kind of you."

"How do you know it was kind?" He lowered his voice and leaned closer. "What if I only did it to turn you up sweet? What if I did it so you would feel sorry for me and grant me the waltz I've been begging for?"

She pursed her suckable upper lip and gave him her profile again.

They ate in silence as Stephen bided his time and considered, yet again, the last bit of information Fielding had given him about the increasingly fascinating widow.

"Even though she no longer lives at the big house, she's still very highly thought of by the earl's people—far more than he is, not surprisingly—and she usually visits the sick, poor, and elderly on Trentham's estate twice every week." Fielding stopped and cleared his throat. "But this past Saturday she did something different."

"Well?" Stephen prodded when the man remained silent, shuffling his big feet on the worn Savonnerie carpet.

"She took her carriage into Cirencester and met a bloke," he finally said, eyeing Stephen with an almost nervous look.

"Who?" Stephen could barely force the one word through the poisonous stew of emotions churning in his gut. Where the devil were such feelings coming from—and *why*?

Fielding shrugged. "I don't know."

The quill Stephen had been fiddling with snapped in two.

"What am I paying you *for?* You'd bloody well better find out, hadn't you, Fielding?" He'd been unable to keep the fury from his voice. That was *all* he needed, some meddling lover to get in his way.

Footmen materialized at Stephen's elbow and brought him back to the present. He released the fork he'd been clutching like a stiletto, allowing the servant to remove it along with the rest.

He turned to Elinor Trentham and stared until she faced him. Without food to hide behind, she could hardly avoid him.

It was she who broke the silence. "Will you be returning to London now that Lord Trentham's ball—and your mania for balls—is no longer keeping you at Blackfriars?"

He smiled at the subtle teasing. "I am returning to London tomorrow."

The flash of disappointment on her face was like a shooting star, here and gone in a flash. Had he even seen it?

"Will you miss me, Lady Trentham?" he asked, prompted by some demon.

Her small breasts rose and fell twice in their snug silk bower, her gaze on her hand as it toyed with the stem of her glass. "My flirtation skills will certainly suffer in your absence, Mr. Worth."

"Is that all that will suffer?" Why did he want her to admit to noticing his comings and goings—especially his goings?

She looked up at him then, her eyes like molten pits of silver. Stephen knew raw yearning when he saw it and the hunger in her look made his entire body hard. She dropped her burning gaze as quickly as she'd raised it. "I'm afraid you'll find society quite thin in London at this time of year."

\*\*\*

Elinor stared blindly at her wine glass. Why was he doing this to her? *What* was he doing to her? She desperately wanted him to go to London and stay there. But then a fist closed around her heart when she thought of days in which there would be no chance to see him, even from afar.

He'd somehow kindled her spirit—and body—back to life with nothing but a few scorching looks and tame innuendo. She might be unschooled in the ways of the *ton*, but she knew many widows led active sexual lives after their husbands died. Was that what she wanted from him? Was that what *he* wanted?

Because there was no longer any doubt in her mind that he wanted something from her. Something more than a blasted waltz. He'd systematically stalked her over the past few weeks. That was the only word for it: stalking. He'd materialized almost every time she'd left her house, except the Saturday she'd spent with Marcus. Thinking about Marcus made her temples throb. She needed to do something about him, and soon.

Footmen arrived with fresh plates and she served herself from the nearest dishes, unaware of what she took. Instead, she stole a sideways look at Worth, relieved to see he'd taken her neglect in stride and was chatting with Squire Lewis's daughter, Laurel. The girl sparkled, her beautiful face like a flower blooming in sunshine. Did he have that effect on every woman in his orbit? Had she simply imagined his interest in her?

He turned to her as though she'd spoken the question aloud.

"I would very much like to show you my collection of miniatures, Lady Trentham."

If not the last thing she'd expected him to say, it was certainly close.

"You would be better served showing it to my father. He is considered something of an expert."

"I don't want an expert opinion, I want yours."

Elinor pushed several peas around on her plate rather than put them in her mouth and attempt masticating. He appeared to be waiting for a response.

"You travel with your collection?"

"I keep the things I like close at hand so that I may gloat over them and touch them whenever I wish." One long, bronzed finger absently stroked the stem of his wine glass. Elinor swallowed. "Besides," he continued, "I plan to settle here and I could hardly do so without my most prized possessions."

"Oh?" She couldn't muster another syllable. Dear God. Was he really going to purchase Blackfriars? She would have to leave the Dower House. And if she couldn't find another cottage nearby—one she could afford on her meager jointure—then she would have to leave *him*.

The thought stopped her incipient hysteria in its tracks. That she would even *think* such a thing was terrifying. He was watching her, his probing green eyes absorbing whatever it was he saw on her face. "Is that why you are returning to London?" she asked softly, "To fetch your possessions?"

He gave her a long, lazy look from beneath dark auburn lashes, as though he knew the heartburn he was causing and was feasting on it, savoring it. "The reason I am running back to London is that I've received information about a large project my bank is interested in financing. I must see if the project is sound. So, you see, my lady, I am *not* going to London to flit about attending society events as you suspected."

"It was *flirting* I accused you of earlier, not flitting, Mr. Worth."

"I'm afraid neither of those activities interests me if you are not involved, my lady."

Elinor couldn't help laughing. Were all Americans this relentlessly aggressive?

"You have a beautiful smile, at least what I can see of it."

Trust the man to notice such a slight thing. Elinor dropped her hand and frowned.

"You are not only flirtatious but persistent, Mr. Worth. That second characteristic must serve you well in business."

Dangerous imps danced in his eyes and a smile that was pure predator curved his lips. "It serves me just as well in my pursuit of pleasure."

Thankfully the man on her other side interrupted to ask a question about Blackfriars and Elinor was able to escape the conversation without making a fool of herself.

The rest of the meal passed in blessed boredom as she fielded impertinent questions from her other dinner partner about Trentham's financial situation, his relationship with the rich American, and his plans for Blackfriars.

Still, it was better than fielding impertinent questions about herself. Wasn't it?

\*\*\*

Stephen had been less than honest when he'd said he loved balls and the world seemed determined to punish him for his untruth. Word of his love of dancing spread faster than the Black Death and he found himself faced with a veritable army of debutantes.

True to her word, Elinor did not dance a single dance. Instead, she sat with all the mamas and companions, watching the dancers, drinking lemonade, and exchanging pleasantries. Stephen wasn't fooled, however. He'd found her silvery gaze on him more than a few times. She was aware of him. Very aware.

By the time the second waltz crept up Stephen had danced every single set and found himself beset by even more eager mamas, each driven to snag the wealthy American for her daughter.

The dancers were already assembling for the supper set by the time he was able to free himself from the throng. He was not surprised to see the chair the countess had occupied all evening was now vacant.

"You little minx," he muttered under his breath, and then flashed a smile at a pair of tittering girls as he made his way toward the double doors.

"I say, Worth," Charles Atwood appeared before him as though he'd sprouted from the intricately tiled floor. "Do you have a moment to meet a few chaps who've come up special from London to meet you?"

Stephen fought back a groan. He already knew what 'chaps' the earl was referring to. After all, it was Fielding's machinations that had led to the men in question's interest.

He gave the earl an apologetic smile. "Not just now, my lord. I've a rather urgent call that requires my attention." He looked in the direction of the necessary and raised his eyebrows.

"Oh, yes, of course. Well, in your own good time, old man. We'll be in the card room."

*Gambling away the money from the sale of your inheritance before you even have it, old chap?*

Stephen made his way to the entrance. "Have you seen Lady Trentham?" he asked one of the footmen who flanked the massive doorway.

"Yes, sir, she just stepped out into the knot garden for a breath of air."

# The Footman

Stephen had been in the neglected garden several times. Although it was late in the year, many of the plants that made up the intricate design were still flourishing. Lanterns had been hung on metal hangers at strategic intervals and the somewhat shaggy garden looked magical under the light of the full moon. Couples lingered here and there, some gravitating to the taller shrubbery, which would shield their behavior. Lady Trentham, the only solo visitant, was easy to spot.

Stephen approached the stone bench where she sat, his evening shoes crunching on the pea-gravel path.

She turned toward the sound. "Mr. Worth," she said flatly.

"Lady Trentham, you do not sound surprised to see me."

"Surprised? No. You are tenacious." She turned away before he could gauge the expression on her face.

"I have come to collect my waltz."

"You shouldn't have. You will ruin your shoes."

"What about your shoes?" He rounded the bench and stood in front of her. When she would not look up, he dropped to his haunches. Her jaw was set and her face was rigid with tension.

"Here now," he murmured, taking her sharp chin in his hand and turning her to face him. "You're serious about this, aren't you?"

She jerked her chin away, her eyes blazing. "Of course I am." She thrust out her left foot and lifted the hem of her dress, the gesture reminiscent of that long-ago night. "Do you think I wish to dance with this?"

Stephen looked down at the small foot beside his knee. It was proportioned normally but twisted at an angle that meant she would have to walk on the outside edge, rather than the bottom. The side of her slipper, a pale peach like her dress, was already scuffed and frayed where it had contacted the ground. He took her delicate limb in his hand and she gasped.

She was so tiny; her foot was barely the span of his hand from his wrist to the tip of his fingers.

"Does it pain you?" he asked, looking up.

She blinked down at him but did not pull away. "Sometimes."

"There is no cure for this?"

"There was none when I was a child. Now the condition is believed to be treatable if the infant's bones have not yet hardened."

"Is this why you study medicine? To prevent this type of thing from happening?"

She jerked her foot away from him. "How do you know that?"

He rose from his haunches and lowered himself onto the bench beside her. "I make it my business to find out what interests me."

"*Why* do *I* interest you, Mr. Worth? I know it is not because of my incredible beauty, wealth, or charm as I am horribly deficient in all three areas. What is it that you want with me? Why can you not fasten your *interest* on someone more appropriate? Someone like Laurel Lewis?"

"Who the devil is she?"

"The girl you sat beside at dinner for almost two hours."

"Oh. I thought her name was Susan."

A strangled sound of disbelief came from between her parted lips.

Stephen smiled and shrugged. "Who can say why I fail to find Miss Lewis of any interest? Why does a person prefer roast beef to lobster patties? Or Scotch to port?"

Her eyes, already large, appeared to double in size. "Are you really comparing women to meat and alcohol, Mr. Worth?"

"Does that offend you? Would you rather I spoke in terms of art? A Fragonard to a Boucher? A Leonardo to—"

"Why." It was not a question; it was a demand.

Stephen took a moment to give the issue the consideration it deserved. Of course he could not tell her the *real* reason he was determined to seduce her. Not yet, at least. That didn't mean he couldn't share some part of the truth.

"You fascinate me," he confessed in all honesty.

Her small body stiffened beside him. "I find that difficult to believe."

"I don't see why. You are an unusual woman. You live alone, you have undertaken to study a subject that is foreclosed to your sex, you have a strong sense of commitment to your dead husband's people even though another man should now be caring for their interests, and you are an attractive woman still in her prime who appears to have closed herself off to the possibility of a husband and children. You are, in a word, fascinating."

She remained silent beside him.

"I'm sorry I teased you to dance with me. It was not done out of spite." That much was true. "I merely sought an opportunity to spend time with you."

Still she did not reply.

"Lady Trentham? Elinor?" Her name came off his tongue as though he'd spoken it out loud a thousand times. Wide gray eyes turned to him and he acted on an impulse that hadn't even registered yet.

Soft, yielding lips touched his and a scent that had teased him for fifteen years invaded his nostrils: lavender mixed with something else, something that eluded him. He feathered her unresisting but closed mouth with light kisses before following the intoxicating scent across her smooth cheek to her jaw and finally to her hair. He inhaled deeply; his eyes closed as the smell triggered thoughts of that long ago night.

Her slim body molded against his, her soft silver eyes looking up, pleading.

*Would you like to kiss me?*

"Tea," he murmured into her thick, fragrant hair, "You smell like lavender and Lady Gray tea." His words acted like the crack of a whip and she jerked away so abruptly she would have fallen from the end of the bench if he'd not reached out to stop her.

"Steady on," he gentled, using the same soothing tone he would employ on any skittish creature.

"Unhand me, please."

"Only if you promise not to bolt."

"A lady does not *bolt*, Mr. Worth."

He chuckled. "That's the Elinor I know."

"You know nothing about me. And I did not give you leave to use my Christian name."

"You may call me Stephen, if it pleases you."

"It does not please me."

"What *can* I do to please you, then?" Only after he spoke the words did he realize he truly meant them. The realization sent a cold, wickedly sharp knife of fear through his body. When had he begun to think of her as anything other than a task? An item to be ticked from a list? A list he'd been carefully compiling for fifteen years.

She pulled her arm from his hand and lurched to her feet. "If you want to please me, you can leave me be, Mr. Worth."

Her limp was pronounced as she walked away, her slim shoulders squared like a soldier's. Stephen watched until she disappeared back into the house, his entire being filled with the most violent craving for a cup of tea.

# Chapter Nine

*The Liberty*
*1802*

Iain had thrown up in his cramped hard bunk, in the narrow dark hallway, and in a miniscule reeking necessary meant to service at least two hundred other men. He had nothing left in his body to expel. At least nothing he could do without.

He rolled slowly off his bunk, careful not to step on the men sleeping in the two bunks beneath him. He'd spoken to none of his fellow passengers during the past days. Indeed, he'd been too sick to speak. And also too sick to leave at his appointed meal times, which were only ten minutes in duration and caused a stampede among the steerage passengers every time the meal bell rang.

He was starving and thirsty. There was nothing he could do about the former, but he'd noticed a water tank on one of the side decks when he'd come on board a hundred years ago. Steerage passengers weren't permitted to loiter on deck outside of a few hours each day, and even then they were limited to only the service portions of the ship. Still, there would be few people out and about at this hour of the night, it was worth the risk for a drink of water.

He eased past dozens of sleeping bodies on the floor of the hold and closed the door as quietly as he could behind him. Only a few badly smoking oil lamps lit the passage and stairs. His damaged eye was still not working properly and images shifted in the manner of a cracked and darkened kaleidoscope unless he closed the eye. He was so exhausted and dehydrated he needed to stop frequently to rest. As a result, it was some time before he made it to the first door that led to the outside.

The fresh air that greeted him was almost as good as a roast beef dinner and he inhaled so deeply he became dizzy. A sound off to one side caught his attention. Two men were bent over a third man, who lay in a crumpled heap on the deck. Iain squinted; one of the men was going through the prone man's pockets while the other removed his shoes. Iain took a step toward them and both men looked up at the sound, one lurching to his feet.

"What the devil are you lookin' at?" he demanded, his voice filled with menace as he came toward Iain. "You'd best get yourself below if you know what's best for you, boy."

Iain was turning away when a low, pitiful moan emanated from the heap of clothing on the deck. A sudden image of John, the boy who'd saved him for no reason that Iain could discern, came to him. Could he really turn away from someone in need?

"Damn and blast," he muttered under his breath.

The kneeling man was still riffling the body and the other man, the aggressor, had already turned his back to Iain.

Iain took a deep breath and then ran toward the kneeling man, who turned just as Iain swung his arm. The blow caught the thief just below the ribs and knocked him back over his victim and onto his accomplice.

As the two thieves tangled in a heap Iain scrambled over the prone body and landed on top of the writhing men. He rained down furious, but largely ineffectual blows, all the anger and fear of the past days exploding out of his fists.

The men skittered and crawled over each other, dodging his blows and dislodging him in the process of backing away. He grabbed the foot of the closest man and received a savage series of kicks in the side of the head before his grip loosened. The last thought he had before he lost consciousness was that he'd better stop putting his head in the way of other men's feet.

\*\*\*

# The Footman

"Wake up, ye thievin' bastard!"

Frigid water splashed onto his face hard enough to go up his nose. When Iain tried to raise his hands to protect himself he realized they'd been tied behind his back.

"Wake up, boy."

He blinked rapidly while he snorted and choked, at the same time trying to expel water from his burning nose. "I'm awake, I'm awake," he said in between gasps. He blinked several more times before he could open his eyes, only to realize he could see nothing out of the damaged one—not even the cracked images he'd lived with the past few days.

Panic squeezed his chest and he blinked again and again and again. When he opened his eyes it was like looking down a long, narrow tunnel.

*My God! I'm going blind!*

"Boy!" Another crack in the head followed.

"Stop," he begged, trying to lean away from the source of the pain, squinting to see his tormentors. Two blurry figures stood in front of him, both wearing the clothing of nautical men.

"Thought you'd crawl out of your hole and find a fat little pigeon to pluck, did ye?" one of the figures asked.

"What?" Iain said, not waiting for an answer. "No! I wasn't trying to—" A fist slammed into his jaw and snapped his head back. The small amount of vision he'd been able to salvage was filled with white explosions. His mouth flooded with the now-familiar metallic taste of blood and one of his back teeth hurt bad enough that he thought it might have been knocked loose.

"Shut it, boy. You'll speak when we tell ye."

"Aye, and that won't be happenin', will it, Bill?" the second man asked. Both men laughed.

"Ye made a big mistake with the pigeon ye picked, boy. 'E weren't no steerage trash like yerself."

"No, that 'e wasn't," the one not called Bill agreed. "'E's a muckety-muck, 'e is."

"Aye, some American bankin' bloke."

"We'll 'ave our first shipboard 'angin', I reckon."

"And soon, too. I doubt t' owd gimmer'll make it 'til mornin'," Bill said, not sounding particularly sad at the prospect of a dead wealthy American banker.

Iain closed his eyes. Good God Almighty. Could he not go more than a few days without sticking his bloody neck into a hangman's noose? A hand grabbed his hair and shook him until his teeth rattled.

"Oye! No sleepin', laddy," Not Bill said.

"There'll be time enough to sleep in the Great Beyond."

Both men were laughing uproariously when the door flew open.

"What the devil is going on here?" The third man demanded in a far more elevated accent.

"We ain't doin' nowt, sir. Just giving our little thief a bit o' the rough."

"You fools! This isn't the man who robbed Mr. Siddons, this is the man who *saved* him. Untie him this instant." The newcomer took Iain's chin and tilted his face to the left and right while the men fumbled with the ropes that bound his hands and feet. "Good God, what have you done to him?" His horrified expression would have been funny if Iain's face wasn't the cause of it.

Bill popped up from somewhere near Iain's bound ankles. "That weren't us, sir. 'E came to us that way."

"Aye, right beaten up 'e was, sir," Not Bill added.

The new man—Iain's savior—grimaced at whatever he saw but nodded. "Yes, most of these bruises seem quite yellow and are several days old." He tilted Iain's chin. "Are you alright, boy? Can you hear me?"

"Yes, sir. Thank you, sir." When Iain tried to smile blood oozed between his lips and dribbled down his chin.

"Sweet Jesus." His savior dropped his chin like a hot coal and shook his head. He glared down at Bill. "Get him cleaned up immediately and deliver him to Mr. Jeremiah Siddons's state room within a quarter of an hour or I'll know the reason why. Is that understood?"

"Aye, sir," Bill said.

"In a jiffy, sir," Not Bill added.

The door shut and a face with more than several teeth missing hove into view over Iain's shoulder. "Now see 'ere, boy, ye've no reason to

# The Footman

go talkin' about this wee set-to, do ye?" Not Bill said, pulling off the rope that bound Iain's wrists.

"I reckon it were nothin' but a mistake," Bill added, dabbing roughly at Iain's face with a filthy cloth. "We'll 'ave ye as good as a newborn babe in less than two ticks."

Iain flinched away and grabbed the rag out of Bill's hand.

"Get me water and something to eat and I'll gladly tell everyone who asks that you were angels of bloody mercy."

# Chapter Ten

*Village of Trentham*
*1817*

"Why don't we cut our studies short today, my lady?" Elinor could tell by Doctor Venable's overly patient tone that it was not a suggestion.

She shut her text and looked up into his serious brown eyes. She hoped that he'd not guessed the reason she was upset and unsettled.

Stephen Worth had returned to Blackfriars four days ago and he'd not yet bothered to seek her out.

Elinor gritted her teeth at the unwelcomed thought.

"I apologize, doctor. I fear I'm wasting your time."

"Everyone is entitled to days when they're not feeling their best, my lady." He paused. "Is there anything I might help you with?"

Elinor couldn't help wondering how the self-possessed, quiet doctor would respond if she told him the truth. *You see, Doctor Venable, I believe I've contracted a particularly acute case of Stephen Worth. It's a relative new ailment from America. I do not believe it has any cure at present. The symptoms include, but are not limited to, an obsession with teasing green eyes, irresistible dimples, heated stares, and elegant, strong hands. In the most severe cases the victim suffers hallucinations in which she pictures herself touching and being touched by said hands and—*

"Lady Trentham?"

Elinor startled. "I've been sleeping poorly." That was not a lie.

"Would you like me to mix you a mild sleeping draught?"

"That won't be necessary, Doctor Venable, but thank you. I daresay it's the weather that has me out of sorts."

Venable glanced out the window at the clear blue sky, a slight wrinkle forming between his handsome chocolate-brown eyes.

Elinor stood. "I promise to be more present at our next lesson."

She politely declined his offer of a ride in his gig and escaped from his surgery with almost unseemly haste.

Her internal dialogue rapidly devolved into an argument as the practical part of her brain castigated the other part—the part that wouldn't stop mooning over a man who'd obviously forgotten her existence. Worth had been gone from Trentham two weeks. Fourteen whole days during which she'd alternately missed him desperately and rejoiced in his absence. Admittedly she'd not done the latter very often. And when he'd finally returned from his horribly, terribly, frightfully long absence she'd waited for her first glimpse of him like a gleeful child looking for gifts on Christmas morning.

And she'd waited.

And she'd waited.

Four whole long days had now elapsed during which he'd made no attempts to see her. How *dare* he make her wait? Had he decided to pursue the delectable Laurel Lewis, who'd made her interest in the beautiful, wealthy foreigner all too apparent to Elinor?

"Americans have such lovely uncomplicated manners, do they not, Lady Trentham?" Laurel had asked when Elinor took tea at Squire Lewis's one day last week.

Elinor had murmured something noncommittal and sipped her tea.

"Mr. Worth, for example," Laurel continued, not requiring any help from Elinor to pursue the topic. "He is not the type to stand on ceremony. At least not with *me*. He told me I should call him *Stephen*." She'd said the word as if it were a rich, delicious dessert that filled every crevice of her delicate little mouth.

"*Stephen!*" Elinor snorted now, so consumed by anger she almost tripped over a deep rut in the road.

"You called, Lady Trentham?"

Elinor yelped and spun around. There he stood in the middle of the road, just like some djinn she'd summoned by speaking his name.

He reached out and took her elbow, steadying her. "I've been looking for you, my lady."

She pulled away from him but he caught her hand before she could hide it behind her, his lips curving into a smile against her chapped, reddened skin.

Again she pulled away and this time he let her. "Yes, well, it is unkind to sneak up on people, Mr. Worth."

"I wasn't sneaking. I've been calling your name for a good minute. You appeared to be transported to another world and were charging along like a mare with the bit between her teeth. Tell me, what was consuming your attention so thoroughly that you didn't even hear me?"

His confident smirk told her he knew *exactly* what had been consuming her. Of course yelling his name out loud hadn't helped.

Elinor ground her teeth and lunged forward, desperate to get away from his solid warmth.

"I can't tell you how much it delights me to be compared with a horse, Mr. Worth."

He laughed and closed the distance between them easily, leading his magnificent animal behind him. "Call me Stephen, I know you can . . . now."

Elinor ignored the dig and forged ahead. Perhaps he would lose interest in tormenting her if she behaved as though she could not hear him? His next words disabused her of that hope.

"I've missed you, Lady Trentham." He took her elbow again, his touch gentle but firm until she stopped walking.

Her heart, which had just been hurling itself against her ribs with such rabid intensity that Elinor thought it might actually escape her chest, became eerily still. She swallowed, too paralyzed by fear to look any higher than his hands. They wore rich brown kid, but she recalled perfectly well what they looked like naked. They were long, beautifully tapered, and bronzed, the very definition of powerful elegance, just like the rest of his body.

"Elinor?"

# The Footman

Her head snapped up, her mouth already open to deliver a scold.

But he was waiting, and his mouth descended on hers with crushing intensity. It was nothing like the wisp of a kiss he'd given her the night of the ball. This was an onslaught. His lips were firm and soft but his tongue was liquid fire as it slid between her lips.

The action was shockingly intimate and utterly unexpected. She gasped and he took the opportunity to slide further in. He held her waist with one big, warm hand, pulling her closer while his other hand cupped her jaw and positioned her mouth for his invasion.

His tongue, lips, and hands were like kindling to the sudden fire that blazed within her.

Elinor wanted. She wanted so *badly*.

The place at the juncture of her thighs, an area she'd ignored for years, pulsed with pure, unadulterated desire. Piece by piece her body liquefied beneath his clever mouth and hands. When he took her waist in both hands and lifted her off her feet, she realized she'd laced her hands around his neck and was pulling him closer, all but climbing the length of his tall, muscular body like a tree, all the while clumsily pressing her mouth against his.

"Elinor," he murmured as he caressed and nibbled the ridiculously sensitive skin beneath her jaw. "You taste delicious."

Once again it was his voice that pulled her back from the brink of madness. She pushed against his chest until he loosened his grasp and gently set her back on her feet and released her.

"What is it, my love?" he asked, his eyelids heavy, his pupils dark with desire.

*My love?* Her knees buckled.

He steadied her. "Are you all right, Elinor?" He bent low to look into her face, which she'd turned away. There were lines at the corners of his beautiful eyes. Elinor swayed toward him, seized by a mad desire to lick and kiss the tiny striations, to feel the texture of his concern with her mouth.

*That way lies madness,* the practical voice in her head cautioned.

Elinor began walking.

"Elinor."

She ignored him.

"Lady Trentham?"

She briefly closed her eyes. Would he never give up? She stopped but did not turn around.

"What?"

"You are going the wrong way, my lady."

For a fraction of a second she thought he meant that walking away from *him* was going

the wrong way. But then she looked up and realized she *was* going the wrong way—back to the village. She dropped her head and stared at the toes of her scuffed ankle boots. Could this encounter possibly *get* any more mortifying?

Girlish giggling wafted from the narrow path that connected with the road only a few feet ahead. Laurel Lewis, along with two other girls and a groom, emerged from the trees.

"Lady Trentham!" Laurel exclaimed, her pretty blue eyes fixed on an object just beyond Elinor's shoulder. "Oh, and what a surprise," she added unconvincingly. "Hello Mr. Worth. *Stephen*," she amended breathlessly.

***

Stephen only escaped Squire Lewis's wife and daughters after submitting to three-quarters of an hour of constant nattering, two cups of watery tea, and half a dozen sugary biscuits. As he rode away, waving and grinning, he worried the smile on his face might become permanent, like a scar from a saber slash or some other gruesome souvenir of war.

For that's exactly what this afternoon had been: war. Or at least one skirmish in a war between him and the Lewis females, who'd fixed their sights on Stephen.

He groaned and the agonized sound startled his horse. "My apologies, Brandy, your master is an idiot."

His time alone with Elinor had ended the moment the featherbrained chits emerged from the trees. What he hadn't expected, however, was how skillfully Elinor would extricate herself from the newly formed party. Before Stephen even knew what had happened, he was riding beside Laurel Lewis and away from Elinor and the Dower House.

Not that the afternoon had been progressing swimmingly even before the Lewis girls had arrived. In fact, Stephen was beginning to wonder if something was wrong with him. He'd thought Elinor had been enjoying their brief kiss—God knows he had—when she'd jerked away and fled like a startled deer. It hadn't been a show of sheer missishness, either. If Stephen had been a betting man, which he was not, he would have wagered a good deal of money that she was more than a little gun-shy when it came to even the mildest forms of affection.

What the devil had Trentham done to make her so? Or was she merely another casualty of a society which steadfastly believed women had no physical appetites other than those that could be satisfied with cutlery and a plate?

Stephen rode his horse slowly in the direction of Blackfriars, mulling over the disastrous end to today's plans. It had been harder than he'd expected to stay away from her a full four days after returning from London. He'd hoped to build the tension between them and avoid her for a week, but, ultimately, he'd not been able to stand the wait one second longer.

He told himself that was only because he was eager to commence his plans. Unfortunately, he lied better to others than he did to himself. Or at least *he* was more skeptical of himself than others were.

"You are not only an idiot, but a weakling, a fool, and several dozen other loathsome things," he told himself. Perhaps if he spoke the words out loud, he'd heed them and come to his senses. Not that it mattered if he and his senses had parted company forever. Even if he fell madly, blindly, passionately in love with the woman, it made no difference. He could not stop.

He *could not*.

No, Stephen had come too far and waited too long to change plans now.

# Chapter Eleven

Cheltenham Minster had seen better days. Tucked away behind a large collection of new shop buildings that had sprung up over the preceding three decades, the church rarely attracted any visitors and was currently without a congregation because of a rather dangerous slate roof. But for Elinor's purposes, the Minster was perfect.

She glanced at the timepiece she kept pinned to her dress. It was teatime, another reason she could count on finding the old church deserted. Where was he? A loud creaking noise came from the vestibule and she twisted round in her pew and then stood.

"I was worried you wouldn't come, Marcus." She'd only taken a few steps toward him when she saw the blue and brown marks on his jaw and temple. "What happened?" On instinct, she reached out to touch his face, surprised when he didn't immediately pull away.

"It's nuffink," he said, jerking his jaw from her hand.

"What happened?" she repeated. She sat down in the nearest pew, grateful when he did the same. She could never be sure with Marcus. Even when he showed up to these little meetings he often chose to leave almost immediately. He was a complex mix of emotions; anger not the least of them.

"I got me a lay as a milling cove." He adjusted the collar of his coat—a rather gaudy brick-red specimen—in a showy fashion while cutting her a sly look.

"Marcus, you know I cannot understand you when you speak such rubbish and *I* know how hard you must work to speak it. Please, in English."

"I've been doing a little pugilism," he said, mulish rather than arrogant now.

"Oh."

"I've been winning, too. Enough to give a bit to Lily and Esme." His expression softened when he mentioned his sisters and made him look younger than his twenty years.

Elinor didn't like that he'd resorted to pugilism but how was it her place to say anything about how he made his living? Especially when she could give him so very little.

"And how are your sisters? Are they doing well at Hempham's?"

He shrugged, his expression suddenly bored, as if he'd shown too much of himself. He looked remarkably like his father but Elinor tried not to let that bother her. After all, it was *because* he was Edward's child that she'd begun helping him in the first place. Edward had done nothing for the boy; at least he'd done nothing pleasant or helpful. The only time she'd confronted her husband about his son—the last time she'd directly confronted him about anything—she'd not been able to get out of her bed for over a week.

After that, Elinor had worked around Edward, rather than deal with him directly. That hadn't been difficult. Unlike the threat he'd issued the day before their wedding—that he would breed her every month—he was often too busy in London with either his business or whores or both to bother. Months went by without seeing his face. Glorious, pain-free months.

"Did you hear what I said?" Marcus's irritated tone told her he'd repeated himself more than once.

"I'm sorry, Marcus. You were telling me about Lily and Esme."

His eyes narrowed and Elinor could see he was torn between showing his displeasure at her inattention and his desire to talk about his sisters. "Esme is going to her first position in three days."

"Is she happy about that?"

"Aye. She's right tired of the rules at Hempham's." He shrugged, a mannerism he used often to express what he found inexpressible. "As for Lily, well." He stopped and scratched his head, clearly baffled.

"What is it?"

"She don't, er, *doesn't* want to leave. She wants to be a teacher." He gave her a look out of the corner of his eye and she could see he was almost bursting with pride.

"That's wonderful, Marcus. Will Mr. and Mrs. Hempham help her?"

"They've already told her she's to have a place at the end of two years if she learns good enough."

"That is *truly* wonderful news." And for more than one reason. Elinor was worried about what Marcus might do if he was burdened for too long with *two* needy sisters. There was no use denying he would do illegal things if he felt pushed. She'd barely managed to purchase his freedom from the authorities the last time he'd been in trouble. And that had been when she'd still been receiving pin money from Edward. Now? Well, now she hardly had enough money to keep body and soul together for her small household.

Marcus shifted on the hard pew, his handsome blue eyes moving around the dim interior of the church in a way that said he was ready to leave. Elinor reached into her reticule.

"It would give me a great deal of pleasure if you would take this. Perhaps you could take the girls out for a treat the next time they have a free afternoon." She handed him the small bundle of notes. He looked from her face to her hand before quickly snatching up the money.

"I don't understand you, my lady," he said, his cheeks reddening as he stuffed the money into the pocket of his colorful coat.

"What is there to understand? You are my husband's child."

"Aye, but I'm not *your* child," he pointed out, his eyes suddenly hard, reminding her that he'd spent the last two years in London, not a safe little village. Elinor flinched away before she could help it and he grinned.

"I'm a man now, not a boy." He swept her body with an insolent gaze. "We've not many years between us, have we, *my lady*?"

"Why are you saying these things to me, Marcus?" she demanded, wanting him to see and hear the hurt he was causing.

He shrugged one shoulder only, as though he could scarcely be bothered to do more. "I'm only sayin' what's in my head."

"Perhaps you shouldn't. Perhaps you should consider what you say before you give your mouth free rein."

He laughed and the hard look slipped away from his eyes. "Aye, you're right. My mouth gets me into trouble. You've been kinder to me than my own Ma. It's just—"

"Just what?"

"The look you have sometimes it makes me feel . . . well, *burdened* is the only way I can think to put it."

"Burdened?"

"Aye. Like you want something from me."

"But I don't," she protested.

"No, nothin' easy like money or a bit of jewelry. More like you want me to *be* something. Something else—something better. I dunno, I sound a fool."

"No, Marcus, you don't." Elinor stared at his darkly flushing face. Was he right? Was she burdening him with her expectations?

He pushed himself up.

"Wait," she began.

"I must be off," he said, already halfway to the door. "Thanks for the blunt. I'll be sure ta tell the girls the treat is on you."

The door creaked shut and Elinor was once again alone.

\*\*\*

"He's a bastard."

Stephen's head jerked up from the list of figures he'd been studying. "*What?*"

"The man Lady Trentham meets every month. Although I suppose you'd call him a boy."

Stephen sighed and put down the list of investors and capital Fielding had brought with him from London. "Start from the beginning, John. He's *whose* bastard? And who is *he?*"

"Marcus Bailey, Bailey being his mum's name. His mum was a whore before she died."

Stephen waited. "Is that it, Fielding? Bailey's mother was whore before she died?" he demanded, irked. "That's better than being a whore *after* she died, isn't it?"

Fielding made a choking noise that might have been laughter, not that Stephen could be sure as he'd never heard the man laugh before.

"Whose whore *was* she?"

"Atwood's."

Stephen couldn't have heard him correctly. "Lady Trentham meets Charles Atwood's bastard once a month?"

"Aye, Edward Atwood's bastard."

"Ah, I see." Although he didn't. What the devil would the woman want with one of her dead husband's bastards?

"Do you really?" Fielding asked, his scarred face curious. Yet another emotion Stephen had never seen his impassive servant display before. Not only that, but the normally terse man wasn't done speaking. "I confess I'm betwattled as to why any woman would want to spend time with her dead husband's by-blow. Maybe you could explain it to me?"

Stephen's eyes narrowed at Fielding's curious expression. "I'm paying you to give *me* information, not so that I might explain things to you," Stephen pointed out. "Just how old is this *boy?*"

"He'll be twenty-one on his next birthday."

Stephen didn't need to think about that too long before deciding it wasn't to his liking. Elinor Trentham had secret meetings with a man of twenty-one? She was thirty-two, a little over a ten-year difference.

"Do you think—" Fielding began and then stopped when Stephen looked up.

"Do I think what, Fielding?"

Stephen couldn't discern even a flicker of emotion on the other man's face. "Nothing, sir."

Stephen ground his teeth while he considered Fielding's silence and what it might mean. "Where does the boy spend his time when he is not meeting Lady Trentham?"

"He stays in London, mostly. Here and there, he's got no fixed abode. He fancies himself a bit of a milling cove." Fielding shrugged. "I've seen him fight, he's not too bad."

"Are you considering a return to your old profession, John?"

"He's a flyweight, sir."

"Doesn't really seem like a fair match, does it?" Stephen mocked, childishly pleased when the other man sighed and shook his head. "What else did you learn about him?"

"He's got two sisters, both in some religious school."

"Atwood's brats as well?"

"I don't think so, although they seem quite close to their brother."

Stephen leaned back in the ancient leather chair and stared at the rib-vaulting above his head. It was a lovely ceiling, but terribly damaged by damp and neglect. He was itching to own this property and bring it back to its former glory, a thing he could not do until he'd driven the earl all the way into a corner. He sighed and looked at his employee. Fielding was watching him with the same speculative look Stephen had seen on eagles and hawks. He knew the expression was nothing more than a defense mechanism, but that didn't make it any less irritating.

"Get the boy's attention," he finally said.

Fielding arched one brow. "Do you care how I go about it?"

"No, just make sure that he is in my pocket—or close to it—when the time comes."

"And is that time going to be soon?"

"Why? Are you in a hurry, Fielding?'"

"Should I be, sir?"

Stephen snorted. "Get your ass back to London. Yarmouth is still short of money. Make an offer on his collection he won't be able to refuse."

"From you, sir?"

"He'd hardly believe it came from anyone else, would he?" Stephen shot back. "How are things going with Lady Elinor's brother, Stuart?"

"I've managed his tables well-enough that he's been doing nothing but winning and winning and winning."

"Good. Now I want you to see that his luck takes a turn for the worse. When the viscount learns his heir is in the basket it will encourage him to sell his collection. It will also encourage him to leverage his properties and take the plunge in my little scheme." He paused, considering a question he'd been avoiding. "What have you learned about my uncle?"

"Nothing yet."

Stephen let out a string of foul words. "How can that be? You've thrown around more money than a bishop in a whorehouse."

Fielding nodded. "And then some. Still, nobody seems to have heard anything from him since the night you boarded *The Liberty*."

"He said nothing to any of the other servants?"

"Only the butler and cook remain from that time."

Stephen rubbed his jaw, recalling the stiff old butler from all those years before. "The butler will be no help. The man hated my uncle. You've not located the two footmen from that night?"

"Not yet."

Stephen couldn't imagine his uncle had been able to have much of a life after his nephew had been accused of raping a peer's daughter. It was difficult to obtain a new position without a reference, and his uncle wouldn't have been able to secure one without Lord Yarmouth. Uncle Lonnie had been literate, but not enough to generate a convincing set of employment letters.

Stephen realized Fielding was still waiting and nodded abruptly. "You can go."

The big man's hand was on the doorknob when Stephen thought of one last thing. "And Fielding?"

"Yes, sir?"

"Bring back a selection of wedding rings when you return."

Fielding didn't turn a hair at his request. "Rundell and Bridge, sir?"

"If they are good enough for Prinny, I suppose they are good enough for me."

The door closed behind him and Stephen took off the spectacles he used for reading and rubbed his aching eyes. Seducing the woman was proving more difficult than he'd planned. It was time to close the net and the only way to do that was to offer marriage.

# Chapter Twelve

*Blackfriars*
*1804*

Elinor hesitated outside the study door and bit her lip and dithered. On the one hand, she did not like to interrupt Edward—or even speak to him, really—even at the best of times. On the other hand, she could not withhold the news from him any longer.

She knocked before she lost her nerve.

"Enter!"

Elinor opened the door a crack and saw that Edward was seated at his desk, his man of business, Mr. Franks, standing stiffly on the carpet before him. Elinor could almost smell the tension between the two men.

"I beg your pardon, my lord. I did not realize you had somebody with you. I can—"

"Come in, Elinor."

She swallowed and closed the door behind her.

"Take a seat. Mr. Franks and I are almost finished with our business." The earl turned his cold blue eyes back to Franks, whose face was the color of a poppy. "I will give you two days. That is when I must make my announcement to the other members of the consortium."

"Two days? But, my lord—"

"Two days, Mr. Franks. Return with Pangborne's agreement in your hand by that time. Understood?"

Franks nodded, his jaw clenched so tight it must have hurt.

"You may go," the earl said. He turned to a small stack of papers, placed them inside a larger portfolio, and locked the documents in his desk before giving Elinor his attention.

"What can I do for you?" His tone was no different than the one he'd used on his employee.

Elinor couldn't help marveling that this cold stranger had been inside her body nineteen times. He hadn't come to her every month as he'd threatened to do. Nor had he coupled with her every time he'd come to Blackfriars. Sometimes he stayed away several months in a row. Sometimes he came to her bed but could not perform. Those had been the worst times. Worse even than the quick, brutal sessions which left her raw and humiliated.

The first time he'd been unable to come into her he'd merely slapped her face. "Don't ever look at me while I am in this room. In fact, cover your face when I come to you."

The next time it happened, some months later, she'd not only pulled the double drapes to mask the light of the moon but also worn her darkest veil—the one she'd worn at Mama's funeral. It did not seem to matter that he could not blame his condition on her appearance. Rather than spare her, it had only increased his wrath.

Doctor Reynald, the old physician who'd served Trentham for fifty years, set her arm the following day. Elinor had made Beth wait until Edward left for London to summon the doctor.

"You must be more careful, Lady Trentham," the old doctor had cautioned while splinting her arm. He would say the same thing several months later when he set her wrist.

Elinor looked from her crooked wrist to the architect of her pain. "I am with child, my lord."

A muscle jumped in the earl's jaw. "How far along?"

"Three months."

His mouth twisted and she could see it did not take him long to perform the necessary math. It was the last time he'd come home. He'd been unable to complete the act. The first time.

Rather than beat her, he'd simply left. Elinor had wept with relief and then fallen into a fitful slumber, only to be awakened several hours later when he'd returned wielding a quirt. He'd taken her three times that night and four times the next, the only visit when he'd come to her two nights in a row.

Beth had cried at the marks on her body but Elinor had not shed a tear—the days of crying over anything Edward did were over. Or so she'd thought then.

"It is past time you are breeding," Edward finally said, his tone saying her lack of fertility was yet another way in which she was a disappointment. "We will tell your father the happy news when he arrives on Friday." He rose and came around the desk. Elinor hastily stood. He took her hand for the first time in years. "You have pleased me, Elinor," he said, an openly hungry glint in his eyes as he lowered his mouth to her naked hand.

Nausea surged through her at the feel of his lips and hot breath. She could see it in his eyes: he was aroused by the memory of what he'd done to her that night. He would do it again.

\*\*\*

Elinor greeted her guests and kept her eyes in constant motion. Edward had made it clear when he'd told her of this ball that it was costing money he did not have.

"I am not giving this ball to engage in pointless frivolity, Elinor. I am giving it only because it is necessary to secure the backing I need."

Although he hadn't told her, Elinor knew he was referring to the same project that had begun with their marriage. The colliery in Somersetshire, which had necessitated their marriage in order to exploit, had not done as well as Lord Trentham had expected. Elinor was unclear as to exactly what the problem was, but it appeared her husband had put more of his wealth into the project than he'd taken out. A fact that greatly displeased him.

"Your duty is to make certain that Mr. Gormley and Mr. Singleton and their respective wives enjoy the evening more than any other event they've ever attended."

"Of course, my lord." Elinor could only surmise the two men were bringing their wives to a function which, in other circumstances—

those in which her husband did not desperately require their money—would be well above their social aspirations.

"I want this evening to go off flawlessly. God knows I've asked little enough of you in the three years we've been married."

"Yes, my lord." Elinor could have said the same about him, but she'd quickly learned such small rebellions had a dreadful cost. And, really, it was far more rewarding to let him think she'd been cowed, his creature. And now that there would be a baby? She smiled to herself. Well, what Edward did would hardly matter anymore.

\*\*\*

The evening had gone smoothly so far. The City investors and their spouses had proven very easy to please. Elinor had dispensed with any pretense at precedence and seated the vulgarly dressed wives beside the earl and Lord Yarmouth. Their husbands she'd seated beside herself and a rather elderly duchess who was hard of hearing and mistook Mr. Gormley for Trentham's cousin, a mistake he made no effort to correct.

If attendance was a gauge of success then the earl was doing very well, indeed. Many of the people filling the huge ballroom had come all the way from London to attend the first ball at Blackfriars in over twenty years.

Elinor knew Edward preferred to entertain in London and on a much smaller scale. Not that Elinor had ever been to any of *those* entertainments. They were not for wives. At least not for the wives of the men attending them. The reason she knew of the affairs at all was because of a chance comment her brother Stuart had let slip on his last visit—only the second time he'd come to Blackfriars. Elinor knew Stuart had only come because he was one step away from a sponging house.

When she'd asked him what had happened he'd become irritable.

"Why don't you ask your husband, if you're so damn curious?"

"Why would I ask Edward about your gambling?"

"Because I lost a packet at one of his bloody orgies, that's why."

"Orgies?" Elinor had blushed furiously at the word.

Stuart's mouth had wrinkled with annoyance. "Oh, never mind."

For once, Elinor had pressed. "Tell me, Stuart. Tell me and I will give you money."

For a moment she thought he'd balk. But then he'd said, "How much money?"

So that was how Elinor learned her husband threw debauches where gambling, illicit substances, and sexual deviance attracted a solid core of gentleman followers.

*** 

It was just past midnight when a footman notified her that a man awaited a word with the earl but Lord Trentham was nowhere to be found. Elinor went in his stead and found Mr. Franks nervously pacing the small receiving room.

"Good evening, sir."

He stopped his agitated striding and his pale cheeks flared. "Ah, there must be some mistake, my lady. I sent word for your husband."

"My husband is not available. Is there anything I can do for you, Mr. Franks?"

He glanced yearningly at the door, as if tempted to sprint through it. "I'm afraid I need to—"

The door swung open and Trentham entered. His icy blue eyes slid from Elinor to Mr. Franks and his mouth hardened. "You are empty-handed, sir."

Franks swallowed so hard it made Elinor's own throat hurt. "I tried, your lordship, but it didn't matter how—"

The earl's jaw tightened until Elinor thought she could hear cracking. "Leave us, Elinor." He did not take his eyes from the cringing man in front of him.

Elinor shut the door quietly and leaned against it for a long moment. The heavy wood muffled the sounds, but she could hear raised voices.

The butler approached from the direction of the ballroom.

"What is it, Beacon?"

"I wondered which champagne his lordship wished to use next, my lady."

"The earl has already marked those he'd chosen for tonight."

"Yes, my lady, but those are gone."

"Gone? But there were hundreds of bottles."

Beacon politely studied his feet.

A loud thud came from behind the door and Elinor stepped away from it.

"Under no circumstances should anyone disturb his lordship."

"Yes, my lady." A knowing look flashed in his eyes before he could lower them.

"I will go and choose the next case."

\*\*\*

Elinor collapsed onto her bed.

"You need to finish your drink before you go to sleep," Beth reminded her from the open doorway of her dressing room.

"I'm not thirsty."

"'Tis not for you, my lady. 'Tis for the baby."

Elinor groaned but pushed herself up. "You are a horrid tyrant," she muttered, picking up the mostly full glass and drinking it in two long swallows.

"There, that's better. They won't—"

The door to her room flew open and smashed against the wall. The earl stood in the open doorway, his normally pristine person wild and disheveled. He fixed his burning blue eyes on Elinor.

He spared barely a glance for Beth. "Out, now."

Only when his hand jerked toward Beth did Elinor notice it had a whip in it.

Beth took a few steps toward the bed and Edward lunged toward her. "I said *out*, you disobedient bitch!" He swung the crop hard against her shoulder.

Elinor flew from her bed.

"Go, Beth," she said in a low voice, edging her body between her cringing servant and furious husband. "That is an order," she barked when the woman failed to move. A muffled cry and slamming door told her when they were alone.

"Turn around and grasp the post."

"My lord, the baby—"

He swung with the same brute force he'd used on Beth, aiming the whip at her midriff rather than her shoulders.

Elinor cried out and clutched at her side.

"Put your hands on the post."

# The Footman

He began whipping her even before her hands closed around the thick wooden spindle of the bed. "You." *Crack.* "Worthless." *Crack.* "Whore." *Crack.*

Elinor's knees buckled and she sank to the floor, raising her arms over her head and shoulders and curling into a ball.

"Get up." His foot struck her hip and she gasped with pain. "Damn you, get up or I swear I will—"

"Trentham?" a familiar voice said from the doorway.

"Father!" Elinor pushed herself onto her hands and knees and turned. The earl had also turned and his back blocked Elinor's view of Lord Yarmouth's face.

"What do you want, Yarmouth?" Edward demanded, his voice labored, as though he'd been running.

"The maid came to my chambers, frantic. I came to see if aught was amiss?"

"And now that you have seen?"

Elinor heard her father take a deep breath, as though steeling himself. "I know you are disappointed, Trentham, but it is hardly the girl's fault."

*The girl.* Elinor knew in that instant her father would not save her. He could not even say her name.

"She is my property to do with as I please, Yarmouth. You have no legal rights over her person. You sold those rights to me, along with a bill of goods that will most certainly leave me a pauper."

"But surely—" her father began, sounding old and tired.

"Enough!" Edward thundered. "I have heard the last I ever care to hear from *you*, my Lord Yarmouth! On anything. Get. Out. Now."

Elinor held her breath.

The soft click of the door was her father's only answer.

"Now," the earl said, turning to look down at her kneeling form. "Where were we?"

# Chapter Thirteen

*Village of Trentham*
*1817*

"Are you in your right mind, my lady?"

Elinor would have laughed at the shocked expression on Beth's face if her wits weren't in such a muddle. Instead, she handed her the brief note she'd composed.

"Send this along with Mr. Worth's gift, Beth." Beth recoiled from the note as if Elinor were handing her a live spider. "*Now*, Beth."

Elinor waited until her angry servant had flounced from the room before collapsing into her chair. She massaged her pounding temples. Why was he doing this to her? A horse? Did he understand the gossip such a gift would cause even though she'd returned it?

She closed her eyes and tipped her head against the high-backed chair.

*Since when are you concerned with gossip?* The meddlesome little voice in her head demanded.

*As of right now.*
*Why have things changed?*
*Because this is different!*
*How?*

# The Footman

Elinor had never minded the gossip that circulated about her and Doctor Venable because it was unavoidable: if she didn't go to his surgery twice a week, she couldn't learn what he had to teach. So, it had never mattered to her if people believed she and the doctor were engaged in an affair, because they *weren't*.

*You're not engaged in an affair with Stephen Worth, either. So why does it matter?*

Because her thoughts about Stephen Worth were *nothing* like her thoughts about Doctor Venable. The thoughts she entertained about the beautiful American were the sort she couldn't—*wouldn't*—put into words. They were the sort of vivid, sensual thoughts that woke her in the middle of the night, breathless and sheened with sweat.

And now this gift. What had he been thinking? As if he only needed to give her a horse and then she could go blithely riding about the countryside like Laurel Lewis.

*You are a far better rider than any of those girls*, the nasty little voice pointed out.

It was true, she was. Riding had been the only activity she'd really been good at when she was a girl. It was unfortunate she no longer could afford such an indulgence. And it was downright cruel of Stephen Worth to tempt her with things she could ill afford. Especially as he was most likely going to send her pitiful finances even deeper into despair when he finally purchased Blackfriars.

His ill-conceived gift was a result of their last conversation, which took place the day after they'd encountered Laurel Lewis and her companions in the lane. Elinor's unfortunate encounter with Worth was largely Beth's fault because she wouldn't stop nagging Elinor about the state of her clothes.

"I've done all I can to the day dresses you have, my lady. Don't hold me accountable if one of them blows away completely in a strong wind."

Bearing that hideous scenario in mind, Elinor had grudgingly taken herself to Trentham's only milliner to be fitted for two new day dresses.

"I hope you chose something in pink?" A familiar voice asked as she stepped out of the shop.

Elinor's steps stuttered but she kept walking. "Lurking outside of milliner shops, Mr. Worth? Can the local constabulary be aware? Surely you have better things to do?"

He caught up with her easily, matching his long strides to her short, frantic ones. "I can't think of a better use of my time than waiting for you."

"I would not have thought you so lacking in imagination, sir." Elinor nodded to Mr. Siskin, who'd come out of his small butcher shop and was polishing his already clean window. No doubt hoping to get a better look at the rich American sprinting after the Countess of Trentham. Elinor winced at the thought of how this must appear.

"I used to be a terribly imaginative fellow." Worth said, breaking into her thoughts with his plaintive tone. "You see what you've reduced me to?"

Elinor laughed—unable to resist his mournful look, no matter that she knew he was merely mocking her. She decided she would pretend their last meeting, including the kiss, had never happened.

"Was your business in London successful, Mr. Worth?"

"It was wildly profitable."

"Are profit and success interchangeable concepts to you, sir?"

"You make a fine point, Lady Trentham. Not all successes involve profit. Take you, for example."

"Me?" She turned to look up at him, which was a mistake. He deployed his dimples.

"Yes, you."

Elinor forced her eyes back to the road.

"Aren't you going to ask me what I mean?"

"No."

He laughed. "I would never have believed you were a coward, my lady."

"I daresay you will weather the disappointment." Her voice was breathless from the effort of trying to keep ahead of him.

"Why don't you ride? Would not these trips to town and the good Doctor Venable's be much easier on horseback?"

"I do not keep a horse."

"Do you not enjoy riding?"

"I have little time for such activities."

"That is not an answer, my lady."

Elinor heaved an exaggerated sigh. "Very well, Mr. Worth. *Yes*, I do enjoy riding." To her surprise, he'd let the matter drop and they'd spoken of other things. That had been two days ago. This morning one of the grooms from Blackfriars, Joe Paling, had shown up with a delightful chocolate-brown mare with pink ribbons woven into her mane and tail.

The groom had doffed his cap and grinned at her. "Ain't she a picture, my lady?"

"She certainly is, Joe. Is there any reason you have brought her here?" she asked, fearing his answer.

"Aye, the American, Mr. Worth, told me she were yours, my lady."

Elinor's face heated all over again as she recalled the man's knowing look.

It had been painful to send the pretty little mare away. Where had he found such a wonderful mount—and one so perfect for her—in less than two days?

The sound of carriage wheels pulled her from her musing.

"What now?" she muttered. She would need to answer the front door as Cook would not hear it from the kitchen and she'd sent Beth to Blackfriars.

The door opened before she could reach it and Beth stepped inside.

"Oh, my lady," she said, a healthy pink glow on her cheeks.

"Whatever is going—"

Stephen Worth's face came into view over her maid's shoulder as he mounted the front steps.

"Never mind," Elinor said, adding in an undervoice, "We will talk about this later, ma'am."

Beth scurried from the foyer as Worth took off his hat and bowed. "Don't be hard on her, my lady. I didn't give her a choice about bringing me with her."

"I hardly wish to discuss my servant's behavior with you in the middle of the foyer, Mr. Worth. Please come into the sitting room."

Rather than look chastened, he grinned at her ungracious invitation.

S.M. LaViolette

Elinor took a seat behind her desk and he lowered himself on the settee with a knowing smile as he eyed the vast expanse of desk.

Yes, thank you very much, she *did* wish to keep a large chunk of wood between them.

"Now, perhaps you will tell me what I can do for you, Mr. Worth?"

"Why did you reject my gift?"

"Didn't you read my note?"

"I read it."

"Well?"

"It makes no sense. You say you have no means of keeping a horse yet Dower House has a fine stable."

"It also has room for a dozen more servants."

He frowned. "Are you telling me your husband left you so ill provided for you cannot afford to keep a horse?"

"That is an impertinent question. My finances are none of your concern, sir."

"I apologize." His serious gaze surprised her, but not as much as his next words. "I would like to make it my concern. I would like to make *you* my concern."

Elinor's lungs ceased working. And her voice along with them.

"I am asking you to marry me, Elinor. Elinor?" He half-rose from his chair. "Elinor, you are very pale. Are you well?"

She swallowed.

"Can I fetch you anything? Er . . . water?" His forehead creased with concern and he looked toward the bell pull.

"I'm fine," she said, her voice breathy but firmer than she'd hoped.

"Are you certain I cannot call for something? Perhaps some tea?"

"You hate tea."

For the first time since she'd met him, he looked nonplussed. That was the moment Elinor knew she'd made a dreadful mistake: she'd fallen in love with him.

For some reason, the admission calmed, rather than upset her. Maybe it was because the worst had finally happened. Or maybe it was because she was tired of lying to herself.

Yes, she'd fallen in love with this wildly handsome, wealthy, beautiful, fascinating, mysterious man. She'd done the stupidest thing a woman like her *could* do. She no longer had anything else to fear.

"How do you know I hate tea?" he asked.

"Every time you drink it, you take it differently."

"Why should that mean I hate it?"

"You are searching for something that will make it palatable to you."

Before he could respond the door opened. It was Beth, and she was carrying a tea tray.

They both burst out laughing.

"What is it?" Beth demanded, hesitating in the doorway. "Do I have a smudge on my nose?"

"You may put the tray on the table, Beth." Elinor left the protection of her desk and took a seat on the low sofa beside the table as Beth left the room. She looked up and found him staring at her with a look that made every nerve in her body tingle.

"How would you like it today, Mr. Worth?"

"Stephen. I know you can say it."

She set the teapot down with a thump. "Why? Just tell me why?"

He rose from his chair and moved to the settee so quickly she didn't realize what he was doing until he was beside her. "Is it so hard for you to believe that I've come to love you?"

"Yes."

He laughed, his green eyes dancing. What sort of man enjoyed rejection this much?

"Why?" he asked.

"I know myself, Mr. Worth. I am *not* that loveable. Certainly not enough to make you ignore the dozens of pretty, young girls who are flinging themselves at your head. I am a widow with no fortune, I am no beauty, I am lame, and I am two and thirty."

"First, I have fortune enough for the two of us. Second, I'll be the judge of who I find beautiful. Third, you do not appear to let your foot get in the way of much. Fourth, I will be two and thirty on my next birthday. And, fifth," he said, cupping her jaw with one big, warm hand, "I never take no for an answer, Elinor." He lowered his mouth over hers.

Layers of ice burnt away beneath his scorching, probing kiss. Her hands slid up his lapels and around his neck and her fingers wove themselves greedily into his hair, his cropped coppery locks far softer than she'd imagined. A deep purring noise emanated from his chest as she caressed the warm, hard lines of his jaw. She was frantic to feel every part of him—*now*—as if somebody—or some*thing*—might try and make her cease her explorations. He responded to her actions by pulling her against the impossibly hard contours of his broad chest while his lips worked across her cheek and nuzzled her neck.

He smelled divine; a hint of cologne mixed with the faint aroma of clean, slightly salty skin. She inhaled him, over and over, unable to take the intoxicating scent of him deeply enough.

His lips returned to her mouth and his tongue moved slowly but implacably between her lips. One of his hands was stroking the side of her body, inching ever closer to her breast, which had become oddly heavy. His fingers drifted over the unbearably sensitive side of her breast while his thumb flicked her already stiff nipple.

She gasped and her entire body shuddered.

"Shhhh, darling," he murmured, his distracting tongue probing her mouth while his hand cupped her more firmly. Elinor was feverish and half-mad, her body unable to absorb the pleasure that flowed from his hands and seeped into her skin, firing her nerves until she felt as though she would combust.

She put her hands on his chest.

"Please. Don't push me away, Elinor." His voice was low and urgent, his breath hot against her skin while he ran kisses down her neck behind her ear.

Her hands balled into fists but stopped pushing.

"That's better," he murmured, his fingers stroking and stroking her aching nipple through her muslin gown until her body thrummed. "I want to make love to you."

His words did what her mind couldn't and jolted her from her trancelike state. She opened her eyes and stared directly into his.

"Wha—?" She spoke into his mouth, around his tongue, which had begun to rhythmically stroke into her, the motion leaving no doubt in her mind what he wanted.

She realized his other hand had shifted her skirts until they were almost at knee level. His green eyes were mere slits beneath his lowered lids. And she knew: he would take her right there if she let him.

Lust, desire, and fierce hunger pounded her with the brutal implacability of a breaker pounding the beach, in its wake it left . . . fear. All would be lost the next time the wave crashed into her and she shoved him back hard, her heart aching with the effort.

He released her and she knew it was not because of the force she used, but because he chose to. His chest was rising and falling rapidly; he was not untouched.

"No."

His brows rose in comical confusion. "No?"

She pushed herself off the divan, backing toward her desk and the safety behind it. Safety she never should have left.

Stephen thrust a hand through his hair, pushing it off his forehead. His expression was already settling into a lazy, insouciant smile. Only the hard ridge pushing against the placket of his breeches and his flushed cheekbones told her what his efforts cost him.

"No, you won't let me seduce you? Or no, you won't marry me?"

"No to both."

"You don't wish for any time to consider my offer?"

"No."

His lips smiled, but the look in his eyes sent chills up her spine. This was not a man accustomed to taking no for an answer.

"I know it is not a question an English gentleman would ask, but may I know why you are rejecting me out of hand?"

Elinor frowned and looked down at her hands; they lay in her lap, tightly clasped, but that had not stopped their shaking. "I do not wish to marry again. Ever."

"Fine. Then let me seduce you."

Her head shot up. "What?"

"You heard me."

"You can't be serious."

He crossed his arms over his chest, the motion causing his elegant coat to tighten and shift intriguingly across his fine shoulders. Her hands recalled the feel of his chest. His body was hard and hot and the memory of it against hers made her inner muscles clench. His eyes burned into her and the banked lust in them was enough to throw sparks.

"Even if I wanted to—"

"Don't lie to me."

She bit her lip. He was right; her desire for him must be as obvious as his for her. "I live in a small community. The code of behavior here is far stricter than in London."

"Then come to London with me."

She opened her mouth and then closed it, shaking her head. "You're mad."

He pounced on her brief hesitation. "I will arrange it. Nobody will ever know we have gone together." His words were clipped but not rushed, as though he were making plans for one of his business transactions, a transaction of whose success he was already assured.

Elinor was terrified by the pull he exerted. He was a force of nature—a wild but inexorable tornado that crushed everyone and everything in his path, until nothing was left to oppose him.

She shook her head so hard it left her dizzy. "No, Mr. Worth. The answer is *no* and it will continue to be so for as long as I live." The words were bald and brutal, like cold, hard lead from a pistol. The only way to fight his devastating pull was to strike out—to push back. To go on the offensive. "I would never marry you, sir, not for any reason. Your attentions are anathema to me and I have never done anything to encourage you—quite the reverse." The hateful syllables tumbled out of her mouth on a wave of shame, fear, and fury—at herself. "I certainly do not deserve your insulting propositions, nor do I appreciate your insinuations that I would agree to your suggestions if circumstances were otherwise. I would never, ever consent to be your—"

"Lover?" He stood, brushing his hand casually across the front of his riding breeches. The motion drew her gaze to the unmistakable evidence of his desire for her. Pulse points all over her body exploded and it was all she could do not to launch her body at him and beg forgiveness for her hateful, untrue words.

But then she looked into his eyes. Only moments before they'd been so hot they'd spit flames. They were now like the dark, cold green of a frozen lake. He was angry; coldly angry.

He bowed, the faint smile on his face unlike any other he'd ever given her. "Well, I guess there is nothing more to say. Please forgive my impertinence, my lady. I apologize for having disturbed you." He was across the room and out the door in a heartbeat.

Elinor stared at the door and held her breath.

Not until the sound of carriage wheels on cobbles vibrated the silence did she truly understand he was not coming back.

# Chapter Fourteen

*Village of Trentham*
*1817*

Stephen left Blackfriars two days later.

Elinor learned this from Mrs. Lewis.

"I cannot credit it," the older woman said when they encountered one another at the dressmakers, which Elinor had hoped to pop in and out of quickly to pick up some ribbon Beth had ordered.

"Perhaps his business here is done," Elinor said in her most repressive tone. She was examining a bolt of cambric but she saw Stephen's face. It was strange how she'd only been able to think of him as 'Stephen' *after* he'd left.

"Rubbish. My husband says the earl just had two new hunters delivered. You know he could never have—" The older woman broke off, her biscuit-colored face turning red as she recalled to whom she was speaking.

*So, Charles was spending money, was he?*

Elinor ignored the other woman's flaming face and fingered a bolt of sarsnet the same shade as a robin's egg.

"Lord Trentham's profligate tendencies have always outrun his pocket, ma'am. Just because he has new cattle is no reason to expect he has parted with Blackfriars." Elinor's tone was sharper than she'd intended, but the fact Charles had exposed himself—and her by extension—to such tittering and conjecture was infuriating. But not nearly as infuriating as the fact Elinor knew less about what went on at Blackfriars than Mrs. Lewis.

"Mama? Mama?" Laurel Lewis emerged from the fitting room, a vision in celestial blue. She saw Elinor and her delicate blond brows descended before she caught her pettish reaction. And then she smiled and dropped a curtsey, the creases on her seventeen-year-old forehead smoothing like ripples on a pond.

"Lady Trentham. How nice to see you."

"You look lovely in that shade of blue, Laurel."

The girl colored far more prettily than her mother.

"Thank you, my lady." She paused. "Have you heard Mr. Worth has suddenly left us?"

Elinor almost smiled. So Stephen had become Mr. Worth again? She wondered what the girl and her mother would think if she told them of Stephen's offers—both of them.

She stroked a hand down the bolt of soft fabric, recalling his eyes—before they went cold. She smiled at the pretty blonde. "Yes, that is what your mother tells me."

"Oh, so you did not know?" Laurel became almost radiant at this evidence of Elinor's ignorance where Stephen Worth was concerned.

"Oddly enough Mr. Worth makes his travel plans without consulting me."

The shop was so quiet you could almost hear the sound of needles piercing fabric in the back room. Mrs. Lewis put her hand on her daughter's shoulder and steered her back into the dressing room.

Elinor turned to the hovering dressmaker. "Beth tells me you have some ribbon for her."

\*\*\*

Elinor cursed her waspish tongue the entire way home. She'd exposed herself before the two people she would have least wished to. Well, perhaps Charles stood higher on that list than the Lewis females.

She'd just removed her bonnet when Beth bustled into the foyer.

"Oh, my lady, did you hear that—"

"Yes, I know, Mr. Worth is gone. Good riddance to him. I'll take tea in my chambers. Here is the ribbon you requested." Elinor left her open-mouthed servant standing in the foyer holding the parcel.

The pain in her chest would have been alarming if she'd not experienced it several times before in her life. It was the pain of profound disappointment, a sensation which had been her closest friend and constant companion all the years of her marriage. She'd mostly managed to avoid the feeling after Edward had died. The only two times it had resurfaced was immediately after his death and the time Marcus had been arrested.

Elinor had hoped she'd endured enough abject disappointment to last her a lifetime. Indeed, she wouldn't have believed she was even capable of the sort of heartburn she was currently feeling. Her mood was swinging wildly between relief, disappointment, and anger: Stephen Worth had finally done what she asked. He had left her, and she hated him for it.

She paced from her sitting room through her bed chamber and into her dressing room. How much could he have truly cared for her if he'd left Trentham without a backward glance? She'd obviously been nothing more than a passing fancy.

*What* could *he do after the horrid things you said to him?* the nagging, persecutory part of her brain demanded.

*Oh, shut up!*

Elinor gritted her teeth against the memory of what she'd said. Besides, he'd looked angry rather than hurt.

She realized she was staring at her peach ball gown and scowled, turning her back and marching into her sitting room. She flung herself onto the padded window seat and stared sightlessly out the window. It was obvious the man was no more than a butterfly, a rake who indulged in mild flirtations wherever he was. No doubt he'd found her resistance to his charms the most fascinating part about her.

Movement caught her eye and she saw Mary, her day maid, leaving the stables. She glanced at the clock on the mantle. It was half-four and Mary usually left by three.

The girl paused in the stables doorway and something in her stance told Elinor she wasn't alone. A giant shape emerged from the darkness and Elinor caught her breath. She'd never seen such a large man before—unless one counted corpulent men. But this man was anything but fat.

Mary played with a strand of her hair, which Elinor could see had come loose and was merely shoved beneath her cap. The giant took a half-stride toward her before dropping his hands to her waist and lifting her bodily for a kiss. He held her effortlessly and Mary was not a slight lass. He slid one hand beneath her bottom and brought her close to his body, which served to bunch Mary's skirts up her legs, baring her to above the knees as she wrapped muscular legs around the big man's waist and offered her mouth up for a kiss.

Elinor's thighs tightened and heat slid from her belly to her sex as she imaged herself in a similar position, but with a different man. She jolted at the raw, sensual image and pulled back from the window. The man must have seen something because one of his big hands held Mary's neck still while he looked up at Elinor's window. Her mouth dropped in shock and she stepped away from the glass. He had the most hideously scarred face she'd ever seen. It was as if his face had been bisected. It was morbidly fascinating and she approached the window for a second look. But they were gone.

Elinor pulled the bell and calmed herself while she waited for Beth to appear. Just because the man looked like a villain did not mean he was one, she reasoned.

The door opened. "Yes, my lady?"

"I just saw a strange man by the stables. He was with Mary."

Beth's face settled into a scowl. "A huge man with a face like a one of them creatures on Blackfriars?"

Elinor frowned, and then realized she meant the gargoyles. "That is very unkind," she chided, staring hard at Beth's flushing face. "Who is he?"

"He's Mr. Worth's man. I would have thought he'd gone with him. He loiters around here often enough. Mayhap Mr. Worth finally gave him the sack."

"You've seen him here before?"

"Aye, he's been sniffing around Mary like a dog scenting a bitch in heat. I wouldn't be surprised if she—" She stopped when she saw Elinor's outraged expression.

"I will thank you not to say such vulgar things in my hearing, ma'am."

Beth froze. The color that had gathered in her cheeks drained away. In all the years they'd been together, Elinor had never spoken so harshly to her. Indeed, she did not know why she'd done so now. Was it because of the desperate need still throbbing in her womb—because *she* was behaving like a bitch in heat? She turned away from both that lowering thought and Beth's crushed face.

"Send Mary to me if she is still here."

The door closed softy and Elinor grimaced. Already she regretted taking out her sexual frustration on her servant. Beth was more than a servant; she was a loyal friend.

Elinor sighed. She would apologize later. She poured herself a glass of water from the pitcher that always sat on the table, a habit she'd picked up from her mother. Lady Yarmouth had frequently needed to quench her temper being married to Elinor's father. The viscount had driven his wife half-mad with his profligate habits, frittering away the money her mother had brought to the loveless union before Elinor was even ten. She'd heard her parents fight only a few times and the words they'd exchanged had cut all the more deeply for their coldness.

Her mother accused her father of wasting their daughter's dowry on expensive mistresses, horses, and art.

Lady Yarmouth, her father had retorted more than once, was barely one step away from the shop and the smell of it on her sickened him.

And so forth.

When she'd been a girl, Elinor had thought the arguments terrible. After a few years of marriage to Edward and several vicious whippings, she'd envied her parents their cold, sterile battles.

"You wanted to see me, my lady?"

Elinor turned at the sound of Mary's voice. It took her a moment to leave the past behind and remember why she'd summoned the girl.

"That man I saw you with. Who is he?"

Mary's plump, pretty cheeks reddened like two apples. "He is Mr. John Fielding—Mr. Worth's man, my lady."

# The Footman

"What is he doing here? I thought Mr. Worth had gone?" Elinor ignored the sudden thudding in her chest and could only hope she wasn't coloring as wildly as the girl before her.

"Oh, aye, Mr. Worth is gone. Mr. Fielding says he's to join him soon, but that—" The girl's voice tapered off and her face got even redder.

"But Mr. Fielding thought he'd see you one more time before he followed his master?" Elinor finished for her.

Mary nodded. "Aye, my lady. But he's gone now," she hastily added.

"Thank you, Mary. That will be all."

Elinor stared at the door after the girl had left. She'd been desperate to ask the girl if she knew where her lover was going or whether he was coming back, but she'd stopped herself just in time.

What did it matter where Stephen Worth went as long as it wasn't here?

# Chapter Fifteen

S tephen handed the courier a thick envelope. "I want this letter delivered to Mr. Haines at 32 Boylston Street before the day is out, Jenkins."

"Right away, Mr. Worth." The boy shot from his office as if his heels were on fire.

Stephen knew he had a reputation as being strict, but he felt like he'd come by it honestly. He worked hard and he expected the same from those who worked for him. Diligence and dedication to his job had taken him from accused rapist to assistant vice-president of the largest bank in Boston in only five years. Of course that wasn't a tale he could use to motivate his workers.

Somebody tapped on the door.

Stephen lifted the quill off the letter he'd been composing. "Come in."

James Powell stood in the doorway.

"Mr. Siddons would like to see you as soon as possible."

Powell was always a miserable bastard and it was impossible to read his pinched face.

"What's this about?"

# The Footman

"I don't answer to you, Worth. You'll have ask Mr. Siddons," the older man sneered, shutting the door to punctuate his point.

Powell had hated Stephen since the first moment Stephen had stepped off *The Liberty* five years ago. Only Powell, of all Jeremiah's employees, knew something about Stephen's humble beginnings. But even he didn't know the whole story or his real name.

Nobody knew that, not even Jeremiah.

Stephen rubbed his chin with the ragged edge of the quill as he considered Powell's virulent hatred. Jeremiah had said more than once that Powell was just jealous of Stephen's meteoric rise in the bank, but Stephen knew there was more to it.

He put the quill in the stand, shrugged into his coat, and checked his reflection in the mirror for ink smudges.

Stephen saw almost nothing of the boy he'd been five years ago other than red hair and green eyes. With proper food and care he'd grown into his tall, lanky form and was now as beefy and well-fed as any American. And it was all thanks to Jeremiah Siddons, president and chief stockholder in Siddons bank: Stephen's friend, mentor, and surrogate father.

Jeremiah was seated at the modest desk his great-grandfather had made, back when the Siddons family earned their money as one of Boston's finest furniture makers.

The old man's face lit up when he entered his office and Stephen felt the same painful twisting in his heart he always did. Part pride, part love, part fear—fear that this great man would one day find out who Stephen really was: a Scottish bastard and accused rapist with a death sentence hanging over his head.

"Sit, my boy, sit." Jeremiah gestured to one of the two ladder-back chairs in front of his desk, which had also been made by some long-ago Siddons. A person would never know Jeremiah was one of the wealthiest men in Boston by looking at his office. It was spare in the extreme, the walls bare and the shelves devoid of knickknacks or books other than ledgers. The wooden floor was highly polished but without any carpets. It was the office of a Puritan businessman, which was exactly what Jeremiah was.

Jeremiah closed the ledger he'd been working on and put it aside. He had hundreds of employees to take care of such matters but he still

117

personally checked on every facet of the bank's operations. He sat back in his chair and clasped his hands over his flat stomach. Even his person was fit and spare and he kept it that way by walking to the office every day of the week, no matter what the weather.

"I understand congratulations are in order for the Fulton-McKenna Bridge project."

Stephen couldn't help the smile that pulled at his mouth. "Yes, sir, it looks like we'll clear a solid twelve percent."

Jeremiah nodded, his sharp blue eyes glinting with appreciation. "And the people who live around that area will no longer have to drive miles merely to get across the river."

"That is true, sir."

"I hope that was part of your motivation for financing the project, Stephen?"

Stephen opened his mouth to agree, but then closed it. There was something in the other man's eyes. Jeremiah almost always smiled, so the only way to tell what he was truly thinking was to read his eyes—something Stephen had studied for five years.

He finally sighed and shook his head. "I'm afraid that thought was not among those motivating me, Mr. Siddons."

Jeremiah gave him a gentle smile. "There's no need to look so downcast, Stephen. I will be the last one to say there is any harm in wanting to make a profit. Even so, a man should wish to leave a more enduring mark in this world than a healthy bank account. The best way to do that is to improve the lot of others."

Stephen had heard this same speech before. He agreed with it—in principle, but it was a luxury for a wealthy man. A man like Jeremiah—not an escaped criminal who never knew when he might have cause to run again or when he might need every dime he could save. Of course, he could not say that.

"I agree wholeheartedly with your advice, sir. I hope I would never engage in a venture that would be harmful."

"As do I, Stephen."

"That said, sir, it is a struggle for me to know what a sound investment is, just yet. Perhaps in time I will be able to juggle both concerns more easily."

"I daresay you will, Stephen. What you said raises another point I wished to discuss with you—your education."

Stephen unsuccessfully fought back a groan.

Jeremiah raised a hand. "Now just listen to me before you get your feathers ruffled. I'm not suggesting formal schooling, you're too old and frankly beyond such things." He paused and looked up at Stephen, and then quickly continued. "So, that leaves another, more attractive option—reading the law."

Stephen's eyebrows shot up. "Sir?"

"I believe the law will appeal to you as you may learn at your own speed. Which I daresay will be fast, judging by everything else you have learned."

Stephen flushed at the praise, bowing his head to hide his smile.

"I have a good friend who is tired of the bench and I have spoken to him about supervising your study." Jeremiah paused. "Stephen?"

He looked up.

"I would ask you to do this for me." For once, Jeremiah was not smiling.

"You know I will do anything you ask of me, Mr. Siddons, but—"

"You wonder why I want such a thing?"

Stephen nodded.

"I want you to have something else to live for, something to strive for. Something with a solid moral core that will guide your decisions."

"Something else?" Stephen repeated, his heart beating hard and loud in his ears. "What do you mean by that, Mr. Siddons?"

Jeremiah opened his desk and brought out a slim folder, which he handed across the desk.

Stephen felt like he was reaching for a live cobra. The page on top was dated nine months ago and filled with small, neat script. He didn't need to read it. Select words and phrases leapt off the page: *accused rapist, Iain Vale, escaped prisoner, Coldbath Fields Prison.*

He turned over the page with shaking fingers and saw a few small newspaper items about a series of escapes from Coldbath Fields Prison in which guards had been implicated and then confessed. He closed the folder along with his eyes.

"You will think I did this to make sure of your character. But I did not. I knew your character before I ever saw you, when the doctor

S.M. LaViolette

told me you'd saved my life at great risk to your own—that if you had done nothing, I would have died. That you gave your eye to save me."

Stephen couldn't look up. He didn't want Jeremiah to see the truth, just how close he'd been to letting those two men get away with what they'd started that night. What a thin line had separated Stephen from him and those men.

"Then why?" His voice was as raw as his emotions.

"There is a reservoir of hate and anger in you, son. I thought it might begin to dissipate when you felt safe, but it hasn't. I thought maybe when you were well-off from your own efforts you might let it go, but you didn't. Each year, as you've acquired more wealth and more security, your hate has only become colder and gone deeper."

Stephen looked up, suddenly furious. "Yes, what of it? I *hate* them. They lied and wrecked my life and that of the only relative who cared for me. Aren't I entitled to some hate?"

Jeremiah nodded. "I understand you, believe me, I do. But hatred is a sword with no pommel, Stephen. You cannot wield it without cutting yourself."

Stephen ground his teeth. How could he explain to Jeremiah what drove him, what made him get out of bed every day, when he couldn't articulate it to himself?

"Is it wrong to want justice?" Stephen's voice broke on the last word.

"No, but it is wrong to live for revenge. And more than that, it is dangerous."

Stephen kept his jaws tightly clenched to keep the hate trapped inside.

"Is it only hatred that drives you, Stephen?"

Stephen couldn't answer because he didn't know. Was it hate that made him see *her* face every time he triumphed over some problem or obstacle? Was it the thought of *her* surprise when he ultimately confronted her with who he'd become that drove Stephen to always want more, that drove him to build his bank account as if it were a monument to something—to somebody? Was *she* that monument?

"You don't know what it is like," he bit out.

"Then tell me."

Stephen groaned. "You would never understand. You've never been so much at another man's mercy that he can treat you worse than a dog." He glared at the man across from him. "First it was my bloody father." He snorted. "Well, I call him that, but he was as much of a father as a ram that impregnates an ewe and moves on to the next. He used my mother, handed her over to one of his tenants, and then let her die wretched, poor, and alone. And then there is *her*." Stephen felt his face twist into a mask of hatred but he could not stop it.

"*She* sent me on this journey because of a goddamned whim. A kiss, Jeremiah! One bloody kiss and I was broken, bleeding, and on my way to the gallows." He stopped, his chest heaving as he panted to regain his breath. "It wasn't enough that I was to scrape and serve and never look them in the eyes. She and her bloody family had me hauled away and disposed of like a piece of rubbish!"

Stephen realized he was on his feet and yelling.

"*Christ.*" He dropped into his chair and dropped his pounding forehead into his hand. A touch on his shoulder roused him from his blinding rage. He looked up into his mentor's kind face.

"Humans beings are terrible to one another, Stephen, they truly are. But there are so many of them, and only one of you. To let other people's cruelty direct your life is to let them chain and control you. It is only when we rise above their treatment that we free our own souls from torment. You are in the grip of hate, son, and it is a crushing, brutal grip."

Stephen snorted. "And you think reading the law will free me?"

Jeremiah smiled, but it didn't quite reach his eyes. "No, I don't think it will free you, Stephen. Only you can free yourself. But I do think it will give that big brain of yours something else to think about. Something more productive."

"Hard work—a Puritan solution?"

Jeremiah chuckled and squeezed his shoulder. "Yes, I suppose it is. Will you try it? For me *and* for you?"

"You always get what you set out to get, Jeremiah. Very well. I will study the law." He gave his mentor a reassuring smile—and privately vowed to do a better job of hiding his agenda from the older man in the future.

# Chapter Sixteen

S
tephen sat in his suite at Padgett's Hotel and read the latest reports from his land agent. Permission for the joint colliery and canal venture had cost him dearly, but it had been necessary to convince his investors of the legitimacy of his enterprise. The project was now clear to proceed—not that it ever would.

He grinned. He would send an offer to Trentham today. The man had been on Stephen's heels when he left Blackfriars and came to London. Stephen could almost feel his brooding presence emanating from his Mayfair townhouse. A townhouse that would shortly belong to Stephen, if everything went as planned.

There was a sharp rap on the door and Fielding entered. The big man refused to learn the polite scratching sound that a good English servant employed.

Fielding looked like he'd crawled from Blackfriars to London on his hands and knees.

"What the devil happened to your clothes?"

Fielding glanced at his mud-stained breeches, scuffed and battered boots, and frayed coat and shrugged. "Nothing."

Stephen tamped down the anger he felt rising. "You look like a bloody street thug. I thought I told you to go buy some decent clothing."

"I did."

"Where the hell are they?"

Fielding held out his arms.

"Christ," Stephen muttered, his eyes roaming to the brandy decanter. He looked at his watch. It was only two o'clock, too damn early to let Fielding drive him to drink. He snatched one of his cards out of his waistcoat pocket and scribbled two names on it before flicking it across to his employee. Fielding was much quicker than he should be for such a huge man and handily caught the small rectangle before it hit the ground. He read the back and his lips twisted into what passed for a smile.

"Am I to bill this to you, Mr. Worth?"

"Yes, dammit. Just get it done. I need you to look respectable when we meet with our investors next week."

Fielding's eyebrows rose.

"Yes, I received word from Shaver today, we're set to go ahead. I'll want to meet to make sure everything is in place with Yarmouth and then I'll need a week to handle some other business." His faced heated and he hurried on. "What about you? What did you learn?"

Fielding knew what he meant without Stephen having to explain. It was the same thing he always asked.

"I found Thomas Jordan and he told me the other footman who was there that night died two years ago. Jordan says your Uncle Lonnie came looking for you when you didn't come home but he didn't find out what happened until after they'd already handed you over to the constable. He says your uncle never said anything to him, he just disappeared a couple days later."

"Yarmouth kicked him out?"

"Jordan didn't know anything about that. He claims the family was too stirred up about other matters to make much of a fuss about your uncle."

"What other matters?"

"Salvaging the betrothal between the girl and Trentham."

Stephen leaned forward, his elbows on his desk. "Oh? So did Trentham baulk?"

Fielding's eyes dropped.

"Well?" Stephen prodded.

The other man took a deep breath, not looking very pleased about what he was about to say. "The viscount took the girl to a quack."

"Why? Did she have some kind of hysteria?"

The thought was a new one to Stephen and he'd believed he'd run every possible scenario through his head over the past fifteen years. Perhaps she'd realized what she'd done and her conscience had suffered for it? Perhaps—

"The earl wanted to make sure the girl was a virgin."

"*What?*"

Fielding nodded, an odd blend of pity and disgust on his usually unreadable face. "Aye, it seems Trentham thought this wasn't the first time you two had tussled."

"Tussled? Christ. It was barely a bloody kiss." His hand stilled its nervous drumming. What did a doctor do to ensure a girl was a virgin? Just thinking the question made him feel queasy and tainted—and oddly guilty.

*Bloody hell!* None of that was his fault; the girl had jumped *him*.

He looked up at Fielding's harsh features and changed the subject. "What about our friend Marcus Bailey? Do we have him firmly on board?"

"Aye."

"He will bring her from Trentham?"

"Aye, just as we discussed."

"Are you sure he understands the rules clearly?"

"He understands them completely." Fielding's sneer was not a pleasant sight.

"Do I want to know what you did to convince him?"

"I doubt it."

"Will anyone get hurt, John?"

"You mean other than the Countess of Trentham?"

Stephen was on his feet before he knew it, his hands gripping the edges of the desk to keep from leaping over it. "Is there something you're trying to say, John?"

Fielding's smirk faded but his jet-colored eyes glinted dangerously beneath his lowered lids. "I reckon I've said enough," he finally admitted.

"Get out of my sight," Stephen snapped, glaring at the other man until the door closed behind him. He dropped into his chair, his entire body rigid with fury.

Fielding was a taunting, evil-natured son-of-a-bitch and Stephen knew better than to let him get under his skin. He was madder at himself than the other man for his loss of temper. Besides, had Fielding said anything other than the truth? Elinor Trentham *would* be hurt. Not physically, of course, but she would no longer be able to hold up her head in public. Certainly not anywhere in polite society.

Stephen poured himself two fingers of brandy and threw it back in one swallow. His throat burned, but not as hot as the fire in his chest. He'd been damned glad to get away from the woman and her confusing presence, but his chest had been tight and hot from the moment he'd left her house. He told himself he burned with anger and resolve, but he was no longer sure what stoked the fire inside of him. The feelings he'd experienced when she'd rejected him had been . . . well, it wasn't worth thinking about.

One thing was certain, he'd run out of time to break her the way he'd hoped and now needed to adjust his plan accordingly. Trentham and Yarmouth wouldn't wait forever and all the other pieces were in play. All except Elinor, the one who'd started this mess to begin with.

For some reason, it was harder and harder to generate the wrath that had once come so easily when he thought of her.

He looked across the room at the enormous mirror and frowned at his reflection. He forced away the image of a successful man and called up one of a frightened, broken, bleeding boy. If Lonnie hadn't had enough money, he'd have gone to the gallows.

It had been Elinor who'd flung herself at him that night. A bored, selfish aristocrat looking for entertainment with a servant, not caring who got hurt.

Well, she'd certainly gotten what she was asking for and more. Little did she know she'd only seen the first half of the play. The second half had been a long time coming and Stephen wasn't about to let his misguided conscience get in the way of business.

*This isn't business, son. This is revenge.*

Stephen ignored Jeremiah's voice. The old man was dead, and the restraint he'd exercised was gone with him. He'd waited fifteen bloody years to avenge the wrongs done to him and his uncle by Elinor and her family. He'd be damned if he stopped now.

*No, son. You'll be damned if you do.*

Stephen hurled the empty glass across the room with all his might. The sound of crystal smashing against the mirror drew hurried footsteps from his bedchamber. His new valet, a middle-aged man with a bald head that reminded Stephen of an egg, gaped at him, his eyes flickering from Stephen to the shattered mirror and back again.

"Is aught amiss, sir?"

Stephen shoved his chair back so hard it toppled over and crashed to the polished oak floor. "Fetch my hat and cane, I need to go out."

Nichols darted back into the other room.

"And Nichols?"

His head popped though the open doorway immediately. "Yes, sir."

Stephen gestured to the shattered mirror. "Make sure there's no sign of that mess by the time I return."

# Chapter Seventeen

*Village of Trentham*
*1817*

Elinor was paying bills when Beth knocked on the library door.

"Someone here to see you, my lady." Her face was pinched and unhappy.

Elinor laid down her quill. "Who is it, Beth?"

A figure appeared behind her maid and gently elbowed her aside.

"Hello, my lady." Marcus wore a cocky smile and an even gaudier suit of clothes than he had the last time.

Elinor stood, her hands already outstretched, a smile forming on her face. "Marcus!"

He hovered in the doorway and she dropped her hands at his wary look. "Would you fetch some tea, Beth?" Elinor couldn't take her eyes off the younger man. Her heart hurt to see him because she knew he wouldn't have come for any good reason. He took her hand with a crooked smile, his eyes sliding away from hers before she could read the expression in them.

"Have a seat," she said, reluctantly releasing him and gesturing him to one of the big leather wing-backed chairs in front of her desk. Marcus ignored the offer, choosing instead to make a circuit of the room. His sharp eyes flickered over her possessions, making her realize how dowdy and threadbare the room and its furnishings had become—just like her.

Elinor sat and watched him strut in his gaudy finery, the sight making her lips twitch. He'd always been a peacock, even as a little boy. The first time she'd seen him, he must have been no more than six, playing in front of his mother's cottage, wearing a paper hat and red scarf and carrying a rough wooden sword.

"Who are you, sir?" Elinor had asked, pulling her horse up when he'd stopped and stared at her mount with far more adoration than old Buttercup had received for years, if ever.

"I'm General Wellesley," he'd declared proudly, his eyes still on her horse.

"Are you just back from battle, then?"

He'd rolled his eyes at that. "Naw, I'm on a sekert mission to kill Boney!"

An auburn-haired woman, still in her dressing gown, had come out then, drawn by the sound of voices. The look she'd given Elinor had been a mix of contempt and fear.

"Come here, Marcus. What are you doing? I told you to stay by the house if you want to stay outside. And now I see you on the road. Get in the house." She'd given the boy a rather brutal shove, her eyes never leaving Elinor.

"I'm sorry, I'm afraid I lured him out to talk. I am Lady Trentham." Her smile and friendly words hardly caused the other woman to thaw but she came a few steps closer, her shapely body swaying in a feminine, sensual manner that Elinor had never quite mastered. "You are new to this cottage? I don't believe I've seen anyone here before."

"We've a right to be here. Just ask Lord Trentham." The woman had turned shrill, her blue eyes narrow and guarded as she thrust out her not unsubstantial bosom, yet another thing Elinor had never mastered.

"I'm sure you have, Mrs. . . .?"

"Bailey. Lydia Bailey." She dropped a grudging curtsey and glanced toward the house. "I'd better get inside; Marcus is more mischief than a barrel of monkeys."

Elinor looked across at Marcus now, as he prowled the room. His tawdry clothing spoke of a young man eager to project a certain image to a group of peers Elinor doubted were worth impressing. In many ways he was still that little boy, full of mischief.

Beth opened the door, her face like an open book. She'd not liked Marcus since the incident with Elinor's jewelry three years prior.

"You can put the tray here, Beth." She gestured to the low table between the two chairs. "Thank you."

Marcus waited until the door closed behind her before dropping into the seat beside Elinor. "Well, that old witch hasn't changed."

"Marcus." She cast him a quelling look before fixing his tea. "Still two lumps and milky?"

"Aye." He reached out to snatch a biscuit from the tray. Elinor handed him his cup and nudged the tray of sweets toward him.

"Have you been ill, Elinor?" He sipped his tea, his watchful eyes on her over the rim of his cup.

She smiled. "Thank you, Marcus—do I look it?"

He grinned in return. "I'm not such a smooth talker as I think, am I?"

They chuckled together, but the tension between them remained high. Why was he here? He hated Trentham and the people of the small village hated him. Elinor couldn't blame either side. Marcus had stolen from people and destroyed the reputation of more than one daughter. The villagers and farmers had never touched him, far too afraid to meddle with the Earl of Trentham's only son, no matter that he was a bastard.

"This is a bit of a grim shack, isn't it?" His lip curled as he looked around her library.

"It is home." She refused to let him draw a rise from her.

"It seems the old man left you as badly off as he did me." He laughed, but there was no mirth in it.

"Why are you here, Marcus?"

"What? You're not glad to see me?"

"You know I am, but I can't help wondering why you've come back to a place you hate."

"Bloody hell, Elinor! Does there always have to be something wrong?" He put the cup down with a clumsy clatter and a tan, milky stain spread across the tray. He jumped to his feet and resumed his pacing, shoving his hand through his dark hair repeatedly, until it stood up like a rooster's comb. He swung around. "It's Esme, she's in some trouble. Bad trouble."

Elinor set down her own cup. "What kind of trouble?"

"She's in a bawdy house and I don't have the dosh to get her out."

"But . . . I thought she was going to be a teacher?"

His harsh laugh made her feel ill. "Aye, so did I. Seems she caught the wrong man's attention and those high and mighty Hemphams tossed her arse onto the street. She didn't come to me first, she— He glanced down at Elinor's waiting face and shook his head. "Never mind what she did. Suffice it to say she's in a right bind."

"Do you need money?" The question was stupid. Why else would he be here?

He nodded.

"How much, Marcus?"

He said a figure that made her eyes close.

"Dear God." Elinor's mind raced as she thought of what she could sell to get the money. There was nothing left. At least nothing that would fetch the kind of money Marcus needed.

She looked up to find his eyes on her, an expression of agony on his face.

"I don't have the money, Marcus, but I know somebody who does."

***

Padgett's was a new hotel and Elinor had never been in it before. The luxurious establishment made her realize just how shabby both Blackfriars and the Dower House had become. Every surface sparkled and shone. Dark wood and cut crystal glinted richly in all directions. Thick woolen carpets muffled the sound of commerce, making the grand entry hall of the hotel seem more like one of the big houses she'd visited as a child than a place of business.

Elinor knew it was horrible of her, but she couldn't help being glad she'd persuaded Marcus to wait in the hackney. He'd changed into traveling clothes that were even worse than his other suits. Elinor did not suppose she was all that much better, but her lavender carriage costume drew far less attention than Marcus's canary yellow waistcoat and royal blue cravat.

# The Footman

"How may I help you, madam?" The man behind the large mahogany desk was dressed far better than Elinor. He reminded her of her parent's town butler, Givens, who'd always made Elinor feel as if she had as smudge on her cheek. She presented one of her cards—a yellowed relic from another life.

"I am here to see Mr. Stephen Worth."

The man's eyebrows descended a few notches as did his nose and chin. The room seemed to warm up several degrees as he read the name on the card.

"Ah. Perhaps her ladyship would prefer to wait in the private parlor while I see if Mr. Worth is in?"

Elinor would have smiled at his sudden about face but that would have ruined her haughty pose.

"That will serve." She used the tone her mother had used on pushing cits or misbehaving servants.

The parlor was every bit as lovely as the entrance, but blessedly private.

"Shall I have tea brought, Lady Trentham?"

Elinor unbent enough to smile. "Thank you, no. If Mr. Worth is not here, I shall leave my card. I have several other appointments that will not wait."

Her not-so-subtle hint to make haste sent the man quickly from the room.

Elinor opened her rather shabby reticule and checked its contents, as if her paltry bundle of notes might have grown larger since she put it in there; it hadn't. She closed the bag and went to stand before a huge gilt-framed mirror. She grimaced at her haggard reflection and tucked a few stray strands of hair under her hat. The lavender smudges beneath her eyes matched her dress and her face, always thin, now appeared positively gaunt. She looked as though she'd been starving herself. Or pining.

Elinor turned away from her unhappy reflection and scratched at what looked to be an egg stain on her best pair of cotton gloves.

"Drat," she muttered, touching her tongue to the stain in the hope a little moisture might help it come loose. Naturally the door chose that moment to open. Elinor looked at the glass and saw her reflection, her tongue still touching the thumb of one glove, with Stephen in the doorway. She dropped her hands and spun around, her faced scalded.

"Lady Trentham." He strode across the room, both his expression and tone unbelievably warm considering the last time they'd parted. He took her hand and raised it to his mouth, his eyes never leaving her face. "I must say this is a very pleasant surprise."

He released her hand and Elinor saw it was the one with the egg stain. She covered it with her other hand.

He gestured to a settee. "Please, won't you have a seat? Shall I ring for tea?"

"No, thank you, Mr. Worth. I am not hungry."

His warm green gaze swept over her face and a wrinkle of concern formed between his eyes. "You look as though you have not been eating well, my lady."

Elinor flushed at his scrutiny and the meaning beneath his words. "Please, sir. I must tell you first and foremost that this is not a social call. I am here on a matter of some urgency."

"Is that so?" He sat forward, his big body coiled and tense.

"I'm afraid I've come to ask you for money," she blurted.

His eyebrows rose a fraction. "May I inquire what is the matter?"

She squirmed under his kind, concerned gaze.

"I would rather not have to explain. I am asking for a loan, but I cannot honestly say I will be able to repay it with any celerity. I understand if you do not feel you can loan me the money under such uncertain circumstances."

"How much do you need?"

She glanced down at her reticule, suddenly horrified at what she was about to do.

"Two thousand pounds."

"Do you need it in notes, or would a bank draft suffice?"

Her head whipped up. "You mean you will just give it to me?"

He flashed a smile that cut her heart to pieces and made her body ache to touch him.

"It would please me to be of service to you, my lady."

Elinor only realized she was crying when she saw the look of horror on his handsome face.

"Please—God, please don't cry." He raised his hands slightly, as if to shield himself from something overwhelming, and the motion was oddly vulnerable.

Elinor sniffed and dove into her reticule. A blinding white square of linen appeared.

"Please, take it," he begged.

She gave a watery laugh at the abject terror in his voice and dabbed the cloth to her eyes. She'd not cried since her second miscarriage, a memory that worked to freeze the tears before more could fall. She swallowed and looked up, her face hot with shame. He was watching her tensely, as if she might dissolve at any moment.

"That was all. I promise. I am not a watering pot—at least not for many, many years. You are very kind and I guess—well, it surprises me after the things I said to you."

He sat back and his body lost some of its tension.

"I wouldn't be much of a man if I let a few words stand in the way of helping you." His lips curved in a self-mocking smile she'd never seen before.

On impulse, she reached out and took his hand. "You have a very kind nature." She squeezed his hand once before releasing him. "You are a good man, Mr. Worth."

He shifted and looked away, an expression she couldn't read on his handsome face. "Where are you staying?" he asked abruptly.

Elinor pursed her lips. How could she tell him she'd not wished to spend any of her paltry savings on hotels?

It turned out she didn't need to say anything.

He gave her a wry look. "You have nowhere to stay, do you?"

"I thought I would find a place after I'd contacted you. But there were delays with the mail coach and we lost several hours fixing a wheel. It was almost dark when we reached the city."

"We?

Elinor's flush deepened.

"The friend I am helping. I don't feel comfortable sharing more than that. It is a rather delicate situation. As well as quite urgent."

He took her meaning and stood. "This sounds like it requires notes rather than a bank draft."

"Yes, I suppose it probably does. Is that a problem?"

"No. I have enough in my safe. Are you sure I can't offer you any help other than money?"

She shook her head. "My friend would be most unhappy."

"You will go with your friend to do . . . whatever?"

Elinor paused. Would she? She could not imagine that her presence would help in a brothel. "I don't think that would be helpful."

"Then I shall have a room made ready for you and—"

"Oh no, please, you mustn't. I'm sure this hotel is well beyond my touch. I will find something more suitable."

"Let me describe how this argument goes, Lady Trentham. You will say no, and I will have to accompany you all over town to find a room you *can* afford because I refuse to leave you unattended. I will miss my dinner and become quite cranky. You will doubtless encounter damp sheets and Beth will have to sleep on the floor. Shall we leave all that undone and merely get you a room here?"

She laughed. "You're very good at getting your way, aren't you?"

His nostrils flared slightly. "I can only recall one time in recent memory when I didn't."

Elinor looked away, stunned by the desire in his eyes. She studied her old, ragged reticule. "I would be grateful for your help, Mr. Worth."

"Excellent. Now tell me where Beth is waiting and I shall fetch her before I get the money."

"I didn't bring her." Elinor glanced up when he didn't answer.

He was staring down at her with a look of fierce disapproval, and something else she could not decipher.

"I see. You were indeed in a hurry. I will engage a maid for you as well. Shall I get your money first or book your room?"

Elinor's face heated with embarrassment. "The money, if you please. I might then give it to the person who is waiting."

"I shall return directly."

Elinor collapsed on the settee. Good Lord. What had she gotten herself into?

***

Stephen waited until one of the hotel staff had escorted Elinor to her room before summoning Marcus Bailey upstairs to his suite.

# The Footman

The boy—and that's what he was, a green boy—sauntered into the sitting room with more bravado than courage. Whatever Fielding had done to him, he was scared.

"Mr. Bailey, won't you have a seat?" Stephen gestured to one of the gilt chairs in front of his desk.

The boy dropped into the chair, his pose slouchy and deliberately unconcerned.

"'Oo are you then?" he demanded.

Stephen's lips pulled up on one side. "I am an associate of Mr. John Fielding."

Bailey sat up in his chair as if he were a marionette and somebody had just yanked his strings. "Oh. Mr. Fielding."

Stephen would eventually have to make Fielding tell him what he'd done to petrify the youngster, but for now, he was grateful for the bigger man's terrifying influence.

"I'm curious about your relationship with Lady Trentham."

The boy looked startled for a moment before a sly look took over his features. He narrowed his eyes and slid down in his seat. "Is that so?"

"It is so." Stephen waited, his arms resting lightly on his chair while he studied the younger man. He could sit for hours without talking, but most men could not. Bailey was no exception.

"I knew 'er back 'ome."

Stephen merely waited.

Bailey sighed and gave Stephen his approximation of a world-weary stare. "She likes a bit o' rough, her kind always does."

Stephen controlled his breathing and forced his hands not to grip the arms of the chairs. "I'm going to give you a moment to reconsider your answer, Mr. Bailey."

Whatever the boy saw in his face made him blench. He raised his hands. "Awright, awright. Don't get in a twist. I used to live on the Trentham estate with my mum." He paused, but not before Stephen noticed his Cockney accent had miraculously disappeared.

Stephen took the decanter from the corner of his desk and poured himself a glass. He looked up at the younger man. "Brandy?"

Bailey nodded, the tip of his tongue skimming his lower lip, as though he was parched. Stephen sat back in his chair and the boy hopped up and snatched the glass from the desk. He slurped down half of it and his eyes widened.

"Nice."

"Do you still have the money Lady Trentham gave you?"

Bailey nodded.

"Tell me what I want to know and you can keep it."

Bailey's eyes went even wider. "All of it?"

"Yes."

Bailey swallowed another sip, this one smaller than the last, savoring it more. The gears of his clever brain turning and whirring loudly enough that Stephen knew he was going to lie. The truth never took this much thought.

Stephen would let him speak; sometimes a lie was more telling in the end.

"I lived on Trentham's estate with my mum. She was—" He sighed heavily. "She was the old earl's whore." He gave Stephen a look that dared him to pass comment. So, the boy had stones after all.

"Go on."

"I'm the old earl's bastard."

Stephen waited.

Bailey sipped. "I wasn't born on the estate. Trentham brought my mum from London, where he'd met her. I don't know why, she wasn't exactly talkative when I reached the age to ask questions." He held up his glass, which was almost empty. "She drank. Nothing so fine as this, of course, but whatever she could get. The earl plunked us in a cottage on his estate. I guess my mum must have thought that meant something good for her, but the bastard only came when he had no other sport." He shrugged and finished his drink. Stephen gestured with his head toward the bottle.

"No," Bailey said, lowering the glass to the table beside him. "I like it too much." The way his eyes caressed the brandy decanter, Stephen knew the man would have a life-long struggle ahead of him.

"Lady Trentham saw me one day while she was out riding." His lips curved into a genuine smile as he looked back on the memory. "I can remember it like it was this morning. It was the first time I'd seen a lady on a horse. Only the earl before then. Of course I thought her nag was a fine one. I learned later she only got his lordship's dregs no matter that she was a far better rider than he. Or that puling gudgeon who calls himself earl now." His jaw tightened and Stephen saw the toxic stew of jealousy, envy, and anger. And why not? He was, after all, Edward Atwood's son, far closer in blood than the old earl's nephew Charles.

Bailey's mouth twisted and he continued. "My mum wasn't much for fun and games." He shot Stephen a hard look. "It wasn't her fault, mind. She'd had a rough life."

Stephen nodded.

"Lady Trentham was half mad for a child—anyone could see it, even me, a lad of barely six." He shrugged. "She fastened onto me like I was her long-lost son. My mum thought the woman was daft, but she didn't stop her." His eyes swept over the brandy. "My bloody father did, though."

He swallowed hard, his eyes shifting around the elegantly appointed hotel room, his shoulders tense. "He learned about Lady Trentham's visits to me." His jaw worked. "He struck my mother in front of me. When I tried to stop him, he flung me so hard against the wall he broke my collar bone."

Stephen could hardly breathe. He could feel the Earl of Trentham's fists on his face, the knee in his groin, the cold, sickening taste of fear that had woken him up in a sweat for years. Yes, he could see the raging Edward Atwood clearly in his mind's eye. That was the only way he could see him, in fact.

Oh, he'd noticed the full-length portrait in the gallery at Blackfriars, of course. But that man had been urbane and handsome. The creature Stephen saw in his nightmares was a visitant from Hell and far larger than the real man.

"What about Lady Trentham?" he asked hoarsely, pouring himself another two fingers.

"I don't know if he said or did anything to her. She stayed away for a month or more and then just showed up again. She always came when my mum was gone."

He gave Stephen a wry, tortured smile. "Oh, there's no use in lying. Mum spent her time at the Crown and Serpent after that beating." Again his look dared Stephen to pass judgement. "She must have known her ladyship gave me things; the old earl hardly gave her enough for us to live on, yet I always had toys, clothes, books, and other treats. Mum never asked. She didn't have the nerve to disobey the earl to his face, but he'd not broken her completely.

"Maybe she stayed away on purpose, knowing Lady Trentham could do more for me. She taught me how to read, how to speak." He gestured to his truly hideous suit and snorted. "She taught me how to dress, not that you'd know it from looking at me." He laughed, but there was no humor in it.

"Mum got really sick in early '12. The earl hadn't been back for almost half a year, and Lady Trentham sent food, money, and even that high-in-the-instep maid, Beth MacFarlane, to care for her, but Mum died all the same." He moved his jaw back and forth. "Lady Trentham took care of that, too. She gave my mum a nice burial and a pretty headstone with angels carved into it. And then *he* came home."

This time it was Stephen who could not abide the long silence. "What happened?"

"What do you want with her? Why did you make me bring her?" Bailey sounded like a very young, frightened boy. "You're not going to hurt her, are you?"

"It's a bit late to be asking that question, isn't it?" Stephen bit out, furious with Marcus Bailey for his part in bringing Elinor Trentham here. For his part in her downfall.

"*Christ.*" Bailey lowered his head in his hands and his shoulders shook.

Stephen was not in the mood for crocodile tears.

"Finish the story," he ordered.

For a moment he thought the boy would tell him to go to hell. It's certainly what he wished for. But Bailey sat up and angrily dashed tears from his cheeks and reddened eyes. Whatever hold Fielding had over Marcus Bailey it was close to strangling him.

"The bastard had me thrown out of the cottage, so I went to see him. I waited until after dark and slipped in a side door Lady Trentham had once showed me, in case I ever had need of her." He shook his head at something he saw in the past. "It was almost like the bastard was waiting for me. He couldn't have been—I didn't even know I was coming myself until I'd had a few drinks and drummed up the courage. He was smiling, as if he was pleased to see me for a change.

"I was only fifteen, but we were of a height and I didn't weigh too much less than him. I was no longer a boy to be buffeted about and I told him so. That made him laugh."

His lips twisted. "He put a stack of guineas on his desk and sat back. *'That's all you'll ever get from me, boy. Take it and go. I never want to see your face again.'*"

Bailey paused, his breathing heavy as he relived the confrontation. His eyes flickered to Stephen. "There were five bloody coins in the stack. *Five.* That's what his son was worth to him. I picked them up and was about to hurl them at his hateful face when he lifted his hand from beneath the desk—the bastard had a pistol on me!" Bailey laughed, stunned even after all these years.

"What happened next?" Stephen's voice was beyond cold to his own ears and the younger man gave him a look of pure venom.

"You'll have it all out of me, won't you?"

"Two thousand pounds should buy me something."

"He had me take off my shirt, stuff it in my mouth, and take hold of his bloody desk. He told me he was going to give me one last lesson before sending me on his way. And then he began to whip me with his quirt." Bailey stared up at Stephen, his eyes crazed. "Would you care to see the scars?" Angry tears squeezed from his reddened eyes and ran down his face. "I collapsed to my knees, almost choking on my own damned shirt but even then the bastard wouldn't stop. And the words that came out of him—they were almost worse than the whip." He gave Stephen a look of horrified wonder. "Such hate and loathing for me. *Me!* His own bloody son. What had I ever done to deserve such hate other than to be born?"

He gulped, pulling at his gaudy cravat, as if he couldn't breathe. "I was half-unconscious when he suddenly stopped—the words and the whip. When I turned, I saw him lying on the floor with Lady Trentham standing above him. She held a poker in her hand. She'd hit him."

Stephen was gripping his chair so hard his hands hurt.

"Lady Trentham checked to see he was still breathing and then began ransacking his desk. She found more money and several other things of value and shoved them at me. She gave me a man's name and address and told me to take only what I could carry and leave that night. I should catch a mail coach and I was to stay away until I received word from her."

He slumped into his chair, his chin almost on his chest. "I learned later that she said it had been a robbery. Lord Trentham had engaged in a struggle, discharged a single shot and missed, and then had been clobbered." He looked up at Stephen. "He lingered in his bed for six months or more but he was paralyzed, couldn't speak or move." A look of self-loathing and hate spread over his face. "Is that enough for you? Will that bloody Fielding let my sisters be now?"

The boy had lied, Stephen was sure of it, but there was enough truth in his tale for his purposes. He pulled another fat packet of money from one of the drawers and tossed it across the desk.

"That is enough to live on, to start a new life, if you don't gamble it away." The younger man's startled look told Stephen he'd guessed correctly. "Lady Trentham is in the room at the very end of the hall. I want you to go to her and tell her everything is going along smoothly. I don't care how you put it; just make sure her mind is at ease. I want you to let her know your business will be finished in three days' time. Indicate to her it would be best if she remained in London. Do not speak of me or this conversation, or you will not live long enough to regret it. Do you understand?"

The younger man shot him a look of hatred doused in fear. "I understand."

"At the end of three days you will return here to me and I will give you a third payment. Altogether the amount will be five thousand pounds—a fortune. Take your sisters and disappear. Do not go to Trentham, do not stay in London. Never go to Lady Trentham for money again. The money should be enough to keep you until you find a more respectable line of business. If I find out you have disobeyed me in any way it will not go well for you. Do you understand?"

Bailey nodded.

"Now go."

The boy stood and tucked the heavy pouch into his coat pocket before turning to the door.

Stephen's mind was already on his next task and he was surprised when the younger man spoke, his hand on the doorknob.

"You're not going to hurt her, are you?"

# The Footman

Stephen frowned at the man's impertinence. But he answered the question all the same.

"I asked her to marry me."

Relief spread over the younger man's handsome features and he nodded, closing the door quietly behind him.

Stephen didn't see the point in telling Marcus Bailey that she'd said no.

# Chapter Eighteen

*Blackfriars*
*1813*

E linor stood beside Edward's bed and listed to his shallow breaths. She'd been doing much the same thing for months. They'd spent more time together in the last few months than they had in over a decade of marriage.

Edward's pale blue eyes, once so terrifying, still burned with loathing, but they now did so beneath a dense fog of pain. He'd not been able to speak or move since that night in the library.

Doctor Venable stood up and replaced the candle he'd been using to examine the earl. "I'm afraid there isn't much more we can do, Lady Trentham. Have you been giving him the sleeping draught I prescribed?"

"Three times every day, doctor."

And each and every time Edward pulsed with impotent fury as she dribbled the liquid down his throat.

"Go ahead and increase it to five times daily." He glanced down at the corpselike body on the bed, frowning, as though he wanted to say something but couldn't think of how to put it.

"Would you care for some tea? I was just about to have some myself." Elinor liked the new doctor for several reasons, not least of which because he knew very little of her history of bruises, cuts, and broken bones. He'd treated her once only, when she'd lost the last child Edward would ever put inside her.

Elinor knew the Doctor Venable had noticed her scars but hoped he'd not inferred how she'd gotten them. What she did know is the attractive young doctor would not need to treat any new injuries.

She looked up at him. "Come, doctor, you must be thirsty?"

He hesitated and then smiled, robbing Elinor of breath.

*Goodness he was a handsome devil!*

"I'd like that, Lady Trentham. I'm afraid I haven't yet found the time to engage a new housekeeper after my last one got married."

A footman stood outside Lord Trentham's chambers.

"I would like tea in the smaller drawing room, Thomas."

Elinor waited until Doctor Venable was comfortable before asking the question uppermost in her mind. "I believe you wanted to tell me something about my husband but did not wish to do so in front of him. Do you think he can hear and understand?"

Venable gave her what Elinor thought of as his doctor smile—a restrained, solemn expression—as though he expected somebody to catch him at it and accuse him of excessive jollity.

"Little is known about a condition such as Lord Trentham's, my lady. I feel it is always best to err on the side of caution. It would be cruel to do otherwise. As for his condition? Even though you've kept his body well-nourished, he seems to be fading." He took a deep breath before continuing. "I'm afraid there is little hope that he will ever recover from this near-vegetative state."

Elinor did not know whether to laugh or weep.

The door opened and one of the maids entered with a large tray.

Elinor turned to the doctor after the maid left. "How do you like your tea, doctor?"

"Strong, please." A slight flush covered his high, sharp cheekbones.

He really was a remarkably attractive specimen. He wore spectacles, but they could not dim the brilliance of his heavily lashed soft brown eyes. Elinor poured a cup for herself and left the tea to steep a moment longer while she prepared a generous plate for the too-thin man across from her.

"I know of a fine cook/housekeeper who is looking for work, Doctor Venable. I could give you her name and direction." She handed him his plate before turning to fix his tea.

"I'd be much obliged to you, my lady. I'm afraid my own efforts in the kitchen are limited to cheese toast." He gave her a shy smile, the rapidly disappearing biscuit he held silent testimony of his hunger.

"Shall I tell her the situation is dire?" Elinor jested, handing him his tea.

"It would hardly be a lie."

They ate in companionable silence for a moment, the doctor's face becoming less pale in proportion to the number of cakes and biscuits he consumed.

"I wouldn't be surprised if your husband had a certain degree of awareness. I believe he knows some of those around him."

Elinor thought of the murder she saw in Edward's eyes at least a dozen times a day.

"I think you are right, doctor. Sometimes I think he is trying to tell me something." And she had a pretty good idea what it was.

The doctor nodded and took a sip of tea to wash down a biscuit before wiping his mouth with a napkin. "I wouldn't be surprised. I'm glad to see you always keep somebody at his side. It would be a shame if he was able to speak at some point and nobody was there to hear him."

Elinor nibbled a corner of cream cake. "Yes, that would be terrible."

Which was why either Elinor or Beth was always with the earl, even when his valet and one of the footmen were changing or bathing him.

"I know this must be very hard for you, Lady Trentham."

Elinor was surprised at the depth of empathy in the man's eyes. They were, for all purposes, strangers. And yet he'd already shown her more kindness in five minutes than Edward had in all the years of their marriage.

Elinor wished she could reassure him. She wished she could tell him the truth, that the past three months had been the best months in a decade.

Freedom. She was free. Free of men telling her what to do. Free of the ghastly monthly visits to her bed. Free of the brutality, both physical and mental. She'd learned more about herself in the past three months than in all her other years combined.

Never again would she place herself in any man's power. *Never, never, never, never.* She would die first.

She picked up an iced biscuit and smiled at the kind man across from her. "Tell me doctor, should I increase the dosage of his pain medication along with the frequency?"

\*\*\*

Elinor had just turned Edward on his side so he was facing her chair. He would remain that way for two hours, and then she would turn him again. She was sedulous in her care of his body and he'd not developed bed sores.

She felt his eyes on her and looked up from her book, which she'd been reading aloud just in case he was awake and aware, a prisoner of his body.

There was more pain than hate in his eyes tonight, and she knew the doctor's last prediction had been accurate; her husband did not have much longer to live. He'd worsened at an alarming rate since Venable had come last night and told her to give him laudanum whenever she thought he needed it.

"Don't worry about over-dosing him at this point, my lady. It's more important that he not suffer."

Elinor took the crinkly bottle from the nightstand and went to sit beside her husband's pitiful, withered body. She propped his head on her shoulder and gently poured a double dose of pain medication past his lips. He swallowed convulsively and his eyes were feverish for the laudanum that made his existence bearable. Elinor gave him several sips of water afterward and then opened the small tin of unguent Beth had made and carefully rubbed some on his dry, cracked lips.

When she'd finished, she laid him back on his side and resumed her seat. His gaunt cheeks had become flushed from the drug and his eyes followed her. Elinor felt a pang of pity for him, even though she knew what he would do to her—and to Marcus—if he were able. On impulse she leaned forward and took his hand.

"I'm sorry you've been reduced to this, Edward."

His lips twitched, as if they were straining to sneer.

S.M. LaViolette

"It's true. I cannot bring myself to take pleasure in your condition, even though you surely deserve it. To be happy about such a thing would make me like you. I wouldn't wish your condition on anyone— even you. It would've been better if you'd died that night." She shook her head as she held his hate-filled stare.

"He is your *son*, Edward. The only child you have, as far as I know. How could you treat him with such brutality? Why do you hate him so?" Elinor had asked him these same questions before. She knew he couldn't answer and wouldn't even if he could. Yet she couldn't help asking. "What would make a man hate his own son?"

A low gurgle sounded in his throat and she leaned forward. His face was an alarming shade of red. She lurched toward the bed and lifted him upright, afraid he must be choking. But the noise didn't stop. She held her ear to his chest, to hear his heart. It beat as regularly—if weakly—as it always did lately. His body shook and the horrible gurgling became louder.

Elinor looked at his face and flinched. He wasn't choking, he was *laughing*. She released him so hastily he flopped onto the bed like a landed fish. She immediately straightened his body, which had fallen at an awkward angle. Touching him was like handling a poisonous reptile. His pale eyes glinted with laudanum, amusement, and contempt.

Elinor shook her head. "I pity you, Edward. You are an evil man."

\*\*\*

The sound of shattering glass pulled Elinor from a deep sleep. She blinked her eyes several times as stared at the rumpled bedding and empty pillow.

Elinor said a very vulgar word she'd once heard her brother Stuart yell when he was drunk.

Edward was gone.

It didn't take her long to find him. He'd dragged himself half-way across the room toward his destination, the bell pull. Elinor crouched down beside him as one weak, shaking hand clawed the carpet, unable to lift his head.

She took his shoulders and easily turned him over. His lips were fixed in a snarl she recognized well. She instinctively flinched away, expecting the blow that usually followed such a look. But he was in no condition to wield even his own body, not to mention a whip or quirt. His head flopped weakly on his shoulders and she laid him back.

"Whore." The word was no more than a harsh whisper.

She shook her head. "Oh Edward. Will you never believe me? Even now, when I have no reason to lie to you? I've only ever been with you, although only the basest mind would ever call what you did to me making love. I kissed the boy—one kiss—and you ruined his life and mine for it. But all that is at an end now. Your days of terrorizing anyone are at an end." Elinor slipped her hands beneath his armpits and slowly pulled him toward his bed. She might not be able to lift him, even though he scarcely weighed more than her. If she couldn't, she would run and fetch Beth. She couldn't risk any of the other servants if he was able to speak.

It took ten minutes of pushing, shoving, and grunting, but she got him back on the bed. He was in pain by the end of it and she cradled him against her shoulder and gave him another dose of laudanum. She held him afterward, even though it sickened her to touch him. A person should not be without human contact when they were in such a poor condition.

His body vibrated with tremors and drool ran from a corner of his mouth. He was dying and he was her husband. His breathing and shuddering eventually disappeared and she laid him back against several pillows, keeping his torso at an angle, which seemed to make it easier for him to breathe.

She was about to resume her chair when he spoke again. "El . . . nor . . ."

She looked at his slack lips and wiped away a strand of spittle. He closed his eyes and shuddered. "Doan . . . touch me." She gladly released him but remained beside him. His breathing quickened. "Boy?"

"He's gone. I've hidden him away in a safe place with a man who has as much reason to dislike you as I do."

The look of curiosity in his pitiless eyes made her smile. She did nothing to explain herself.

"You . . . you . . ." he swallowed, his body shaking with frustration. "You . . . hiding . . . killer." The last word was hardly more than a puff of air.

"Yes, that's true. Unfortunately no court in the land would listen to the truth, that you incited your own son to violence. That he only struck you in self-defense."

"I get . . . you . . . both." His breathing was choked and ragged so she lifted him higher.

"You need to calm down, Edward. You're wearing yourself out."

"Both," he rasped, before his eyes fluttered shut.

She shook her head. "It doesn't matter what you say—if you ever say anything. I will not let you ruin Marcus's life as you've ruined mine. As you ruined that poor boy's all those years ago. Marcus will not suffer for what you drove him to do. I'll confess to it before I'll let you hurt him."

Elinor realized she was talking to herself. His eyes were closed and his breathing was heavy and labored, the sound of a man heavily drugged.

She made him as comfortable as she could before taking her seat, staring at his sleeping form. Was this the end of her brief happiness? Would she wake tomorrow and find Edward could speak? That all her efforts to save Marcus had been for nothing?

Elinor watched his vulnerable, sleeping form and wondered just how far she would go to keep him from talking.

# Chapter Nineteen

**London**
**1817**

There was a sharp knock on the hotel door.

"Go see who it is, Molly." Elinor stared at her reflection in the glass while the maid went to see who was outside. She knew it wasn't Marcus, as he'd already come and gone. His news hadn't been bad, but it had not been good either. He wanted her to wait three days; the man who had his sister was gone from London and Marcus couldn't deal with any other.

"Will she be safe in the meantime? Have you seen her?" Elinor asked.

Marcus's face had been red with shame. "Aye, I've seen her. They've promised to let her be until the man returns."

She squeezed his shoulder. "You're a good brother, Marcus. You mustn't blame yourself."

He jerked away from her hand as if she'd burnt him. "I've got to go, Elinor." He'd lurched for the door.

"Wait, won't you have something to eat? You must be starved; you've done nothing but run since we left Trentham."

"I'm not hungry!"

Elinor winced away from his angry face and words. He sighed, plowing his already disheveled hair with his hand. "I'm sorry, Elinor. But I can't stay. Please don't ask me to."

"When will I see you again?"

"I can't say. Maybe tomorrow."

She'd watched him leave with a heavy feeling of dread. If everything was going well, then why did he look so guilty and nervous?

Elinor looked up now to see the maid, Molly, holding a note toward her.

"It's a message for you, Lady Trentham."

*Will you have dinner with me?*

It wasn't signed and she'd never seen his handwriting before, but she knew the bold, black script must be Stephen's. She looked up. "Is a servant waiting?"

"Yes, my lady."

"Tell him my answer is yes."

\*\*\*

Elinor shouldn't have been surprised when the man led her to a room down the hall rather than to the dining room below.

"Mr. Worth will be with you in a moment, Lady Trentham. May I get you something to drink?"

"No, thank you."

He nodded and left. Elinor examined the room. It looked very similar to hers, but with books and papers and other personal items scattered about. This was obviously where Stephen lived when he stayed in London. She saw a fancy ivory pipe on a silver salver and picked it up. It was carved in the shape of a peacock and quite lovely.

"A nasty habit."

She jumped guiltily and set down the pipe.

"But elegantly done, I see." She looked up to find him towering above her. He'd shaved and bathed; he smelled delicious and looked even better.

He motioned to a table filled with cut glass decanters. "What will you have?"

"You choose."

He crossed the room in several long strides and she watched him hungrily as he poured out two glasses of something dark red, realizing just how much she'd missed him. He was dressed in black except for his waistcoat, which was the color of a frost-covered leaf. His linen was almost blinding, and she could see glints of gold at his cuffs as he walked toward her.

"Madeira."

His hands brushed hers and Elinor gulped a mouthful quickly, as if to quench the sudden flames in her chest. He gestured to a beautifully set table, complete with a floral display that probably cost more than it took to feed her entire household for a month.

"I thought we might dine in here. I hope you don't think my suggestion is inappropriate?"

"I think it looks lovely."

He seated her and pulled the velvet cord that hung in the corner of the room before seating himself.

"Are you hungry?"

"Famished."

"I thought you might be, so I ordered one of everything on the menu."

She laughed.

His eyebrows arched.

Elinor stared. "Surely you are jesting?"

He shook his head slowly from side to side, his expression tying her stomach in knots.

***

"I shall never need to eat again." Elinor watched the servants carry away the last of the food, much of it untouched, and closed her eyes.

"You were hungry."

"You noticed?" It was a struggle to open her eyes and doubly so not to yawn.

"I made sure to keep my hands at a safe distance from your plate."

She laughed. "What an ungentlemanly observation."

He merely smiled, swirling his glass before taking a drink. She didn't think he'd eaten half as much as her. She supposed it had been necessary for one of them to carry the conversation, and her mouth had been too full to talk through most of dinner.

"I trust your business went well?" he asked, setting aside his empty glass.

Elinor grimaced. "I'm afraid I need to talk to you about that." She was glad the subject had come up so quickly; she'd dreaded the thought of bringing it up herself.

"Oh?" He propped his elbows on the table and leaned forward. "Was the money not enough?"

She felt herself flushing already at what she was about to say. "It's not that. It's something else. I can't really say as—"

"You needn't tell me anything, Lady Trentham. Just let me know what I can do to help."

Elinor's stomach twisted at the kindness in his voice, in his eyes. She wanted to throw herself under the table and hide.

"Please, call me Elinor."

The right side of his mouth quirked. "Only if you'll call me Stephen."

"It would be a pleasure, Stephen." His eyes darkened and she glanced away. "I need to stay in London another few days."

"Of course." He spoke without hesitation. "Would you like me to send for Beth?"

This further display of kindness was almost too much. She closed her eyes and shook her head, unable to speak. She felt a soft brush at her side and saw he'd dropped to his haunches by her chair. He took her hand and she gripped his fingers tightly, drawing strength from the sheer substance of him.

"No. Don't bring Beth. She is very . . . unhappy with me right now."

Stephen lifted her hand to his mouth and kissed the tips of her fingers, one by one. "It won't last. Nobody could stay angry with you."

Elinor could hardly breathe and she couldn't take her eyes from his mouth as he trailed kisses across the knuckles of her work-reddened hand. He lowered his eyes and auburn lashes fanned his cheeks.

"What happened here?" He brushed the knob on her wrist, his green eyes almost black when they looked up.

"I was clumsy and broke it." She didn't protest as his fingers lightly massaged her deformed wrist and moved up her arm. "That too," she said, when he felt the misshapen bone in her forearm. "It was a riding accident."

He lowered his head and feathered kisses from her wrist to the inside of her elbow. Elinor's toes curled in her slippers. Never had she felt such tender softness. She bit her lower lip to keep from moaning when his tongue flicked against the sensitive skin of her inner arm.

Just as suddenly as he'd come beside her, he was gone, moving across the room to the window and resting one arm against the frame like a man holding back something dangerous. His absence was like a bucket of cold water. Had she done something?

"Stephen?"

"I'm sorry, Elinor. I didn't mean to take advantage of the situation—to take advantage of *you*." He kept his back to her.

Elinor stood and went to him, humbled by his slumped shoulders, horrified to think he'd believed he was forcing himself on her. She laid a hand on his arm and he jumped as though she'd prodded him with a hot poker.

She looked up into eyes as tortured as any she'd ever seen and her hand was on his jaw before she knew it had moved. She massaged the taut, smooth skin and his eyelids fluttered closed.

"Do you know what you're doing?" he asked, his body swaying toward hers.

She reached up with her other hand and laid it over his heart. It was beating strong and fast and with a power that sent a shock straight to her core. She stood on her toes to reach his lips with hers. The merest touch was enough to bring his arms around her and his mouth crushing down. He held her with a ferocity that squeezed the air from her body and she opened to him. His tongue swept the inside of her mouth, her lips, and then tangled with hers. He pulled away suddenly, his lips moving with feverish intensity across her cheek and coming to rest just beneath her ear.

"I want to be inside you so badly." His words shocked her entire body, not least the part between her thighs.

"Will you take me, Elinor?" His hot mouth wrapped around her throat and his teeth grazed over her pounding pulse until she trembled all over. He pulled back, his eyes black, his lips parted. "Is that a yes?"

"Ye—yes."

He swung her into his arms, cradling her in a way she couldn't recall anyone doing, even when she'd been a child. Her arms slipped around his neck and he looked down as he pushed open the door to his bedchamber.

"You're sure?" he asked, almost as if he wanted her to say she wasn't. This last sign of kindness undid her and she covered his mouth with hers. He groaned at her clumsy kiss and she felt his lips curve into a smile as he laid her gently on his bed.

"Turn over, sweetheart, let me get this off you."

His hands went to the fastenings of her gown and her body stiffened. He leaned over her, until their eyes met.

"Don't you want me to take off your clothes?"

She swallowed at the desire she saw in his eyes. "Is it necessary?"

He gave a surprised laugh and sat back. "Necessary?"

Elinor was so mortified she could hardly breathe. Why hadn't she simply let him do what he wanted? What did she know about any of this? Everything he'd done had felt so good. But she couldn't let him see her without her gown. It wouldn't be like her arm. He'd never believe those other marks came from a riding accident.

"Elinor?" He tilted her face toward him. "Have you never made love without clothes on before?"

She'd thought she couldn't be more ashamed, but she'd been wrong. She closed her eyes against his curious stare. "No."

A pause that felt a dozen years long stretched between them.

She heard him inhale. "Would it bother you if I were to see you?"

She nodded, no longer able to speak.

"Have you seen a man naked?"

She shook her head.

He made an odd noise and she opened her eyes. He was looking at her as if she were some manner of . . . freak. She turned away.

"Oh, darling. I don't mean to make you feel self-conscious." He pulled her to his chest, the endearment as powerful as his gentle arms and the strong, steady hand stroking up and down her back. "How about a compromise?" She shrugged and he laughed softly. "Have you stopped speaking to me?"

"No." The word was muffled against his shoulder.

"Good, I should hate that. Your voice is one of the things I like best about you."

She pulled away until she could see his face. "It is?"

He nodded, his expression serious.

"You don't think I'm . . . waspish?"

He hesitated and then nodded again, a tiny smile making his lips even more kissable.

She laughed and pushed on him, which was like shoving an anvil. "You beast."

He pulled her close and nuzzled her throat.

"Now it is you who have stopped speaking. What compromise, Stephen?"

He jolted slightly at the sound of his name. "No dress, no stays, no drawers, no stockings." His voice rumbled against her throat, the words causing her body to turn liquid and hot.

"Drawers *and* chemise."

He grunted, his fingers already going to her back. "Done."

"What—what about you?" His hands on her back made speaking difficult. His fingers paused.

"What about me?"

"What will you wear?"

"What do you want me to wear?"

She swallowed. "What do you usually wear?"

He chuckled.

Her breathing hitched and hiccupped. "Oh."

"Haven't you seen a man's cock before, love?"

The word made her woozy. When she didn't immediately answer he tried to pull away and look at her. This time it was Elinor who held him firm. "No."

"No, you haven't seen one?" He sounded stunned.

"No, don't look at me."

"Why not?"

"I could never have this conversation with you looking."

She felt him hesitate. "Are you quite certain about this, Elinor? We do not have to *do* anything. We could just lie here together and talk."

Elinor considered his offer, which was more than kind considering how they'd ended up on this bed. He must think her daft—a woman married for a decade who made such a fuss about the marital act. How could she tell him she'd never experienced such a thing? That all she'd had was brutality and harsh neglect? Would he even know what she

S.M. LaViolette

meant? Everything he'd done to her—from his kisses, to the way he'd gently held her foot at the Blackfriars ball, to the way he was behaving right now—was so different from what Edward had done they were like two different species.

She realized he'd pulled her closer and was rubbing her back, holding her lightly. He really *would* just hold her. But if he did so, she would never know where these feelings swirling around her body might lead.

"Could we extinguish the lights?"

His hand froze on her back. "Is that what you'd like?"

"Would you mind terribly?"

He chuckled. "Yes, I would, but I would be glad to do it for you."

Elinor turned away while he rose and extinguished the various lights. When he was done, only the light from the city below illuminated the room.

"The windows?" Elinor reminded him, when she heard him approaching.

"The windows?" He sounded plaintive.

Elinor lifted a hand to smother a laugh. "Please."

He cursed under his breath, but yanked the heavy drapes closed, making the room as dark as a moonless night. She heard a thump.

"Bloody hell!" he muttered. She couldn't entirely stifle a laugh. "I'm so glad I amuse you, my lady. I'll have a bruised shin, now."

"I'm sorry."

"You sound it."

"What are you doing?" she asked when he didn't return to the bed.

"Stripping."

Elinor swallowed. "Oh."

"Don't touch your dress. Or your stockings," he ordered, his voice coming from someplace close. "That's my job. You may remove your shoes."

"You are too kind," she muttered, kicking off her kid slippers.

"What was that?" His voice came from right beside her ear and she squeaked.

"You move like a cat."

His hands went to the back of her dress. "I'm going to push it down, lift your bottom." She complied and a big, warm hand pulled the garment beneath her.

"You never answered my question." His voice was husky as he slid a hand up one of her legs.

Elinor had hoped he'd forgotten asking it.

"Yes, I've seen one." She didn't tell him it had only been a drawing in Doctor Venable's textbook. She knew all the pertinent parts and what they did; it had been the most mortifying part of her instruction, thus far.

He deftly released one stocking and then the other, rolling each down slowly.

"Mmm." The sound was low and predatory and it made all her muscles tighten. Intellectually she knew what was happening: blood was flowing to her clitoris and causing it to become engorged. She knew where it was; she'd seen it both in drawings and on herself. She'd touched it from time to time and knew what it did when stimulated. But it had never felt quite like this before.

His hands settled on her thighs.

"Drawers?" He sounded hopeful.

"We had a deal, Mr. Worth. Are you trying to breach your contract?"

"No, just renegotiate."

"Isn't that breaching the contract?"

He picked her up by the waist and tossed her further back on the bed, just like a doll.

A laugh broke out of her.

"I thought you were studying medicine. Have you taken up the law, too?" His weighty, muscular body made the bed shift as he moved closer.

She felt his hands on her ankles and the laughter froze in her chest.

"Shh," Stephen murmured, immediately releasing her legs and crawling up beside her, stretching out along her body. "Don't be frightened, Elinor. I would never force you." He unerringly found her jaw in the darkness and slowly traced one finger to her chin. He leaned in and kissed her gently, his tongue probing suggestively between her pursed lips. She opened and took his thrusting organ into her mouth.

He moaned and inched closer, his free hand moving from her jaw, down her neck, and settling lightly on her breast.

She gasped into his mouth at the feel of his palm over her nipple.

"Easy, sweetheart." He circled his hand over her and her body answered without any help from her mind, arching to meet him. "Yes, that's right," he coaxed, nipping her lip sharply before pulling away from her mouth. Resentment surged through her. Where was he going? Why was he leaving her?

Something warm and unbelievably soft hovered over her breast. He dropped lower and sucked her nipple into his mouth.

"Stephen!" His name tore from her mouth before she could stop it. He tongued her stiff peak, his lips curving into a smile against her sensitive skin before he commenced suckling her through her chemise. She bucked in his grasp until he locked his arm around her and held her fast, his wicked, wicked mouth moving to her second breast. Her intimate muscles contracted and she almost cried out at the sensation. She was so unbearably sensitive, so tight, so . . . something. He chuckled against her nipple and she realized she'd been pushing her hips against him.

"No, don't stop." He kissed her throat, her ear, her temple while his finger went to her nipple and pinched it through the damp cloth. She shuddered and gasped, her body no longer hers to control. "Such sensitive little things," he murmured, his hand moving to her other breast, tweaking the nipple harder. The sensation between her legs began to overwhelm her reason and she pushed against him, desperate. His hand slid down her hip with glacial slowness.

"Oh, Elinor, I could make you come just by sucking your sweet nipples." His vulgar words were like a key unlocking the madness inside her body.

"*Please.*" Elinor's shame at what she was saying and doing was no match for the need driving her.

"Hmm?" His hand continued its journey, brushing the bones of her hip like the wings of a butterfly.

She shook her head back and forth, unable to take any more sensation, unable to verbalize what she wanted, what she needed.

"Is this what you want?" His finger pushed through the slit in her drawers, into the curls that guarded her sex.

# The Footman

Elinor's mind shut down.

***

Stephen held her shuddering body against him, one finger deep inside her sheath as his thumb teased another climax from her responsive body. She'd come so quick and hard it had stunned him. He was so bloody aroused he couldn't think straight.

*Slow down, you great rutting pig!* a voice from the far-flung reaches of his mind ordered.

Yes, slow. He needed to go slow. She would be angry at her body once she realized it had broken free of her control. Stephen had seen the same reaction before, times beyond counting, widows whose husbands had merely come to them in the darkened room, filled them like anonymous vessels, and left them confused and unsatisfied and still in the dark.

He cupped his hand around her swollen mound and slowly removed his slick finger, unable to resist touching her pearl one last time. She flinched as though he'd touched her with a hot poker.

"I'm sorry, love. Too sensitive yet?"

She nodded her head against his chest.

Stephen swallowed back his lust, his body shaking with need, his mind offering all kinds of suggestions, all of them ending with some part of him buried in some part of her. He brought his hand to his face and inhaled her musky scent. His mouth watered to take her stiff peak between his lips and suck until she screamed. Instead, he put his middle finger in his mouth and sucked it clean.

"God, you taste so sweet," he groaned.

She jolted against him and he could tell he'd shocked her—again. He grinned and put his wet finger to her lips, pushing gently until she parted and took him. "Can you taste yourself, Elinor?" She trembled but her tongue touched the pad of his finger and then drew back, like a shy serpent scenting danger. He pushed and she took him deeper.

He ground himself against her while stroking into her velvety mouth, the motion suggestive, making it obvious what he wanted.

Stephen thought he'd imagined it at first, that it was just the torturous rub of a sheet against his enflamed skin.

But then her hand settled around him and he jerked violently.

*"Good God!"*

159

Her hand disappeared.

"No!" He snatched at her wrist in the darkness and wrapped her small, rough fingers around his throbbing organ. "Stroke me, Ellie. Please," he begged, rolling onto his back, one hand covering hers, guiding her movements.

Her hand tightened. "Nobody has ever called me that before—Ellie."

"Mmmhmm," he moaned. "Elinor is too stern, too proper. She wouldn't do this. But Ellie would."

She chuckled, the sound low and wicked. "I like it."

He thrust his hips against her fist.

"My rough hands don't hurt you?" Her voice was more tentative than he'd ever heard it.

He laughed, thrusting with barely restrained violence, like a boy with his first grind. "You'll only hurt me if you stop."

He released her hand and fisted the bedding at his sides until his knuckles ached, fighting the inevitable as his balls tightened and snugged to his body, eager to free him from his misery.

Even with her awkward fumbling—or maybe because of it—he came fast and hard, crushing her hand with his and pumping savagely into their doubled fists to finish himself. He vaguely heard his voice shout something crude as she milked him. He stilled her hand, just before everything faded to black and his mind went to that place where nothing mattered and he became nothing.

He must have slept because the next thing he noticed was cold spunk on his stomach and a small, warm body snuggled against his side. He turned toward Elinor but could see nothing in the utter darkness. Her breathing was heavy and regular, telling him she'd fallen asleep.

He dropped his head back onto the pillow.

*Well.*

He stared at the blackness above while he considered tonight's work.

*One down, two to go,* his baser side crowed.

Part of him wanted to stifle the crass, snide voice, but another part knew the chivalrous reaction was nothing but a side-effect of ejaculation. It had been a while since he'd come—either in a woman or in his fist. He'd been hard for Elinor countless times, but he'd never acted on it with another woman or relieved himself. He didn't want the pretty whores, eager servants, or lustful widows who'd slaked his need for the past fifteen years.

He'd only wanted her since that first morning in her shabby little house.

He still wanted her and that bothered him. He'd hoped to satisfy the beast inside him by bedding her.

*You haven't been inside her yet*, the evil little voice reminded him.

No, not yet. Maybe that's why he still felt hollow—he needed to complete the ultimate act of possession and then it would all be over. He'd slip out of the strangling, choking leash that had dropped over his head a decade and a half ago and tightened every year. Yes, that was what he needed, to be inside her.

The thought of fucking her had made him harden again.

*Why rush? You've been waiting for it for half your life.*

Why was he rushing? Tonight was proof he could have her in any way he wanted before all was said and done.

Stephen thought of the Chinese monks he'd once read about. They believed ejaculation made a man weak, drained him of his power and his male essence. Stephen thought that was probably a load of horseshit, but he had to admit going without a woman had made him one mean bastard and kept him sharp.

The very opposite of how he felt right now, which was like a fat, lazy housecat on a warm hearth. He wrapped his hand around his nagging arousal and absently stroked himself while his lips found her shoulder and covered it with soft kisses.

His body, and a big chunk of his mind, urged him to take her now, but the other part of him—the cold, driven part that always made sure he got what he wanted—told him to wait.

*Stay with the plan, Stephen.*

*Yes, the plan.*

Wasn't that what Stephen was always telling Fielding when he tried to rush things?

He released his insistent organ with a groan, shoved aside the covers, and rose, careful not to disturb Elinor. He felt around in the dark for his robe and used it to wipe the cold 'essence' off his stomach.

He tossed the soiled robe on the floor and carefully made his way across the dark room to the door, opening it only a crack. A glance at the bed showed him she was still sleeping.

He edged sideways through the gap and went to the study, closing the door before striding across to the decanter on his desk and pouring out a good three fingers. He collapsed into his overstuffed chair, leaned back, and rested his heels on his desk, savoring the fine spirits and trying to forget about his semi-erect cock.

Stephen couldn't have said how long he sat there when he heard a knock.

"Come in." Fielding stepped inside and Stephen felt a smile tug at his lips. "Well, look at you."

Fielding scowled. "I could say the same for you. I suppose it would be too much to ask for you to put on some bloody clothes?"

Stephen grinned. "Is my naked body exciting you?"

Fielding strode across the room and snatched a glass off the desk, turning to the side to fill it. "The sight of your hairy bollocks is enough to shrivel my own."

Stephen threw back his head and laughed. "Lord, what a bloody prude you are. You never would have survived at Eton or Harrow."

"It's a good thing I was born on the wrong side of the blanket then, wasn't it?"

Stephen dropped his legs and tucked his lower half beneath the desk. "There, is that better?"

Fielding grunted and lowered his considerable bulk into the biggest chair.

Stephen looked him up and down. "You look like a bloody lord. Better, actually, since most of them can't afford to dress so well." His gaze snagged on the other man's glossy black boots. "Hoby?"

Fielding actually smiled. "You sent me to the top of St. James."

"You profligate son of a bitch. You'd better prove worth it." Stephen ignored Fielding's laughter and dug around the papers cluttering his desk before finding what he wanted. He flicked the envelope over to the big man, who caught it with nimble fingers.

"Take that over to Trentham's town house."

"Tonight?"

"Yes, *tonight*. And wait for an answer."

162

# The Footman

"And should I bring that back *tonight*?"

"No, don't bother me again until morning. Come first thing." He looked around the room. "Where the devil is Nichols?"

Fielding tossed back the rest of his drink and stood. "How should I know where your valet is? Perhaps he's tired of looking at your naked arse as well."

Stephen stood, causing the other man to turn abruptly away. He smiled and scrubbed his hand across his chest before stretching and falling into a huge yawn.

"Fielding," he called as the other man reached the door. "Since I can't find Nichols, you'll do just as well. Tell them I want a cold supper sent up—just in case she wakes up hungry. Send it in an hour." He absently scratched himself. "Make that two hours and have them send two bottles of the best red they have. And a bottle of champagne."

Fielding muttered something that sounded a lot like, "*Go sod yourself.*"

"What's that you say, Mr. Fielding?"

"I said, 'Right away, sir.'"

He slammed the door on Stephen's laughter.

*\*\*\**

Elinor was dreaming and it was the best dream she'd ever had. She tried to stay completely still and keep her eyes closed, as if that would somehow help her hold onto the moment. But then the delicious waves began. Again and again, she tensed her body, inside and out, but that just made the sensation more powerful. She cried out, her back arched until she hurt. Her hands were tangled in something soft but heavy between her legs.

Her eyes flew open and met utter darkness.

"Go back to sleep, Elinor." Stephen's voice was muffled by the blankets.

Elinor realized her hands were tangled in his hair, and that he was . . . down *there*.

She pinched her thighs together and he yelped.

"Dammit! My *ear*."

"Sorry." She unclamped her thighs and yanked on his hair.

"Christ! Not so bloody hard, Elinor."

"What are you *doing*?" She dragged his head from beneath the bedding, suddenly wishing she could see his face. And just as suddenly glad she could not.

"I was happily feasting until you interrupted me." He sounded sulky, and his hands had begun to roam her body in a way designed to distract and confuse.

"Feasting?" she squeaked.

"Mmmhmm. I was starving and you taste delicious." He took advantage of her surprise to tug his hair from her grasp and lower his mouth to her chest. "Sweet, like honey." He nibbled her stiff nipple before sucking most of one breast into his mouth.

"But . . ."

He released her breast. "But?" he repeated, licking her just like a cat. Well, not *just* like a cat.

"That can't be normal, Stephen?" Even so, her body pulsed for the return of his lips and tongue between her aching thighs.

"It's normal for me. I think of it all the time." He slid a hand into her damp curls and her legs tensed, only to find he'd wedged his knees between them. He traced the swollen seam of her lips and a low, desperate sound came from deep inside his body while he mercilessly tongued her breast.

Elinor groaned, her body rendered boneless by his relentless mouth.

"That's better," he praised, moving from breast to breast, suckling and nibbling, his finger parting her. "Mmmm, wet." The words were a puff of air against one breast just before he bit her nipple.

She cried out, the pleasure so intense her head rang. He slid a finger inside, not stopping until his knuckles rested against her sex. "You're so fucking tight." Her face flared at the profanity but her inner muscles tightened even more around his finger and he chuckled. "You like that, a bit of dirty talk?" He grazed the underside of her breast with his teeth and slowly pulled out, his hand negligently rubbing against the sensitive triangle of flesh above her entrance.

Elinor spread her thighs wider and he chuckled, rewarding her with deep, rhythmic thrusts, *accidentally* touching her enflamed clitoris each time. The wet sounds coming from where his hand worked made her face so hot she thought she must be visible in the dark.

Stephen's breathing became harder and harsher and a second finger joined the first.

She startled and his hand immediately froze. "Am I hurting you?"

She swallowed. "No."

He eased his fingers deeper. "You're so tight, I want to make you ready."

"Ready?"

*Shut up, shut up, shut up,* her mind jabbered while her body adjusted around his fingers.

"Mmmhmm, ready to take me." He worked her with controlled, patient thrusts and it wasn't long before she was floating on the now familiar current of pleasure that flowed from one small spot to the rest of her body, her limbs unbearably heavy and her head light.

"That's right," he murmured, as pleasure wrapped around her body like a fist and squeezed her in its ruthless, velvet grasp. "Let go, sweetheart." She cried out and he held her, his fingers coaxing and beckoning until a second and larger dam broke, its savage waters carrying her away. She was consumed by bliss when something slick and hot nudged her entrance.

"Let me in," he whispered, his voice hoarse and desperate in the darkness.

She spread her thighs in answer.

"Ah," he groaned, coming into her in one long, smooth thrust.

Her eyes flew open and frantically searched the dark, her body wide awake and so utterly filled by him she couldn't draw a breath.

"Elinor?" His big body shook as he tried to hold himself motionless. "Does it hurt?"

"No. But it feels—Well, it has been a long time," she finished lamely. She did not mention that he was entirely different from Edward. Entirely.

"Should I stop?"

She squirmed. "Maybe take some out for just a moment."

He laughed hoarsely and pulled back. "Better?"

Elinor exhaled raggedly and fought to calm her breathing. "You're terribly big."

This time his laugh was more genuine. "What a generous lover you are, darling." He slid in a little more and she tensed, waiting for the pain. But it never came. "More?"

She took control of her body and forced her muscles relax. She imagined the textbook, and the pictures it contained, and the tension drained from her body. "Yes, more."

He pushed deeper. "Tell me when to stop."

There seemed no end to him, but the sensation of fullness was not unpleasant—quite the opposite. He felt nothing like Edward, who'd often become soft after entering her.

"Pretty soon I won't be able to stop," he said through clenched teeth, his shaft sliding deep, stretching her.

She tilted her hips. "I don't want you to."

He shuddered, his body straining as if against some invisible barrier, as he rhythmically pumped into her, harder, deeper. "So good, Ellie," he muttered. "So tight." His stroking was becoming increasingly savage and uncontrolled.

Elinor struggled to hold back the wave building inside her. She was so near her climax, but she wanted to make him come apart—just as she had—so she opened herself wider and then tightened her inner muscles.

"God, yes!" His hoarse yell shook the room and he hilted himself and then held her full. She could feel his shaft pulsing against her taut, sensitive flesh; the rest of him was eerily still as he emptied himself deep inside her body.

*La petite mort*, the French called it and now Elinor knew why. After all, she'd just experienced the same thing herself several times in rapid succession.

He toppled to his side like a fallen tree, his body still buried in hers. He caught her with one muscular leg and pulled her on top of his heaving chest. One of his hands moved absently up and down her arm.

"Elinor," he muttered.

She relaxed against him and lowered her head onto his chest. He was slick with sweat and she ran her tongue over the damp, shuddering skin. He groaned. She found his nipple and took it into her mouth, just as he'd done to her earlier. He jumped and his hand stilled her.

# The Footman

"Not just yet, love, but soon." He flexed the part still inside her to illustrate his point. "You make me feel like a boy of seventeen."

Elinor knew that was a compliment and smiled against the sensitive skin of his chest. He laughed and tweaked her ear. "Pleased with yourself?"

Her smile grew larger; yes, as a matter of fact, she was.

# Chapter Twenty

"Elinor?" A deep voice whispered in her ear. "Are you going to sleep forever?"

She opened her eyes and saw light streaming into the room. And Stephen sitting on the bed beside her, a cup of something—she sniffed, coffee? Yes, a cup of coffee in his hand.

"Do you want it?" He waved the cup in front of her.

Elinor growled and pushed herself up.

"That doesn't sound very friendly."

"Give me the coffee or I'll breathe on you."

He laughed. "Take it." He sat back and watched as she drank.

"*Ah.*"

"There is the sound of a satisfied woman."

She flushed, suddenly recalling the other sounds she'd made last night. "What time is it?"

"It's a quarter to one."

She made yet another unladylike noise. "Oh, no!" The coffee sloshed in the cup as she handed it to him and scrambled to get out from beneath the bedding. He moved to the side as she swung her legs off the bed. Her naked legs. She pressed back against the headboard, suddenly realizing how light it was in the room.

"Stephen?"

"Hmm?" he paused in the act of lifting the cup to his lips.

"Where are my clothes?"

His lips curved and he took a sip, smiling while his eyes probed the dimness and he stared at her body.

"Clothes?" he teased.

Elinor's chest tightened. "I would like to get dressed."

His eyebrows rose. "Where are you going?"

"Nowhere, I just wish to put on some clothes."

His playful look altered subtly at her cool tone, as if he suddenly sensed her tension. He stood; his smile gone.

"Of course. I shall ring for your maid."

"But—" She hesitated, not wishing to offend him further.

"You needn't worry about discretion; I pay her very well for it." He put the coffee on the nightstand.

Elinor could tell she'd hurt him and wished she could tell him what she truly feared. But she couldn't. "Stephen?"

He stopped, his hand on door. "Yes?" he said without turning around.

Elinor shivered at the frost in the air. "Thank you."

"What are you thanking me for, Elinor?"

"For everything. For . . . last night."

He opened the door and left her alone, just as she'd asked.

\*\*\*

The door to the bedchamber opened and Stephen put aside the paper he'd been reading and stood. Elinor hesitated a moment before coming toward him.

"You look lovely," he said.

And she did. Her normally pale cheeks were tinted and her eyes were a luminous silver. She looked like a woman who'd been well-pleasured. He began to harden as he recalled the pleasuring.

She stopped beside the table, her mouth curling into a smile. "More food?"

He looked down at the array. "I ordered—"

"—one of everything on the menu," she finished for him. They both chuckled and the tension between them eased. She sat and poured herself a cup of coffee. "Would you care for more?"

"No, thank you. Unlike some people, who shall remain nameless, I've been awake since five."

"Five!" She paused in the act of pouring cream into her coffee to stare.

"I'm an early riser."

"It must be that famed Puritan work ethic." She pulled apart a strawberry pastry and delicately licked some jam from her fingers before wiping them on the napkin. She stopped when she noticed him watching. "I'm sorry, I eat like a savage. I'm afraid it's the result of living by myself for so long. I hope it won't give you a disgust of me?"

"No, disgust is not what I'm feeling right now." He gave his thoughts free rein and her color deepened. He shifted uncomfortably in his chair. "What are your plans for the day?"

She chewed, swallowed, and sipped her coffee. "The maid brought a note my friend left at the desk for me. There is nothing for me to do but wait."

Stephen nodded. Marcus was behaving like a very good boy. "Then perhaps you would let me entertain you?"

Her smile took his breath away. How could he have ever believed she was anything less than beautiful?

Where the *hell* had that thought come from?

Stephen looked down at the linen-covered table, searching for something. An anchor for his thoughts, a club to cudgel his errant brain back into line—*anything*.

"You're not engaging in important business today?" she asked.

Stephen cleared his throat, looked up, and smiled. "Oh, but I am—you are the *most* important business, Elinor."

She laughed and shook her head.

"Is there anything in London you would care to see?"

"It's been years since I've seen any of the sights. I'll be guided by you."

"You didn't come for the Season when you were married?" He didn't want to ask anything that would allow the ghost of Trentham into this day, but the words would not be held back. His curiosity

# The Footman

about her married life was like a fever that never completely left his body. He thought of her tentative—almost frightened—lovemaking and his jaw tightened. Jealousy and fury churned inside of him as he imagined Edward Atwood putting any part of his loathsome body on or into the woman across from him. The repulsive vision triggered a primitive, possessive feeling that was centered in his groin—as if he could fuck her hard enough and often enough to erase any other man from her memory.

"Stephen?"

His head jerked up.

She was staring at him, a wrinkle of concern between her beautiful eyes. "What is the matter?"

He gave her a reassuring smile. "Nothing. I just recalled something I had to do."

"It must be something unpleasant."

"Why do you say that?"

"You looked quite . . . murderous." A slight shiver wracked her slender frame.

He gave her the smile that never failed to comfort either women or business rivals. "I'm merely angry at myself for my wretched memory. But never mind that, I can take care of it in a trice. When was the last time you were in London?"

She wagged a finger at him. "You really *were* distracted. I said I hadn't been here since before my marriage."

"You *never* came to town?"

Her smile dimmed. "I prefer the country."

"But Trentham had a London House?"

"Yes, it is still in the family. My husband spent most of his time here."

Stephen started at the word husband.

"I believe Charles is here right now," she added before popping the last of her pastry into her mouth.

Stephen realized he was drumming his fingers on the table and stopped. So, the marriage had been the standard aristocratic arrangement? He ruthlessly quashed any pity the realization generated. So what if she had a cold, passionless marriage? Being beaten to a pulp and thrown in jail on a false charge of rape and facing the hangman's noose had been less than enjoyable. Losing the vision in one eye hadn't exactly been a trip to Astley's Bloody Circus. Fleeing for his life with no more than a few bob in his pocket hadn't been terribly entertaining, either.

Stephen felt her eyes on him and looked up. He fixed a charming smile on his face. "I hope you've fortified yourself, my lady, because I plan on taking you about town in high fashion."

***

Another note awaited Elinor at the hotel when they returned. She waited until she was in the privacy of her room to open it—not that she *wanted* to open it. She was torn almost in half with her conflicting wants. After today—and last night—she wanted only to stay with Stephen. To run away with him, maybe to Boston or to someplace else where she could start a new life and forget all about the horror of her marriage. Where she could trust him enough to give him not only her body, but also her heart.

But she couldn't. No matter where she ran, the thought would always be with her: the knowledge of what a man could do once you were completely under his power.

Besides, she loved Marcus and he loved his sister. How could she even think of running off until Marcus had Esme back safe? She opened the note.

*I'm sorry, Elinor, but he's not yet returned. I'm told it will be another day, certainly no more than two. I'll be in touch as soon as I know more, please wait. Marcus*

Elinor exhaled the air she'd been holding inside, weak with a mix of happiness and shame. She would not have to leave Stephen yet.

Molly bustled into the sitting room.

"I shall be having dinner with Mr. Worth tonight. Will you please draw a bath for me?"

Molly dropped a curtsey. "Shall you want to wear the new gown, my lady?"

"New gown?"

Molly nodded and hurried back into the bed chamber, where a gown of the most glorious silvery silk lay across the bed.

"Where did this come from?" Elinor asked, knowing the answer even though her brain could not fully accommodate it.

Molly handed her a card. "This was in the box."
*Elinor,*
*Wear it to make me happy.*
*S.*

She smiled. He certainly knew what to say in any situation. The dress was yards and yards of gossamer thin silk in a shade that was a cross between silver and pewter; chips that sparkled like diamonds were scattered around the sweeping hem. The bodice was almost severe in its simplicity, a perfect foil for the extravagant skirt. Elinor had never seen a dress so beautiful.

"And slippers, too, my lady." Molly held up a matching pair of satin shoes, complete with glinting diamonds.

Elinor felt the tears begin to form behind her eyes. "I'll take the bath now, Molly."

Once the maid left, she sat on the bed beside the glorious garment, her mind drifting back to the equally glorious day. She felt just like a princess in a fairy tale, and, like them, she knew there would be a price for such happiness.

She fingered the delicate silk. He'd taken her to the park, where they'd watched a foolish puppet show surrounded by children and shared a paper cone of sugary sweets. He took her next to Baker Street to see the famous wax figures of Madame Tussaud, laughing at her when she'd turned away from the more savage of the famous Frenchwoman's creations.

Afterward they'd gone to eat in a tiny bistro in an area of the city that was far more risqué than respectable, and they'd scandalously dined alone in a private dining room. Stephen had been stunned by her lack of experience with French cuisine and had embarrassed her, once again, by ordering one of everything for her to try.

Not once during the day had he mentioned the night before—or the night ahead. Nor had he said anything of his plans. Elinor wondered if he'd forgotten about his proposal of marriage and now believed she would become his mistress. Would she? Wasn't she already?

She continued to consider their possible futures through her bath and afterward, as she watched Molly fix her hair in the simple chignon she favored.

She didn't see him settling in the village of Trentham, even if he did purchase Blackfriars, a subject neither of them had raised in spite of ample opportunity. He was far too restless to live the life of a quiet country gentleman. Something inside of him seemed to be always questing, pushing, burning. Perhaps it was because of her limited experience with men, but she couldn't help feeling there was a real Stephen Worth hidden somewhere beneath his driven personality, charming smiles, and acts of kindness.

Flashes of something else occasionally caught her attention but were gone far too quickly to identify. He was a complex man, utterly unlike Edward in every way. While she was thrilled by the obvious differences between the two men, it had been, at least in one sense, far easier to understand Edward and his brutal, selfish desires.

What did Stephen want from her?

Not that it mattered. She was beginning to suspect she would give him anything he asked.

\*\*\*

Stephen was not alone when Elinor arrived for their dinner.

"I'm sorry, I didn't mean to interrupt." She looked from Stephen's stern face to the rather amused face of his employee—the hulking, dark-eyed man called Fielding.

Stephen's face immediately shifted into a smile. "You're not interrupting. Let me introduce you to John Fielding, who came with me from Boston. He was just delivering some information about a few business matters. John, this is Lady Trentham."

The big man gave her what could only be called an amused smirk. He dropped a slight bow.

"My lady."

Elinor tried not to stare. She'd known he was scarred, but she'd only seen him from a distance. Up close he was . . . well, mesmerizing was as good a word as any. He was an incredibly handsome man, even with the cuts that almost bisected his face. His eyes were the blackest she'd ever seen. Even in the well-lighted room she could see no distinction between the black of his pupil and his iris. He kept his shock of thick, dark hair long enough to pull back in a soldier's queue, a style one rarely saw anymore. It was somehow barbaric and suited him to perfection. Everything about him was unusual and drew the eye.

"Are you enjoying your visit to England, Mr. Fielding?"

He snorted rudely and Stephen stiffened, the look he shot the other man nothing short of murderous.

Fielding sneered. "I love it here, my lady." His accent was not American, nor was it English. She'd never heard anything quite like it.

"Will you be joining us for dinner?" Part of her wanted to hear him speak more while the other part wanted to hide from his eyes, which stripped her all the way down to the bone.

He turned to his employer, his eyebrows raised, his smile verging on a grin.

Stephen shook his head. "I'm afraid Mr. Fielding has some rather important business to attend to, my dear."

The other man gave him a knowing, mocking look—certainly not the kind of look a well-behaved servant would give his employer—and then bowed to Elinor. "Maybe another time, Lady Trentham."

"Will you excuse me a moment, Elinor?"

She nodded at Stephen and looked out the window over the darkening city as the two men stepped into the hall.

A moment later, the door clicked shut and she turned around.

"I'm sorry about that," Stephen said. "Fielding can be a little—"

"Overwhelming?"

"Exactly."

"What manner of work does he do for you?"

Stephen busied himself pouring two glasses of wine. "Whatever I need done. Why?" He glanced up, looking more than a little overwhelming himself just now.

"No reason. He just seems. . . unusual for such a mild-mannered pursuit as banking."

He gave her a crooked smile and handed her a glass. "Do I look mild-mannered?"

"No, but you don't look like a savage, either." She immediately flushed. "I'm sorry, that was—"

He waved away her stumbling apology. "Fielding would be the first to agree with you. He constantly warns me not to try and turn him into a housecat."

"I can't imagine that happening," she murmured, sipping her wine. "This is delicious."

"I'm glad you like it. I thought I might have to order one of everything on their wine list, but there wouldn't have been anywhere left for us to sit."

"Where did you ever get the idea I had such fastidious tastes?"

"Nowhere, but I want you to have only the best." His eyes dropped to her dress. "I didn't want to say it in front of Fielding, but you took my breath away when you came in."

"The gown is lovely. You have excellent taste."

"Yes, I do."

She flushed, unable to say anything that did not lend itself to innuendo. "You would spoil me."

"In every way, Elinor." His eyes burned into hers and she felt naked before him.

The door opened and broke the erotic spell he'd begun to weave around her. Elinor exhaled with relief. His was an incinerating type of personality and she was far too tempted to fling herself into the fire.

"Ah, dinner is served." His ironic smile said he knew her mind.

He dismissed the servants after they'd laid out the food. Tonight he'd only ordered the things she'd eaten yesterday—exactly. She looked up from the dishes and met his knowing smile.

"You remembered."

"I remember everything."

Something about his admission made her shiver.

"I will be your servant tonight." True to his word, he fixed her a selection of food before seeing to his own needs.

Elinor was again ravenous, although she'd eaten more in the past twenty-four hours than she had in the prior week.

She caught him watching her and laid down her fork. "You are not eating."

He shrugged. "I prefer to watch you."

"It makes me uncomfortable."

"That I like to watch you?"

She nodded.

"Why?"

"I am simply not that interesting. Not only that but—"

"But?"

"I can't help feeling you're . . . cataloguing me." She flushed.

Stephen sat back in his chair. "Cataloguing you? What an odd choice of words. Whatever do you mean?"

"Never mind. I spoke foolishly. Tell me about life in America."

He stared at her so long she thought he wouldn't allow the change in subject. But he nodded. "Very well. What would you like to know?" He took a sip of wine but left his food untouched.

"Anything." Elinor resumed her meal. If she drank only wine she would not be fit company for long.

He tipped his head back and stared at the ceiling before looking at her.

"Earning money is not looked down upon in the United States. In fact, it is something of a religion."

"A religion?"

"Yes. Or, if not exactly a religion itself, then certainly a companion to several religions. Take the Puritans, for example."

"Mr. Jeremiah Siddons was a Puritan, correct?" She saw his look of surprise. "I've read of him, of course. He's quite well-known here. I don't understand your relationship to him, however."

Something in his eyes flickered. Pain? Loss? "He was no blood relation of mine."

"But haven't you—"

"Yes, I inherited the empire he built. Mr. Siddons adopted me. He had no children of his own. His wife died many years before and he never took another."

"He had no other family?"

His smile was slow and dangerous. "Oh yes, he had plenty of family."

Elinor swallowed. She didn't want to pry any deeper into anything that would cause such an expression. "What of your parents, did you never know them?"

"My father died when I was very young. My mother not long after. The only relative I knew was an uncle, who has long since been lost to me."

Elinor felt like every question she asked led her deeper and deeper into a quagmire; even though he gave no sign of it, she did not think he was happy with her questions. She ate, searching her mind for a less volatile topic. A rather large one came to mind.

"You said Mr. Fielding came with you from America, yet his accent is not similar to yours."

His body seemed to relax, and with it, the tense atmosphere that had built in the room.

"He is not American. I brought him from Hobart Town, five years back."

"Hobart Town? Why does that sound familiar?"

Stephen reached for the bottle and gestured to Elinor's glass. She shook her head and he refilled his empty glass.

"It's a town of sorts on Van Diemen's Land." His eyes were as hard as an outcropping of granite.

Elinor swallowed but refused to look away. Why was he telling her these things and looking at her as if she were to blame?

"He was sentenced to seven years transportation for stealing food. He was fourteen." He tipped the glass back and drank fully half of it.

"That's *dreadful*." It was a horrific punishment for such a small crime. "But now he is free and moved to America?"

"He served his time, just like many others. If they survive their sentences, they can find their way back—if they have the money." He shrugged. "Most do not, of course."

"How is it that you came to know him?"

"I was there to broker a timber agreement with the man who ran the prison. Fielding stood out and I paid his way back."

"That was kind of you, Stephen."

His eyes glinted. "I can be kind, Elinor." He stood and put down his glass. "Will you waltz with me?"

"What?" She laughed and then realized he wasn't jesting. "Here? Without music?"

He held out a hand. "I shall hum for us."

She put her hand in his, mesmerized by his intent stare. He drew her close and laid one hand at her waist. She shuddered under his touch, remembering last night.

"I've never danced with anyone other than my dancing master, Mr. Foster."

"I am not Mr. Foster. Put your feet on mine."

"What?" She looked up almost a foot to meet his eyes. "I will ruin your shoes."

"I'll buy another pair."

"At least let me take off my slippers."

"Elinor . . ."

She heaved a sigh and stood on top of his lovely black shoes.

"Your valet will be furious with me," she muttered.

"It will give him something to occupy his time."

Stephen began to move, his steps as smooth and unhampered as if he wasn't carrying almost six stone on his feet.

"Relax." His breath was hot in her hair and she felt his nose against the top of her head.

"Are you sniffing me, Stephen?"

"Mmm." He moved like flowing water, whirling and spinning her until she laughed, dizzy with the sheer joy of it. She hadn't been lying about Mr. Foster. She'd taken dancing lessons, just like every other girl of her age and class, but she'd never danced in public. Her come out ball had been her only ball until those few she'd hosted for Edward at Blackfriars; Edward had never asked her to dance.

Stephen swung her toward the bedroom door and stopped with his back against it.

"Open it," he whispered into her hair, his pounding heart the only clue that carrying her weight was not as effortless as he made it seem.

The room beyond was lighted only by a single candle that burned by the door. He lifted her chin and stared at her with eyes that were dilated and darkened.

"One candle?"

Elinor nodded. It would matter little to what he could see.

"No chemise?" She shook her head and his smile dropped from his face almost comically. "Oh Elinor, that makes me very sad."

"I shall try to make up for it."

"I will hold you to that promise."

And he did. Several times, in fact.

***

Elinor woke with the first rays of sunshine, but she was still not early enough to catch Stephen. She bathed herself, wrapped up in a plush robe, and combed the tangles from her hair before ringing for her maid.

Molly appeared so quickly Elinor realized she must have been waiting nearby. In her arms was an afternoon dress that looked like crushed strawberries and cream. There was also a silk chemise and stays in the shade of a young girl's blushes.

Elinor's face heated at the sight of the expensive, very personal gifts, but she said nothing as the maid dressed her in the new finery. What could she say? She was behaving as a mistress; why should she be surprised that Stephen would want to dress her as one? After all, her own clothes were so old and poor he would hardly want to be seen with such a specimen. No, she'd become his lover with hardly a backward glance at her morals. Whatever else happened, she might as well enjoy the fruits of her decision and be grateful she'd not gone through her entire life without learning the true joy of making love with a generous, caring man.

The image that looked back at her when Molly finished dressing her was almost unrecognizable. The deep pink was a shade she never would have chosen, but it suited her completely, giving her pale skin a pearl-like glow. Her eyes, her finest feature by far, appeared larger and darker and altogether more interesting than she'd noticed before.

The knowledge that Stephen had selected every single stitch of clothing on her body made her feel even more exposed than she'd felt in his arms last night. Her color deepened as she recalled the things they'd done—the things *she'd* done.

"Thank you, Molly." She turned away from the glass. "There were no messages for me this morning?"

"No, my lady."

"I shan't need you until later."

The girl dropped a curtsey and Elinor nervously smoothed the front of her gown before opening the door that led into the sitting room. The room was empty, but the door leading to the study was open. A quick inspection of the rooms showed her that she was alone. She was just about to leave for her own room down the hall when the door opened and Mr. Fielding entered.

He didn't look surprised to see her. "Good morning, Lady Trentham."

Elinor nodded, too mortified to speak.

"Mr. Worth asked me to tell you that he would return as soon as possible."

"Thank you, Mr. Fielding." She hesitated. "I was just about to order breakfast. Would you care to join me?"

One side of his mouth pulled up, as if he could hear the struggle that had gone inside her before she'd issued the invitation.

"Thank you, I've not yet eaten. Oh." He reached into his breast pocket. "This was waiting for you at the front desk. I took the liberty of bringing it up. Shall I order breakfast while you read it?"

"Thank you." Elinor went to the window and opened the familiar paper with shaking hands.

*Elinor,*

*I've just received word that the man who makes all the decisions will be here tomorrow afternoon. I have an appointment to meet with him and will let you know the outcome immediately afterward.*

*Marcus*

That meant today was her last day in London. She closed her eyes, struggling against the tears that prickled beneath her lids. Three days. That was more time with him than she'd ever hoped for.

*You could marry him*, the young girl inside her suggested.

Elinor wasn't entirely surprised by the thought. More and more she'd thought with her sixteen-year-old brain and her pre-Edward heart.

But the years of experience—the lifetime—between that girl and the woman she was now could not be ignored. She would never, ever marry again. She couldn't. She'd barely survived the last time. Only a fool would give herself over to another man, no matter what he seemed like on the surface. She knew better than anyone what could lurk beneath a polished, handsome façade.

"Lady Trentham?"

She turned to find Mr. Fielding standing beside a large breakfast trolley. "My, that was fast."

"Mr. Worth had them on notice to prepare two breakfasts per hour, just in case you might wake and be hungry." He told her this without any look of surprise, as if his employer's profligate and eccentric behavior was normal. His disturbing eyes dropped to the letter she still clutched in her hand. "Bad news?"

"No, nothing like that." She looked at myriad covered platters and smiled. "Goodness, I hope you will be able to help with this, Mr. Fielding."

He merely pulled out her chair.

Elinor's appetite, so hearty only last night, had vanished. Even so, she filled her plate and poured them both coffee, amused when her hulking breakfast companion put three spoons of sugar in his coffee.

He saw her smile and shrugged. "I have a terrible sweet tooth." He stirred the viscous liquid, the spoon laughably delicate in his huge hand—a hand with six fingers. Elinor looked quickly down at her own cup, hoping he'd not noticed her staring.

She'd read about polydactylism but had never actually seen it. She risked a glance up. He was eating, his eyes assessing as they rested on her.

"I understand you are English, Mr. Fielding?" It wasn't much of a question, but she could see he had no intention of generating any conversation.

He chewed slowly, the dreadful scars pulling the muscles of his face tight, rendering him even more inscrutable. His injuries hadn't just vandalized an attractive face; they'd also robbed him of the ability to express basic human emotions. Even a smile looked angry and frightening when distorted.

He swallowed most of the coffee in one gulp.

"The Dials," he grunted, before putting a heaping forkful of egg into his mouth and chewing, his eyes glinting like water at the bottom of a very deep well.

Elinor had heard of Seven Dials, of course, one of the most iniquitous parts of the city. She considered his harsh visage and took a bite of toast. He didn't seem to be angered by her questions. Besides, anything was better than sitting across from him in awkward silence while he skewered her with his uncomfortable gaze.

"Mr. Worth said he met you in, er, Van Diemen's Land?"

He'd been sawing on a thick slab of ham and paused. Elinor swallowed, perhaps she'd overstepped . . .

He resumed his sawing. "Aye, that's where we met." He popped the cube of meat into his mouth and masticated, his mouth quirked in a way that could have been either angry or amused. She doubted many people—particularly women—would dare ask questions about his past.

"Will you be returning to Boston with Mr. Worth?"

That made him pause. One eyebrow—without a doubt his most expressive features—cocked in the shape of an inverted 'V'.

"Is Mr. Worth returning to Boston?"

Elinor's face became hot.

He lifted another forkful of food to his mouth and chewed.

"Oh, will he stay?"

He swallowed and smiled.

It was not a comfortable expression and Elinor babbled on. "I know he once mentioned purchasing an estate here. He even mentioned Blackfriars at one point. I have not heard anything on the matter in some time."

His smile dropped away like a sheet of ice shearing from an iceberg.

"You'd have to ask Mr. Worth that." The words were as close to a slap as could be delivered without actually putting hand to cheek. Rather than act as a deterrent, as he'd most likely planned, she felt something rumble in her chest and it wasn't hunger.

*So what if he was the most enormous man she'd ever seen? She would not fear him.*

"Mr. Worth tells me you handle a variety of business for him, Mr. Fielding."

He was holding a slice of bread in his six-fingered hand and slathering it with butter. Something in her tone must have alerted him to possible danger. He paused, knife still in his hand even though the bread wore a good quarter-inch layer of butter already.

"That is true, my lady."

"Does that include seducing my housemaid, Mr. Fielding?"

He gave a quick bark of laughter and the smile that twisted his face was wicked rather than repentant. "I do occasionally get personal time, my lady."

"Mary Bevins is a good girl, Mr. Fielding. Trentham is both a remote village, untouched by the moral laxity of London, and an intimate one. Any stumble she makes will be swiftly and harshly punished."

"I would imagine that is very true, Lady Trentham." He lifted the bread, now laden with huge gobbets of strawberry preserves in addition to half the contents of the butter dish and took an enormous bite. He chewed in the leisurely manner of a man who was accustomed to people waiting to hear what he said. He was, in every way she could discern, utterly unsuited to the life of a servant. She could only imagine Stephen spent a good deal of his time bringing him to heel. He swallowed his mouthful of food and finished his thought. "It is not my habit to leave specimens of myself in my wake."

Elinor supposed she deserved his mocking smile. Luckily she was saved from having to answer his scandalous comment by Stephen's entry. He stood in the open doorway and surveyed the tableau that greeted him. His recovery was smooth and quick, but Elinor had the impression he was not pleased to find her dining with his employee. Did he have so little faith in her constancy, or an unrealistic belief in his employee's universal appeal to women?

He tossed his hat and gloves onto the settee and came toward her, his expression giving no sign of his momentary displeasure.

"You are awake early today. I thought I'd come back and find you still abed." He raised her hands to his mouth and kissed both.

Elinor's face had already been hot at Fielding's comment but it seemed there were a few degrees of heat left to go. She gestured to one of the two free chairs. "Will you not join us?"

"Thank you, no. I ate earlier." He lowered himself into one of the wingback chairs off to the side. "But please do finish your breakfast. You will need it for today."

"That sounds . . . ominous."

He laughed. "I only meant that I have a full roster planned. I thought you might enjoy a visit to Hampton Court?"

"How delightful!"

His eyes flickered to his employee. Mr. Fielding tossed back the last of his coffee and scraped his chair back.

"I'll go see that the carriage and barge are prepared and waiting." He tossed his napkin onto his half-full plate.

"Afterward you can finish that business in Mayfair. We shall proceed as planned tomorrow."

The big man froze, his body emanating an odd, dangerous awareness. "If we're going forward so quickly, I will need some time to see to my own affairs."

"Naturally."

Fielding left without another word.

Stephen swept Elinor from head to toe, his eyelids drooping to half-mast and his lips curved into a very smug smile. "You look exceptionally lovely today, Elinor."

"Thank you, both for the clothing and the compliment. You certainly know what looks good on a woman."

"I know what looks good on you."

Elinor replaced her napkin on the table, hardly able to see clearly for the haze of innuendo he'd generated with little more than a few words and heated stare.

"Today is my last day in London."

He crossed one long, pantaloon-clad leg over the other.

"Ah, I see. We should make it count, then."

Elinor found that she could not hold his knowing look and dropped her eyes. What had she expected? That he would renew his offer of marriage? Why should he when she'd already become his mistress? Besides, it wasn't as if she'd say yes, was it?

"Elinor?"

She saw his feet and realized he'd come to stand beside her chair. She refused to look up and expose the agony roiling inside her. A large warm hand cupped her chin and tilted her face up. He looked like a handsome stranger rather than a man who'd made love to her—been inside her body—three times the prior night.

"Is aught amiss, my lady?" His eyes, usually so warm and laughing, were a cool, crystalline green.

She shook her head. "No." The word was a dry croak.

"Very well. Shall we venture out into the world?"

***

The journey to Hampton Court by river took several hours. Stephen had 'borrowed' the luxurious river barge from an aristocrat who'd dipped rather deep at a card table with Stephen. The man had been

S.M. LaViolette

glad to exchange the use of the barge for forgiveness of his debts. The decision had been a good one. Stephen and Elinor had relaxed and lounged on the journey up, spending only an hour in the famous gardens before returning to their barge.

"I hope you aren't disappointed with such a brief visit," he said, handing Elinor onto the ramp that led to the river boat.

"Oh, not at all. The journey is almost more fascinating than the destination."

Stephen smiled at her enthusiasm. He'd taken an entirely different kind of female on the trip earlier in the year and her interest had lay in the contents of a velvet box rather than his company or the view of the shore.

"Would you care for some refreshments?"

She smiled up at him, her eyes luminous. "Yes, please."

Stephen led her to the pavilion that was set up in the yacht's stern and offered a view of both sides of the river without the wind, which had picked up around mid-day. He settled her onto one of the comfortable divans and poured them both a glass of wine.

"Thank you," she said, taking her glass.

"A toast." He paused, staring down at her expectant face. An odd feeling surged in his chest, a tightness that was somehow pleasurable.

*You're happy, Stephen.* It was Jeremiah's voice. And it was so clear and loud it was as if the old man were standing right behind him. Stephen resisted the urge to turn and look over his shoulder. Instead, he ignored his old mentor's phantom voice and looked down at the very real woman who waited for him.

"To a day of unparalleled pleasure." He clinked his glass against hers. She smiled and took a sip before putting the glass on the table. Was that surprise he'd seen in her eyes? Had she been expecting more?

*Excellent*, his cool inner voice hissed like a serpent. *Her expectations will only make it better.*

Stephen's chest became unpleasantly tight, as if somebody had clamped an invisible vise around his body. He sat down beside her, his legs suddenly leaden and weak.

When he looked at her again, he saw a hint of sadness in her expressive eyes.

# The Footman

*She believes you will renew your offer for her. She is half-way to being in love with you; just look at the sparkle in her eyes. You have done well!* The voice was louder this time. It had been his constant companion for fifteen years and had every reason to rejoice in his imminent success.

And the voice was correct, Stephen *had* done well. He would complete the job tonight and reap his reward in the morning.

"You sound as though you are reaching completion on one of your business ventures?" she asked, interrupting his internal celebration.

He forced a smile. "Yes, we are about to finish three ventures."

She lifted her glass. "We should toast to your success, then."

Stephen raised his glass and touched hers, his hand shaking so badly he hurried to put the glass down.

"Oh! Don't set it down without taking a drink," Elinor warned. "It's bad luck, or don't you have that superstition in America?"

Stephen took a drink, the £100 bottle of wine tasting like bilge water.

He was slipping, he could feel it. He was sliding down a very long, slippery slope.

*Take control of yourself, Worth!*

Stephen swallowed down the bile that threatened to choke him and threw back the rest of the wine. When he turned to her he was wearing his brightest smile. "And how would you care to spend our last evening together in the city, my lady? I will leave the decision completely up to you."

# Chapter Twenty-One

*Boston*
*1812*

"In conclusion, I shall wait until the second week of January before I take action regarding the three tracts of land outside Gloucester. Yours, et cetera, Stephen Worth."

Stephen waited until his secretary finished scribbling.

"I'd like to get this out today, Bates."

Bates nodded and stood. "Was there anything else, sir?"

"No, that's it. In fact," Stephen smiled at the earnest-faced young man, "why don't you go ahead and leave work a little early today? Have you bought that pretty betrothed of yours a gift yet?"

Bates grinned and flushed, the red making the freckles that covered his face even more prominent. "No sir, not yet."

"Well, you'd better take care of that. Christmas is only two days away."

"I'll do it today, sir. And thank you."

The door opened before Stephen could answer and Jeramiah looked in. "I'm sorry, Stephen, I didn't know you had company."

Stephen stood. "Mr. Bates was just leaving to purchase a gift for his fiancé."

Jeremiah laughed, his hand already extended toward the younger man.

The Footman

"And how is Miss Perkins?"

Bates grinned, clearly pleased the old man remembered the name of his girl. "She's doing very well, sir."

"Excellent. Please give her my best, and the same to your mother and father."

Bates left the room glowing.

Stephen waited until his employer sat before resuming his own seat.

"You could have sent for me, Jeremiah."

The old man waved his words away good-naturedly. "I like to walk about the office and see everyone. It keeps me feeling young."

"It certainly keeps you looking young."

Jeremiah laughed. "Flatterer."

But Stephen wasn't flattering him. He looked remarkably healthy for a man in his eighties.

"How about you, Stephen? How are you doing? Are you still squiring Miss Cullen about?"

"No. I'm afraid that's over." Stephen straightened the papers on his desk.

"That is too bad. She's a wonderful girl."

Stephen couldn't argue. Nor could he explain why he'd stopped seeing the dark-haired beauty. He shrugged. "But she's not the girl for me."

Jeremiah nodded, some of the twinkle leaving his blue eyes. Stephen worried the older man was about to pursue the topic of his love life—or lack thereof—but his next words put paid to that concern.

"I wanted to ask you about the Corcoran project."

Stephen felt like swearing. Instead he asked, "What would you like to know?"

Jeremiah's smile was gentle. "You needn't cover for James, Stephen. I can guess what happened."

Stephen sighed heavily and threw himself back in his chair. "If that is true, I wish you wouldn't ask me about it, Jeremiah."

"I'm not asking you to speak out of school, Stephen."

"Then what are you asking?"

"You must stop cleaning up after James. It is not your job."

Stephen shoved his hand through his hair, absently realizing he needed a haircut.

"I wasn't cleaning up. I saw the problem before it happened so I stepped in and straightened things out. Isn't that what I should be doing as president?"

"Absolutely. However, you don't need to allow James to handle such important projects."

"James Powell was your second-in-command before I displaced him, Jeremiah."

The old man chuckled. "Ah, is that what he told you?"

"Isn't it the truth?"

"I suspect it is James's version of the truth." Jeremiah sighed, suddenly looking every one of his eighty-odd years. "He was my Anne's only brother—the baby of her family. She doted on James as if he were her own son." He glanced up. "We were already married when James was born. He was an afterthought for her parents and they were glad to give him to me and Anne to raise. Perhaps we spoiled him, gave him too much too fast and didn't make him work for it." Jeremiah shook his head. "It doesn't really matter now. What matters is he is not a strong man, nor a smart one. But, most importantly, he is not a good man."

Stephen opened his mouth to say something—he didn't know what—but Jeremiah stopped him with a raised hand.

"I learned long ago about his penchant for young girls. I like to think I've spared more than a few of Boston's poorer girls by the control I've kept on his actions, but that is mere self-congratulation. The truth is I couldn't give him to the authorities when I found out about him because I knew it would break Anne's heart. I did the best I could and kept him as close to me as possible." He shrugged. "I reasoned he couldn't get up to mischief if I was always close at hand." He looked up, his eyes suddenly as hard as agates. "That doesn't mean I ever intended to leave him either the bank or my personal fortune. He will be taken care of, don't get me wrong, but I will ensure his access to money is carefully hedged with stringent requirements for his continued good behavior.

# The Footman

"So," he said, his expression shifting subtly back into its usual lines. "All that is to say you needn't allow him free rein—or any rein at all—when it comes to Siddons business. Understood?"

"Understood, sir."

"Good." Jeremiah's slight frame relaxed into the chair, clearly relieved to be finished with the unpleasant topic. "Tell me, will you be joining us for Christmas dinner this year?"

Stephen opened his mouth to decline—the same as he did every time Jeremiah invited him to one of his family affairs, which were full of people who considered Stephen an upstart and usurper—but the old man looked so hopeful.

So, he smiled and nodded. "I'd be honored, sir."

Jeremiah face seemed to light from within. "I'm so *glad*. It will be a pleasure to spend the day with you. What's your man Fielding doing?"

"Your guess is as good as mine, sir."

"You did a good deed when you rescued him from that dreadful place, Stephen."

Stephen shrugged, not wanting to receive credit for what he'd done. Rescuing Fielding from the penal colony was one thing. Telling the other man the truth about his past and fueling Fielding's lust for vengeance, was quite another.

"Why don't you bring him along on Christmas, there is always room for one more."

"I'll pass along your invitation, sir." Stephen had a hard time imagining the menacing Fielding handing platters of ham and turkey to Jeremiah's Puritan relatives.

Jeremiah began to push up from his chair and Stephen was up and around the desk beside him before he could make his feet. He took the fragile arm in his hands and gently lifted him.

"Thank you, son," Jeremiah said, looking up at Stephen with the expression that always made a lump form in his throat.

"You're a stubborn old man," he said gruffly. "Next time call me to your office."

Jeremiah laughed and quietly closed the door behind him.

\*\*\*

Stephen easily dodged the book aimed at his head.

"You bastard!" James Powell screamed, his hand landing next on the small wooden carving Jeremiah had made with his own hands and given to Stephen for his last birthday.

Stephen raised a hand, but not his voice. "Throw that and I'll throw you out the window, James."

James froze at the threat in his quiet words. His hands dropped and he fell back against the door to Stephen's office, lines of anguish on his narrow face.

"Why are you punishing me? Don't you have enough?"

"I'm not doing this punish you. I'm doing it because you've made a hash of the project, James. If somebody hadn't stepped in, Siddons would be in front of a judge right now."

"You're so *arrogant*. How did you even know about this—because you're having me watched? Just wait until I tell Jeremiah what you're doing."

Stephen sighed, but kept his mouth shut. How could he tell the older man that Jeremiah was the one who made Stephen remove James Powell from any position of authority at the bank? He couldn't, not without destroying him. "Look, James, I'm working on a new storefront on Newbury Street. Why don't we—"

"Go to hell. Go straight to hell." James's face was a chalky white and his body trembled with rage. He pointed a finger at Stephen, his voice pure venom. "You don't offer me scraps. Ever. You might think you're the boss here, but you're not. And one of these days you're going to make a mistake. When you do, I'll be waiting." He slammed the door behind him so hard the glass shook.

Stephen took off his spectacles and dropped his head into his hands. What a bloody mess. He would need to talk to Jeremiah about James. This was the third confrontation in two weeks. This could not go on.

He heard the door open. "Go away, James," he said wearily, not bothering to look up.

"I'm sorry to bother you, sir."

Stephen's head jerked up. "What is it, Bates?" he demanded when he saw the man's pale, rigid face.

"It's Mr. Siddons, sir. I'm afraid he's had an accident."

# Chapter Twenty-Two

I t was wicked, but all Elinor wanted was to spend her last evening alone with Stephen. *Alone in bed.* Elinor shook her head, causing Molly to make a startled sound.

"I'm sorry, Molly."

"I'm almost finished, my lady. These buttons are quite the smallest I've ever seen."

Elinor looked at her reflection in the mirror, no longer surprised at the creature that looked back. Every garment he gave her made her look prettier than the last. In another week she might actually look beautiful.

*But you don't have another week. You only have tonight.*

She felt ill at the thought and pushed it away.

*You were already in love with him before you came. Now you can barely imagine life without him.*

That realization was like an old enemy that had lost the power to upset her. Besides, maybe it wasn't love? How would she know the difference between love and lust, never having felt either before? Not that it mattered what she called it—love, obsession, lust—it would not be easy to forget.

"There, all done." Molly stepped back and surveyed her from a distance, shaking her head slowly. "Oh, you do look beautiful, my lady."

"The gown certainly does." Elinor held out the gauzy skirts, clouds of cobalt blue silk so vibrant it made her look a decade younger.

Molly picked up a black velvet case from the dresser. "This was inside the dress box, my lady." Her eyes sparkled, as though she, and not Elinor, was the recipient of the gift.

Elinor's hands shook as she took the box. She'd never received jewels from a man before. She opened the box and found a note inside.

*Even these are a pale imitation of your eyes. S.*

Elinor lifted the card and gasped. "Oh my goodness."

"May I see?" Molly was bouncing up and down like a little girl. Elinor wordlessly handed her the box.

"Crickey!" She looked from the jewels to Elinor. "But what are they, my lady? I've never seen the like."

"They are star sapphires."

"I've heard of 'em, but not seen any. Why, they're the most beautiful stones I've ever seen."

"They are." And likely monstrously expensive. And he'd given them to her.

Molly lifted the delicate silver necklace from the box as though it was a religious icon.

"Oh, it will look lovely with that dress." She put the necklace around Elinor's throat and stood behind her, her eyes wide in the mirror. "I can see why Mr. Worth chose it, Lady Trentham, it makes your eyes a silvery-blue. There are earbobs in the case, as well."

Elinor merely stared. Who *was* this man and what did he want from her? Was this it? These three nights?

Never before had Elinor felt the lack of her life experience so severely. She had nobody to ask—except Beth, who would be horrified to learn Elinor had turned down a proposal of marriage only to become his mistress.

"My lady?" Molly asked.

"I'm sorry, Molly." She smiled into the maid's curious, yet kind, eyes. "Thank you, that will be all for tonight. If you could pack for me, that would be lovely. I shall be leaving first thing in the morning."

Elinor stared at the door into the other room. He was waiting for her. He'd asked her what she wanted to do tonight and she'd told him she wished to spend it here, with him, dinner and a quiet evening in. Their last evening.

The sitting room was empty.

"I'm in here," Stephen called from the study, where he was leaning over something on the desk. "I want to show you something."

He looked up and his lips parted.

"My God," he breathed, the reverence in his tone causing a bolt of pure lust to shoot through her body. His pupils dilated as they skimmed over the jewelry and settled on her face. "You are magnificent." His reaction was more than any woman could ask for. It was certainly more flattering than any admiration Elinor had ever received.

"I imagine I'm a very interesting color right about now."

"Don't try and dismiss my compliment, Elinor. Come here." He took her hand and led her to the big mirror beside the front door. He stood behind her, his hands huge on her shoulders.

"Look at you. No." He shook his head when she looked at him instead. "Not me, you." He framed her face with his hands. "Really look at yourself."

Of course she saw the lovely clothes and jewels, but the real difference was *inside* her. She was in love, and it shone from her like a beacon. Did he see it? She looked at him. His brow was wrinkled and his eyes bright with—before Elinor could identify the emotion a curtain dropped and his face relaxed into its smooth, handsome façade. He kissed her neck, watching her in the mirror.

"Beautiful." He murmured the word against her skin.

She pulled herself away from the distracting reflection. "These jewels . . ." She fingered the stones at her throat, just in case there was any confusion. "I cannot accept them."

He smiled and ran a finger lightly across her jaw. "Oh?"

"They are too valuable a gift."

"I'm sorry. Is there some unwritten rule that says how valuable a gift should be?"

She pulled away from his diverting touch. "Don't fence with me, Stephen."

He was still smiling, but it was now fixed. She'd seen the expression before, whenever he did not get his way. He shrugged. "Do what you like with them—except give them back to me. Donate them to a workhouse, gift them to the hotel maid, leave them to Beth in your will, I don't care." He turned on his heel.

"Stephen?"

"Yes?" He threw the word over his shoulder.

"I'm sorry. What I should have said was *thank you.*"

He stopped and turned, his lips no longer tight and flat. "You're welcome. Now, come into the study and look at what I brought to show you."

Spread across the huge desk were dozens of miniatures. Elinor looked from the tiny portraits to his expectant face. "This is quite an impressive collection."

"It is not the entirety. I have some on loan to a few museums, one in Boston and one in New York."

Elinor smiled at the pride she heard in his voice. It was rare that he allowed any emotions to show. "Which is your favorite?"

"Ah, that's easy." He picked up a miniature with a spectacular emerald-and-diamond frame and handed it to her.

"It's a Hilliard," she said, recognizing the style immediately. Her lips parted and she cut him a quick glance. "Is this Sir Walter Raleigh?"

He nodded, his eyes glinting with some intense emotion.

Elinor gave a small grunt of surprise. "This is quite a treasure. How did you ever get it, Stephen?"

"You would have all my secrets from me, my lady?"

Elinor stared at the near-priceless miniature. Her father could only dream of owning such a work of art. How much would such a thing cost? How much did the jewelry around her neck and in her ears cost? The answer to those questions was too disturbing to contemplate; he must be very, very wealthy. She replaced the portrait on the desk and another caught her eye. She picked it up. "My father has a Cosway that is similar to this one."

"Not anymore." He was watching her with the raptor-like expression she'd seen more than once. It was avid and it made her uncomfortable.

"He sold it to you?"

He nodded, his sly smile verging on unpleasant.

"Why? He loves his collection more than he loves anything—even life, probably."

"He needed money. Apparently, he loves something more than his miniatures."

Elinor studied his face, as if she might find answers if she looked long enough. There were none—at least none she understood.

"Here, make yourself comfortable." He pulled a chair to the desk and Elinor sat and looked at his collection. She recognized five more miniatures that had once belonged to her father but didn't mention them. What her father did no longer mattered to her and hadn't for years. If he was in financial difficulties she would not be surprised. He'd always lived a lavish lifestyle and speculated rashly on business matters, without ever bothering to learn what he was investing in. He would consider such advance research demeaning and too close to actual work.

"You have an impressive collection." She sat back in her chair and looked up at Stephen.

"Thank you." He seemed to be waiting for her to say more. When she did not, he continued. "I took the liberty of ordering dinner for us. It will arrive at nine. I hope that is not too late."

"No, I am still replete from the two lunches and teas we shared aboard the boat today. Why do I feel as though you are trying to fatten me up?"

"Because I am. I would guess you don't take adequate care when it comes to feeding yourself. Not that I do not think you are perfection already."

Elinor laughed. "Flatterer."

"It is not flattery." His eyes roamed over her with a hunger that made her believe him. "You look so lovely. Are you sure you wouldn't care to go out so that I might show you off? It is not too late to take you out to a play or perhaps dinner."

S.M. LaViolette

"Not unless you wish to. Is that what you generally do when you are in London? Go to plays and such?"

"Sometimes. Mostly I attend business dinners with other men."

"Is that all you do, Stephen? Business?"

"I've been doing something else these past few days."

She flushed. "I meant, do you not have any hobbies or pastimes?"

"Hobbies like the male members of your class, you mean?" He smiled but she nonetheless sensed a hint of hostility behind the question. "Horse races, pugilism, cock-fights, gaming, riding to hounds, and the like?"

Elinor laughed. "They do sound rather vapid when listed that way. But surely there must be other leisure activities. What do men do in America for entertainment?"

"I don't really know. I've always worked. I ride, of course, and I've done my share of boxing and gambling, but mostly I work." He took a drink of wine, his green eyes amused. "What a boring fellow you have before you."

Elinor cast her eyes ceilingward. "Ah, I see you enjoy fishing, too."

"Touché, my lady. What about you? What do you do for enjoyment?"

"I read, garden, stitch—and other traditionally female pursuits."

"You left out studying medicine." He propped his elbow on the table and dropped his chin into his hand. "Won't you tell me about that?"

Elinor glanced down at her hands. She'd only been away from Doctor Venable's surgery for a few days and already they were less calloused and chapped. "What do you want to know?"

"What made you decide to do it?"

Elinor could hardly tell him the truth, that she'd often needed to treat her own injuries.

"As you know, the Earl of Trentham's demesne is quite large."

"Yes, approximately 54,000 acres."

Elinor raised her eyebrows and he smiled.

"You forget I have investigated Blackfriars as a potential investment."

"No, I have not forgotten." But she didn't want to talk about his plans for Blackfriars—at least not tonight. "When my husband was

198

still alive there were more tenants than there are now. Our doctor at the time was rather old and couldn't see to all the people who needed him. I found myself in a position to help people, but without the requisite knowledge. I did what I could and learned many folk remedies from the people themselves, but I did not have a chance to do more until Doctor Venable arrived."

"And then your husband died. Did he approve of such activities for his countess?"

"No, he would not have allowed such a thing."

"I've never asked about your marriage." He stopped, hesitant for the first time Elinor could remember.

"I wish you would keep it that way." Elinor knew she'd spoken rather sharply, but the last thing she wanted on this final night of magic was to allow thoughts of Edward to spoil it. "It is a subject I do not care to talk about," she said in a softer tone.

"Then I shall not press you. But tell me, what is your goal with your study of medicine? Do you hope to become England's first lady doctor?"

"No, I merely wish to be of use."

He raised his brows quizzically.

"I can see you find that notion amusing."

"Not amusing, merely interesting. I have not met many women of your class with such aspirations."

"Perhaps they simply have not shared their thoughts with you."

He straightened in his chair and took another sip of wine. "No doubt you are correct. An American businessman is an unlikely confidant for a female aristocrat."

"It is not your status as an American businessman that prevents such disclosures, but the fact that women with unordinary aspirations are viewed with disapprobation by our class. At least by the male members."

"Ah, so any kind of ambition is viewed as a dirty little secret?"

Elinor felt her face darken at the innuendo in his tone. "That is not strictly true. Marriage is an acceptable ambition for women."

"But not for you?" His tone was no longer teasing.

"It is an ambition I realized long ago."

"And one you no longer aspire to." It was not a question. He turned his glass slowly in his hands, his eyes never leaving her face. How she wished she had the courage to ask him what he was thinking. Or to tell him why she'd refused his offer. Or to beg him to ask her again.

But then she imagined the disgust on his face when he saw her naked body for the first time.

"No, I no longer aspire to marriage." Elinor turned back to the miniatures and picked up the first that came to hand. "Tell me about this one."

\*\*\*

"Shall I leave you alone with your port?" Elinor asked after they'd finished their meal.

Stephen smiled, genuinely amused by her offer. "I wish you wouldn't. I will gladly forgo a glass of port for the pleasure of your company."

Her cheeks stained a rosy pink at his words, making her look even more desirable.

"I propose you don't do without either."

"Drink port in front of a lady? What rebels we are." He poured a glass and offered it to her. "Care to join me?" She shook her head but her eyes lingered on the glass. "Come, Elinor—it's a night to break taboos."

She grinned and took the glass, for the first time forgetting to cover her mouth. The great flaw she'd always covered was nothing more than a small chip in one of her front teeth. It gave her smile a piquancy that complemented her serious features.

"It's charming, Elinor."

Her smooth brow wrinkled. "I beg your pardon?"

"Your tooth. The slight imperfection is charming. You should never hide it." Her hand rose to her mouth even as the words left his. "Please, Elinor. For me?"

She dropped her hand and took a deep breath, the action drawing his eyes to her décolletage. The tops of her small white breasts were pushed into gentle swells and he knew she would be wearing the silk undergarments he'd chosen for her.

In fact, everything on her body had been chosen by him, for his pleasure. He wanted nothing more than to tear off the gown and tongue her until she screamed his name and begged for more.

Her chest expanded and then froze, two hard points pushing through the thin blue silk. Stephen looked up. Her eyes were wide, her lips parted, and two bright spots of color appeared on her sharp cheekbones. Stephen threw back the contents of his glass and placed it on the table with a shaking hand. He stood and closed the distance between them.

"I want you, Elinor." His voice was so hoarse he hardly recognized it.

She stared up at him, her eyes dark and enormous. "I want you, Stephen."

Her low, husky response drove the last clear thoughts from his mind and he swooped down on her, lifting her by her slim waist and placing her on the table. He took her face and held her still while he explored the hot, sweet depths of her mouth. Her kisses were those of a woman who'd quickly learned what she wanted.

Small, strong hands burrowed between their bodies and deftly unbuttoned his coat. He groaned with almost unbearable pleasure when she pulled his shirt from his trousers and ran her cool hands up his stomach to his chest.

He pushed his fingers beneath the taut silk of her bodice and slid a finger beneath each breast, lifting them over the top of the fabric until two hard, rosy nipples were within reach. He sucked one into his mouth. Her body shuddered and shook beneath his mouth and he moved to her other breast, suckling the small peak until it was a hard little pebble.

Her hands wove tightly into his hair and pulled him down. He grinned against her wet nipple and gently pushed her back until she lay on the table.

He shoved glasses and the decanter away and she jolted when they crashed to the floor.

"Stephen?" She started to push up onto her elbows and he looked up from the breast he was teasing.

"Do you want me to stop?" He bit her nipple to make his point.

She sucked air through clenched teeth, her eyelids fluttering while her chest arched and a guttural moan tore from her throat.

Smiling, Stephen pulled the bodice fabric lower, until the perfect mounds were thrust high and proud. He tongued the sensitive skin beneath her breasts, teasing and nipping and sucking while his hands pulled up the yards and yards of diaphanous silk that made up her skirt. She stiffened when he reached her stocking-clad legs and he stroked her from ankle to thigh. Their eyes met and she spread her thighs for him, the wanton action making him groan.

"My God you're lovely." He slid a finger into her tight, wet heat and she whimpered, her slim hips thrusting off the table, taking his questing finger deeper and grinding against his hand.

Triumph and fierce possession ripped through him as she responded to his touch with eagerness and hunger. He wanted more, he wanted all of her. He shook with the need to taste and explore and fill every part of her willing body.

Stephen released her nipple and pulled away from her almost painful grip. Her hands slid from his hair, her eyes like slivers of moonlight.

Stephen smiled down at her sulky face and lifted her slippered feet to the tabletop. Her knees sagged open and he found her peak and circled her with relentless flicks of his thumb, until her body lifted off the table.

He was unable to resist the honeyed scent of her one second longer. She cried out and bucked beneath him as his mouth settled over the tiny bud that controlled her pleasure. He worked her without mercy, until she was drenched and engorged and ready.

***

Elinor thought she might simply go mad.

She'd lost count of the number of times he'd taken her to the brink of pleasure and ruthlessly shoved her over. Every nerve in her body was raw and sensitive and yet she was still greedy for more.

His hot wicked mouth disappeared from her sex and she looked up. His lips were slick and red, his green eyes black as he flicked opened his pantaloons.

He grabbed her hips and pulled her toward the edge of the table, until she could feel his crown pushing against her. His face was taut and beautiful with raw desire.

"Take me in your hand and guide me inside."

She let her legs open even wider and reached between her spread knees for him. She'd no sooner positioned him when he entered her with one long, hard stroke.

Elinor closed her eyes as he began to move in deep, controlled thrusts.

He stopped, buried inside her. "Look at me, Elinor." His eyes burned with the fierce determination of a man who would conquer and possess. His gaze dropped to where they were joined and his eyes narrowed in sensual gratification. A small, tight smile curved his lips as he claimed her with a brutal thrust. Elinor grunted and tilted to take more.

"That's right, darling," he encouraged, rocking into her almost playfully as she raised her hips and offered herself to him. "Take all of me." He punctuated his words with a savage thrust that took her breath away.

"You are mine." He drew out with agonizing slowness and then slammed into her like a battering ram, his glittering eyes fastened to hers. "Say it, Elinor." He bared his teeth with the force of his thrust. "Say it." Pleasure gathered at her core and rippled outward to the rest of her body. "Say it," he demanded, his voice rough with desire.

"I'm yours, Stephen." The words were torn from her chest as she detached from her body and began to float away.

The last thing she saw before she closed her eyes was a fierce, exultant grin and green eyes that blazed with an expression that looked oddly like despair.

\*\*\*

Elinor swam up from the liquid depths of sleep slowly. Her body had not felt so well-used and exhausted since she'd ridden to hounds as a girl. But even riding had not exercised all the muscles she was feeling this morning.

She heated all over at the memory of last night, and what she'd done to get so tired. The shocking episode on the dining table had been the most adventurous part of the evening, but not the most enlightening.

Stephen had woken her twice more in the night to make love, the last time just before dawn, when he'd slipped between her legs and held her from behind, taking her with exquisite slowness as they lay on their sides. Afterward they'd stayed intimately joined.

"You are a remarkable woman, Elinor." He'd kissed the back of her neck, his voice oddly tender in the darkness. "I'll never forget this time we've had together."

Tears had rolled down her cheeks at his words and she'd cried silently as he drifted into sleep behind her, his body still inside hers as his breathing became deeper and more regular.

Her eyes prickled at the memory—and the knowledge that she would leave him today.

She heard the murmur of voices out in the sitting room and pushed herself up to look at the clock. It was ten already. It was possible Marcus had already left a message downstairs, although not likely. Either way, it was time for her to be up and about.

She dispensed with Molly's services and was able to have a quick sponge bath and dress herself in less than a half-hour.

Once she was as ready as she'd ever be, she opened the door.

Only to find her father, brother, and the Earl of Trentham seated in the sitting room.

# Chapter Twenty-Three

*London*
*1817*

hat in the—" her nephew Charles began, his eyes round with surprise.

Stephen, whose back was to her, turned around and smiled. "Ah, good morning, Elinor. Look who is here." His green eyes danced, as though the presence of her father, brother, and loathsome nephew in her lover's hotel room was something she would enjoy. The room seemed to grow and recede and she gripped the doorframe.

Stephen hastened toward her; his brow wrinkled with concern. "Are you unwell, Elinor?" He hovered over her and she stared into his eyes, which held nothing other than polite solicitude.

"Why—" She broke off, unable to find the words to complete her question. Instead she squeezed her eyes shut, like a child refusing to see what was in front of her.

Charles chuckled. When Elinor opened her eyes, she saw he was openly grinning.

"I say, Worth, I'd heard you'd been sniffing around her skirts but I didn't believe it." He laughed again and raked Elinor with a dismissive glance. "Can't say I understand why you'd want to bed her when you've got the Lewis chit panting after you, but," he shrugged.

Stephen whipped around. "Lord Trentham." The words were like a blade on a whetstone. "I'm going to give you exactly five seconds to apologize for your last comment before I kick you down five flights of stairs."

Charles flinched, his eyes swiveling from Stephen to Elinor and back. He coughed and gave Elinor a weak, chinless smile.

"No offense, old girl."

"You don't have the power to offend me, Charles."

"What the devil is going on, Worth? Why have you brought—" Her father met Elinor's eyes and broke off. His narrow face, which had lost most of its color when she entered the room, began to darken. Elinor thought he looked almost as shocked as she felt. Almost.

Her brother merely sat with his mouth open, his eyes moving from face to face. A distant part of Elinor's mind observed that Stuart was much altered. His thinning brown hair and the dark pouches of skin beneath his gray eyes were those of a far older man.

Elinor turned to Stephen, who was now watching her with breathless avidity rather than concern. She realized he'd taken her hand and she yanked it from his grasp before stepping away.

He straightened to his full height and gave her a slow, knowing smile that sent a sickening bolt of fear directly to her heart. In that moment, she knew; this had all been a game, a sick, twisted game, with her as one of the game pieces.

"Did you bring me here to prove what I already know, Worth? That my daughter is a whore?" Viscount Yarmouth demanded.

Elinor flinched, suddenly reminded of that night so long ago.

Stephen's terrifying smile grew wider and his eyes narrowed to dangerous slits. "I will give you the same warning I gave Trentham," he said silkily. "Guard your tongue, my Lord Yarmouth, or I will remove it from your mouth." He raised his voice, "Fielding, get in here."

The door to the study opened and the big, scarred servant stood in the opening, a slim portfolio in one hand, his face even grimmer than usual.

Elinor's brother shot to his feet. "Caplan? George Caplan?" Stuart gasped, his face as pale as his father's.

"Ah, you recognize my associate, do you?" Stephen asked, smiling at Stuart in a way that made the other man blench.

The American took the brown leather portfolio from his servant. "Thank you, Mr. Fielding. You may take a seat." The big man's eyes flickered from his employer to Elinor and he hesitated. "Take a seat, Fielding," Stephen repeated, his clenched jaw the only sign he wasn't as calm as he looked or sounded.

For a moment it looked as though Fielding would disobey, but he shrugged and dropped into the chair Stephen had recently vacated.

"Elinor?" Stephen said, gesturing to one of the chairs around the dining table, the table on which he'd done such intimate things to her only a few hours before.

"I will stand, thank you," she said coldly.

He gave her a slight smile, as though her small rebellion amused him. "As you wish." He opened the portfolio, extracted two sheets of paper and placed the rest on the table. "Let's begin with you, Lord Trentham." He paused and a nasty grin distorted his handsome features. "Tell me, are you still Lord Trentham even though you no longer are Lord *of* Trentham?"

Charles was no longer looking either smug or amused. He snatched the papers from Stephen's hand.

His eyes flickered down the page like racing hares. He reached the bottom and staggered backward, gripping the chair with his other hand. When he looked up, his eyes were wide with horror. "My God."

"Read the second page, Trentham." Stephen's eyelids had lowered while his smile grew slowly broader.

Charles collapsed into his chair before turning to the second page. If Elinor had ever dreamed of revenge against the man who had been nothing but petty, cruel, and vindictive, she would have considered that emotion duly satisfied by the expression on his face. Charles shook his head, as if the motion could dislodge a pernicious thought from his brain.

Elinor knew the feeling.

He looked up. "I don't understand."

"Well, it's called speculation, Lord Trentham. It's when a—"

"Not that, you bloody upstart cur!" Charles sprang to his feet and crushed the pages in his fist, as though they were Stephen's head.

"This must have cost you tens of thousands of pounds. Why would you beggar yourself just to break me?"

Stephen chuckled. "It would take a great deal more than that to beggar me, Trentham."

Charles's jaw sagged and he could not stop shaking his head from side to side. "You're mad—utterly insane. What will your investors say when they learn of this?" He waved the crumpled pages in the air.

"I didn't use bank money, *Trentham*, I used my own. I am answerable to only myself."

To Elinor's surprise Charles lunged at the bigger man. Fielding was on his feet so quickly he was nothing but a blur. He caught Charles and held the far smaller man in an inexorable, but gentle, grasp and turned to his employer. "Are you finished with him?"

Stephen's grin threatened to split his face in two. "Quite."

"You fucking bastard!" Charles shrieked, struggling futilely in the huge man's grip. "I'll see you in court! I'll take this to the Lords! You'll be driven from the country!"

"Come, my lord," Fielding murmured soothingly as he picked up the squirming earl and carried him toward the door as if he were nothing more than an awkward toddler throwing a temper tantrum. He opened the door and deposited the still raving peer on his feet in the hall.

"I won't rest until you rot in jail, you—"

Fielding closed the door and cut off the rest of what Charles said. Even so, Elinor could still hear his ranting, although she could no longer understand the words.

Stephen gave Fielding an abrupt nod and the giant sighed heavily and took the seat Charles had just vacated. His black eyes came to rest on Elinor.

"What have you done, Worth?" her father asked, his voice shaky and weak.

"Take a look for yourself, Lord Yarmouth." Stephen plucked another few pages off the table and handed them to the viscount.

Elinor's father took his gold *pince nez* from his breast pocket and began to read. The color drained from his face as he made his way down the page. By the time he reached the bottom he looked positively corpselike. He flipped to the second page, which he merely skimmed, and then gave Stephen a smile so bitter Elinor hardly recognized him.

"I see. I suppose you now intend to redeem the notes?"

"That is the nature of a loan, my lord. I shall give you until the end of the month. I am in no great hurry." Stephen's expression was so guileless and kind that Elinor's heart began to fracture in her chest. He'd looked at her that very same way times beyond counting, the last time just last night as they'd talked about her medical ambitions.

It had all been an act, a mask he wore for this inexplicable performance. Her hand crept to her stomach, which churned with sickness and despair.

Stuart sprang to his feet and snatched the pages from his father's shaking hand but then seemed unwilling to read them.

"What does he mean? What loan?" he demanded, his gaze flickering from Stephen to the viscount and back.

"It means your father owes me a great deal of money. As do you, I'm afraid to say."

"What?"

Under different circumstances, Elinor might have found her arrogant brother's stricken expression amusing. Stephen strode to the now hateful portfolio and extracted a collection of notes. He waved them in front of Stuart's face.

"Perhaps you recognize these?"

Stuart seized the stack of chits from his hand and riffled through them, his entire body shaking violently. "I don't understand."

"It's simple, really. I bought those notes—every single one I could find." Stephen looked down at his large employee. "And of course my associate Mr. Fielding helped you create several of them."

Stuart looked from Stephen to the silent man in the chair. He pointed a trembling finger at Fielding. Comprehension dawned, turning his face an ashen gray.

"You planned all this." It wasn't a question. "You were always there, always at the table beside me, encouraging me to keep playing. You . . . you *wanted* me to lose."

"Actually, Mr. Fielding did not care one way or another if you won or lost. I, however, cared a great deal." Stephen was no longer smiling and Elinor saw, for the first time, the beast he kept hidden and chained far behind his handsome mask.

Hatred and rage oozed from his eyes like poison from an inflamed, suppurating wound. Elinor was morbidly mesmerized by the fury that festered in his fever-bright eyes. She could not look away. One thought echoed in her mind: *Why? Why was he doing this? What had she done—what had they all done—to deserve such malice?*

Lord Yarmouth grabbed the papers from his son's hand and flicked through them. When he looked up, his smile was still bitter but also triumphant.

"You've wasted your time, Worth. My son has *nothing*. And you've already taken everything I have to give. Everything else is protected from your grasping hands."

Stephen laughed and it made Elinor's skin crawl. "Oh, Lord Yarmouth, please don't tell me you think the flimsy entailment will protect you."

Her father crumpled in his chair, as though he'd been struck by some invisible hand.

"Why?" Elinor asked, her voice raw with the pain that threatened to tear her in half. "Why are you doing this?"

All three men jolted, as if they'd forgotten her very existence. Only Fielding was not surprised. For the first time Elinor saw an expression she could read on his ravaged face. It was pity; pity for her. And it terrified her more than anything else that had happened in the nightmare that was the last thirty minutes.

Stephen went to the table and took the last pieces of paper.

Elinor stared at the pages he held toward her and put her hands behind her back, as if she could avoid his poison by not touching them.

"Take them, Elinor." He sounded kind, gentle almost. His eyes were no longer filled with hostility but something else—regret?

Elinor was proud her hand did not shake when she took the pages from his hand. The words swam before her, refusing to organize themselves into any order that made sense. Finally, one sentence pushed its way through the fog. She looked up and saw the face she'd grown to love. Stephen was no longer gloating.

"This is the deed for the Dower House."

He nodded. "It is yours now. Nobody can take it away from you."

Elinor's eyes flickered wildly around the room as her mind sought purchase in the hideously confusing situation. "I don't understand." The inadequate words were the best she could do.

"When I bought Blackfriars, I separated the Dower House and put it in your name. Along with an annual allowance." He hesitated and—for the briefest of moments—his expression began to shift and become more . . . human. But in the blink of an eye his handsome features hardened and his eyes glinted like glass. "It is a standard arrangement with English gentlemen when they part from their mistresses."

His words were like a knife that cut from her throat to her belly, slicing her in half. The words *five thousand pounds per annum for life* leaped off the page. Her head began to throb and the papers fluttered from her hands like large white leaves.

"Elinor?" Stephen's voice came from a long way off, and she was glad. She wanted to be somewhere else, somewhere far away from him. Anywhere. She stumbled past him, shaking off his hands and heading for the door.

"Elinor, you come back here this instant." Her father's voice was sharp and high—and frightened. It worked like a match to a fuse and male voices erupted behind her as she flung open the door.

Marcus stood in the hall, as though he'd been waiting for her. Elinor took two steps and collapsed against him.

"Thank God," she whispered into his shoulder. "Thank God you are here."

"What the hell are you doing here?" Stephen's voice demanded behind her.

Marcus's body turned rigid. "I've come to give you back your money." He held Elinor at his side while he fumbled in his coat pocket and pulled out a bulky pouch. He tossed it toward Stephen and it landed on the thick carpet with a heavy thud. "Take it, I don't want it. I want no part of your dirty games." He squeezed Elinor's shoulder so hard it hurt. "Come on, Elinor. I'll take you home."

She stared up at him, dazed. "You . . . you know him?"

Marcus's face was a dull red and his eyes refused to meet hers. "I'm sorry about this, Elinor. This is all my fault. I brought you here. I promise I will make it all right."

"But what about Esme? Is she safe?"

His lips twisted into a scowl. "She was never in danger—you were. I was just too selfish and stupid to see it. Come on."

Stephen's voice came from her other side, but she refused to look at him.

"Elinor, you can't trust him." His voice was low and earnest. "He sold your secret for just—"

"I lied!" Marcus screamed, his voice breaking. "Alright? I lied! It was me, not her. I'm the one who hit him. So you can bloody well turn me in for it. Come on, Elinor." Marcus grabbed her arm and yanked her roughly down the hall. "The maid already packed your things and they are waiting for you in the carriage. I'll take you home."

"I'm not finished with you, Bailey!" Stephen yelled behind them.

"Marcus—" Elinor began, stumbling as she tried to keep up with his long strides.

"I'll explain it all to you on the way home."

Elinor didn't tell him that she no longer had a home.

# Chapter Twenty-Four

*London*
*1817*

"Here ."

Stephen looked up to find Fielding holding out a glass of brandy. He took it, drank it in one gulp, and handed it back. "Get me another."

Fielding gave one of his heavy sighs, the ones he thought were a substitute for actual conversation.

"Just get me the damned drink, Fielding."

The next glass had twice as much in it.

"So, that's that," Fielding said.

Stephen drank half the glass, baring his teeth as the expensive liquid burned down his throat.

"Yes, Fielding. That is that."

"How does it taste?" the big man asked, sounding curious. "Is it as sweet as you'd hoped it would be?"

"You'll find out for yourself soon enough, won't you?" Stephen snapped, glaring up at him.

Fielding's scarred face was contemplative. "I want some time for myself."

Stephen snorted. "Oh, do you?"

The other man refused to rise to the bait. "I'll need a month."

"Take however long you please, I don't need you."

Fielding nodded again. "Is there—"

"Just get the fuck away from me, Fielding, before I discharge your big ass," Stephen snarled, choosing at the last moment to hurl the empty glass at the dormant fireplace instead of his servant's head.

Fielding was a big target, but he was adept at dodging both fists and projectiles.

Stephen heard the soft clink of glass on wood, a few footsteps, and the click of the door latch. He was finally alone and could savor his victory in private.

He dropped his pounding head against the back of the chair. Whether he closed his eyes or kept them open, he saw the same thing.

Gray eyes, wide and shocked and filled with horror and loathing.

\*\*\*

Marcus knocked on Doctor Venable's door and then turned back to Elinor.

"I'm going inside with you," he insisted, not for the first or even fifth time.

The door opened before Elinor could answer him. Doctor Venable stood in the opening, his normally impeccable person in a charming state of dishabille. He wore no sleeping cap and his dark thatch of curls corkscrewed out in all directions. His blue silk banyan was old and threadbare but of excellent quality.

"Lady Trentham?" He blinked large brown eyes at her and Elinor realized he'd come to the door without his glasses. It occurred to her that it was a very good thing for the female residents of Trentham he kept such sensual eyes and lush lashes safely hidden behind distorting spectacles.

"I'm sorry to disturb you, Doctor Venable, but I'm afraid it can't wait."

He stepped back into the house. "Please, come inside. Are you ill?" His handsome face creased with concern.

"No, I am well." She gestured to Marcus. "This is Marcus Bailey, my stepson."

Venable nodded, his face going from concerned to impassive in a heartbeat. He would have heard of Marcus, there were plenty in town eager to spread gossip about the old earl's bastard. "Would you like to come inside, Mr. Bailey?"

Marcus ignored the doctor's polite greeting and took her hand. "Look, Elinor—"

"Please wait for me in the carriage, Marcus."

They had a long, silent staring match. In the end, he swore, clomped down the wooden steps, hopped into the carriage, and slammed the door so hard the two postilions jumped.

Doctor Venable closed the door to his house far more quietly.

"I should get dressed, Lady Trentham. Will you make some tea?"

"Gladly," she said, relieved to have something to do.

Fifteen minutes later they were seated in Doctor Venable's small sitting room with a pot of tea. The man across from her bore little resemblance to the one who'd opened the door a scant quarter of an hour earlier. He'd brutally restrained what she now knew to be unruly black curls and hidden his soulful eyes behind split-lens spectacles.

"What can I do for you, Lady Trentham?" he asked in his usual cool, collected tone of voice.

"Please, won't you call me Elinor? We've met twice a week for years, you've proposed marriage, and I am about to beg a rather large favor."

One corner of his shapely mouth lifted in a wry smile. "Since you put it that way, please call me Jago."

"Ah, you are Cornish."

"I was." Before she could ask him what he meant he repeated his question. "What can I do for you, Elinor?"

"I need to leave Trentham, immediately."

His expressive black brows rose, but not much. He was almost eerily unflappable. His next question only served to underscore his preternatural calm. "Where do you wish to go?"

Elinor laughed.

His brows continued their upward journey and the corners of his sensual lips pulled down. "Did I say something amusing?"

"I'm sorry, Jago. It's just that I found your question rather unusual."

"How so?"

"Most people would have asked me *why*, first."

"I see. Well, the 'why' is not my affair." He hesitated, his eyes dropping to his still full teacup. "I would take this opportunity to renew my offer of marriage."

Elinor gave him a smile of genuine gratitude. "Thank you, but I must decline. What I need is someplace I can go—someplace far away from here. Somewhere I might be of use. You've spent almost four years teaching me, it is time I put my knowledge to use." She had all the skills of a midwife and more; surely someplace would have need of her?

He took a sip of tea and considered her request. "I have not much money, but I'd be—"

"I have enough money. Well, I believe I *will* have enough if you can help me dispose of some jewelry. What I need is help finding a place to go—somewhere remote. A place the rest of the world has forgotten and left behind."

His full lips twisted into a resigned, bitter smile. "I know just the place for you, Elinor."

***

Stephen had no idea what day it was, or even what week, he only knew he was out of brandy. He grabbed the bell pull and yanked so hard it came off in his hand.

"Dammit." He staggered toward the bedroom and almost tripped over the shards of a broken bust and the shattered remains of either this morning's breakfast or last night's dinner, or both.

"Nichols," he bellowed, flinging open the bedroom door. His valet was hiding in the dressing room; Stephen could see the toes of his shoes. "I can see you, Nichols."

Nichols stepped out from behind the door, his shoulders hunched and his bald head shining with sweat. "Yes, sir?"

"Get your ass downstairs and tell them I want a new room."

"Very good, sir. Er—"

"What?"

"When would you like to move?"

"Yesterday, dammit."

"Very good, sir." He turned and darted toward the door.

"And Nichols?" The room tilted sickeningly and Stephen pressed his knuckles to his pounding temples.

The valet froze like a startled hare, his narrow shoulders rigid as he spun on his heel. "Yes, sir?"

"Tell them to send up a whore."

Nichols flinched back, as though Stephen had tossed a rabid ferret at him.

"I'm not sure the management provides that sort of service, Mr. Worth."

"Well, find me one yourself. What the hell am I paying you for, man? Certainly not to keep my clothing neat." Stephen spread his arms out, displaying his rumpled, stained, and torn clothing for his valet's inspection.

"About that sir, wouldn't you like—"

"No, I bloody well wouldn't. Brandy and two whores, Nichols, and I want all three within the next hour or you can find yourself another damned job."

A loud knock on the door interrupted whatever platitude his valet was about to utter.

"Answer the door on your way out," Stephen muttered, flopping face down on his bed, his head pounding so loudly it sounded like the rickety dancefloor of a country inn.

An amused voice spoke from the doorway. "Well, look at this."

Stephen struggled up onto his elbows and peered over his shoulder at the door, his eyes grainy and dry. "You back already, Nichols?" he asked, blinking until he could make out three figures in the doorway: a short, bespectacled figure flanked by two other figures. Figures that looked far too large to be whores. Unless Nichols had hired stevedores from the docks as retribution for Stephen's dreadful treatment.

"I'm not Nichols."

Something about the shorter man was familiar. Stephen squinted until his vision was less blurry and immediately wished he hadn't.

"Christ," he groaned, "If I'm going to hallucinate somebody I bloody hell wish it would be a naked female."

Two of the three figures laughed.

"Sorry, but I'm no hallucination."

All three of the figures came closer.

"Powell?" he said, not really needing to ask.

"Hello, Iain."

The big men stopped beside the bed but Stephen kept his eyes on the smaller man as the room swayed and tilted.

"What did you say?" Stephen asked.

"These men are here for you—for Iain Vale."

Stephen stared harder, as if he would be able to hear better if he could see better.

The larger of the two figures spoke.

"'E says you're Iain Vale—the same man what escaped fifteen years ago from The Steele. Is that right?"

Stephen looked from the big man to Powell, who came close enough that Stephen could finally see his face. His features, always rat-like, were even more shriveled and vindictive than usual. But for once, the little man was smiling. He actually looked . . . happy. "I've got you now," he said with a demented grin. "You're going to be so very, very sorry you ever crossed me."

"You're too late, James. I'm already so very, very sorry." Stephen laughed. And once he started laughing, he couldn't seem to stop.

# Chapter Twenty-Five

Newgate Prison was nothing like Coldbath Fields, at least not as Stephen remembered it.

He threw his linen napkin onto his plate and took a drink of wine. It was amazing; a man could get everything inside prison that he could get on the outside. If he had enough money.

The hatch in his door opened.

"Beggin' yer pardon, Mr. Worff, but there's a gent here to see ya."

Stephen hadn't invited anyone, but he knew the person must have paid the guard well and denying a visitor would snatch money from the man's hand and make him unfriendly. Right now Stephen needed all the friends he could get.

He slid down in his chair, holding his cut crystal glass between negligent fingers. "I believe I'm at home to visitors, Mr. Marley."

The guard laughed at his weak jest and his keys rattled in the door.

"Now only fifteen minutes, mind," Marley said to somebody Stephen couldn't see.

The door opened and Marcus Bailey stepped into dimly lighted room.

Stephen was genuinely surprised. "Well, well, well. Who would have believed that you would pay to see me, Bailey? Indeed, who would have thought you'd even have the money to do such a thing?"

Marcus nodded sourly. "Aye, go ahead and laugh—I deserve your scorn, and more besides for what I did."

The smile slid from Stephen's face at the other man's words.

"Is she alright?"

Marcus shrugged. "I don't know."

Stephen sat up straight. "What do you mean, *you don't know*?"

"Just that—I don't know. She's gone."

"Gone where, you bloody fool?"

"I don't need to stay here and listen to that."

Stephen rolled his eyes. "Fine. I'm sorry I called you a fool. Where is she, Mr. Bailey?"

"I said I don't know. She just up and left." He scowled at Stephen. "She said the house wasn't hers anymore."

Well, Stephen shouldn't have been surprised. He must have been out of his right mind to believe she'd take a gift from him after what he'd done. "Where did she go?"

"I don't *know.*"

It was all Stephen could do not to leap over the rickety table and throttle the younger man. "Tell me the whole story, without leaving anything out."

"And what's that worth to me?" Marcus asked, his eyes narrow and sly.

"I'll give you the same as I did before."

"More."

Stephen snorted, his hands itching to grab the young bastard and squeeze his neck. "Why should I pay you anything, you little weasel?"

"Who else is going to tell you what happened that day?"

Stephen gave the question some consideration; Bailey had a point.

Stephen had stupidly given Fielding all the time away he wanted and now he had no idea how to reach the man. Thus far he'd managed to get Nichols to do his fetching and carrying, but the man was limited, to say the least. He'd paid off jailers, magistrates, and anyone else who might move his case along. Stephen knew his money would hold out forever, but he didn't know how long their greed would protect him from Yarmouth and Trentham, both of whom were baying for his blood.

"Fine, Bailey. How much do you want?"

"I read in the paper you're worth over two million pounds—*you*, not the bank." Marcus spoke softly, as if the words themselves were somehow rich and powerful.

"What of it?"

"The paper said you were nothing but a footman when you raped her."

Stephen gritted his teeth. "I did *not* rape anyone."

Marcus shrugged, as though that fact was immaterial when compared to everything else.

"You made all that money yourself, after you went to America?"

Stephen sighed and topped up his glass. It appeared he'd have to answer some of Marcus's questions before they could get to his. Well, it wasn't as if he was going anywhere.

"Yes, Marcus. I was a humble footman here and then I went to America and made pots of money. Is that what you wanted to know? Or perhaps you want me to tell you that *you*, too, can be rich if you go to America? Would you like me to buy you a ticket on the next ship headed to Boston?"

Marcus frowned at his nasty tone. "All the money in the world won't save you if they find you guilty of raping an aristocrat."

Stephen took a swallow of wine. "Thank you for the legal advice. Now, why don't you tell me something I don't know, like what happened with Elinor?"

"Ten thousand pounds."

Stephen waved his hand. "Fine. Now talk."

Marcus looked stunned, and not a little chagrined—as if he should have asked for more.

"I kept some of the money you gave me," Bailey admitted.

"How shocking."

Marcus half-stood, his face a mask of frustration, fury, and pride. "I don't need to suffer this abuse from you!"

Stephen stretched out his legs, took a big drink, and smiled. He knew men and he knew greed. He'd promised the man ten thousand pounds. He'd need a bloody pry bar to get him out of the cell.

Marcus tried to stare him down before slumping into his chair. "You're one cold bastard, aren't you?"

Stephen ignored both the boy's question and his grudging admiration. "You'd gotten as far as your confession. What happened next?"

"We made it to Trentham just past midnight. I told her everything that happened, including me telling you that she'd killed the earl." He offered this last bit belligerently.

Stephen didn't bother to tell the man what he thought of his belated chivalry. "And?" he prodded.

"She wanted to stop at the doctor's house before she went home."

Stephen put down his glass. "After midnight?"

"Aye. The doctor invited her in and they had a cup of tea. Alone."

"And what did you do while they were drinking tea in the good doctor's house after midnight?" Stephen wanted to break and rend and tear and destroy something, anything.

Marcus threw up his hands. "She told me to wait in the carriage, what else was I supposed to do?"

"Go inside with her? Protect her goddamned reputation?"

"Are you mad, Worth? Or Vale, or whatever the hell your name is? You *destroyed* her reputation entirely, utterly, and completely. You kept her in your bed for three days and nights, like some bloody pasha!"

The boy had his history wrong but he made his point all the same. Stephen wanted to smash the young bastard's head against the table, but not as badly as he wanted to smash his own head.

"What else?" he grated, dumping the last of the bottle into his glass.

"That night is the last time I saw her. The carriage dropped me off at Mum's cottage after I left her at the Dower House."

Stephen narrowed his eyes. "That's *my* cottage now."

"Well, it ain't like you need it, is it?"

Stephen ignored the question. "When did you next go to the Dower House?"

"Not the next day but the one after that."

"Whom did you talk to?"

"The old gimmer who opened the door. I don't know his name."

"Was Beth there—her maid?"

"No, she must have gone with her."

"How do you know that? She came to London without her."

"Trust me. The old crone hates me and wouldn't have missed a chance to rip up at me if she'd been there."

He didn't want to ask, but he had to. "Did the doctor go with her?"

"I don't know, but he wasn't at home."

Stephen repressed a howl. Fury churned and burned in his gut and threatened to push him over the edge, a luxury he could not afford just now. He shoved the good doctor from his thoughts and concentrated on Elinor.

So, she'd left after being home less than two days? At least she'd taken Beth with her, wherever she'd gone. Had she drawn on the account he arranged under her name? He squeezed the glass so hard his fingers burned. Bloody hell! He needed Fielding, he needed answers. He looked at the young man across from him.

"That was three weeks ago, why the hell have you only come to me now?"

The boy shrugged. "I dunno."

"Do you have *any* idea of where she might have gone?"

"No. But that wasn't part of the deal—you didn't say I had to—"

"Oh, shut up," he snapped. "You'll get the money I promised you." Stephen eyed the other man without bothering to hide his contempt. He was a dishonest little toad but he was all Stephen had right now, other than Nichols, whose usefulness didn't extend much beyond delivering money to his guards and food and drink to Stephen. He tossed back the dregs in his glass and glared at the younger man.

"How would you like to double your money?"

***

It was five days later when Stephen had his second visitor.

"Ah, Mr. Powell. I expected you sooner."

The little man shuffled into the cell through the slim crack in the door. Stephen could tell by the jailor's face that Powell hadn't been one of his more lucrative customers.

"Ten minutes," the guard snarled at Powell before slamming the door, the loud *clang* making Powell jump.

"It appears your charm hasn't diminished any," Stephen said, grinning at the other man's reddened face. "What can I do for you today, James?"

"It's more a question of what I can do for you." Powell looked nervously at the only free chair in the room—which was within arm's reach of where Stephen sat.

Stephen waved to the chair. "Please, have a seat. Don't worry, I won't hurt you." He gestured to the half-full glass on the table. "I'd offer you a drink but I only have the one glass."

Powell scowled. "Isn't it a little early for drinking?"

"I don't know. What time is it?"

Powell grabbed the wooden chair and yanked it another three feet away before sitting down. "I didn't come here to discuss the time of day with you, Vale."

"Oh, why did you come?" Stephen asked pleasantly.

"I came to see if you were ready to make a deal."

"A deal? That sounds intriguing, do continue."

"I think you'll find that even money won't buy you more time. Yarmouth has managed to call a special session of—" He paused, his brow wrinkled in thought. He waved his hand dismissively, a mixture of embarrassment and irritation on his thin face. "Whatever the hell they call the government body that expedites legal matters in such cases." He shook his head. "It hardly matters. What *does* matter is your highly paid barrister will no longer be able to buy you more time." He stopped to give Stephen the full benefit of an unpleasant grin.

Stephen took a sip and waited.

Powell's face turned an even darker shade of red. "The only way you can get out of this is if the original charge is recanted." Again he paused.

Stephen decided it was time to move matters along. After all, Powell only had a few minutes left to begin extorting. "Let me guess, James, you would be willing to facilitate the matter on my behalf for the right fee?"

"After what you did to that woman, you'll need an advocate. A damned good one, at that. I want half."

"Half?"

"Half of the company, fifty-one percent."

Stephen chuckled. "*Tsk, tsk, tsk.* That's rather dreadful math for a banker, James. Half would be fifty percent, I believe."

Powell sneered. "Mock all you like, it won't change what I'm asking for. I'm not greedy, I don't want it all. You'll still have forty-nine percent and that's better than being dead."

"Ah, but that isn't *all* of it, is it?"

"Trentham and Yarmouth want you to give back everything you took from them."

"And?" Stephen prodded. He didn't imagine either man would pass up such a rare opportunity to improve their fortunes.

"They each want one hundred thousand pounds."

Stephen laughed—a genuine belly laugh, the first in weeks. The keys rattled in the door as he wiped the tears from his eyes, shaking his head. "I must thank you, James."

"For what?" Powell's eyes shifted from Stephen to the open door, as if he was afraid it might close and trap him inside if he didn't hurry.

"For the best entertainment I've had in ages."

"Is that all you have to say, you bastard?"

"Were you really expecting something else?" Stephen asked curiously.

Powell's rat-like face twisted with rage. "Jeremiah should never have left it all to you. It was mine before you came. *Mine!*"

"It was never yours, James. Even if I hadn't come along. Jeremiah knew you weren't capable of handling the bank and so do you."

"You're a bastard and you don't know anything!"

"I know what he told me."

"You're a goddamned liar who'd rather swing than part with just a fraction of what you have."

"You're partly correct, James. I'd rather swing than give *you* even a penny of my money or one share in the bank."

Powell shook his head in disbelief and wonder. "You're mad, absolutely mad." He backed toward the door, as if he didn't want to take his eyes off Stephen. "What's wrong with you? What kind of man would throw away his life like this?" He edged through the door without waiting for an answer and it slammed shut behind him.

Stephen listened to the key grating in the lock and the sound of receding footsteps. He lifted his glass to the empty chair.

"That's an easy question to answer, James. The kind of man who doesn't have anything left to live for."

# Chapter Twenty-Six

*Redruth, Cornwall*
*1817*

Elinor cradled the basin in her arms like a newborn babe.

"You're with child, my lady."

She looked up to see Beth standing beside the bed, her hands fisted on her hips, her worn features pinched with anxiety and fear.

"I'm not Lady Trentham here, Beth. Please, it's Mrs. Atwood," she reminded the older woman, not for the first time.

Beth made a noise of strangled frustration and began to tidy the already neat room, her motions jerky with suppressed anger.

"I will be fine, Beth." Elinor didn't have to feign the happiness in her voice. She *would* be fine. Better than fine, in fact. She was pregnant. Her heart pounded with furious joy. The little voice in her head, the one which seemed so determined to tear down anything good, was babbling about miscarriages somewhere in the background, but, for once, she was able to ignore it. She'd lost her babies in the past because of Edward, there was no question of that. This time . . . well, this time, she'd take care of herself.

"I'm going to have a baby." Elinor didn't realize she'd spoken out loud until Beth came back to the bed, a hopeful light in her brown eyes.

"Does this mean we can go home, my lady?"

Elinor smiled. "We *are* home, Beth. And it's—"

"Yes, yes, I *know*. It's Mrs. Bloody Atwood."

Elinor raised her eyebrows at her unprecedented cursing and the older woman flushed.

"I beg your pardon my, er, Mrs. Atwood. It's just—"

Elinor lowered the basin to her lap and took Beth's hand.

"I know you miss Trentham. So do I. But that life is gone now. We need to embrace this new life."

"It just seems wrong that Mr. Worth would buy Blackfriars and then throw you out of the Dower House." Her eyes dropped to Elinor's stomach. "Especially since—" she stopped, clearly not wishing to spell out the obvious.

Elinor felt a pang at the lies she'd told, but she knew what Beth would say if she learned that she'd rejected both Stephen's offer of marriage *and* his gifts of money and property. And she really didn't want to tell her servant the truly wretched way they'd parted. Not when she still didn't understand his behavior herself.

Elinor waited for the pain and fury that usually accompanied thoughts of their last day together, but she felt nothing. She was no longer angry at him: what was the point? She knew better than most, after ten years with Edward, there was no point in anger. While she might not be angry, she doubted she would ever stop wondering over what he'd done.

Still, that was a subject to fill her long, empty nights, not her mornings and days. She handed Beth the basin and pushed herself up higher, shifting the cushions behind her. "I'll not over-exert myself this morning and have my breakfast in bed. Some dry toast and tea, rather than coffee."

Beth inclined her head. "Aye, my la—ma'am."

Elinor's smile slid from her face when her servant left the room. She wished she could share her worries with Beth, but they were not Beth's worries to bear. They were in this fix because of decisions Elinor had made. Bad decisions, just like every other decision she'd made in her life, starting with that kiss so long ago.

The thought of Marcus and what he'd done made her heart burn. Oh, she wasn't angry with him, nor was she really surprised. The money Stephen had offered would have looked like a fortune to the younger man. Marcus had always stood just outside the door of wealth and status and Stephen had allowed him to step a foot inside. Still, she could no longer trust her stepson. Not because of what he'd told Stephen about that night with Edward. After all, it was Elinor who'd made him promise to stick to the lie she'd carefully constructed. But she couldn't trust him with any other secret, certainly not where she'd gone, even though she doubted anyone would care, including Stephen.

Oh, he'd be surprised when he learned she'd left the Dower House, but she couldn't imagine he would be upset or try to find her. He'd given her the Dower House because it had been the easiest way to dispose of a woman he was finished with. Or perhaps he'd thought to keep her within convenient reach of Blackfriars, just in case he might want her on occasion.

The way her heart leapt at the thought of seeing him—no matter how degrading such an arrangement would be—convinced her that leaving Trentham was the best decision she'd ever made. Elinor told herself that she wouldn't have gone to him if she'd stayed, but that was a lie. As pathetic as it was, she loved him, even after what he'd done. Love, she'd learned, was like a weed that refused to die, no matter how viciously and ruthlessly a person tried to exterminate it. No, she'd needed to get away. The only way to resist such humiliating temptation was to completely remove herself. What could be more completely removed than Redruth, Cornwall?

The town Jago Venable had found for her was the most desperately poor area Elinor had ever seen; too impoverished to have its own doctor. Elinor's skills would be put to good use—if the insular, suspicious Cornish would just allow it. Thus far she'd treated only two patients, neither of them human. Jago had warned her that animal doctoring was often expected in such rural areas, where a cow or pig had more value than people.

So, Elinor hadn't complained, but had stitched a nasty wound on a pig that weighed more than her small cottage and helped deliver a foal who'd required turning. Both families were better off than most of those around Redruth and Elinor knew their word was respected and her fame would soon spread.

As she'd done in Trentham, she'd accepted food in exchange for her labors since money was all but unknown in a town as poor as Redruth.

Bartering served her purposes just as well as money, if not better. Jago had sold the necklace and earrings Stephen had given her and the money from the sale had left her speechless.

"I probably could have gotten more for the necklace and earrings," Jago admitted when he'd handed over the small fortune. "But I did not have the time to visit more than a few jewelers."

"You've already done enough for me, my friend. Besides, this will last us for years."

That money, in addition to the humble jointure Edward had left her, would be adequate to support her, Beth, and a child. But what about when that child grew older?

Elinor absently pleated the bedding between her fingers as she considered her baby—Stephen's baby. He could give children everything money could buy. But was he capable of giving anyone love?

He'd not been content to merely acquire Blackfriars; he'd also tried to destroy anyone related to it in the process. That was not normal and Elinor knew quite a bit about men who were not normal. She'd sworn never to get involved with another man after Edward, and then she'd thrown herself at the first man who showed her any interest.

Even as she thought the words, she realized she wasn't being quite fair to herself. Stephen Worth had come after her with all the formidable assets at his disposal. What woman could've resisted him?

A light knock on the door pulled her from her pointless introspection.

"Yes?"

The door opened and Beth peeked inside.

"You've got your first human patient, my—uh, Mrs. Atwood."

Elinor almost leapt from the bed. She gave Beth the first genuine smile in weeks.

"I shall be right there."

***

Elinor finished splinting the stocky man's arm while his two sons held him steady.

"Be him okay, missus?" The elder of the two young men asked, lines of concern disturbing his smooth brow as he eyed his father's swaying form.

"Mr. Williams will be fine once the drug wears off, which should be in an hour or so. Don't leave him alone tonight," she cautioned, looking up as she gently placed his meaty arm in a sling she'd fashioned from a triangle of material. It was the last of their old bedding and Beth had been very unhappy when she'd delivered it to Elinor.

"What will it be next, *Mrs. Atwood?*" Beth had demanded, tossing the sheet onto the rude wooden table where Elinor mixed her medicines. "Perhaps you might want to break up our chairs to use for splints? Or maybe use your bedroom as an infirmary?"

Beth had become increasingly belligerent in the two weeks since her first patient—when people had begun to virtually pour into Elinor's small surgery.

Elinor tied off the last knot and smiled at the two men—boys, really.

"Tell him not to disturb the splint, even though his arm will itch like mad. Give him a stick if he needs to scratch.

Both boys flushed a charming, rosy shade as she spoke to them.

"Aye, mum," they muttered in tandem.

Elinor suppressed a smile at the accent, which still tickled her. Oftentimes the dialect was unintelligible to her, and people still spoke Cornish in this remote backwater.

"Uh, how much do we owe, missus?" The taller one—Ronnie, she thought his name was—asked.

Elinor named a price that was half what Doctor Venable would charge. Even so, the two young men turned pale. The Williamses were a family of rag and bone pickers, a poor occupation in the best of places, it was barely enough to keep body and soul together in Redruth.

"I'll offer you an alternate manner of payment," Elinor said. "I have a pig who needs a home. I'm afraid she's become too large to continue living inside." Not only that, but Beth had threatened to pack her bags and leave if Elinor did not get rid of Daisy, who'd come to her as payment for delivering a baby.

Both men smiled, obviously relieved. "Aye, we can build a sty, mum."

"Good, the sooner the better. If you let me know what you require I will—"

Ronnie shook his head. "We'm bring what we need."

They spent another ten minutes discussing dimensions for Daisy's new house before Mr. Williams began to wake. The two boys promised to return the next day and Elinor collapsed into a chair after they left.

The past two weeks had heralded a radical change in her status. Most days she woke at dawn and didn't stop until dark, often going out in the middle of the night when the occasion demanded it. She was bone-tired, but she was not unhappy. Never had she felt so . . . necessary, so important.

Unfortunately, Beth had every reason to worry—and not just about running out of sheets or bedding. Since moving to Redruth, Elinor had acquired six hens, a piglet, untold baskets of potatoes and other vegetables, and enough dried meat to last them for several years. The actual money she'd made would not be enough to buy another sheet to replace those she'd used up in her small surgery. She needed more money and every day the thought of the money Stephen had put aside for her chewed at her mind like a rat gnawing on a corpse.

Could she take the money? *Should* she take the money? After all, he'd set it aside for her. Even if she only took one year's worth it would be enough for sheets and food and pig housing for the rest of her life.

She heard the clatter of horse hooves outside her door and opened her eyes, grateful to have something to distract her from the nagging question of the five thousand pounds.

The door opened and a familiar, handsome face stood in the gap.

"Why, Jago, whatever are you doing here?" She pushed herself to her feet as he came towards her.

"You would do better to remain seated, my— Mrs., er, Atwood."

Elinor couldn't help laughing. "Oh no, not you too. One would think my name was Mrs. Myer-Atwood."

The doctor gave her one of his rare smiles, his gaze flickering around the small room.

"What do you think of my surgery, doctor?"

"I think you've done quite nicely. How is business?"

"Busy."

"I hope you are not overtaxing yourself." His eyes dropped to her midriff and heat surged up her neck.

"Beth wrote to you," she said, barely getting the words out between her clenched jaws.

"Don't be angry with her; she's concerned for you."

Elinor would deal with her loose-lipped maid later. "Please tell me you have not come haring half-way across the country because I am with child?"

His smile grew at her waspish tone. "No, I've not come for that. Although I would—"

Elinor held up a hand. "Thank you, Jago, but I must respectfully decline your very kind offer."

The sudden slashes of red across his high cheekbones were the only sign she'd guessed correctly.

"I do appreciate your concern," she added in a kinder voice.

He nodded.

"So, if it isn't my delicate situation, to what do I owe the pleasure of your visit?"

"It's about Stephen Worth."

*** 

The small hatch in the cell door opened. "Another visitor for you, Mr. Worth."

Stephen squinted up at the gun slit window. It wasn't night, but it was close. He shoved himself up against the wall, his hand already seeking the glass that was never far away. He tossed back the dregs and grimaced at the sour, metallic taste it left in his mouth.

The keys rattled in the lock and he pushed his hair off his forehead but didn't bother to get up. The jailor growled to somebody and a low rumble answered before the door creaked open.

John Fielding ducked under the lintel, his shoulders brushing the doorframe.

He flipped a coin over his shoulder in a manner calculated to show maximum disdain for the jailor, who caught the flickering gold coin handily and left—without closing the door.

Fielding limped toward him.

"What the hell happened to you?" Stephen demanded, glaring up at his giant employee.

Fielding held up one big bandaged paw. "Had a bit of an accident."

"Did it prevent you from reading any papers for almost seven damned weeks?"

"Actually, it did." He turned his head, allowing Stephen to see the white bandage beneath his coal black hair.

"Hmmph."

"Thank you for your concern."

"I pay you to be concerned, not the other way around. Where were you?"

He shrugged his massive shoulders. "Here and there."

Stephen gritted his teeth. There was no point in letting the bastard get under his skin; Fielding enjoyed it too much. "May I ask if you are now back at work?"

"You may."

Stephen stared.

"I am. In fact," he dug a big hand into the breast pocket of his ruined coat and extracted a folded piece of paper, "I just got this from your barrister."

Stephen snorted. "I'm surprised he's managed to generate anything; I've only paid him more money than he's made in his entire bloody life." He snatched the single sheet, unfolded it, and his eyes dropped to the bottom. He looked up to find Fielding staring. "Have you read this?"

"Aye. You can leave whenever you're ready."

Stephen lifted the letter. "The date on here says three days ago. When, exactly, was that idiot going to bring it to me?" His head was pounding and hot and more than a little muzzy. Three Fieldings stood in front of him instead of one.

"The barrister was instructed to give you the letter after four days had passed. After I read it, I convinced him to give it to me immediately. I also convinced him to take some personal time— somewhere far, far away from you."

Stephen pointed to the wine crate. "Make yourself useful and open a bottle."

Fielding cocked an eyebrow at him, sighed, and moved toward the half-full crate. He squinted at the label and his second eyebrow joined the first.

"This looks quite nice."

"It's too bad you can't join me. I only have one glass."

Fielding snorted, made short work opening the bottle and filled Stephen's tumbler.

Stephen grunted, took a gulp, and set the glass down on the grimy flagstone floor so hard he thought it might break. "Hand me my spectacles."

The letter was addressed to several officials, as if the sender hadn't been quite sure who should receive it and wanted to cover all eventualities.

*Dear Sirs:*

*I am writing this letter in the presence of three witnesses, one of whom is magistrate for Trevingey—*

Stephen looked up.

"Cornwall," Fielding said, tearing his attention away from a particularly realistic carving on the wall that depicted a man hanging by the neck from a gibbet.

"Cornwall?" Stephen repeated.

Fielding grunted and turned back to the wall art.

*I am writing this letter in the presence of three witnesses, one of whom is magistrate for Trevingey and can attest to the truth of the matter contained within.*

*I, Elinor Elizabeth Mary Constance Trentham do hereby swear the following is a true and accurate description of what happened on the evening of June 22, 1802.*

*On that day I was living with my mother and father, Lord and Lady Yarmouth, who hosted a ball to celebrate my betrothal to Edward Atwood, Earl of Trentham.*

*Iain Vale was a new footman in my father's household. That day, June 22, was Mr. Vale's first day in that capacity.*

*I encountered Mr. Vale twice that evening while he was working. Both times I engaged in inappropriate and purposely inflammatory conversation with him. It was during the second instance that I put my hands around his neck and physically surprised him into kissing me. He was trying to put me away from him when my betrothed, Edward Atwood, Earl of Trentham, arrived and placed the most severe interpretation on what he found.*

*Utterly unprovoked, Lord Trentham attacked Mr. Vale from behind and knocked him to the ground. In spite of my attempts to convince Lord Trentham otherwise, he kicked, beat, and abused Mr. Vale until he lost consciousness. My father arrived and believed Lord Trentham's rendition of events, rather than mine.*

*Mr. Vale was taken away by the local constable and never, within my knowledge, offered an opportunity to give his version of events. Neither was I.*

*Realizing an innocent man was incarcerated on charges that could result in transportation if not death, I conspired to gain his release from Coldbath Fields Prison. I provided the money and hired a man whose name I cannot recall to implement the escape plan.*

*In sum, Iain Vale was the victim of a sixteen-year-old girl's capricious and thoughtless act. Mr. Vale's suffering was compounded by fifteen years of silence on my part.*

*I take full responsibility for my actions, including, but not limited to, bribing an official of Her Majesty's government. I have tendered my confession to Magistrate David Philips of Trevingey and he has ordered me to present myself to the proper authority in London and await His Majesty's pleasure.*

*Sworn and signed,*

*Elinor Trentham*

Stephen re-read the letter before looking up. "Did you see her?"

"No, she went to a special session before the magistrates and left not long after."

Stephen wasn't surprised the authorities had ignored the opportunity to charge a countess with a crime.

"When did you get here?"

"A few hours ago." Fielding made a vague gesture with his chin. "I've got the coach waiting outside." He glanced around at the crates of spirits, stacks of books, and wheels of cheese, his eyes lingering on a large wooden cask of olives. "That is, if you still want to leave."

Stephen ignored his servant's sarcastic comment and looked down at the letter he held crushed in his hand.

He should be feeling elated. He was a free man. He could be Iain Vale again. He could remain Stephen Worth. He was not only personally wealthy; he was in sole control of a financial juggernaut. He could do anything, go anywhere.

But it turned out that the one thing he wanted—the brief happiness he'd shared with Elinor—he'd utterly destroyed.

# Chapter Twenty-Seven

***Blackfriars***
***1817***

tephen woke up in the Blackfriars library. For some reason, he was wedged between the dark green leather sofa and an end table. His hand was still wrapped around a bottle, but it was empty.

He groaned and let his head fall back on the oak floor, and then groaned again. He had no idea what day it was—or what time it was. For a moment, just the merest of seconds, he wondered why he'd gotten drunk last night.

And then it hit him, the reason he got drunk *every* night: Elinor.

"God." His voice was gravelly from lack of use or too much alcohol, or both. Every day he hoped the pain he felt at the thought of her would go away. And every day it was worse.

*You're pathetic,* his faithful inner critic offered. *You paid her back; it's what you wanted* for years. *Quit sniveling.*

Stephen knew the voice was right. He'd wanted revenge, and he'd gotten it.

*Repent.*

Stephen blinked at the voice, not the usual snide, cruel mental companion. It was Jeremiah's voice. He closed his eyes and willed the old man to come back—to tell him what to do. But all he heard was the gurgling of his own stomach.

He released the empty bottle and pushed up onto his hands and knees. Lurching to his feet turned out to be a horrible idea.

He'd just finished vomiting in a coal scuttle that sat, inexplicably, in the center of the threadbare Aubusson carpet when somebody knocked on the door.

"What?" he yelled, wiping his mouth with the back of his hand before flopping back onto the settee.

Fielding's head appeared in the crack. "Somebody here to see you, Mr. Worth."

Stephen snorted and held out his arms. "Do I look like I want to see anybody?" He glanced down at his body. He'd lost his waistcoat and coat somewhere and his once-white shirt was wrinkled, stained, and stank of sweat. His gray trousers had an eight-inch rent over one knee and his feet were bare. He had no recollection of dressing himself. Or undressing himself.

And every last drop of moisture had gone from his body. He needed a drink.

"Sir?"

Stephen looked up and saw Fielding still waiting for him.

"Go away. And have somebody send in a fresh bottle."

"Do you want to receive your visitor in here?"

"What did I just say, Fielding?"

"You're going to want to see this person, Mr. Worth."

*Bloody stubborn irritating interfering bastard.* "Tell me something, John."

"Sir?"

"Are you going to bother me until I do what you want?"

A long pause followed and then, "Yes, sir."

Stephen gave a loud bark of laughter that made his pounding, desiccated skull throb.

"Well, what are you waiting for? Send whoever the hell it is in. And then send in another bottle."

Fielding's black eyes moved up and down Stephen's body in a manner that spoke volumes. "You don't wish to—"

"No, dammit! I don't wish you to do or say another fucking word. I want you to show whoever it is into this room and bring me a damned bottle of brandy."

Fielding didn't answer but the door swung wider.

Three identical gray-haired men in ill-fitting suits entered. All three had removed their hats and were holding them in big, work-worn hands.

Stephen squinted until he saw only one man.

"Well?" he demanded when the man remained silent. "Who the hell are you and what the hell do you want?"

"Iain?"

Stephen peered harder and his heart jerked like a rabbit in a snare. "Uncle Lonnie?" he gasped.

The face shifted into a smile—a very familiar smile. It was true there was more gray than brown and there were more wrinkles than a decade and a half ago, but it was unmistakably his uncle. He eyed Stephen from his head to his feet, and then back to his head.

"Iain, just look at you."

Stephen gawked, too stunned to speak. He pushed off the divan so quickly he tripped and would have sprawled flat on his face if the other man hadn't sprung forward to catch him.

"Easy, lad," his uncle soothed, using the same voice Stephen had heard him employ with skittish horses hundreds of times.

"Uncle Lonnie," he repeated dumbly, placing his feet shoulder-width apart to remain standing.

"Aye, lad." He squeezed Stephen's shoulder and leaned closer to look at his face. "What's wrong with ye, boy?"

Even Stephen's drink-addled brain could hear the disapproval in his uncle's voice.

He bristled and pulled away. "There nothing wrong with me." Stephen glared at the older man's judgmental expression; this was hardly the heart-warming reunion he'd envisioned for fifteen years. But then again, what part of his carefully conceived plan *had* lived up to his expectations thus far?

Lonnie Clark's eyebrows lowered and a vertical line formed between his hazel eyes.

"You'd better sit, my boy. You look as if you might fall down." He gestured to the sofa and then lowered himself onto a smaller divan across from it.

Stephen tamped down his irritation at his condescending tone. "You look well, Uncle."

"Aye, I am well."

"What—?" Stephen coughed and tried again. "What happened?" He didn't need to explain what he meant.

The library door opened before his uncle could answer. Fielding entered holding a silver tray with a bottle and two glasses.

Stephen scowled as the huge man lowered the tray onto the table with a rough *clunk*.

"What the devil happened to my butler?" Stephen demanded.

"You threw a bottle at him the last time he came into the room." Fielding poured two glasses and offered one to Stephen.

He waved it away. For the first time in weeks, he had no desire for a drink.

Fielding's black brows arched but he remained silent and gave the glass to the older man.

"Much obliged," Lonnie said, not wasting any time before taking a healthy swig. He grinned. "Ah, now that's fine. I suppose you drink this well all the time?"

Stephen ignored the question. "You can leave now," he said to Fielding. He turned to his uncle after the door closed. "I thought you were dead."

His uncle's eyes widened. "Why'd you think that?"

"Because I couldn't find you anywhere."

"Why'd you even try? What did I tell you about coming back?"

Stephen struggled to suppress the irritation that simmered in his empty, churning gut and threatened to explode.

"Where were you?" he asked coldly.

His uncle's eyes narrowed. "You may be a big man with buckets o' money, but you don't talk to me that way, boy."

Stephen closed his eyes and counted as high as it took to stop the vein from pulsing in his temple. When he opened them again it was to find his uncle sipping his drink with the expression of man determined to enjoy a rare luxury.

# The Footman

Memories of his uncle's monumental stubbornness drifted through his mind and came floating back to him. Stephen recalled how his uncle could make a mule appear reasonable. He exhaled gustily, crossed his arms, and made himself more comfortable.

Lonnie made him wait a few moments more before speaking. "I left that same night, right after dropping you at the docks. Lady Elinor set up everything. She gave me some jewels, all her pin money, and a letter."

Even though Stephen knew it had been Elinor who'd paid for his escape he still found it difficult to breathe, as if something large had just landed on his chest. His vision rippled with waves of heat and his head blazed like a furnace. "Why didn't you tell me?"

His uncle shrugged, his hazel eyes flickering from the worn carpet to the dusty, ragged drapes, to the half-filled bookshelves.

"Looks like you need to hire a better housekeeper, son."

Stephen's hands clenched so tight his bones hurt. It took every ounce of strength he had not to yell. "Why didn't you tell me all this that night?"

The older man's eyes sharpened and the look he gave Stephen was less than friendly.

"Because she told me not to, Iain. Can you imagine what would have happened to her if anyone found out what she'd done? Already she was in terrible trouble with the viscount and that other monster. Just think on what woulda happened if she'd been caught springing you from jail."

"She had nobody to blame but herself!" Stephen roared, no longer able to take his uncle's accusing looks or his own shrieking conscience. "She threw herself at me, dammit!"

"She was a sixteen-year-old girl, Iain."

"And I was a fifteen-year-old boy!"

His uncle nodded grimly. "I know, lad. Neither of you deserved what happened that night. It wasn't the girl and it wasn't you. Her father should have known better; if not him, then surely the viscountess. But some form of madness possessed them all. It was a nightmare."

"You're bloody right it was a nightmare."

His uncle's eyes turned accusing. "You've done alright out of it, haven't ye?"

Stephen could hardly breathe. "Money?" The word came out a disbelieving gasp. "You think *money* made up for having to leave the only family I had left and run half-way round the globe?"

"Of course I don't, lad. But it is what it is. In other words, it's life, Iain. And it's messy and doesn't always go the way you want. But the fact is you're still alive. You're also a healthy, rich, and powerful man. A body can't say the same for her, though."

An odd jolt of energy ran up Stephen's spine and made his head snap up. "What do you mean?" He scowled. "And what the devil do you know about her, anyway?"

"I know plenty. I'm married to Beth MacFarlane's sister, Mary."

"What?"

"Aye, Beth MacFarlane, Lady Trentham's maid. When her ladyship wrote me a letter of recommendation, she said her maid grew up outside Manchester, in a small village called Moston. She said Beth's sister worked in Baron Mainwaring's house and was well-treated. His lordship needed a man in his stables and I took the position. It wasn't stablemaster, but I worked my way up. That's where I met my Mary and she agreed to become my wife a year later."

"You married." It wasn't a question.

"Aye, I've three boys." He grinned, his face glowing with pride. "One of 'em I called Iain."

"And Elinor wrote you a letter of recommendation?" he said stupidly, unable to think of anything else.

"Lady Trentham, aye. She was quite the little forger. By the time she finished puffing me up I could have worked in the royal stables."

Stephen could only stare. All these years. All these *bloody* years he'd believed his uncle either dead or destitute at the hands of Yarmouth and Trentham. The entire time he'd been secure, married, and fathering a veritable brood of children. All thanks to *her*.

Stephen looked up from his clenched hands. "Why are you here now?"

His uncle blinked. "I just found out you were back, din't I?"

"So, you read about me in the papers, eh?"

"No, Beth wrote to Mary—when they finally learned who you were."

"Ahh," Stephen drawled, pleased by how insulting he could make a single syllable sound. "Come to see if there was any money to be had?"

Only his uncle's tense jaw and the white knuckles of the hand holding the glass betrayed the anger inside him.

"I guess you had to grow up without anyone to teach you manners, Iain, but—"

"Stephen. My name is Stephen Worth and I'm not a boy in need of learning manners. I did what you told me to do and I chose a new name for a new life. Iain Vale is dead."

The air crackled between them. For a moment Stephen thought his uncle would either leave or grab him and administer a thrashing. In the state Stephen was in, he couldn't do much to stop him.

His uncle nodded, his eyes unreadable. He placed the glass gently on the table. "Well, thank you for the drink, son." He picked up his hat, which had been perched on the sofa beside him, and held it carefully by the brim, the way a man unaccustomed to such finery would treat a hat he wore only a few times a year. An honest man, not a man who'd come looking for anything other than his nephew.

Stephen dropped his head as a wave of suffocating shame washed over him. He was behaving like a mad dog, biting the hands of those who loved him. This was his *Uncle Lonnie*, for God's sake! A hand landed on his shoulder and his head jerked up. His uncle stood in front of him, a tentative expression on his familiar face.

"You're being eaten away, boy. I can see it as plain as the nose on your face, even as I sit here watching. You've hate in you and it's like an acid corroding your soul. You need to let bygones be bygones."

"It's too late for that." Stephen shook his head. "I've—I've done horrible, unforgivable things."

"It's never too late."

"You don't know, Uncle. You just don't know."

His uncle sat down on the sofa beside him. "And I won't, son. Not unless you tell me."

# Chapter Twenty-Eight

Elinor put the bloody cloths into the worn pillowcase before washing her hands in the basin of lukewarm water. It was only three o'clock and she was already exhausted. She thought fondly back to the days when she'd had only a pig or mule to doctor.

She dried her hands on the rough cloth and smiled. It was hard work, but at least it left her too tired to think when her head hit the pillow at night.

For once in her life she was making a difference; she *mattered* to these people. The thought made her frown. If only she could advocate for them. Unfortunately, the advocacy of a widow who was about to have a child out of wedlock was hardly likely to carry much weight with the local mine-owner, Peter Cantwell. When it came to his employees and tenants, Peter Cantwell treated people like cheap and shoddy tools he expected to have to replace.

The Redruth mine was among the most dangerous in Cornwall, an area not renowned for safety in such matters. Cantwell owned two other mines, each of which were far more productive and lucrative, meaning the Englishman gave very little of his attention to the conditions or maintenance at Redruth. Hardly a day went by when

Elinor didn't treat a miner who'd suffered a crushed limb or had been poisoned by the foul air in the deep, unstable tunnels.

The door to the surgery opened and Beth's face appeared in the doorway. Her cheeks were flushed and her eyes sparkled.

*What was this?* Beth had not smiled since they'd come to Redruth.

"You've a visitor, my—er, Mrs. Atwood."

Elinor froze.

Beth bustled into the small surgery, frowning at the basin of bloody water.

"Come, you must change into a different gown." She took Elinor's hand and her eyes flickered dismissively over the old brown day dress she wore.

Elinor pulled her hand away.

"Who is it, Beth?"

"It's Mr. Worth." She worried her lower lip. "Or perhaps he prefers to be called Mr. Vale?"

Elinor's heart stumbled into action and her lungs strained painfully for air. "I don't wish to see him," she said in a high, brittle voice that sounded nothing like her normal voice.

*You're lying, Elinor.*

"Tell him I am from home." It was all she could do to force the words through clenched jaws.

"My lady," Beth admonished, forgetting where she was and who she was supposed to be speaking to. "You cannot do that."

Elinor gave Beth her most haughty look, the only useful thing she'd learned from Edward. "You heard me."

Beth bit her lip. "I've already told him you were here."

"Beth!"

The older woman winced, her cheeks beet red with shame. "I know, my lady. I'm sorry, but I couldn't help it. I was so surprised to open the door and find him standing there. It was quite shocking to see a man dressed so beautifully out here in the wilderness," she added, almost to herself.

*Ha! Overcome by fashion.*

Elinor gritted her teeth. He was a persistent man. Most likely he would not leave her in peace until he said whatever it was he'd come to say.

"Very well, I will see him."

Beth's smile was radiant.

"Don't look so pleased. I'm not changing my clothing," she said, taking childish pleasure in dashing her maid's happiness.

"But—"

Elinor left before she said something cutting. She took a detour past Daisy's yard on her way to the cottage. Jory Williams, the youngest Williams boy, was expanding the chicken coop that abutted Daisy's house.

He stopped hammering and touched his forelock when she approached.

"How goes the construction, Mr. Williams?"

He flushed delightedly at the grown-up form of address. From his size, Elinor had guessed him to be eighteen. It turned out the boy was not yet fifteen. Like every other lad in the area it was his hope to get work at the mine. Until that day, he helped his family in their meager business.

"It'll be t'only 'en 'ouse in Redruth with a flowerbox." He chortled, his eyes on the small rectangle Elinor had asked him to attach to the little wooden house.

Elinor felt something brush against her fingers and looked down to find Daisy rubbing against her hand. The pig was flourishing in her new home but she still gave Elinor a yearning look whenever she came to visit.

Elinor scratched the huge sow between the ears. "Daisy will like a flowerbox," Elinor said, her mind on the man waiting for her in the cottage.

Jory Williams thought that was hilarious. "She'm more likely to eat flowers, missus!"

"He is maligning you, isn't he, Daisy?" She scratched the furrows on Daisy's forehead.

Daisy's eyes closed and she wore an expression of pure porcine bliss and gave a deep grunt of contentment as Elinor's fingers encountered the perfect spot behind one ear.

"Whatever are you doing, my—er, Mrs. Atwood?" Beth popped up behind her, her chiding voice making Elinor jump. "He's waiting for you," she hissed, giving the boy a hasty glance, grimacing at Daisy, and pushing Elinor toward the house. "You should wash your hands after touching that filthy animal."

"Daisy is cleaner than most humans," Elinor protested, allowing her maid to shove her toward the little cottage.

Beth grunted, a sound which was remarkably like Daisy's. Elinor doubted her maid would appreciate the observation.

A magnificent post-chaise sat in front of the cottage and Elinor wondered how she'd failed to hear six horses approaching.

Mr. Fielding leaned up against the carriage box, his expression oddly pensive and his disturbing, flat gaze fixed on one of the postilions, a tall, blond lad who was eating an apple beside one of the jet-black leaders. The horses' ears were pricked forward and Elinor absently wondered how the boy would share out one apple core between six horses.

"Mr. Fielding," Elinor greeted the silent giant with an abrupt nod but did not stop.

"Ma'am." He lifted his hat and bowed, his lips bending into their usual amused sneer.

Beth caught her arm as she opened the front door. "Are you sure you won't—"

"No."

"I'll bring the tea tra—"

"No. He won't be staying that long."

Beth drew back, aghast. "But, my lady—"

Elinor turned on her argumentative servant. "If I hear one more word about my clothing, tea, or Mr. Worth, you'll be accompanying him back to Blackfriars in that magnificent carriage when he leaves. Are we understood?"

Beth chewed the side of her cheek more ferociously than a dog worrying a soup bone.

"And my name is *Mrs. Atwood.*"

Beth made a sound that was part huff and part squawk and spun on her heel, disappearing into the little kitchen.

Elinor took a deep breath, exhaled, and then did it again before flinging open the door to the parlor-cum-library-cum-sitting room.

\*\*\*

Stephen's back was to the door and he was examining the books that covered one wall of the small room when the sound of wood slamming against plaster made him startle and turn.

"Why are you here?"

Elinor stood in the open doorway, her hands on her hips. She was wearing the most hideous garment imaginable and her hair looked as if she'd combed it with a pitchfork.

She was the most beautiful woman he'd ever seen.

He realized he was gaping and closed his mouth. "Elinor."

"You may call me Mrs. Atwood," she snapped. "Now, why are you here?"

"Wouldn't you like to sit?" His heart leapt like an exuberant puppy under her steely gray glare.

"You won't be here long enough." She tapped one foot, her eyes never wavering from his face.

"I spoke to my Uncle Lonnie."

She lifted one brow but remained silent.

"He told me where you were. He also told me that you are with child. My child."

She gave him a look he'd never seen before: a sly, nasty smirk.

"Sure of that, are you?"

Stephen considered his next words very carefully; the subject was more dangerous than a nest of vipers. "The only other man you've spent any amount of time with was Venable and I already spoke to him."

Her eyes widened. "And *he said* he was not the father of my child?"

"No, he said nothing. He did give me this, however." Stephen tilted his head so that she might see the purple stain on his jaw.

She barked a laugh. "I hope he did not hurt his hand."

Stephen knew he deserved that, even though her words were like broken glass in his guts. "No, he's fine. The man knows how to throw a punch."

"I hope you did not engage in a brawl with him. He is too important in Trentham to be laid up with injuries."

The implied message being that Stephen was not. Well, he had to give her that; nobody's life would be the worse if he was too injured to walk around.

"No, I didn't strike him. I deserved what he did and I honor him for it."

Elinor snorted and dropped into a chair. "He had no right to fight for my honor. I don't need any *man* to guard something I am more than capable of defending."

Stephen would have sworn ice crystals formed in the air between them. He gingerly took a seat without being asked. "I know you must be angry with me and I—"

"You don't know the least thing about me and that is exactly the way you planned it." Her chest rose and fell violently, belying her cool voice. "You came back for revenge, and you got it. I don't fault you for blaming me for that night. I was, without a doubt, entirely at fault for what happened. Believe me, you cannot abhor my behavior any more than I have done these past fifteen years. If you've come to thank me for my letter, please save your breath. It was the very least I could do and cost me nothing."

"That's not why I came," he cut in when she paused to catch her breath. "I came to beg you to forgive me."

His words seemed to breathe more life into her.

"I forgive you—freely and completely. I understand what you did and why you did it. I daresay I would have done something similar had I been in your shoes. I hold you in no blame and you may go about your life."

"I want to go about my life but I want *you* in it. I know I've behaved badly—"

She snorted.

"—terribly," he amended. "But surely we can get beyond that now that there is to be a child—*our* child."

She gave him a look that should have flayed the skin from his bones. But the words she spoke next were worse. "You are not the kind of man I would allow near a child of mine."

Stephen flinched away as if she'd thrown hot coals at him. Anger flared in him. "That is unfair, Elinor. You know I'm capable of good and kind behavior."

"When you want something in return."

"But that could be said of all people." Her eyes narrowed and he hastened to continue. "I'm not trying to excuse my behavior, merely saying I have it in me to do better. You know I could give our child anything their heart desired."

"You could give *my* child creature comforts, but could you give love, Mr. Worth?" She paused and cocked her head. "Or is it Mr. Vale?"

Stephen grimaced at the tiresome subject of his name. "I will continue to go by Stephen Worth. And yes," he added, "I *am* capable of love." He pushed up from his chair and sank to one knee in front of her. "It took losing you and almost facing a hangman's noose to accept the truth about myself, Elinor—that I love you. I know now that I was in love with you even when I behaved so unforgivably.

"When I was in Newgate and thought I'd lost you forever I didn't see the point of going on. I was grateful to face judgement and punishment. And then you came forward and saved me without even being asked. Instead of taking that opportunity—that chance—and coming to you *then* and begging forgiveness I went to Blackfriars and wallowed in my own misery and self-pity. It wasn't until my uncle told me what you'd done for him—and what was done to *you*—that I wanted to crawl into the deepest, darkest crack in the earth and hide."

"Perhaps that is where you *should* have gone instead of coming here."

Stephen nodded. "I deserve that. I deserve everything you can throw at me."

"You are under a great misapprehension, sir. I have no intention of throwing *anything* at you. I hope never to have anything to do with you again. Now, if you've quite finished—" She started to rise and Stephen took her hand and raised it to his lips.

"For weeks I *did* crawl into a deep, dark place. However, the more I thought about it—about what I'd done to you—the more I realized I owed you an apology, even if you didn't want it, even if you couldn't forgive me, even if you refused to see me." He took a deep breath and held her cold stare. "I humbly beg your forgiveness, even though I know I do not deserve it. You refused my offer of marriage once before, but now things are different—there is a child's future and wellbeing and reputation to consider. If you would consent to be my wife, I would spend the rest of my life proving my love and making myself worthy of you." He kissed her palm.

She met the outpouring of his soul with a look that could have withered crops. And then she removed her hand from his and folded it in her lap.

"I've already said I forgive you. As for your offer, I must decline. I told you before I would not marry you."

He stared at her with open amazement. "Surely you don't wish to raise our child as a bastard? Do you know how difficult his or her future will be?"

Telltale slashes of color drew attention to her too-thin face and sharp cheekbones. "Never use that word in my presence. And, no, of course that is not what I wish. However, I wish even less to be under the control of a man—any man—but most *especially* a man who has demonstrated a *boundless* capacity for revenge, cruelty, and spite."

Stephen's face became so hot his vision was blurry, as if his eyeballs were stewing. He dropped his gaze, no longer able to withstand her penetrating stare.

For the first time in years his clever mind abandoned him and he forgot how to negotiate and bargain. His thoughts careened into one another like billiard balls. He wanted her, but she did not want him. She was all he wanted, but he could not have her.

He swallowed several times to get rid of the obstruction that blocked his throat. What could he do to prove he would never hurt her again? What reassurances could he give her? He *always* found a way to get what he wanted. Surely there had to be a way?

The thought had not even completed itself before an answer sprang into his mind.

He looked up. "I will put every last penny I own into your name. You will control my personal fortune, my property, even my share in the bank."

A look of surprise ghosted across her face but disappeared just as quickly.

She pursed her lips. "I don't want your money or possessions, Mr. Worth. No matter what you give to me, under the law you would still be my lord and master. I will never place my physical well-being—or that of my child—into any man's keeping. Ever. Again."

Stephen opened his mouth but no words came. He could only gape like a village idiot. It was like facing a vast, unscalable fortress wall and she was at the top, looking down the dizzying distance between them. She was like a mythical princess trapped in a castle and waiting for her hero to rescue her.

Stephen had no idea what to do. After all, hadn't he already played the villain in this particular fairytale?

# Chapter Twenty-Nine

Elinor looked at the kitten lying in the straw-lined basket and frowned. Beth would have a conniption fit when she saw the newest member of their small family. Still, she'd been complaining of the mice in the pantry.

The little beast yawned and curled into a tighter ball. It was a white-and-ginger striped female.

"They'm the best hunters, missus," Petroc Tregaron had insisted when he'd handed over the basket along with a half dozen eggs.

Mr. Tregaron, who worked at the Bal Dorkoth mine over in Camborne, had come all this way to have his ten-year-old son's arm set.

More and more Elinor had patients from farther afield as word of her skills or, more likely, her generous payment terms, spread. She often woke in the morning to find people sleeping outside her cottage to be first in line for treatment.

Mr. Tregaron and his son, Alan, had been asleep up against Daisy's fence. The big sow had been lying on the other side of the sturdy wooden fence right beside them, her intelligent eyes open and observant. The pig was interested in everything and anyone around her and seemed to enjoy visitors.

Elinor handed Mr. Tregaron a small vial of laudanum. "There is enough in here for tonight, to help him sleep." She turned to Alan. "No work with that for at least two weeks," she warned the boy as she opened the door and the pair prepared for the long walk back to Camborne.

"Aye, missus," Tregaron said, both he and the boy nodding vigorously. But Elinor knew the Tregarons could not do without the income their eldest son earned. Alan might only be ten but he'd already been working for a year in the copper mine, his duties menial ones like cleaning, sweeping, and fetching and carrying.

Mr. Tregaron couldn't have been more than thirty but his skin already bore the red splotches that heralded an early death. Life spans were short for Cornish miners and he was already quite old by local standards.

Elinor carried the kitten and walked to the cottage alongside them.

"Come back immediately if there is any swelling," she reminded them as they made their way toward the dirt path that led back to the main road.

She watched them as she stroked the little cat, its small body vibrating with pleasure at her petting.

A lone figure approached the Tregarons from the direction of the main road. Whoever it was, they were still some distance off. Few people came down this road so it was likely another patient. Elinor would not have much time to enjoy her meal before she would be needed.

She sighed and looked at the cat's sleeping face. "Are you ready to get this over with? We might as well go and face Beth now."

\*\*\*

Elinor had just finished defending the newest addition to the family and sat down to a bowl of porridge when there was a knock on the door.

Beth dried her hands on her worn blue apron. "You just eat, my lady. I'll tell whoever it is you'll be with them in half an hour."

"A quarter of an hour," Elinor called after her. She forced herself to spoon the porridge into her mouth slowly. She'd noticed lately that she'd gotten into the bad habit of eating too quickly. Often that made her sensitive stomach rebel and left her weak and ill, a state of being that was not good for her unborn child.

The door to the kitchen flew open. Beth's face was flushed, her eyes sparkling.

Only one thing made her dour maid so happy. Elinor scowled and pushed away her bowl, no longer hungry. "Tell him I'm busy."

"My lady!"

Elinor wanted to yell at her servant. She also wanted to get into her bed and pull the covers over her head. Why wouldn't he leave her alone? Instead, she pushed back from the table.

She pointed her index finger at her maid. "No tea," she said in the most dangerous, menacing tone she could muster.

Beth made small, unhappy noises which Elinor ignored.

He was waiting in her sanctum sanctorum.

She crossed her arms and glared at him, forcing herself to ignore her heart's drunken lurching at the sight of his face. Naturally, he looked delicious in buckskins, dusty black boots, and a dark green coat that looked to have been poured over his broad shoulders.

"Mrs. Atwood." He came toward her with outstretched hands, which he dropped when he met her frosty glare.

"What are you doing here?"

"Why, paying a neighborly call."

"You are hardly my neighbor. Blackfriars is days away."

He pulled his dimples on her like a cutpurse brandishing a knife. "I have a confession to make. I've purchased a property not far from here. We are most certainly neighbors."

Elinor's eyes widened. "What are you talking about?"

"I came to tell you I purchased a small manor not far from here— Oakland. The sale took place not long after the last time we saw one another but it wasn't completed until today. You are the first person I am telling."

"Oakland?" Elinor squinted hard, as if the action might stimulate some rational thought. Why did she feel as though she'd just walked in at the tail end of a complex lecture on steam power or celestial navigation? "But doesn't that belong to—"

"Peter Cantwell."

"But isn't he the one who—"

"Owned two of the mine largest mines in Redruth," he offered, his smile somehow managing to be innocent and improper at the same time.

"*Owned?*"

"I purchased those, too." He rocked back on his heels.

Elinor sat back in her chair as though a large hand had shoved her. Without being invited, he lowered himself into the chair beside her.

"Is anything wrong, Elinor?" He leaned close, a notch of concern between his emerald eyes.

"Mrs. Atwood," she corrected absently, her heart not really in it. He was her neighbor? He would be here all the time, only a few miles away? She closed her eyes.

"Mrs. Atwood? Are you ill? Should I fetch Beth?"

She opened her eyes to find him on one knee beside her chair, his face only inches from hers. The urge to lean forward and touch her lips to his was strong—like a child reaching toward a flame.

Their eyes locked and her face flared. He *knew* what she was thinking.

But then a vision of his face as it looked that hateful morning flashed through her mind and she jerked away from him before she could get singed.

"Are you sure you don't want something, Elinor?"

*Just you.*

She scowled down at him. "It's Mrs. Atwood. And please return to your chair."

"Of course." He pulled away but before he bowed his head she caught a small, triumphant smile on his shapely lips. She'd given herself away. He could see the lust in her eyes or read it on her face or smell it emanating from her pores.

Elinor fled from the disturbing thoughts. "Why have you done this, why? I thought you wanted Blackfriars—why aren't you there?"

"I'd hoped you'd take the Dower House in the spirit it was given," he said, his guilty expression telling her he wasn't being entirely honest.

"You think I'd take a *house* from you after what you'd done?"

He dropped his eyes, his magnificent head bowed.

# The Footman

"You drove me from my home, and for what? A whim?" Elinor struggled to hold back a degree of fury she hadn't even known existed. "Wasn't crushing and humiliating me enough?"

His head whipped up. "I was horribly wrong to do that to you and I regret my behavior *profoundly*. If I could go back in time—" He made a frustrated noise. "I *can't* go back. All I can do now is try and make things right. I told you the last time we spoke: I love you. I want to be with you. If I can't be *with* you, at least I can be near you. At least I can be nearby if you should have need of me."

*I love you.* The words generated an excruciating mix of joy and agony in her chest that threatened to choke her. It didn't matter that she tried to numb her feelings, to dull the sensations he evoked in her. Her resistance to him wavered and would soon break if she were forced to endure much more of him. The only way to protect herself was to drive him away.

She looked into his serious green eyes and forced a sour, twisted expression onto her face. "I'm not a lady here. And I do not *need* afternoon callers. I work, Mr. Worth. I might not make very much money at what I do, but I like to think I make a difference. No matter how much you wish otherwise, I will not be available to sip tea and eat sugar buns with you whenever you are bored."

His expression remained impassive even though her cool tone slid well over the line of politeness and into the territory of rebuke.

"I, too, will have things to keep me busy. I expect the mine to take up a great deal of my attention. I did not come to waste your time, my, er, Mrs. Atwood, I wanted you to be the first to know of my purchases and also to deliver an invitation."

"Invitation?" Elinor bit her lip at the interest she heard in the single word. Why could she not control her reactions around this man?

"Yes. I'm organizing a small celebration for my workers. It has come to my attention—in the short time that I've lived in town at the Arundell Arms—that the locals used to celebrate the end of the harvest." He gave her a wry smile. "Back when there was something to harvest other than copper and tin. They call it Allantide after the—"

"Allan apple. Yes, I already know this. What of it?"

S.M. LaViolette

"I was sure you did." He looked amused, rather than irritated, by her rude interruption. "There hasn't been an Allantide celebration in years. I thought I'd not only do something for the children, but also their parents. I will hold an afternoon function for people of all ages and a dance that same evening at Oakland. There's a rather nice ballroom. Or at least there will be after it's been buffed up a bit."

Elinor's chest tightened at his words and an image filled her mind: that of dancing with him in his room in London. And of making love afterward.

*Good Lord you are a ninny,* the cool, supercilious voice in her head accused. *Haven't you already learned your lesson from this man?*

Elinor must have made an odd face because Stephen—*yes, fine! She still thought of him as Stephen! What of it?*—stared, his brow wrinkled with curiosity.

She extended her hand, palm up.

He glanced at it before looking at her face. "I'm sorry, I don't understand?"

"The invitation. You may give it to me."

A dull flush crept up his neck and she drank it in like a gin addict embracing a pint of Mother's Ruin. Yes, she was a bad person to take such enjoyment from his discomfort, but she didn't care.

He cleared his throat. "I, er, well, I don't have the invitations made up yet."

Elinor stood and he shot up beside her, taking her hand before she could back away.

"I just needed to see you, Ellie." The desperation in his voice was like an aphrodisiac. Blood and heat and desire pulsed in every part of her body.

She swallowed hard and closed her eyes.

*It's just your body's physical response to stimulus. It was no more significant than sneezing when you tickle your nose with a feather.*

Except it was.

The memory of the first time he'd called her by that name came back unsolicited. Blinding white anger followed on its heels and she yanked her hand out of his.

"You have no right to call me that. *No* right." Her breathing was ragged and shallow and she stepped away from his intense green eyes and large, looming body. "It's past time I went back to work. You can show yourself out."

He said nothing.

Elinor closed the door on him and briefly leaned against it, her bones turning to water.

*Good Lord. She would never be able to resist him.*

***

Stephen watched her back out the door, her gray eyes wide and frightened like a startled doe. The door shut with a decisive *snick* and he slumped into the chair and exhaled.

Well, that had gone better than he'd hoped.

He'd expected her to refuse to see him at all. Or perhaps shoot him, if she had a firearm about. Luckily, Beth was on his side.

"You just go and sit in the library, Mr. Worth. I'll bring her to you." The older woman had assured him with a conspiratorial smile. No doubt she wanted her mistress to be back in an environment more suited to her gentle background. She was probably also concerned about the unborn child. So was Stephen. He didn't think Elinor realized the burden of being labeled *bastard*.

Stephen had been born in wedlock, of course, but his mother had already been showing when his parents married. Everyone in the small village of Dannen knew who pretty Becky MacArthur had lain with. Not only that, but Stephen's red hair and tall lanky build would declare his relationship to the laird who'd owned everything and everyone for miles around.

Local boys had teased and tormented him about his status until he'd grown big enough to hand out thrashings and end the taunting.

Stephen didn't want his own experiences for his son or daughter.

His entire body tightened and hummed just thinking the words *son* and *daughter*. A child—*their* child. Could there be anything more arousing than putting a baby inside the woman you loved?

*God!* How he wished he could strip her naked, lay her body out before him like a banquet, and feast on her. Would she be showing? Would the gentle swell of her stomach be more pronounced?

Stephen was rock hard.

*Idiot.*

He stood and was rearranging his cock when the door opened and Beth's face appeared in the crack. She smiled, her cheeks flushed.

"I just heard about the party, Mr. Worth."

Stephen grinned at her unrestrained excitement. He also buttoned his coat closed and hoped like hell it hid his aroused state.

"Do you enjoy dancing, ma'am?"

She gave a girlish laugh as she opened the door wider. "I'm too old to dance."

"You're never too old to dance. In fact, I'm going to claim a dance with you right now and get an unfair jump on all the other gentleman."

She shook her head, her brown eyes twinkling as she walked into small entry hall beside him. "None of that new-fangled waltzing, mind."

"Of course not," he agreed, retrieving his hat and walking stick from the tiny console table near the front. He smiled down at the older woman, who wasn't much larger than her diminutive mistress.

"Thank you for today, Beth."

Her flush deepened and she waved a hand. "Oh, 'twas naught. Don't you worry, sir, I know—"

"Beth!" The sharp voice shot toward them from the direction of the stairs.

Beth grimaced. "I'd better—"

"Yes, you had. Thank you again, Beth."

Outside the cottage several people were clustered near the animal enclosure. A large boy was building something that looked like a crooked, miniature barn. When he saw Stephen, he paused his hammering and touched his cap.

"Are you a builder full-time?" he asked the boy.

"Ach, no, sir. This be payment for missus. She fixed me tas."

"Tas?"

"Me da."

"Ah." He'd heard Cornish spoken a few times since coming to the area but locals seemed cautious about speaking it around outsiders.

"Are you interested in any work when you finish this?"

The boy's face lit up. "Aye, sir."

260

Stephen couldn't help smiling at the enthusiasm. "Come see me at Oakland next week. I'm sure I'll have something that will suit you. What's your name?"

"Jory Williams, sir." The boy could hardly spit out his name he was grinning so hard.

"I'm Stephen Worth." Stephen held out his hand and could see the gesture startled the younger man. It wasn't done in Britain to shake hands, but he considered himself an American.

"Aye, sir. Everyone hereabouts knows of ye."

Jory's hand was almost as big as Stephen's. The boy would be a giant if mine work didn't kill him before he reached his full size.

He turned to leave and noticed Elinor talking to the group of patients. He glanced at the little building where she did her doctoring and frowned. She needed a larger building, a place for people to wait. A ball of anger heated and expanded in his stomach. Why wouldn't she let him help her? He could build her a proper hospital and fill it with supplies and equipment. He could—Stephen realized he'd been glaring at her and stopped.

She studiously avoided meeting his eyes when he went past her, but Stephen felt the heat of her gaze on his back as he walked away.

# Chapter Thirty

*Redruth, Cornwall*
*1817*

Elinor didn't know what irritated her more—the constant chattering about Stephen Worth and all the wonderful things he was doing for the people of Redruth, or her nagging, incessant, burning desire to always want to hear *more* about him.

True to his word, he'd not been to see her since their last meeting. But his presence in the small community made it feel like he was practically living under her roof. She was torn between relief at not having to see him in person and irritation that he seemed to have forgotten her.

"He's cleaning up that wretched mine," Beth said, her tone nonchalant as she placed Elinor's meal on the table that was set for one. Her maid steadfastly refused to sit down to eat with Elinor, no matter how ridiculous it was for the two of them to eat exactly the same meals in two separate rooms at exactly the same time.

"Is this the guinea fowl Mrs. Polgaren gave us?" Elinor asked, ignoring the comment about Stephen, no matter how tempted she was to use hot irons on Beth and extract every last drop of gossip about the annoying American.

Beth heaved an irritable sigh. "Yes, it is. And the potatoes Mr. Bevan paid you with and the cream is from the—"

"All right, all right, Beth. I don't need to know the provenance of every item on the plate."

"No use using those smart foreign words on me, *Mrs. Atwood*. If you're wanting to have such conversations you should have them with one of your own kind." Beth punctuated her advice by plunking the butter crock on the table and flouncing away, the swish of her skirts louder than words.

Elinor made a childish face at her back before turning to her meal. She refused to wish that she'd let Beth tell her more about Stephen. She already knew plenty.

Stephen Worth had increased wages at the mine, taken steps to implement safety measures that were long overdue for most Cornish mines—but particularly the ones around Redruth—and he'd also employed a veritable army of people to refurbish Oakland. He was a one-man whirlwind.

He was obviously determined to demonstrate his kindly, giving nature to her.

"Ha!" As if such transparent acts were likely to convince her that he'd changed his stripes.

The sound of hooves pulled her from her contemplation of the rich American. Beth bustled out of the kitchen just as Elinor stood.

"You just eat, my lady. No doubt it's some needy soul come to interrupt your dinner. I'll get it," she muttered under her breath as she went to the vestibule.

Elinor sat. It hardly took two people to answer the door.

Her mouth was full of food when the door to the dining room flew open.

"It's Doctor Venable, my lady. Should I have him wait?"

Elinor finished chewing, swallowed some water, and wiped her mouth with her napkin. "Do we have any food to offer him?"

"Don't you worry, my lady, I've got plenty."

"Show him in."

Beth disappeared and the handsome figure of Jago Venable filled the doorway.

"I'm terribly sorry to interrupt your meal. I told your maid I could—"

Elinor gave him a genuine smile. She was always glad to see him, even though his visits were generally not social calls. "Come in, Jago. Please."

He glanced down at his dusty clothes.

Elinor stood. "If you don't come in and eat, I won't eat. And then Beth will lecture and scold you."

He gave her one of his gradual, serious smiles. "Well, we don't want that. I'll sit. Thank you, my lady. Er, Mrs. Atwood."

"Elinor."

He nodded. "Elinor."

"Did you just arrive?" she asked, making small talk until Beth brought food.

He gestured to her plate. "Please, eat. There is no point in your food becoming cold out of politeness." He saw her hesitate. "If you don't eat, I will leave and come back after dinner," he said, a mocking smile on his face as he echoed her chiding tone.

Elinor laughed and picked up her fork. "Well, we don't want that. You are a persuasive negotiator, Jago. While my mouth is full of food why don't you tell me why you are here? Not that I'm not pleased to see you, of course."

"I'm here on family business."

Elinor lowered her forkful of food. "You have family here?"

"Yes, this is where I am from. My brother was the Earl of Trebolton."

"Trebolton. But didn't he—"

"Yes, he died in a carriage accident at the beginning of the year."

"I'd heard that," she said, and then frowned. "But why have you only come now?" She grimaced. "I'm sorry, that was a forward question."

He smiled. "It was a logical question. I've been coming here each month to spend a week, just until I could find a replacement doctor for Trentham."

"Oh, Jago—I wish you'd told me, perhaps I might have helped you search for somebody."

"I had somebody in mind but needed to wait until he was free; he just arrived in Trentham a few days ago. So," he shrugged. "Here I am."

# The Footman

The door opened and Beth entered bearing a tray heaped with bread, half a fowl, most of a meat pie, a mountain of potatoes, and a tall glass of amber liquid that could only be beer, no doubt yet another payment from some patient or other.

Jago's jaw dropped. "Oh, Miss MacFarlane, you needn't have gone to so much trouble."

"Pish-tush," Beth muttered. "You look like a skellington, doctor. Doesn't that fool Mary Fardle know how to feed a man?"

Jago smiled at Beth's chiding. "Mrs. Fardle is an exemplary housekeeper and cook. I'm afraid I'm often too busy to partake in the wonderful fare she prepares."

Beth shot Elinor a dirty look. "Oh, aye, I'm familiar with that, doctor."

Elinor fought the urge to roll her eyes. "Thank you, Beth. We'll ring if we need anything else." *Like a lecture on eating habits.*

Beth sniffed loudly at this obvious dismissal and closed the door with a firm click.

"I'm sorry, Jago. I'm afraid Beth and I have settled into the way of two old spinsters and don't hesitate to give each other the word with the bark still on it." She watched him cut a piece of meat and put it in his mouth. She'd have to let him eat before she could indulge her curiosity. Instead, she had news of her own.

"Stephen Worth has bought a house not far from here. He has also bought the Redruth mine."

Jago chewed and washed his food down with a gulp of beer. "I know."

Elinor blinked.

"My sister-in-law sent me a letter," he explained. "She lives at Lenshurst Park with my two nieces."

"Ah, yes of course. I have not met Lady Trebolton, but I've heard of her good work in the area."

"She is a kind and very sweet-natured woman. I believe you would like her, Elinor. And my nieces are charming girls."

"These past months must have been a terrible time for them all. How did you find things at Lenshurst Park?"

He put down his fork and took a deep swallow of beer. "I've not yet gone there."

"You came *here* first?"

His pale cheeks tinted. "I felt I owed it to you. I should have told you all those weeks ago, when I brought you here, but—"

Elinor waved his concern aside. "It doesn't matter." Something occurred to her. "I thought the family name of the Earls of Trebolton was Crewe?"

"It is. Venable was my courtesy title—Viscount Venable. I took the name as a surname to spare my family the embarrassment of being associated with my low profession." He picked up his fork and for a few moments the clink of cutlery was the only sound in the room.

Elinor was no longer hungry but continued to eat; it was better to have something to do than to figure out what she should say next.

Jago saved her that worry. "I know how deeply you care for the people of Trentham—I just wanted to come here first to reassure you that they are in excellent hands. I'm sorry I must abandon them."

"You are not abandoning them, Jago, you are being called to your duty. There is plenty of good that can be done in this area. As you well know."

His smile was fleeting and bitter. "As I well know," he echoed. "You have seen Worth?" he asked, his already flushed skin darkening a little more.

She nodded and stared at her half-full plate. If she didn't eat, Beth would scold her. She took another forkful of food and chewed.

"Did he tell you of our meeting?"

Again she nodded, taking a drink of water to wash down food that now stuck in her throat like gravel.

"I'm sorry, Elinor."

"Why? Because you struck him?"

He gave her an almost boyish grin. "No, I enjoyed that. I'm sorry for what my actions told him, though. I didn't know if you'd want him to think—"

"You did nothing wrong, Jago. He'd already learned enough from his uncle to put everything together."

"Are you sure you won't—"

"Yes, Jago, I'm sure I won't marry you, but again, thank you for your kindness. You are an important man and there will be many contenders for your hand." She grinned. "Even more than when you were just a humble doctor."

He grimaced. "Please don't remind me. That is a part of my new role I do not relish."

That was the first time Elinor had ever heard the man even vaguely reference women. What had happened to make him so bitter about women or marriage? The thought surprised her. Surely she should be the first person to sympathize with somebody who didn't want to marry? But Jago was a man, what danger did a *man* face in a marriage?

"There is something else I must tell you, Elinor." He removed his glasses and began to polish them with a small cloth he pulled from a waistcoat pocket. The action was a nervous one and the removal of his spectacles—his vision—told her he didn't want to see her when he shared his news.

"What is it?"

"It's Worth. He's offered me a great deal of money to design a hospital."

"But . . . but that's *wonderful*, Jago! Why do you look so nervous?"

"He wants to build the hospital in Camborne."

"Oh, he wants to build it here." She would no longer be necessary.

"You will still be necessary, Elinor," he said, as if reading her mind. "And I don't believe he is doing it to, er, lessen your contribution but perhaps to relieve some of the pressure."

Elinor's emotions were like a tangle of embroidery silks. How could she *not* be happy the area would have something many larger, more populated towns and counties did not boast? How could she be so childish as to feel as if he were disturbing her world? Was that really why she was here—to gather admiration from people? Or was she here to make their lives better? A hospital would without a doubt improve people's lives. She looked up and found Jago watching her.

"This will be a very good thing for the area."

"Very good." He swallowed. "The amount of money he has pledged is, well, it is astronomical. Enough to have a proper hospital and a dispensary. And he has placed the design and implementation under my control. Do you know what this means, Elinor? A hospital created by the people who will actually work there?"

"It is a dream come true—better, really. I am glad for you, Jago. You are a good doctor—and a good man—Mr. Worth couldn't have chosen better."

He flushed. "I hope this is not forward of me, Elinor, but I will need your help."

It was her turn to blush. "*My* help? What do I know of hospitals or their design?" Her eyes narrowed. "Did Worth put you up to this? Is this part of the condition for—"

"Your name was never mentioned. Do you really think I would conduct negotiations with you as some sort of powerless pawn?" For the first time in their almost five-year association the retiring doctor looked haughty and proud. He looked, she realized, every inch what he was: an earl.

"I apologize, Jago. Of course you wouldn't. And I would be pleased to help in any way I am able."

He seemed to deflate before her very eyes and she realized just how worried he'd been about the disclosure. She also realized he'd cleaned his plate.

"Would you like some desert? I know Beth has an apple tart."

He shook his head. "As delightful as that sounds, I'd better complete my journey."

"You came all this way on horseback and without any possessions?" she asked as she accompanied him toward the vestibule.

"Worth's man—Fielding—was bringing Worth's carriage and another coach and offered to take my few possessions. It would have been wasteful and churlish to refuse the kind offer. They have gone on ahead to drop my things off at Lenshurst." He picked up his dusty hat and gave it a few turns before meeting her eyes. "Please know that I am always your friend first, Elinor. My association with Worth is—"

Elinor put her hand on his and squeezed lightly. "I know that, Jago. I'm not at war with Mr. Worth and I don't fault you for your association with him. He's a powerful, wealthy man who seems interested in doing good." She smiled wryly, "At least at the moment. I think you are just the man to advise him."

"I don't know about that, but I certainly will help him spend his money on a hospital."

# The Footman

Elinor watched as the doctor cantered down the rutted drive under the moonlight. It did not surprise her to hear he was the son of an earl. She'd always known he was a gentleman. Obviously there was more to his story than she would have guessed. An estrangement with his brother at the very least.

As for the hospital? She'd been honest with him, but not entirely so. Stephen had embarked on a campaign and she was the ultimate objective. This time, unlike the last, he was leaving acts of kindness in his wake. But he was still working on a plan. A plan that involved her but did not consult her. He might have changed—although she wasn't sure of that—but his methods had not.

# Chapter Thirty-One

*Redruth, Cornwall*
*1817*

"I t needs to go up a little on the right," Stephen said.

The workmen jostled the priceless painting while trying to lift it and Stephen fought the urge to squeal like a little girl as the gilt frame smacked against the wood paneled wall.

"That's good enough," he yelled the instant they came anywhere close to what he wanted. He would level the damned thing later himself. Maybe he'd get Fielding to—

Like a djinn summoned by Stephen's thoughts, Fielding's voice came from behind him.

"Why is it okay to show women getting their kit off if you throw in a few cherubs, some harps, and a table full of food?"

Stephen turned to find his huge employee eating an apple. His black eyes moved from the painting to Stephen as he chewed, his expression curious and patient.

Stephen snorted when he realized he was waiting. "Oh, I apologize. Was that a question you actually wished me to answer?" He didn't wait for a response. "Did you bring everything I asked for?"

Fielding made him wait while he chewed before finally swallowing. "Aye."

Stephen began walking before he gave into his urge and throttled the man.

"You haven't changed your mind?" he snapped without looking back to see if Fielding was following.

"No."

"Well, come and get your final pay packet and then you can bugger off."

A low chuckle floated behind him. "You miss me already, I reckon."

"Ha!" Stephen flung open the door to his library. The room was the first he'd seen to after buying the place. Peter Cantwell had squeezed a fortune out of his mine but he hadn't spent a groat on Oakland or its tenants.

Naturally, Stephen had investigated the man before making the offer and knew exactly what Cantwell spent his money on: gaming and young girls. *Very* young girls.

He could only hope he and Fielding had instilled enough fear into the loathsome pedophile that he wouldn't look at anyone under fifty until he was far too old to do anything about it.

Stephen had stripped the house to the bare bones before he could spend a night in it. He didn't like to think of touching anything Cantwell had put his hands on. The library and master suite had been the first to enjoy a complete renovation but he was almost finished with the house's common areas and was applying some of the finishing touches, like those he'd just been supervising in the gallery.

He flung himself into the plush leather chair behind his desk and took a small ring of keys from his waistcoat pocket. Inside the lowest drawer was a pre-prepared packet for his now ex-servant. Stephen tossed him the money.

The burly man caught the leather pouch and peered inside before closing his massive fist around it.

"So, what are your plans, John?"

"Well, *Stephen,*" he said, using his Christian name for the first time, a habitual sneer twisting his lips. "I reckon I'll go and take care of my own business now."

Stephen opened his mouth and then hesitated.

"Save your breath to cool your porridge," Fielding advised.

Stephen shrugged. "Fair enough. I was only going to tell you to consider my own experience before you do anything . . . irrevocable."

Fielding gestured to the decanter on his desk.

"You could give me a drink along with my lecture."

"An excellent idea." Stephen poured them both a glass.

Fielding took the cut crystal glass in his six-fingered hand. "My situation is not the same as yours, Worth."

"Revenge is revenge, John." He raised his glass and touched it against Fielding's. "Here is to letting bygones be bygones."

The other man's hideously scarred face twisted into something that made Stephen's blood turn cold.

"And here's to taking back what is yours."

They drank.

Fielding drained his glass in one long swallow and set it down with a thump. He smirked. "Good luck with the *new leaf* you're turning over. If you find yourself tempted to give away all your possessions and go live the life of a holy man, let me know. I'll be glad to take your traveling chaise, those chestnuts, and Blackfriars off your hands."

Stephen laughed and stood. "You will be the first person I think of." He extended his hand and they shook, as equals, for the first time since the day they'd met six years earlier, when Stephen had freed him from the brutal penal colony. "Don't be a complete stranger, John."

Fielding rolled his eyes and strode to the door, slamming it behind him without another word.

He let out a heavy sigh and sat back in his chair. Fielding was right about one thing: Stephen would miss the inscrutable, willful, annoying, rude, disobedient man.

He would also hope the other man's long banked rage didn't flame, burn out of control, and almost ruin his life—and the one he loved—as Stephen's had.

"But people don't listen to advice, do they, Jeremiah?" He smiled across at the portrait of the old man he'd had shipped from Boston once he knew he was going to remain in England.

The painter had captured Jeremiah Siddons's most riveting feature: the lively, intelligent twinkle in his blue eyes.

Stephen lifted his glass in a gesture that was half toast and half prayer for the friend who'd just left.

# The Footman

"Be wiser than me, John, and maybe you'll also be happier."

***

John Fielding tucked the money into the inner pocket of his coat and ignored the slightly whiney inner voice that told him he should stay and forget about Falkirk and vengeance.

But it wasn't a matter of making a choice: he *had* to finish the matter before he could move on with his life.

He liked Stephen Worth well enough; Lord knew the man paid better than any other employer on either this miserable little island or in the entire state of Massachusetts. But John didn't need money. He'd already earned a packet in his years with Worth. A man would have to be an imbecile not to. It had been very simple, actually. Every pay period he'd asked Worth to invest half his pay for him. At first the other man had wanted to explain finances and investments. John had finally told him, as bluntly as he could, that he didn't give a damn about the *how* of making money, he just wanted enough to do the things he needed to do. To pay back the man who'd tossed him like garbage into the gutter: his father, the Duke of Falkirk.

Just thinking the name lit a fire beneath the cauldron of anger that always simmered in his gut. He felt his face twist into what must surely be a hideous expression as he jogged down the immense, curved staircase, ignoring the frightened gasp of a maid as he passed.

John wasn't a religious man, but he believed in at least one part of the Bible, and he had no intention of letting bygones be bygones. He'd already tried that. He'd also tried fighting—letting men beat on him until the pain was *almost* enough to make him forget the tight, burning ball of hatred that had taken up permanent residence in his belly.

When pain hadn't worked, he'd tried drinking to drown the nagging, clawing, soul-destroying obsession. But hate, it seemed, could float to the surface, as vile things often were wont to do.

No, he would have no rest, no peace, no *life* until he'd visited the iniquity of the fathers on the children, to the third and the fourth generation if necessary.

John didn't think he was God, of course, but if it was good enough for the Lord, it was good enough for John Fielding.

He'd left his soft leather bag—his only luggage—packed and waiting in the foyer. He ignored the nervous glances of the footmen and snatched up the bag on his way out the door and headed for the stables.

John always saddled his own horse since the damned beast had bitten and kicked every other person who'd ever touched him. As he trod the buckled cobbles around the side of the manor, he absently observed the army of workmen busy transforming the grounds and structure back to its former glory. Oakland couldn't hold a candle to Blackfriars, but Worth had still managed to work his magic on the place and bring out its ancient, quiet dignity. Or, at least, Worth's gobs of money had.

Fielding had enjoyed watching the old place shed years of waste and neglect and become something worth having. It had made him think he might like a place of his own. Not yet, of course—not until he finished his business—but one day.

The jovial Cornish lad, Jory, had the massive stable door on two sawhorses and was affixing wide metal straps around its ancient timbers. He paused in his hammering and gave John a pleasant smile. Unlike most people, the boy always looked John in the eyes.

"Good afternoon, Mr. Fielding."

John grunted and ducked under the low lintel into the cool, dimness of the stables. The entire building was old, but the worn oak planking was truly ancient and grooves ran down the middle of the broad aisle where thousands of men must have walked over the years. They would've all believed their lives were important and somehow more vivid than those who'd come before them. And yet they were dead now and none of their dreams, desires, or petty differences signified a good goddamn anymore.

John knew he was no different than any other man—alive or long dead. Did his wants and needs and plans even matter in the long, long scheme of life? Was Worth right? Was John pursuing a hollow victory—just as Stephen Worth had done? John didn't think so. His employer's situation had differed from his in a key way. Worth should have realized he loved Lady Trentham long before he hurt her. He also should have recognized that she was not the villain of the piece, but just another victim who—

"There now, that's a good fellow. You're just misunderstood, aren't you? Aww, there's a gentle, good boy." The voice was a soft, low crooning and it came from the stall where John kept his horse. The stall he'd forbidden anyone to enter except himself. He froze and listened.

"Do you want another, hmm?" A low chuckle. "Well, just one more. We don't want you getting a sour stomach right before your trip, do we?"

John recognized the voice: it was one of Worth's postilions—the newest one, a tall, thin blond lad named Ben Piddock. John had hired Ben when Worth's other postilion suddenly left. Piddock had been loitering around one of the bigger posting houses on the North Road on their last trip to London. There was something odd about the boy, something—

Piddock came out of the stall and careened right into him.

"Ooof!" His slight body flew backwards and he bounced off the wall, staggering to catch his balance.

John automatically reached out to help and his hands twitched as his brain tried to identify what it was he'd just felt.

"Oh! Mr. Fielding, sir. I'm very sorry." Piddock's blue eyes were as large as proverbial saucers.

"You're not supposed to go in there."

Ben cleared his throat. "I just had a few apples I brought for the horses and he'd not had one, so, er—" He petered out under John's gaze.

John kept the boy pinned with a glare as he considered pursuing the issue. He finally shrugged. What did it matter that Piddock had disobeyed? John was leaving anyhow. He shouldered past the boy and went into the stall. His horse was waiting for him, his ears flat back, as always.

"Fetch my tack," he threw over his shoulder. If the boy wanted to linger around John's possessions, at least he could make himself useful.

"Aye, sir."

Fetching tack was a stable boy's job and most postilions would have rebelled at such an order. Ben obviously knew better. John bent down and began checking his horse's hooves. It was a job he never delegated to others. Never entrust your safety to anyone but yourself; he'd learned that the hard way.

The sound of raised voices jolted John from his thoughts and made the horse nervously shift its weight and nicker. He was still holding the rear hoof and the sudden weight shift almost knocked him over.

"Damnit," he muttered, dropping the hoof and staggering backward.

"Mr. Fielding! Mr. Fielding!" It was Ben's voice, but oddly shrill.

"What the devil is it?" John snapped, pushing himself off the splintered stall wall and straightening slowly, his knees cracking like pistols.

"A cave in at Redruth!" The words reached the stall just as Ben skidded to a halt, his mouth open as he gasped for breath.

John grimaced. It seemed he wouldn't be leaving today, after all. "Take the fastest horse in the stables and go to Lenshurst Park. Get the earl and tell him to bring his doctor bag and come immediately to the mine."

Ben nodded, turned, and sprinted deeper into the stables to fetch a horse.

John picked up his saddle, which the boy had dropped in his excitement. As he did so, his brain made the connection it had been unconsciously struggling with since colliding with young Piddock earlier. *Breasts.* That was what he'd felt when the boy ran into him: Breasts.

# Chapter Thirty-Two

Redruth, Cornwall
1817

Elinor was enjoying a rare moment of privacy, reading up on splinting broken bones in the medical text Jago had given her, when the door to her sanctum flew open.

Beth stood in the open doorway, her face like parchment. "There's been an accident at the mine."

Elinor didn't need to ask which mine and was on her feet at the word *accident*. "I'll get my bag. Gather up all that bedding you were making into bandages. We'll take the gig in case we need to move anyone." She pressed her knuckles to her temple and stared at the doorframe as she composed a mental list. "And somebody needs to get a message to—"

A hand touched her shoulder and she looked up. "Yes?"

"It was Doctor Venable, er, Lord Trebolton who sent the message, my lady. And he didn't send it from the mine—he sent it from Oakland."

Elinor blinked. "Oakland? But I thought you said—"

"Mr. Worth has been hurt, my lady."

Beth was making no sense.

"Stephen was hurt at Oakland?"

"No, at the mine."

S.M. LaViolette

Elinor felt like she was taking part in a poorly written farce. She opened her mouth, but nothing came out.

Beth took her arm. "His lordship sent a carriage for you. I'll fetch everything you need and grab your hat and cloak."

"And my bag," Elinor added absently as she hurried toward the front door. Stephen was hurt.

"And your bag," Beth echoed.

Elinor recognized the tall, blond postilion who'd been eating an apple and sharing it with the horses. He stood beside the lead horse, scratching its ears. A footman waited beside the carriage door and moved to open it when he saw her.

She ignored the open carriage. "Tell me what happened," she demanded in a voice that didn't sound like it belonged to her.

The footman and postilion exchanged glances and, to Elinor's surprise, it was the postilion who spoke.

"One part of the stull collapsed while the men were reinforcing it. It was lucky Mr. Worth had stopped operations and there were only the six men." The boy paused and drew a shaky breath. His cheeks were as smooth as a girls' and his voice was at that fluty phase right before it changed. "Mr. Worth and Mr. Fielding went down to the area where the men were trapped. They made a sort of lever and were able to lift a corner. Mr. Worth was helping the last man from the wreckage when one of the pitch pine timbers snapped and fell on him."

Elinor felt as though she'd just been pushed off a cliff. "Is he—"

"He's alive, ma'am. Doctor Venable, that is, er, Lord Trebolton," the boy corrected, his cheeks reddening, "is with him. He sent me to fetch you, ma'am."

Beth bustled up beside her. "Come, my lady," she said, adjusting Elinor's cloak and lowering her hat onto her head. Dressing her, as if she were a child. The realization shook Elinor from her daze.

"Thank you, Beth." She tied the ribbon closed herself and glanced at the postilion. "What is your name?"

"Ben Piddock, ma'am." The boy pulled his forelock and cast his eyes downward.

*What long lashes he has!*

Elinor blinked at the foolish thought and nodded to the two servants.

278

# The Footman

"Let us make haste."

*** 

Oakland was barely a shadow by the time the carriage rolled to an abrupt stop in front of its entrance. The sky had been clear when they'd begun their journey but clouds obscured the moon midway and the postilion and footman had stopped to light the running lanterns for the second half of the journey.

The darkness fit Elinor's mood, which was gloomy and oddly . . . guilty.

*Ridiculous! I had nothing to do with the mine accident.*

*No, but he would not be doing all of this if not to curry favor with you,* her chastising conscience pointed out.

Elinor gave a snort of angry disbelief.

Beth leaned toward her, her eyes narrow with concern. "Is aught amiss, my lady?"

"It's nothing, Beth."

*Nothing but a guilty conscience.*

***

The front door swung open before Elinor had even reached the top step. A tall, bone-thin man dressed in the conservative black suit of an upper servant stood in the opening.

"Welcome, Mrs. Atwood. I am Palfrey, Mr. Worth's butler." He took her hat and cloak, surveying her from slitted gray eyes, his beaky nose tilted up like a hound sniffing the air. "If you will please follow me."

"Well!" Beth hissed in Elinor's ear as they followed the stiff-backed man up a flight of stairs. "He's right proud of himself, isn't he?"

Elinor couldn't help smiling. Beth still wasn't accustomed to her drop in status. As the maid of the Countess of Trentham she'd wielded respect—probably more than Elinor herself. As the maid of an eccentric woman who played at being a doctor? Well . . .

The house was a lovely example of neo-Palladian architecture that must have been built early in the prior century. It was a tasteful size for a country house and Elinor could see as the butler led them down the second story hallway that the wood paneling had been waxed and buffed to a shine and the coved ceiling was freshly painted. The dark wood floor was almost black with age and the carpet runner was ancient, the threadbare sections outnumbering those with any pile. Elinor found the worn carpet somehow endearing and found herself mourning its inevitable removal.

She shook her head at the foolish thought. This was probably the first and last time she would ever be in this house. What did she care if the new owner stripped the grand dame of a house down to her knickers and dressed her in newer, richer clothing?

The butler stopped at the second-to-last door and opened it.

Elinor hesitated as she approached the open doorway, an almost overwhelming sense of doom making her motions jerky and slow.

*Please, God, let him be all right.*

\*\*\*

Stephen was Iain again. Or Iain was Stephen. Either way, he was back to being just the one person and it was a relief. He was ill, in bed, and didn't have to do his morning chores.

His mother bustled around him like a fussy hen and he basked in her attention.

Her hand on his forehead was cool and soothing.

*"Has he regained consciousness?"* Her voice was muted and odd sounding.

Iain tried to tell her he was awake, but his mouth wouldn't open. That was strange.

Another voice—one Iain didn't recognize—answered. *"He's been unconscious since I set his arm. He refused to take laudanum—at first. We managed to get it down him once he began to fade."*

*"Any other injuries?"*

*"—to the head."* The voice faded in and out and in and out. *"—give him laudanum, but the—I felt it worth the risk."*

*"—think it is serious?"* Iain's mam asked.

*Ahhh, Mam, how he'd* missed *her!* A voice cut through the warm blanket of love that had wrapped around him.

*"—observation—needn't stay, Elinor—just wanted—appraised of the situation."*

*Elinor?*

A sharp female laugh cut the heavy air. *"Who else can nurse him? Fielding?"* The voice was tart and had no Scottish brogue. If not his mother, then who? Who?

Again he tried to open his mouth, or at least his eyes, but he was so *tired* it was all he could do to think. He was *tired*, he needed—

"*He's shivering, Jago.*"

"*—the drug—unpredictable and hallucinate—healing sleep—side effects.*"

Gentle hands drew a blanket up to his shoulders and tucked it in.

"*—stay—Beth holds—esteem.*"

A low chuckle—male this time—and a cool hand on his forehead. Somebody moaned.

"*Hesveryhot.*"

Iain squinted and concentrated to stop the words, but they wanted to slam into each other.

Opening his mouth was *so* difficult.

"*Murrrthhhh—*"

"*Hestryingtospeak Jago.*"

"*Idaresayhesjusttalkinginhissleepcomeletusgivehimsomepeaceandquiet.*"

Iain shut his ears. The noises weren't loud, but they were frustrating. His stomach growled. When was the last time he'd eaten?

A strawberry-filled cream cake the size of a dinner plate floated into view.

Cream cakes were his favorite.

Iain tried to reach for it. But his hand wasn't working. The cake floated away and warm tears slid down his cheeks.

"*Oh, Stephen—*"

Who was Stephen?

Who would milk the cow in the morning?

***

Rather than argue, Elinor let Beth take the first shift.

"That Mrs. Kennett is a right bossy one," Beth huffed, bustling around the small suite of rooms they'd been given and putting away Elinor's few items with more force than was necessary. "And you should have let me tell her to give us another room. It isn't right for you to have to share with me, my lady."

"You heard her. This is the only guestroom that has been finished, Beth. Apparently Mr. Worth is renovating the entire house to make it fit for him to live in," she added under her breath.

"Surely there's room in the servant's quarters?"

"There's a bed in the dressing room. Besides, we shan't both be in the room at the same time, one of us will always be with Mr. Worth."

"Hmph! Not if that Mrs. Kennett has anything to say about it. The way she makes it sound neither of us has the—"

Elinor thought she might just go mad. "Beth!"

The older woman's head jerked around, her eyes wide with surprise. "Yes, my lady?"

Elinor forced herself to speak calmly. "Shouldn't you relieve Mr. Worth's valet? Doctor Venable told him one of us would take over shortly."

Her eyes widened. "Oh, of course. If you don't need anything?"

"I'm fine. Mrs. Kennett is having a tray sent up and then I will get some sleep. I'll relieve you around five."

"You needn't, my lady. I'm perfectly—"

"I shall see you at five, Beth."

A loud sniff and head toss and Elinor was alone.

She collapsed onto the bed and groaned, wishing she'd taken Jago's suggestion.

"You could return home and leave Beth here," he'd said to Elinor once they'd stepped out into the hallway and left Stephen in the care of Nichols.

Elinor had been more than a little tempted by his suggestion.

She only realized her hand was resting on her stomach when she glanced down. She clenched her fingers and lowered her hand to her side before looking up, her face and neck hot.

"I will stay." She glanced away from his keen eyes, which had obviously caught the gesture. Neither of them said anything, but she knew they were both thinking similar thoughts: Worth was the father of her unborn child.

Venable nodded. "I will feel better if you are here to keep a close eye on him, at least for the next forty-eight hours until we can rule out the chance of any damage to his head. I noticed some unusual pupil dilation in one of his eyes."

Elinor caught her breath. "But that could—"

"Do not jump to the worst conclusion. Anisocoria can mean many things, Elinor. It's even possible it is a condition that predates this accident. In any event, watch for signs of concussion and send somebody to fetch me if necessary."

Elinor smiled. "You are an earl now, Jago. I can hardly send a servant to *fetch* you."

He shoved his shaggy black hair from his forehead and made a noise of frustration. "It would be a relief to do something I am competent at. Besides, it appears I may need to continue my profession if I'm to keep Lenshurst Park in candles."

She grimaced. "As bad as that, is it?"

"It is not good."

Elinor knew all too well how an estate could weigh upon a man and turn him bitter or mean. She could only hope her friend would avoid that fate.

"Well, I had better get along," he said when the silence became uncomfortable. "Don't hesitate to send for me if you need me."

Elinor knew she wouldn't send for him. After all, there was very little anyone could do for Stephen if he did have any sort of head injury. Only time and rest could heal such things.

She stared up at the blue brocade canopy above her bed and considered the conversation. She hoped Jago had exaggerated the extent of his financial problems because there was only one way to pull a large estate out of such problems—as Elinor knew only too well. She hated to think Jago would be forced to marry for money.

*** 

"He slept through the night," Beth said, the lavender half-moons beneath her eyes proof that she herself had not slept a wink.

Elinor squeezed the older woman's shoulder. "Go get some sleep, Beth."

For once her maid did not argue.

The sun had yet to come up and Stephen's room was lighted by a single candle and that behind a screen beside his bed. He lay in the same position he'd been in last night—as if he'd not moved. His chest moved up and down evenly and his brow was cool and dry to the touch; his fever seemed to have abated.

Elinor sat in the chair beside the bed and put her book on the table. It was too dim to read and she would prefer to watch him, in any case.

His copper hair was striking against the white bed linen but his skin was pale, nothing like his usual vibrant coloring. She could see his freckles, which were normally obscured by his heathy glow. His mouth—those strong, shapely lips—was far softer in repose and there were faint crescents etched at the corner, lines that came from that mocking, lopsided smile he was so adept at flashing. His jaw and chin glinted with flecks of red and gold and Elinor's fingers twitched to stroke him.

She sat on her hands.

His right arm lay atop the blankets, splinted from his fingers to his elbow. He wore a nightshirt, which he'd not done during their three days together. It was fine white linen, open at the throat, exposing a tangle of auburn hair. She'd never seen him in even this much light. The darkness she'd hidden in when they'd made love had hidden him, as well.

She bit her lip. What a pity she'd missed all those opportunities to explore him with her eyes. He was lovely, muscular and bronze and—

She realized her breathing had quickened and forced herself to look away from him, studying instead the toes of her blue slippers. Beth had, naturally, packed her nicest day dresses and her best two pairs of slippers, neither of which she'd worn during the months she'd lived in Redruth.

*You should leave,* the prudish, hectoring voice in her mind advised.

Elinor knew that to be very good advice. Even asleep he could discountenance her. What would it be like when he was awake and—

"Ellie?"

Her head shot up.

His green eyes were wide with surprise. "What are you doing here?" he asked, his voice hoarse. He lifted his arm, as if to shove back the hair on his forehead and winced. "What happened?" He looked at his arm, a wrinkle of confusion forming between his eyes.

"You don't remember?"

"Remember what?"

"Yesterday—at the mine?"

He blinked rapidly.

*Oh God, please don't let him have lost his memory! Please don't—*

"The men were trapped." He shot her a frantic glance. "Are they, did they—"

Elinor was almost dizzy with relief. She shook her head. "They're fine, Stephen. All of them. In fact, you are the only one who was seriously injured."

He looked at his arm.

"It was a clean break and should heal nicely."

He carefully laid his arm down. "Did you . . ."

"No, Doctor Venable set it. You don't recall any of it?"

He stared at the ceiling, as if searching for answers. "The last thing I remember is Fielding and I levering up the fallen section and then," he paused, his forehead creasing, "and then there was a loud snapping sound."

"One of the timbers gave way and you were caught by it."

He nodded, turning away from the ceiling to look at her. "My mouth—there's an odd taste?" He wrinkled his nose.

"Laudanum. Doctor Venable gave you some when he set your arm."

"Ah, that explains my head."

"Does it hurt?"

"Like the devil." He grimaced, lifting his left hand to rub his temple.

"Would you like me to fix you a headache powder?"

He shook his head and then made a pained face. "I'll just wait it out."

"Would you like something to eat?"

"What I'd really like is some coffee."

Elinor hesitated. "One cup—but only if you eat something along with it."

His mouth twitched into a smile; there was the blasted dimple. Elinor went to the door before she gibbered like an infatuated fool. A footman sat on a chair beside the door and shot to his feet.

"Yes, ma'am?"

"Would you please have the kitchen send up breakfast?"

"Yes, ma'am. Beggin' your pardon Mrs. Atwood, but is he—"

"He's alive and well and wants his coffee."

The young man grinned, his expression one of relief. "Very good, ma'am." He was half-way down the hall before she'd even turned around. Elinor had noticed the servants appeared to adore their master.

When she returned to the bed, he'd pushed himself up and was leaning against the massive mahogany headboard. He looked remarkably awake. And remarkably handsome.

She frowned and went to the table Nichols had set up beneath the window. There were several vials labeled in Jago's careful hand. Two doses of laudanum and a headache powder.

"Elinor?"

She schooled her face into an impassive expression and turned.

"Yes, Mr. Worth."

His eyes reproached and caressed and pleaded. "Elinor."

She scowled. "I did not give you leave to use my name."

"I love you." He spoke the words in a quiet dignified way that sucked the air from the room.

She opened her mouth but no sounds came out.

"Don't worry, I won't press my suit." He threw both dimples at her this time. "At least not while you are here as an angel of mercy. But I don't see the sense in pretending we are strangers. Besides, you used my name only a few moments ago."

The door opened and saved her from further gaping.

"Good morning, Mr. Worth." It was Mrs. Kennett, herself, carrying the tray.

Elinor could only stare. How had the woman even made it from the kitchen to the bedroom in such a short time? Not to mention how she'd managed to assemble a tray of food.

The housekeeper turned her beaming face from Stephen to Elinor and it was as if a cloud passed over the sun.

"Mrs. Atwood," she said flatly.

Good Lord! What had the woman heard about Elinor to cause such frosty treatment?

Stephen didn't seem to notice. He grinned up at the older woman. "Mmm, it smells delicious, Kenny."

Mrs. Kennett preened at the nickname.

Elinor couldn't decide if she wanted to vomit or choke the smug, boyish look from his face. She did neither, instead, moving toward the bed to assist with the tray.

"Sit up," she ordered more sharply than she'd intended.

He did so, his face a study in complacent satisfaction, as if having two women fretting over him was his natural due.

Elinor rammed a cushion down between his back and the headboard and he grunted and gave her an innocent, questioning look.

Mrs. Kennett came between them, her expression of mortification proclaiming more loudly than words what she thought of Elinor's violent nursing.

"Here, you are, sir. Cook has made your coffee nice and strong, just as you like it." She lifted a lid from one of the chaffing dishes. "And here are two nice eggs with some soldiers."

Elinor glanced down; sure as anything, there were uniform slices of toasted bread along with two boiled eggs with their tops already removed, as if the invalid might not be able to wield a butter knife.

She rolled her eyes.

"Thank you, Kenny." He went to rub his hands together and then stopped, glancing from his incapacitated right hand to the tray.

"Do you need assistance eating, sir?" Mrs. Kennett asked in a nauseatingly worshipful tone.

Elinor would pack her bags before she'd witness such a thing.

Stephen shot Elinor a sly look, as if he could hear her thoughts. "Thank you, Kenny, but I shall do just fine with my left hand." His smile grew. "And Mrs. Atwood will be here to assist me if I should need help."

Mrs. Kennett made a *hrmphing* sound that showed what she thought of that. She cast several suspicious looks in Elinor's direction before finally closing the door behind her.

"Disgusting," she muttered.

"I beg your pardon?" Stephen looked up from the cup of coffee the housekeeper had poured for him.

"Nothing."

He smirked. "Would you like a cup of coffee? It seems Kenny brought a pot."

Elinor considered rejecting the offer—just so she could reject the offer—but decided a cup of coffee was more important than putting him in his place.

She poured herself a cup and sat down.

They sipped in silence.

He dipped one of his "soldiers" into the decapitated egg and offered the yolk-drenched tip to her, his auburn eyebrows forming elegant arches.

She snorted. "You'd best concentrate on feeding yourself."

He grinned and bit the toast in half. Elinor studied him while he chewed, unable to look away. His hair stuck out at odd angles, he had a plaster on his forehead and bruises on his cheekbone and chin, yet he was still as enticing as an open flame.

Elinor wished suddenly—and *fiercely*—that their child would inherit his coloring, his physical beauty, and, yes, even his clever, relentlessly scheming mind.

He cocked his head at her and swallowed his mouthful of food. "What are you thinking about to make you look so intense?"

"I was thinking I need to go and feed Daisy and Matilda," she lied.

His eyebrows dipped. "Daisy and Matilda?" He slathered another sliver of toast in egg yolk and again offered it to her.

She shook her head. "My pig and cat."

"Mmmmmph." He chewed and washed down the mouthful of food with a swig of coffee before wiping his mouth. "Send one of the servants to do that."

Elinor's eyes narrowed at his arrogant, peremptory tone and he lifted both hands in a placating gesture and then winced, lowering his right arm back to the bed.

"I'm sorry, Elinor, I didn't mean to command. I only meant to offer."

She bit her tongue, reminding herself she was here to help him rest, not to bicker with him.

"I would have a bite of toast and egg."

He brightened and quickly prepared another soldier. When he handed it to her she took the toast with her fingers, ignoring his obvious disappointment that she hadn't allowed him to feed her.

"I'd like to thank you for coming, Elinor."

# The Footman

She chewed, glad her mouth was full of food so she didn't have to answer.

"I know you're very busy and this is an inconvenience." He paused. "As much as I would love for you to stay, I want you to know Mrs. Kennett and Nichols would be able to take care of me. I daresay I will be up and about tomorrow, if not today."

Emotions warred inside her at his words. Did he *want* her to go?

"Although I do wish you would stay."

She blinked. Was her face really that easy for him to read?

She finished her piece of toast before speaking. "Doctor Venable is concerned you might have a concussion."

"Oh?"

"Yes, he noticed some unequal pupil dilation in your eyes, which is sometimes a sign of head trauma."

"Is that so?" he asked politely, as if they were discussing the weather rather than possible brain damage.

"Yes, that is so," she said a bit tartly. "I'm to stay and observe you until the immediate danger has passed."

"Excellent!" He smiled as though she'd just told him his horse had won pots of money at Epsom.

Elinor's lips twitched.

"How long am I in immediate danger?" He poured himself a second, unauthorized, cup of coffee.

She looked pointedly at the cup. "If you survive until tomorrow you will most likely be fine."

"Any chance of a relapse?" He raised his cup, a hopeful look on his face.

"Only if something else hits you on the head."

# Chapter Thirty-Three

Mrs. Kennett came to relieve Elinor a full hour before the agreed-upon time.

"He's been sleeping since he finished his lunch," Elinor told her after they'd stepped out into the hallway to converse. Indeed, Stephen had fallen asleep directly after breakfast and only woken long enough to eat again and fall asleep. The rest was not only good for him, but also good for her frazzled nerves. It was far easier to watch him sleep than to talk to him.

The housekeeper nodded stiffly and Elinor once again wondered why the woman seemed to dislike her.

"Doctor Venable—that is, Lord Trebolton—asked that I stay through tomorrow. My maid will be going back to my cottage, so there will only be me for dinner. I will relieve you at ten o'clock."

Mrs. Kennett opened her mouth, an argumentative gleam in her eye, but then must have seen something in Elinor's expression that made her close it and nod.

Elinor left the woman to tend to her patient and went to find Beth.

She wasn't surprised to find her in the dressing room, but she was not asleep. Instead, she was ironing Elinor's best gown.

She looked up when Elinor entered the generously sized room. "Good afternoon, my lady. You'll be wanting a nap. I'll finish this later so you can lie down."

"I'm not sleepy, Beth," she said, sitting on the royal blue velvet bench in front of the vanity. "I'm going to take a walk first. Did you happen to bring my half-boots?"

Beth grimaced. "Aye." She rummaged through the bag and extracted Elinor's homely, worn walking boots.

"Thank you, I will manage them, go ahead and finish your ironing." Elinor kicked off her slippers. "When you are done with the dress, I'd like you to go back home. Somebody will need to feed Daisy and Matilda is probably frantic by now."

To her surprise, Beth merely nodded. "Aye. Doctor Venable already sent Mr. Worth's postilion over yesterday to check on them."

Elinor looked up from her half-laced boot. "Ben Piddock?"

Beth nodded. "It seems the boy is going to work for his lordship."

That was odd—why would Jago want a postilion if he was having money problems? And why would he hire Stephen's employee if he *did* want a post boy? She shrugged and resumed lacing her boot. Men and horses and carriages and such; who knew what they did or why they did it?

She took her cloak from the peg and tied on her rather worn bonnet.

"I'll send fresh clothes back with the footman, my lady."

"Oh, I shouldn't bother," Elinor said, tying the faded brown ribbon beneath her chin. "I doubt I'll need more than what you've already brought. I'll most likely be leaving tomorrow."

Again Beth surprised her and merely grunted, rather than arguing.

The gardens around Oakland were reputed to be some of the finest in the area. Elinor could see they'd suffered from long-term neglect although a veritable army of gardeners swarmed both the park that lay off to west as well as the cultivated areas on the south and east sides. She opted for the small section of wood that lay between the house and the road.

The sun was unseasonably warm and she'd not gone very far before she regretted bringing her heavy cloak. Still, it was too beautiful and she was too restless to go back to the house so she tossed the flaps over her shoulders and pushed deeper into the spectacular stand of Cornish Elms.

Spending time with Stephen today—even when he'd been sleeping—had made her realize she could not live in such proximity to him before he would eventually wear down her defenses. Unfortunately, she could also not go back to Trentham, either. That left her with the choice of going somewhere new.

She gazed up at the thick canopy of leaves over her head. Although it was heading into winter in the rest of England the trees in Cornwall still held on to much of their foliage. She'd grown to love Cornwall in the brief time she'd lived here. She did not want to move. She also didn't think Beth could survive another move. Oh, she'd come with Elinor—she was too loyal to leave her—but she'd be deeply unhappy.

Elinor knew Stephen Worth wasn't the only one hoping she'd change her mind and marry him. Beth was another, and Elinor even got the feeling Jago's true feelings were that she owed it to her unborn child to give him or her a father—although not necessarily Stephen. Yes, Jago would marry her and she knew he would be a kind and good husband. But it was hardly fair to marry one man when you were in love with another.

She stooped and picked up a twig, viciously stripping it to bits as she trudged through the trees, chased by thoughts of marriage and duty.

She'd married for duty once before and look where it had gotten her. Oh, it was true her first marriage had not been her choice to make. But she could have fought it, even if it would have left her an outcast in her own family. Instead, she'd married Edward to save the family fortunes. Was this any different?

Stephen was not the monster Edward had been, but he was still a man and he would expect his wife to obey him. She'd never seen him become heated. Indeed, even at his angriest he'd become cold rather than violent. He wouldn't beat her, or, God forbid, their child. His servants and employees adored him, so he wasn't cruel. Edward had been notoriously unkind, selfish, and brutal—nothing about his treatment after they'd married had been a surprise.

Still, Stephen's coldly, carefully plotted revenge was something she could not—indeed, *should* not—forget. Even though he'd come to care for her in their time together—and she knew he had—his feelings had done nothing to stop his unforgiveable behavior.

*Is it really so unforgivable? Yes, he behaved like a beast, but he certainly had motivation after what your family did to him. He could have shamed you publicly but didn't. If word of your three nights got out it would be Charles or your family who said anything—not Stephen.*

Elinor snorted at the weaseling voice. *So, I should be grateful he didn't behave more appallingly and forgive him, is that what you're saying?*

The sound of a baby crying broke into her futile mental argument and she stepped off the well-worn path, following the sound through the trees to a tiny cottage. Elinor caught her breath—it was utterly charming, like the oversized dollhouse she'd had as a child. There was a tiny porch with vine-covered trellises and a rocking chair where a woman sat with a squalling bundle. Elinor was about to turn around when the woman looked up and smiled.

"Hello," she called, her voice that of a girl, or at least a very young woman.

As Elinor came closer, she saw the other woman was beautiful—one of the loveliest she'd ever seen. "I'm sorry to disturb you. I didn't mean to trespass."

The girl—she couldn't have been more than sixteen—giggled. She tossed an escaped blond curl over her shoulder. "You'm not trespassing, mum. This be Mr. Worth's land." She gave Elinor a shy glance from beneath lashes that were thick like tiny blonde brooms. "You'm the doctor lady, aye?"

Elinor smiled and bent low to look at the child. "Yes, I'm Mrs. Atwood. And your baby is very lovely." She spoke the truth. The child had the same shock of strawberry blonde hair and china blue eyes as her mother. "What's her name?"

"Emblyn, after me *mabm vejydh.*"

Elinor's eyebrows shot up and the girl laughed at whatever she saw on Elinor's face.

"What your sort call a godmother, mum."

"Ah, I see." Elinor glanced at the blue-and-yellow gingerbread trim that edged the top of the porch. "And is this your godmother's house?"

She shook her head and one of her curls brushed the baby's cheek and made her gurgle. "No, mum, my own home, Mr. Worth seen to it. Oh!" Her hand flew to her lips, which were pink, bow-shaped pillows.

"Is something the matter?" Elinor asked.

The girl kept her hand over her mouth tightly, as if more words might slip out, and violently shook her head. Her enormous blue eyes shimmered with tears.

"My goodness, there is no need to be afraid. Please, don't cry, I won't—"

"Kerensa! What are you doing?"

Elinor jumped at the voice, knowing before she turned who it belonged to.

"Mrs. Kennett," she said, not bothering to hide her surprise.

The older woman's eyes swiveled between Elinor and the girl and back. "I didn't leave Mr. Worth alone," she said, defensive. "Doctor Venable was there and said I might return in an hour." The look she fixed on Elinor told her it was her turn to explain her presence.

Elinor refused to do so. Instead, she turned to the girl—Kerensa. "It was a pleasure to meet you and your baby." She smiled into the girl's wide, startled eyes, and nodded to the housekeeper. "Mrs. Kennett."

Elinor felt two sets of eyes on her back as she left the small glade.

\*\*\*

Stephen eyed Venable from beneath lowered lids as he re-wrapped the bandage on his right arm.

"How is your head feeling today, Mr. Worth?" The doctor asked the question without looking up.

"A bit muzzy, but otherwise I feel fine."

He saw the other man's lips curl. "And your vision? Any problems?"

Stephen hesitated. What was he getting at? "No, it's the same as usual."

Venable glanced up. "Which means you can't see out of one of your eyes?"

Stephen's mouth opened.

"I guessed as much from our brief, er, confrontation in Trentham."

294

Stephen snorted. "You mean when you gave me a leveler?"

"Come, Mr. Worth, you've got a good three stone on me and we both know the only reason I knocked you down was because you let me. You never even flinched when I swung—I thought about it later and realized you never saw my fist coming."

His dry words and wry expression made Stephen laugh. "I deserved what you did and more."

"Yes, you did," Venable agreed, fastening off the bandage that held the splint in place.

"So why are you helping me, Venable—or Trebolton now, I guess? That *is* what you're doing, isn't it? Getting Elinor here by falsely claiming my brain is addled?"

The quiet aristocrat flushed at Stephen's taunting tone. "To be perfectly honest, Worth—or is it Vale now, I guess?" He smiled, his tone a mocking echo. "I'm not entirely sure your brain is *not* addled after what you did to her."

Stephen's blood rushed to his head at the other man's words. But he bit his tongue. *You deserve that and more*, he told himself. Yes, he did. He took a deep breath to calm the near-deafening pounding in his head.

"You're correct, my lord." He looked down at his left hand, which had clenched into a fist without him realizing it.

Trebolton stood. "Yes, well, all men are fools at one time or another. Tell me about your eye," he said, turning away to place his instruments and rolls of cloth in his black leather bag.

Stephen shrugged. "What do you want to know?"

"When did it happen?"

"The night of June 11, 1802."

Trebolton nodded, not looking terribly surprised. But Stephen knew he'd read Elinor's statement to the magistrate. "What happened?"

"The former Earl of Trentham kicked me in the head. When I woke up, my vision had an enormous black spot in the middle. I suffered a couple more knocks a week later and then there was nothing."

"Any changes with this latest blow to the head?"

Stephen glanced up quickly. "No. Will there be?"

"Probably not, if there hasn't been already. Sometimes a subsequent trauma will change things, but usually not so long after the initial injury. My guess is the damage is permanent after so many years." He paused. "Does she know?"

"About my vision?"

Trebolton nodded.

"No, I didn't tell her."

The earl opened his mouth but then closed it without speaking.

"What?" Stephen demanded.

"I was going to say that perhaps you *should* tell her. And then I realized it was none of my business." He snapped his bag shut and stood. "I shan't call again, unless she sends for me. You may get up any time you like."

Stephen nodded.

"By the way, Ben Piddock came asking for a job at Lenshurst Park. It seems your man, Fielding, gave him the sack."

Stephen knew he'd sustained a knock on the head, but he distinctly recalled the surly man quitting. Fielding had sacked an employee on his way out the door? He frowned up at the earl. "Now I'm without a postilion?"

"So it would seem," Trebolton said coolly.

"Why do *you* need a postilion?" he snapped, annoyed by the other man's superior tone. He immediately wished he could take back the impertinent question. He'd heard about the earl's situation and knew the man was as poor as a church mouse.

Trebolton turned without answering, clearly finished with both the matter *and* Stephen.

He was about to close the door when Stephen stopped him. "Why?"

The earl sighed loudly but turned. "Why did I hire the boy?"

"Not that, why are you helping me?"

"I'm doing it for her—not for you." Trebolton's spectacles glinted and Stephen couldn't see his eyes. "She doesn't know how hard life will be for her and the child if she continues alone. And she will not marry me, although I have asked repeatedly." He shrugged. "Perhaps she will marry you." He turned away, leaving Stephen with his mouth hanging open.

# The Footman

"You *cheeky* bastard," Stephen muttered, glad the other man was gone after delivering such a bomb. He might be injured, but he might not have been able to resist trying to deliver his own leveler.

He considered the doctor's parting words. As annoying as it was to hear he'd had the audacity to ask for Elinor's hand in marriage, Stephen did feel a bit more optimistic to hear he wasn't the only one she insisted on *not* marrying.

There might be hope for him, but he had so very little time to make his mark on her heart and no idea how to do it.

# Chapter Thirty-Four

E linor had just stepped out of her bath—a luxury she'd not
enjoyed since leaving the Dower House—when there was a
knock on the door and one of the maids entered.

She curtsied to Elinor and held up a gown—one of
Elinor's best gowns. In fact, it was the one she'd worn to
dinner that last evening in London, the only item of clothing
she couldn't bear to part with.

"Beggin' your pardon, ma'am," the girl said, her eyes going to
Elinor's towel-clad person and blushing. "But Miss MacFarlane sent
this along for you."

"Thank you. You may hang it in the dressing room and go."

The girl hesitated.

"Yes?"

"Well, it's just that Mr. Worth has invited you to join him for
dinner, ma'am."

"I will be joining him at ten. But I will have eaten by then."

The girl looked unhappy.

Elinor let out a heavy sigh. "I take it he meant in the dining room?"

She nodded, her expression of relief almost comical.

"Very well. And you are here to assist me?"

Again she nodded, a hopeful smile spreading across her face.

"What is your name?"

"Betsy, ma'am."

"Well, Betsy, you'd better start with my hair."

\*\*\*

The girl chattered nonstop while her clever hands dressed Elinor's straight, heavy hair.

"Have you worked at Oakland long?" Elinor asked when there was a break in the conversation.

The girl looked up from the small cask of jewelry Beth had sent along with the dress and undergarments. "Only since Mr. Worth bought the place, ma'am. Me parents would never let me work here before." She rooted through the sparse collection of jewels. Elinor felt a pang when she recalled the star sapphires and how lovely they'd looked with this gown.

"Why is that, Betsy?" she asked, forcing her thoughts away from the lovely jewels and the fact she'd sold them.

"'Cause of Mr. Cantwell." The girl pulled a simple strand of pearls from the jewel box and frowned at them.

"Because of Mr. Cantwell?" Elinor persisted, nodding when Betsy held up the pearls for her approval.

"Aye, mum," Betsy said, her eyes on Elinor's reflection and her mind on something else as she lapsed into the local patois for "Missus." "It wern't good for girls here. Leastways not young ones."

Elinor half turned, until she'd garnered the girl's attention. "You mean Mr. Cantwell interfered with his servants?"

The girl's face flamed and her eyes widened, as if she'd only just realized what she'd been saying and whom she'd been saying it to.

"Oh, please, mum, I'd get that much of a wallopin' if Mrs. Kennett knew I'd said such things. Please don't—"

"Shhh, Betsy," Elinor said, turning back to the mirror. "Of course I won't run and tell tales to Mrs. Kennett."

"Oh, thank you, mum. I've a way of runnin' on, so me tas says." She stepped back to admire her work and it was clear that Elinor would get no more out of her tonight.

\*\*\*

Stephen was surprised when Elinor actually came to dinner. He'd told the stables to be prepared with a carriage if she decided she wanted to go home. He wanted her here, but he would not keep her if she meant to go.

She wore the purplish-blue gown—the one that made her look like a serious, beautiful fairy. She was as slim as she'd been that night and he couldn't help wondering if she wasn't eating enough.

He went to meet her as the maid left her at the door. He held out his arm and she laid one small kid-gloved hand on his sleeve. He was surprised to see her wearing the matching gloves he'd bought, as she'd not done so the first time.

"I wore them for Betsy, not for you."

He looked up to find her piercing gray eyes on him.

"Ah," he said, grinning at her ability to read his simple male mind. "I've heard it said more than once that women dress for other women, rather than men. I didn't know that included one's maid."

"You've obviously never had extensive dealings with a lady's maid." Her eyes flickered over the long dining room table, which had settings for only two, and her expressive sable eyebrows arched.

He pulled out her chair. "Yes, we are dining *a deux*. While I feel well enough to dress and leave my bed I'm not sure I am up to formal entertaining."

She snorted and snapped her napkin before laying it across her lap.

Laughter—even if it came in the form of a sarcastic snort—was better than silence. He was a pitiful husk of his former self in many ways, one of those being his ridiculous hunger for attention from her. Attention of any kind. He loved her scoffs, rebuffs, abuse—anything was better than nothing. Yes, he was pathetic, but he'd never been happier in his life than when he was with her. He smiled at the thought and nodded to the footman to begin serving before turning back to her.

"I wanted you to know I'm not disobeying orders by being up and about. Both Doctor Venable *and* Lord Trebolton told me I was free to leave the sickroom."

"I'm pleased to hear that. He must believe the concussion threat has passed."

"Well, here's the thing . . ." He paused, wondering where he should begin—*if* he should begin. After all, wouldn't she leave once she knew he was in no danger? Of course she would. But he'd used lies once and they'd not worked. He was a pragmatist in all things; this time he would employ the truth. He could hardly do any worse than before, could he?

"Yes? The thing?"

"There never was a concussion."

"Oh?"

"The damage to my eye is of long standing. I told the doctor that today. It is from an old injury."

The door opened and a stream of servants paraded into the room.

"I thought we could serve ourselves so we might talk more freely," Stephen explained as dish after dish was arrayed before them. "Courses are so . . . intrusive."

This time she lost The Battle of the Smile and allowed her lips their full range of motion. He drank her in as she studied the food, his own lips curving as he watched realization break like dawn on her features.

"You remembered all the dishes I liked," she said once the servants had deposited their burdens and gone. Her tone was one of wonderment.

"Of course I did."

She shook her head. "Why?"

"Because it is what I do when things are important to me: remember them."

"But after all these weeks—months?" She made a small sound of disbelief, her gray eyes wide.

"I love you, Elinor."

A flush crept up her neck, flooding her pale cheeks with color.

He reached for her with his uninjured hand on impulse and then stopped. "I'm sorry, I didn't mean to cause you distress. May I serve you?"

"Please." Her skin was bright pink but she'd schooled her features and he could not read her. So instead he fed her.

They ate, making only general conversation about food, until she asked him the question he'd been expecting.

"Did the damage to your eye happen the night Trentham attacked you?"

Stephen laid down his fork and knife. "It began that night."

She closed her eyes.

This time when his hand moved, he did not pull back. Instead he took her chapped, delicately boned fingers in his and had to steady himself against a wave of emotion that left him weak with relief and a sense of—homecoming.

*God. How he missed touching her—any part of her, every part.*

"Elinor." He waited until she opened her eyes, dizzy with gratitude that she hadn't pulled away from him. "You are hearing it just now, but for me it happened a long time ago. I have learned to live with it." He'd also learned that the loss of vision in one eye was nothing to the loss of her, but he didn't think she would find the argument persuasive just now.

"You cannot see at all from that eye?"

"No."

Her face crumpled. "Oh, Stephen. No wonder you hated me. No wonder you wanted revenge."

He squeezed her hand hard enough to hurt.

"Don't think that for even a second. That is the excuse I used for *years*. Life leaves its scars on us all, Elinor." He paused, wanting her to know he'd learned things about her past, but also wanting her to know it was hers to share, or not. He released her hand, but she didn't pull it from under his. "Can I tell you a story?"

She nodded, her mouth quivering as she struggled to gain control of her emotions.

"My mother was pregnant with me before she married the man who became my father in everything but blood. Our village was small and everyone knew I was The MacLeod's bastard—including me. It ate at me to see my real father and my real half-brothers—boys who had everything I didn't thanks to what side of the blanket their mother had shared with our father." He slanted her a bitter smile. "Instead of being grateful for what I had—parents who loved and cared for me— I could think of nothing but revenging myself against the man who'd tossed me aside.

# The Footman

"My adoptive father died when I was twelve and things became harder. Even so, The MacLeod allowed us to keep our small farm." He shrugged. "Joe Vale was dead and so was The MacLeod's wife. I supposed I expected—hoped—my father would finally marry my mother now that he was free. When he didn't—when he took a young girl to wife, instead—I stole from him.

"He could have seen me hanged, but instead he banished me and my mother from the only home I'd ever known. Not long afterward, she took ill and died in a hovel in Edinburgh—courtesy of me, her thieving son."

Elinor opened her mouth, no doubt to protest, but Stephen raised a hand.

"The story isn't finished. Before she died, my mother sent a letter to my uncle in London. He was a good man with no wife and children of his own and he graciously took in his fifteen-year-old nephew. He taught me what he could about his trade—he was a stable master— and supported my wish to go into service." He smiled at her. "Once again things did not work out the way I'd hoped. But the thing I never realized until a few months ago—when I ended up in that cell in Newgate, alone, and without any hope of ever being with you—was that it was my destiny to be on that particular ship to America. Because of *me*, Jeremiah Siddons lived another fifteen years. Because of what happened between me and you, I was able to save one of the kindest and most generous people I've ever known. What I'm trying to say, in a very long-winded fashion, is that my life has really been very charmed. I am only devastated that it took hurting you for me to realize it."

***

Elinor felt like an animal that had been caught in a trap. But instead of sharp jaws that snapped closed, this trap was slow and silken and she wandered deeper and deeper into its clutches with each moment that passed.

They'd finished dinner and Stephen had given her a tour of the house before they'd ended up in the library. The entire time it had been on the tip of her tongue to ask him to send her home in one of his carriages. But the words never came.

*Get out now,* an insistent voice in her head advised.

Elinor ignored it and instead perused the shelves full of books. There were many gaps but also many new-looking bindings.

"Was there much here when you bought it? Or are these yours?" She took a volume of Chaucer from the shelf.

"Most of these are mine."

His voice came from right beside her and she jumped. He didn't notice and was looking at a shelf too high for her to see. He plucked down a large, aged-looking book and turned to her. "I think you might find this interesting."

The library was well-lighted and they were close enough that she could see his eyes clearly. One pupil was slightly larger than the other. How was it that she'd never noticed the size difference before?

"They're not always that way," he said, smiling. "And I have no idea what causes the sightless one to dilate or not. I believe most of the time they are quite similar."

Elinor flushed. "I'm glad to hear that or I would have thought myself abysmally unobservant." She looked down at the book in his hand. It was *De Re Anatomica Libri XV*, by Realdo Colombo. She looked up.

He was intent, his nostrils slightly flared. For some odd reason the knowledge that his beautiful green eyes were damaged squeezed her heart until she felt weak. On the surface he looked perfect; yet he was flawed all the same.

She took the book from his left hand and carried it to his desk before opening it.

"It's phenomenal," she said, turning fragile pages that were almost two hundred years old.

He came behind her, the heat of his body like the touch of his hand as he leaned over her shoulder and pointed to one of the illustration plates. "Have you ever encountered one of these in your work?"

It was a fat, capering cherub, which the author had prudently inserted into a description of internal organs and dissection, no doubt to pacify the Catholic establishment of the time.

Elinor laughed. "Beth has already squabbled about making room for a pig and a kitten; if I took in a naked, winged man that might be the final straw."

He chuckled and the low sound teased her body like the feather-light caress of fingers across the strings of an instrument.

She needed to leave. *Now.*

"This is lovely. Thank you for sharing it with me." She closed the cover.

"I bought it for you, Elinor." The words were hot against her temple, and her body—without any instruction from her brain—turned with agonizing slowness, like a weathervane in a steady, unrelenting wind.

His mouth descended on hers with swift brutality and she met him with a force that equaled his own. Teeth clicked and tongues tangled; it was carnage.

She couldn't get close enough. She wanted to be *inside* him.

Elinor didn't recall grabbing his shoulders but she was already halfway up his body when she must have jarred his arm.

He yelped and jerked away.

"I'm sorry, Stephen."

He muttered something unspeakably vulgar and then used his left arm to sweep the desk clear of books and papers.

Foolscap and parchment fluttered through the air like a startled flock of birds. Elinor flung out a hand to grab the ancient book before it joined the rest but her fingers scrabbled uselessly on the embossed leather cover.

Stephen leaned across her, plucked the book off the desk, and tossed it onto a nearby chair, ignoring her gasp of protest.

"Get on the desk." His voice was a hoarse growl. He drove her back with his body, not stopping until she felt hard, unforgiving wood against her bottom.

She hastily scrambled up onto the clear surface.

He gave a low grunt of approval. "Lift your skirts, Ellie."

Her entire body became hot and it was a wonder she didn't glow through her clothing.

"Please, I want to see you."

*See her?* Her bodice clung to her damp, heated torso like hot, clammy hands. Her fingers plucked at her skirts but her brain clutched at one last straw.

"The lights, they're—"

"Please."

The simple word was like a scythe through wheat and any vestige of resistance fell before his hungry intensity.

She lifted the hem to her thighs and he looked down at her, his eyes flickering across the scars that crisscrossed her upper thighs. Elinor held her breath, but he made no comment. Instead he pushed the gossamer skirts higher with his good hand. His fingers flicked lightly over the tops of her stockings and he pressed his body closer, spreading her knees with his thighs, his hand moving toward the part of her that ached for him.

He slid a finger inside her body and his eyelids fluttered shut. "Oh, God."

Her hips lifted off the desk to take more of him, giving up the fight to maintain or regain any kind of control.

She thrust against his hand and they both groaned.

"Ellie." His hand stilled.

She opened her eyes at his desperate whisper.

"I want to be inside you."

She nodded, too shaken too speak.

He lifted his right hand and frowned at the splint. "You'll need to unbutton me, sweetheart. I'm afraid it's either you or Nichols."

Elinor sent a button flying before getting the others open. She clawed at his tight pantaloons and yanked them down.

Her eyes riveted to the hard evidence of his arousal. She'd felt him in her hand and had taken him inside her body—but she'd never seen him. She slid her fingers around him and he hissed.

His head fell back and she looked up the long, bronzed column of his throat to the surprisingly white, vulnerable skin beneath his jaw. His hips pushed gently against her hand and his body shuddered. It was perhaps the most powerful moment of her life. He'd placed himself in her hands and closed his eyes, entrusting himself to her entirely.

Elinor spread her thighs and guided him closer. He bent his knees and gasped when he felt the entrance to her body.

"Oh, Ellie." He slid his good arm around her and entered her in a hard thrust. "Hold on to me," he rasped.

She wrapped her legs around him and he began to move.

Their eyes locked and his arm tightened like a strap as he held her steady and drove them both higher.

It didn't take long for either of them to reach the blissful plateau. For her part, Elinor had been humming and pulsing for him from the moment she'd learned he survived the accident—the moment she realized what it would feel like to *lose* him for good.

***

Elinor lay in the crook of his arm, his heart beating a steady, solid tattoo below her cheek. She could feel the tension in his body and knew what he was going to say even before he spoke.

"Elinor."

"Yes, Stephen."

"Tell me about the scars."

She sighed. "There's not much to tell that you don't already know from personal experience. Edward was a violent, cruel man who needed a victim. That was you once, Marcus on occasion, and me for almost ten years. He left his marks and some of them were more painful and lasting than others. But it wasn't a living hell all the time. I was able to do things for our tenants nobody else could do. I had Beth to love me and later I had Marcus to love." She smiled. "You might not think it, but he was a delightful child and gave me a reason to live during some of the darkest times."

"You never wanted children of your own?" His voice was as taut as a newly strung violin but he stroked her shoulder with calm, soothing strokes.

"I was pregnant several times."

He stopped stroking and squeezed her until it hurt. She wanted nothing more than to go to sleep in his arms tonight, to wake up in them tomorrow, and to do so every day for the rest of her life. But the story she'd just told him only reminded her of why she could never place herself in any man's care ever again.

"I love you."

She smiled—why couldn't she enjoy hearing those words from the man she loved?

He inhaled deeply. "I beg of you—please, will you marry me? Not only for the sake of our child, but because I want to spend the rest of my life with you."

Tears leaked from the corner of her eyes and one gleamed on the smooth fabric of his black coat before disappearing.

"No, Stephen, I will not."

His hand resumed its gentle stroking. "You know I will not give up on you, Elinor. I love you too much. I will ask you again. And again."

Elinor closed her eyes but the tears just fell faster. "Stephen." She said his name first, hoping it would ease the harshness of the words she was about to speak. "Tonight must be the last time this happens. If you really love me, I want you to promise to go away—to leave Redruth. I've carved out a life of sorts for myself here and I cannot stay unless you leave. If you will not go, I have to go."

His chest still rose and fell in even, deep swells like a calm sea, but every muscle in his body was as hard and brittle as glass.

"You want me to leave Oakland—for good?"

She said the words before she couldn't. "Yes, I want you to leave Oakland. For good."

His arm tightened slightly and then slid away. Her hair had come loose during their exertions and he brushed it back from her face and leaned over her, his expression one of near agony that made her heart catch.

He kissed her temple. "Then I will leave Oakland. For good."

# Chapter Thirty-Five

**B**eth slammed the door to Elinor's small study with enough force to make her jump.

It had been this way for days, ever since Elinor came home from Oakland. Her maid's face had been a study in disappointment, dismay, and anxiety. Whatever the other woman's hopes had been, Elinor's return had dashed them.

Since that night they'd lived together like two prisoners sharing a small cell. Elinor's only escape from the aggrieved haze that hung over the house was to escape to her surgery. Unfortunately, young Jory Williams was currently hammering on the roof of that edifice, thanks to the appearance of an extended family of starlings. Luckily there were no fledglings and she'd instructed Jory to patch the hole and look for any others.

Until he was finished, she was trapped in the cottage. With Beth. The worst part about Beth's war of silence was that she'd heard nothing about Stephen in five days.

She looked down at the ledger she'd been working on and bit her lip. A large black blot of ink in the middle of her medical expenses column was a testament of her inability to concentrate. She'd been working on the same column for at least an hour. Or *not* working on it, depending on how you looked at the manner.

When she wasn't wondering about Stephen's whereabouts, she was recalling their last night together. Every time she remembered he was blind in one eye because of her actions she felt as though she'd been kicked in the stomach. That knowledge had opened the door to her imaginings. What must his life have been like? What hardships had he known that she couldn't even imagine?

It was true that marriage to Edward had possessed its share of horrors, not the least of which was physical and emotional violence, but she'd never gone hungry or wondered if she would die somewhere half-way around the globe, alone. Stephen had been only fifteen.

The gut-wrenching guilt she'd experienced for years after that night had faded. In its place was a sad understanding of how easy it was to hurt and be hurt and of the dangers inherent in baring yourself to another person.

What Stephen had done to her in London had hurt her deeply.

Oh, she knew he was composed of more than anger and vengeance. His behavior at the mine had proven what she'd known deep down—that he could put others above himself.

But one impulsive act of selflessness could not cancel fifteen years of plotting and revenge. The frightening truth was that he was accustomed to having his own way and stopping at nothing to get it. If she were to place herself in his care, she could never be sure that—

*Thud! Thud! Thud!*

Elinor's heart shot into her mouth.

The door swung open and slammed against the wall. Beth stood in the opening, her fisted hands on her hips.

"You have a patient, *Mrs. Atwood.*" She spun on her heel and was gone before Elinor could speak.

As peevish as Beth had become, at least she'd put a chair in the foyer for her patient—who was none other than the girl Kerensa. She turned a tear-stained face to Elinor and leapt to her feet, her baby in her arms.

"Oh, Mrs. Atwood, please help. Emblyn is dying!"

\*\*\*

"It's called *cynanche trachealis*," Elinor said, filling the basin with steaming water. "Don't worry, it sounds far worse than it is. Emblyn will be fine, we just want to clear her breathing a little. Hold her upright and support her head, Kerensa."

Elinor arranged the cloth so that it formed a loose tent over the baby and captured the steaming water from the basin.

"Rub her back and talk to her," she told the girl. "Babies get scared just like anyone else and right now she can't breathe very well."

Elinor set the kettle on the hearth and pulled the bell pull before going to sit across from the terrified mother. They were in her study and Kerensa looked as frightened as a startled doe. It had taken Elinor a full five minutes to quiet her fears and get her to take off her wrap and sit.

The door opened almost immediately and her dour maid's face appeared in the gap.

"Could you bring us some tea and another kettle of hot water, Beth?"

Beth grunted but at least she didn't slam the door. Elinor could only assume she'd restrained herself for the baby.

"Now, we'll just sit here and chat softly and she will be soothed by the sounds of our voices." The infant's breathing was still rough, but she'd begun to breathe more deeply and the bark-like quality had given way to a hoarse, raspy sound that was not nearly so horrific sounding.

Elinor gave the younger woman a reassuring smile. "See, she sounds better already."

She nodded uncertainly, her blue eyes wide, like those of a porcelain doll.

"How did you get here, Kerensa? Did you walk all that way?"

"No, Billy Martin bringed me."

Elinor was certain that her earlier suspicions had been correct. Kerensa was what the local people would probably call piskey mazed or touched by pixies. What kind of man would father a child on such a girl?

"How old are you, Kerensa?"

"Five and ten." She squinted. "Or mayhap six and ten. What month be it?"

"It is November."

The girl nodded and crooned to the baby, apparently forgetting why she'd asked.

Elinor realized she was gripping the arm of the chair in a vise-like grip and relaxed her hands. Who would do such a thing to a simple girl? She grimaced. Why even think such a question? The girl was uncommonly beautiful; there were probably plenty of local boys who'd be bewitched by such a lovely creature.

"Be you going to marry Mr. Worth?"

Elinor blinked at the question, her face heating. "No. Who told you such a thing?"

The girls smile turned oddly sly. "I hear things." Her eyes flickered around the room, as if she were hearing things right now. "The angels talk. They'm said they'd send Mr. Worth to help."

"Oh? To help you with what?" Kerensa's eyes slid to the baby cradled against her shoulder. "With Emblyn?"

The girl nodded. "He made the master stop his interfering and then he gived me the doll house." Her blue eyes sparkled with a combination of love and hero-worship.

"What master? Peter Cantwell?"

Kerensa nodded. "He wanted to put another *baban* inside of me."

"Dear God," Elinor whispered, blinking back tears. Out loud she said. "And did Mr. Worth stop him?"

Again the sly smile transformed her ethereally beautiful features into something earthy and teasing. "Aye. He," she paused, her smooth brow wrinkling with confusion, "*gweskal?*" She swung her free hand to illustrate.

"He hit him?"

She nodded vigorously, her face wreathed in smiles, the expression making her truly glorious.

Stephen had beaten Peter Cantwell for assaulting this young girl? Her head whirled as Kerensa sang to the baby. They were still sitting that way when the sound of raised voices came from the hall.

"No, Mrs. Kennett, you may *not* go in there."

"I know my goddaughter is in there with a sick baby and nothing—especially not *you*, Miss No-Better-Than-You-Should-Be—will keep me away from them!"

Elinor hastened to open the door before the women began trading blows.

"Mrs. Kennett," she said, smiling from the housekeeper to Beth and back again. "Please, do come in." She stepped back and the housekeeper swept inside.

Elinor reached out and squeezed Beth's hand. "Thank you." For the first time in days, Beth smiled back at her.

Elinor turned to find Mrs. Kennett holding Emblyn, cooing and bouncing the baby, who was responding with a rather raspy chuckle. Obviously Emblyn would be in good hands.

"Just a bit of the croup, is it?" she asked Elinor.

"Yes, she will be fine. Kerensa was worried about her."

Mrs. Kennett glared at her goddaughter. "She should've come to me."

Kerensa's lips quivered and Elinor was afraid she would begin crying and upset the baby. "Kerensa, why don't you take Emblyn to the kitchen and have some tea. I know Beth just made some gingersnaps."

The girl grinned like the child she was, her smile fading slightly when she looked at her godmother. The housekeeper grudging handed over the baby. "Mind you keep her warm and upright."

The door shut and Elinor gestured to the chair the girl had just vacated. "I wonder if I couldn't have a few words with you, Mrs. Kennett?"

"It depends."

Elinor glanced at her tight-lipped face. What would be the best way to approach such a subject? It turned out she didn't need to bother.

"I daresay you're wondering about Kerensa's cottage and what it means?"

"Well—"

Mrs. Kennett didn't seem to hear her. "It's not the way it looks. Mr. Worth has naught to do with her, he just provides her with the cottage and enough to go along."

Hostility was rolling off the other woman in waves. Elinor smiled. "Not for a moment did I believe Mr. Worth was keeping Kerensa as a mistress."

"Hmmph."

"The truth is, your goddaughter mentioned how she came to be in the cottage and who the father of her child is."

"Pffft! That girl can no more keep her tongue behind her teeth than she can add up two and two. She were sworn to secrecy about that," Mrs. Kennett said, her veneer of sophistication slipping with her lapse in speech. "Now Mr. Worth will be unhappy when he finds out." She shot Elinor a particularly look. "Not that he'll find out anytime soon seeing as he's left Oakland. For good."

A wave of heat washed over her face. Elinor was always amazed that servants knew what they did. But what else could you expect when one person lived in a house and was served by dozens of others?

Elinor studied the hostile woman across from her and carefully considered her next words.

# Chapter Thirty-Six

*Blackfriars*
*1817*

S tephen was inspecting the first of the renovated guest rooms when the massive iron-strapped door flew open and bounced off the stone wall. Elinor stood in the doorway, her eyes blazing, her chest heaving, her hair disheveled and loose. Stephen's jaw dropped; she looked bloody glorious.

And angry.

Fear knifed through his joy. "My God, is anything wrong with the baby?" His eyes dropped to her midriff when she didn't answer. "Elinor?"

She planted her fists on her hips. "Don't you dare *Elinor* me. You *left* Redruth, Stephen! You left *me!*"

Stephen blinked and cocked his head. He could not have heard what he thought he'd heard. "But, darling, you asked me to leave."

"*Darling.*"

The way her eyes widened and the odd hissing sound that escaped her lips made the word sound oddly menacing. In fact, his words seemed to be causing her to double in size. He held up his hands.

"Elinor—"

"You *said* you would never stop loving me. You *said* you'd never give up."

He blinked. "I haven't. I won't."

Her gray eyes opened even wider but she seemed, at least temporarily, to have run out of words. He took the opportunity to inhale the sight of her. Dark smudges beneath her luminous eyes and the chalky pallor of her skin told him she was tired, most likely from the long journey. Why had she come all this way?

Just thinking the question was like whacking a hornets' nest with a stick. Questions, hopes, fears, worries, and concerns buzzed in his skull, each one armed with its own particular sting.

Beyond all common sense, hope was the first emotion to pierce his confusion; joy surged in his chest. Why had she come? Surely it could only be for—

Stephen forced his elation back down while schooling his features into an impassive mask. For some reason, he thought Elinor would object if he broke into song or howled in triumph.

Instead, he gestured to the sitting area. "Would you like a seat?"

Her eyes flitted toward the collection of chairs and settees. And then they jumped to the room beyond: a bed chamber. A room all but filled with an enormous four-poster bed. She jerked her eyes away, swallowed, and limped heavily toward the sitting area.

Stephen wanted to scoop her up in his arms and carry her when he saw her drooping shoulders. Instead he closed the door before turning to face her. "When did you arrive in Trentham?"

"Just now."

His eyebrows inched up his forehead and it took some effort to bring them back down. He cleared his throat. "Would you care to rest? Perhaps you'd like to freshen up? Or maybe I should ring for some tea and—"

"I didn't come for rest or to take tea."

Stephen lowered himself cautiously into a chair across from her, as if he were approaching a gentle forest creature and didn't wish to startle it.

She looked up at him with eyes that were dark with anger. "Why didn't you tell me about Peter Cantwell?"

It was the last question on earth he'd expected her to ask. "I'm sorry?" he asked, unable to come up with anything better.

She frowned and he realized the skin over her cheekbones had pinkened. And then he knew what she was asking and his own face heated.

She set her jaw and waited.

Stephen took a deep breath and held it. He did not want to talk to her about Cantwell. Hell, he didn't even want to *think* about Cantwell. Still . . . if it would get her to stay—he would talk about anything she wanted.

"I first heard about him when I was staying at the inn in Redruth. The owner's daughter had worked at Oakland for a few months several years ago. She gave birth to a child and then drowned herself not long afterward."

"Go on."

Stephen exhaled noisily. "It's not a pretty story."

"I've already guessed as much."

"Why do you want to know about such things, Elinor?"

"*You* know about them."

"Yes, but I didn't *want* to. And now that it has been taken care of there is no need for *you* to have to hear about it."

"I want to know what you did after hearing about the girl at the inn."

"Elinor—"

"Please, Stephen."

"Fine. After I heard that story I had Fielding look into the man. It wasn't difficult to put together a picture—an ugly picture. He'd, er . . ." Stephen looked at the floor, the chair legs, the wall—anything but Elinor. *Hell!* He shoved a hand through his hair.

"I've been married to a brutal, cruel man, Stephen. You needn't worry about shocking me."

He sighed, but he answered. "Cantwell tampered with more than one lass in the area. In fact, it had gotten to the point where people no longer allowed their daughters to work at Oakland or even wander near the property—which is what the girl Kerensa did, just wander by." Stephen swallowed back the bile that rose in his throat. What kind of deviant would rape a woman of *any* age or condition—but especially one who was no more than a child? He pushed his hair back again. He needed to get it cut, it was driving him mad.

"How many did Fielding find?" she asked, as relentless as any inquisitor.

"Lots, Elinor; lots of girls. Some ran, some found a man to marry them and make their child legal." He paused and looked away. "Three of them took their own lives." He sighed. "Obviously there was nothing I could do for them, or most of the others. But I could help Kerensa and that, in turn, eased the burden on Mrs. Kennett, who'd been using most of her wages to keep the girl at a room in Camborne.

"There were two others, girls who'd been driven to the edge of a decent life. Those I brought here to Trentham, where they've started new lives, calling themselves miner's widows." When he was finished with his dismal recitation he sat back and looked at her. Her face could have been carved from alabaster, but tension flowed from her in tangible waves.

"And Cantwell?" she asked.

Stephen didn't bother to stop the bloodthirsty smile that twisted his lips. "Ah, Cantwell. Well, it turns out he was in the bag from gambling and other unsavory habits. Fielding recommended we find an unused mineshaft for him." A soft snort made him stop. She was unsuccessfully fighting a smile. "I see you are of a like mind, my lady."

"It is difficult to see the purpose for such a man. However, I'm pleased you stifled Mr. Fielding's first instinct—I should hate to see him hang. What did you end up doing?"

Stephen flexed his fist at the memory of his favorite part of his first, last, and only interaction with Cantwell.

"I told him I'd relieve him of the burden of Oakland and that he was no longer welcome anywhere in the neighborhood. I then found him a position on a ship leaving Plymouth."

Elinor's brow creased. "A position?"

"Yes, it seems there are many ships willing to take on even older, inexperienced sailors." He coughed. "I believe there is a rather nasty phrase for it. In any event, I told him I'd paid the captain well to keep an eye on him. I also told him that if I found out that he'd ever hurt anyone again, I would kill him."

\*\*\*

Elinor's body experienced two distinctly different reactions at his words: one was a gradual lifting of the tiny hairs on the back of her

# The Footman

"Are you saying you're going to play solicitor with me, Stephen?"

He kissed her ear, jaw, and nose, the touches as light as the wings of a butterfly. "Truth be told, I'd much rather play doctor with you, sweetheart."

"Stephen, you're incorrigible," Elinor gasped, barely able to catch her breath between kisses.

"Am I?" he whispered against her neck.

"Yes, you are."

"What are you going to do about it, my delectable countess?"

Elinor wasted no time showing him.

# Epilogue

S tephen took his infant son from his wife and patted his back until he'd elicited the necessary burp.

Elinor adjusted her dressing gown. They were in the nursery, a room Stephen had made more comfortable with the addition of adult-sized furniture, since they enjoyed spending so much time with their son. They'd developed an informal sort of ceremony, where they'd meet in the evenings and discuss the day's events while preparing young Jeremiah for bed. Stephen employed a houseful of servants, but this particular job was one he didn't wish to delegate.

"Do you want me to take him?" Elinor asked after they'd spent a few pleasurable moments gazing at the perfection of their child.

"No, I want to hold him," Stephen murmured, shifting Jeremiah until he was resting comfortably in the crook of his arm. His eyes, a bright blue that Elinor said would likely change color in time, were heavy lidded and his breathing was already deep and regular as he slid into sleep.

"He needs a haircut," Stephen said, bringing up a bone of contention.

"Absolutely not," Elinor said, reaching over to smooth back the unruly thatch of copper colored hair that stuck out in all directions.

Jerimiah slept like the proverbial log and they'd had many conversations over their dozing son.

"The other children will tease him for having such vulgar hair," Stephen warned. "Trust me, I know that from personal experience."

She made a dismissive clucking sound. "It's the reason I agreed to marry you, Stephen: I wanted my own little brood of red-haired hellions."

Stephen cleared his throat. "Actually, darling, *I* agreed to marry *you*."

She laughed and shook her head. "You'll never get tired of reminding me about that, will you?"

"No," he agreed. "How did you and Jago find things in Camborne?" The two had gone to visit the hospital and look over the weekly progress. Stephen had done the visits with the reserved earl for the last month of her pregnancy, when Elinor had been too uncomfortable to go out, but only two weeks after Jeremiah's birth she'd been ready to resume her duties.

"Things are moving along quite nicely—the nursery will be done in only a few weeks."

"Are you sure you don't mind giving up your work?" he asked, not for the first or even twenty-first time.

"I can already see there will be plenty for me to do both here and in Trentham," she said, her eyes distant, as if she were imagining all the work ahead—and loving it. "Besides, if Jago can give up his practice to take up his responsibilities, then so can I."

Stephen let the matter be. For the moment, at least. They could always revisit the subject in the years to come.

"I worry about Jago, Stephen."

"I do, too, love. But he won't take help from me." Lord knows Stephen had tried to find ways to ease money into the other man's pockets, but the new earl was a proud, stubborn man. A lot like Stephen's wife, as a matter of fact. He glanced at Elinor. "I wish I'd been able to see the two of you working together. The way you argue now, it must have been something when you were actually treating a patient."

She smiled. "I'm afraid I'm less respectful than I should be."

"And stubborn."

"Yes, *and* stubborn," she admitted. "But I believe Jago enjoys our arguments."

So did Stephen. The two could bicker endlessly over some medical point they'd read in the journals Jago continued to have delivered.

Stephen kissed Jeremiah's forehead and then whispered loudly enough for Elinor to hear, "Your mother is stubborn, Jeremiah. Let's hope you've inherited your father's easier temperament."

Elinor laughed, but then her expression became serious. "I saw you received a letter from Mr. Fielding."

Although it might have been disloyal to his friend, Stephen had told Elinor about John Fielding's plans. They'd discussed the situation often, trying to come up with some way to dissuade the other man from his chosen path of revenge.

"He didn't say much," Stephen told Elinor. "But then he never does—not even when he's sitting across from a person." He cut her a worried look. "I'm afraid he's going full steam ahead with it all. I was thinking that perhaps—"

"You want to visit London?" she guessed.

Stephen nodded. "I know I can't change his mind, but I feel like I should at least try."

"I'm fit to travel."

"What about the young master?" he asked, smiling down at the boy in question. "Can we bring him, too?" He glanced up, no longer teasing. "I don't want to leave either of you—not even for a week."

As ever, the loving smile she gave him did odd things to his chest. "I wouldn't let you leave us behind."

"Oh?" he said, his heart speeding at her arch expression. "And why is that?"

"Jeremiah and I have no intention of allowing you to shirk your duties."

"Which duties would those be?" he asked, even though his body was already responding to the raw desire in her hot silver eyes.

She reached for the baby and Stephen handed the precious bundle over with the same reluctance he always felt upon relinquishing their son.

She cocked one eyebrow. "I suppose I should take you to our bedchamber and remind you."

"Oh?" he asked, surprised he could squeeze out the word. "And what will we do there?"

She heaved a sigh. "I can see I'll have to give you a lesson, just to remind you, of course."

Blood rushed south, leaving him rock hard and slightly dizzy.

Stephen knew by her wicked grin that she'd seen what her gentle teasing had done to him—and that she was relishing her power. He went to stand behind her as she put Jeremiah in his cradle. When the baby was settled he pressed evidence of his desire against her and slipped his arms around her slender body. They stared down at the sleeping infant in silence for a moment.

"He's perfect," Stephen said softly before turning her to face him and tilting her chin until their eyes met. "And so are you, Elinor—my love, my gift, my life." He kissed her parted lips and the heat quickly built between them. When he pulled away, he wasn't the only one short of breath. "Now, about that lesson . . .?"

She smiled up at him, took his hand, and led him toward their chambers and what Stephen hoped would be the first lesson of many.

S.M. LaViolette